Hope For Mr. Darcy

The Hope Series Trilogy

Book 1

By
Jeanna Ellsworth

www.heyladypublications.com
Cover photography and design by Perrywinkle Photography

Check out Jeanna Ellsworth blog and other books by Hey Lady Publications: https://www.heyladypublications.com
Follow Jeanna Ellsworth on Twitter: @ellsworthjeanna
Like her on Facebook:
https://www.facebook.com/Jeanna.Ellsworth
Like the book's Facebook page:
www.facebook.com/PrideandPrejudice.HopeSeries
Connect by email: Jeanna.ellsworth@yahoo.com

Dedication

To all the beautiful, brave people who have ever sat alone at a restaurant reading a book about Mr. Darcy, and looked up and reminded themselves to never give up *Hope for Mr. Darcy* to enter their life.

CHAPTER 1

Oh dear Lord! How did I ever get myself into such a predicament? How could I have been so blind? Mr. Darcy leaves tomorrow! I pride myself on my prudent judgment, and yet I was so wrong!

My head! My neck! It is so stiff and I am so chilled!

Mother was right, my ramblings in the countryside will surely be the death of me. But I must hurry back! Jane, my sweet sister, I must speak with you! You were right all along.

I must write to him!

Dizzy. I feel dizzy.

This is all too much to bear. I am too tired.

But I must! I must write back!

*****

Charlotte Collins had been watching the storm come. There was a sliver of sun along one horizon, but dark rain clouds were quickly filling the sky. It was clear that her dear friend, who had been so insistent on going for a stroll in the sunshine, was about to get drenched. The trees were whipping angrily, one branch tapping in an almost decipherable pattern. Once. Twice. Pause. Twice again. Repeat.

She looked away from the window and returned to her embroidery. She had never been any good at passing time when she was worried. Welcoming the rhythmic pull of the threads in and out, she continued working a brown-toned crucifix on her prayer pillow.

She completed an entire row before she allowed herself to look out at the rain that pelted the window. The tapping tree branch had turned silent. She impatiently put the embroidery aside and went to the fire and added a log. Elizabeth would surely need to be warmed after being out in the rain. All this worry was not good for Charlotte, she knew that, but what else was there to do but wait?

Tap. Tap, tap. Pause. Tap, tap. There was that odious tree branch again. And where in heaven's name was Elizabeth? She stood mesmerized by the fire as the new log caught hold and filled the room with warmth. Then suddenly Charlotte could not contain herself any longer.

She took her shawl and grabbed the umbrella. If she had to listen to that tapping one more time, she would go insane! Making sure not to open it indoors, she stepped out onto the porch and opened the umbrella. The last thing she needed was more bad luck.

The rain was coming down very heavily, and the sound of the tapping faded away with the howl of the wind. She took a moment to pause and wondered whether searching out her friend was the wisest course of action. Elizabeth had a strong constitution, and by now she knew the grounds around Rosings and the parsonage well.

Charlotte put her hand on her belly. It would do her no good to go out in this weather. Her mother's words echoed with each clack of thunder, *"You must produce an heir, and until you do, you must do exactly as your husband says. Fate does not bode well for the Lucas women. It took me seven attempts to produce two daughters."*

Her heart unwillingly took a step back into the house. She could not go out in the storm. Elizabeth was resourceful. She would have to be.

But just as she turned and shook out the umbrella, the tapping resumed, grating on her nerves with ferocity. If her mother had told her how impatient and irritable being with child would make her, she would have never gotten married. Charlotte was a sane, rational sort of lady. One who prided herself on her level head and sound mind. But this anxiety and fear constantly consuming her was too much. Never before had she been so irritated with God's green earth.

Tap. Tap, tap. Pause. Tap, tap. *That was it!* She could not handle it one minute longer. She opened the umbrella one more time and went outside to the west window that faced her personal parlor. Storm or not, that tree branch had tapped its last tap. She sloshed through the mud, carefully lifting her enormous skirts, only to nearly trip on a soaking wet bonnet—Elizabeth's bonnet. Charlotte felt her heart race, and she shifted her eyes around. There by the window was Elizabeth, sitting quite unladylike, cross-legged, just under the eaves of the parsonage.

Charlotte nearly burst with all the emotions roiling in her heart. And roil they did. First she was angry that Elizabeth had endangered herself so recklessly while Charlotte sat worried and alone. That woman's independent nature was too much sometimes! Then she spied the mud-caked hem of her friend's petticoat, and a surge of frustration blossomed as she wondered how her maid was ever going to get it clean. But just as her indignation reached its full height, she focused on Elizabeth's face, which made only the subtlest movement to look back at Charlotte.

Fear instantly dissipated all of her other emotions. Elizabeth was unwell, quite unwell. Compassion swelled in Charlotte's heart as she saw her dear friend's expressionless eyes trying to focus. Guilt came crashing in. Why hadn't she have gone looking for Elizabeth sooner? How long had her friend been sitting here in the rain?

"Dearest, are you hurt?"

Elizabeth blinked and hit her head back against the window. Thud. Thud, thud. Pause. Thud, thud.

So it wasn't a branch after all. "Oh dear, you have been out here all this time? I thought that sound was a tree branch. Let me help you. Can you stand?"

"I should have seen the signs," Elizabeth muttered.

"Storms have a way of creeping up on us; do not be so hard on yourself."

"I must write and explain."

"Who must you write to?" Elizabeth made no reply, only thudding her head again. "Come, Lizzy," Charlotte entreated. "Stand up and let us get you inside."

"No, it cannot wait! Jane . . . Bingley . . . all a misunderstanding. She needs to know. He knew nothing!"

"Who? Mr. Bingley?" Charlotte carefully bent down and helped Elizabeth up as much as she could, then they huddled together under the umbrella.

Elizabeth suddenly turned panicked eyes on Charlotte. "What must he think of me?"

"But Mr. Bingley adores Jane and thinks very highly of you. Whatever the matter is, I am sure it can be resolved. You just wait and see. He will come back to Netherfield. Now, stop this nonsense and start walking."

Elizabeth wiped her brow and took a few stumbling steps forward and then stopped again. "I must write to him! I cannot leave the letter unanswered!"

Charlotte felt her insides lurch nervously. How long had Elizabeth been out here under the eaves in the rain and wind? The edges of her dress were soaked through. She seemed so flushed, and her hairline was damp with perspiration. Charlotte nodded and listened as Elizabeth continued rambling on about some letter that simply could not wait. Twice she turned to Charlotte and insisted that it had to be done immediately. It was unnerving to hear Elizabeth speaking this way, murmuring about regrets and misunderstandings. She always took such pride in her ability to judge a person.

Charlotte tried not to admit that Elizabeth had judged Mr. Collins precisely right. She let out a sigh with this thought.

Elizabeth turned sharply and dropped her friend's supporting arm. In a frantically raised voice, she declared, "I must write, Charlotte! I have not a moment to lose! . . . All I believed came from the most devious of sources! Did you know that Wickham—? No, never mind. This is my mistake, and I shall fix it. I shall."

With that, Elizabeth picked up her skirts and tried unsuccessfully to run into the parsonage. She stumbled a few times, but it wasn't until she nearly knocked her head on a tree branch that Charlotte noted how uncoordinated she was. It was as if her shoes were three sizes too big and her head was too heavy for her neck. Charlotte, still under the protection of the umbrella, made her way to follow after her with the strangest of feelings.

Elizabeth was quite unwell.

She watched as Elizabeth rushed into the house and, without even attempting to remove her muddy shoes, walked right into the sitting room and went directly to the writing desk. She pulled out a paper, dipped the pen in the ink, bent over the chair and started writing.

Charlotte sighed, closed the umbrella, and wiped her feet. Walking over to Elizabeth, she said, "Please, my dear, come lie down. You can write later after you have refreshed yourself and taken a rest. You look very unwell."

Elizabeth stood upright and waved the pen at Charlotte, once again raising her voice. "You have no idea how confused I have been! He, he . . . He is not what I thought he was! . . . None of them are. Not Darcy, not Wickham, not Bingley! . . . That is why I must write at once!"

"Very well, very well, but do sit down. I doubt Jane will be able to read your hand if you write standing up." Charlotte pulled out the chair at the writing desk, and Elizabeth quickly acquiesced.

"Jane? Yes, I must write to Jane . . . Why is it so cold in here, Charlotte? . . . I must write." Elizabeth sat down and began to write furiously.

Charlotte feared Elizabeth's grip would snap the pen in half, but she could see there was no deterring her from writing to Jane. Charlotte went to the fire and put on another log. A servant came in and begged her attention. As she took one last look at Elizabeth, worry overcame her once again and her insides flipped in her abdomen. Elizabeth was fidgety and distressed, and frequently wiped her brow. Charlotte could hear her mentioning Mr. Darcy's name in some form of muttered self-chastisement. She was indeed behaving quite singularly. Charlotte pursed her lips, but left the room and attended to the servant's concerns.

When she returned fifteen minutes later, Elizabeth's hair had fallen from its bun, and she was perspiring dreadfully. She was muttering and fretting over some sort of misunderstanding once again and saying strange things that made no sense.

"I was wrong . . . I do not know how to say it . . . please understand . . . oh! Colonel Fitzwilliam! He will know." Elizabeth turned to Charlotte quickly, but even that small movement seemed to unbalance her. She steadied herself with the arm of the chair and the edge of the desk. "Charlotte! I must speak with Colonel Fitzwilliam!" Elizabeth seized Charlotte's shoulder in supplication, and giant tears sprung up in her eyes. "Not a moment to lose! He must deliver my letter!" she pleaded.

Charlotte reached a hand to Elizabeth's face and confirmed that she was indeed feverish. Her eyes, upon closer inspection, were hazy and unfocused. "There, there, Lizzy. Please just lie down. Do not fret."

"But the letter . . . It must be given to him. He knows! No . . . he does *not* know. That is the problem. He needs to know. All this time I was wrong . . . He must get the letter."

Charlotte was making good progress with getting Elizabeth over to the chaise. "Very well, I will make sure that Colonel Fitzwilliam posts Jane's letter. Now, sit down and let me take your shoes off."

"Quickly, Charlotte!" Elizabeth cried. "Ring the bell! Fetch him!"

Charlotte could tell there was no sense arguing at this point. She rang the bell and told the servant to inform the Rosings party that Miss Elizabeth was requesting Colonel Fitzwilliam and Mr. Darcy. Elizabeth instantly relaxed and allowed herself to be pampered with a pillow under her head and another for her feet. Charlotte watched and waited the mere seconds it took for Elizabeth to transform from her agitated state to complete exhaustion. Elizabeth closed her eyes, and Charlotte again heard her mutter strange things under her breath.

"Oh, Jane! Do not go! . . . He will come! He did not know! . . . Oh, I must send the letter!"

Charlotte hurried out in the hallway and told the departing servant to call for the apothecary as well.

*****

"She did not say, sir. I was just asked to fetch you and the colonel for Miss Elizabeth. I am supposed to tell you it is of the utmost importance."

Colonel Fitzwilliam watched as Darcy dismissed the parsonage servant. His cousin had a strange look in his eyes. "I believe I know what this is about, Colonel," Darcy explained. "I think I can safely say that she requests only *your* company. In fact, I very much doubt that Elizab . . . I doubt Miss Elizabeth wants me there."

Colonel Fitzwilliam eyed his cousin as he walked to the sideboard and poured himself a stiff drink. After he downed the first glass, Darcy turned around to face him and offered Fitzwilliam a drink as well. "Is there some reason why I would need a drink before daring to brave the ladies of the parsonage?" the colonel inquired.

Darcy paced silently, then turned back to the brandy and poured himself another drink. He sipped it this time. With his back to his cousin, he opened the conversation as smoothly as the colonel had ever heard him speak. His voice spoke of complete control with forced, practiced words. "I believe Miss Elizabeth will be requesting your confirmation of a certain event that happened last spring."

"Which event in particular? I take it you are not referring to the humorous escapade involving a cat atop my horse in Salamanca."

Darcy sipped his brandy again, and the colonel saw him grimace from the burn in his throat. Then Darcy opened his mouth and replied, "No. Georgiana's near elopement. More precisely, Wickham's attempts to get her dowry."

The colonel stood up quickly and closed the distance between them. "You cannot be serious, Fitz. You mean to say you told her of—"

"Yes." Darcy turned around to face him. "Yes, I did. And I cannot tell you why. Do not ask me. You know I would never reveal such a damning story if it were not absolutely necessary. Please believe me that it was. Now I beg of you, please, just go to her and confirm my story."

The colonel examined his cousin. Darcy had not bathed yet today. The stubble on his face was still present from the day before. He examined him from head to toe. Although they were the same height, Darcy was not carrying himself in his usual stance. His shoulders were all wrong. In fact, upon closer examination, it was suddenly obvious that he had either not slept last night or his valet had suddenly become unbelievably negligent in his duties. Perhaps dressing in the same clothes day after day was the new fashion. It was a real possibility; his valet was a little odd. But based on the anxious pleading in his cousin's eye, the colonel suspected that Darcy's valet was not responsible for his new look.

"Darcy, what the devil has gotten in to you? Are you foxed?" he asked, eying his cousin's drink.

"No, certainly not—"

"Then are you under some sort of legal obligation to make a fool of yourself in front of Elizabeth Bennet?" he demanded. "If you are, keep me and your sister out of it."

"Richard, please. I never beg you for anything. Ever. Please do not ask me about Miss Elizabeth. Believe me when I say I cannot tell you anything more. It may be *selfish and disdainful* of me, but that is apparently what I am known for."

Colonel Fitzwilliam heard Darcy's voice crack and then saw him try to stand erect and square his shoulders as if they were in a standoff.

This would not do. Richard did not like going into battle unprepared. The whole situation had a foul odor that reminded him of those blind days of trusting your superior officers to ward off danger. But Darcy wasn't his superior. He need not take orders from him.

"Please, Richard," Darcy mumbled, rubbing his eyes with his fingers while shaking his head. "I just need you to do this for me. I know I deserve no faith, God knows I do not, but please, go to her and confirm what happened."

Fitzwilliam hesitated. "We promised each other that no one would ever know about Georgiana. This was not your story to tell."

"Miss Elizabeth will not tell anyone. I am sure of it."

Somewhat irritated, but curious, Colonel Fitzwilliam considered the facts before him. Darcy had said it was *selfish* of him to reveal Georgiana's story. How very odd. What a strange choice of words . . . What was the next thing he had said? That it had been *disdainful* of him? Even more odd. They had a relationship that was closer than brothers. It was even closer than Darcy's friendship with Bingley. Darcy had never held anything back from him before. He was sure of it. Why now? Why all this secrecy?

"Very well, Darcy, but if I go to the parsonage for you, you *will* explain yourself later." Darcy reluctantly nodded. Colonel Fitzwilliam walked over and took the bottle of brandy away from Darcy and told him, "Take a bath, and tell that valet of yours that you need a shave and a change of clothes. Has Poole even seen you this morning?"

Darcy shook his head and took the brandy back and poured more into his empty glass. "Just go. And keep her thoughts on the subject to yourself. I can well imagine her opinion of me."

"Her opinion of *you*?"

"Of . . . the Darcy family," he stammered. "Of all of us. Of Georgiana and Wickham after this incident."

"Very well." The colonel bid his cousin a reluctant farewell and started on his way to the parsonage.

Colonel Fitzwilliam had his own views of their little Easter trip to Rosings. In the last five years, ever since Darcy's father died, they had traveled each spring to their Aunt Catherine's estate at Rosings for Easter week. Never once did they meet with the rector during those five years. And they had certainly never entertained eligible young ladies. Aunt Catherine had her own plans for Darcy: he was to marry her daughter, Anne. This was the entire expectation and purpose of the annual invitation to visit. But this trip had been different. Darcy had seemed almost eager for the trip this year. Colonel Fitzwilliam supposed it was because he was finally considering offering for Anne. That was until he met Miss Elizabeth.

Two weeks ago they had barely finished washing up after their travels from London when Darcy proposed calling on the new rector. Darcy had forewarned him that the man was "entirely senseless" but suggested that a visit would be mildly entertaining. In fact, he had insisted that they pay their respects immediately. Colonel Fitzwilliam had agreed, although suspiciously, for it was very unlike Darcy to take interest in someone outside of their intimate circle. His cousin was a very private man, as today's conversation had so clearly proved.

And to have taken interest in such a man! Surely no one in Kent was more insipid or uncouth than Mr. Collins of Rosings Park. But while Richard couldn't help but be intrigued by the ridiculous creature who seemed to have more words than thoughts tumbling out of his mouth, he didn't fail to notice where his cousin's eyes rested. Darcy feigned surprise at seeing Mr. Collins's guest, a Miss Elizabeth Bennet, but when he paid little attention to the rector, the colonel was immediately suspicious.

When it was revealed that Darcy knew Mrs. Collins and Miss Elizabeth from his visit to Hertfordshire, his suspicions were confirmed. It was apparent to the colonel's well-trained eye that Darcy harbored tender feelings for Miss Elizabeth. It did not take long to see why. She was quite distinct and intriguing. She was intelligent and insightful, and there was a fire of confidence in her eyes. She was an easy conversationalist, and the draw to engage her in topics was quite strong. For her opinions, which were always spoken with a bit of cheekiness, left the colonel wondering if his own views had any validity at all.

Colonel Fitzwilliam could sense the pull she had on others, but that wasn't what consumed his mind as he walked to the parsonage.

Darcy was pulled. For the first time ever, his cousin had sought out a lady's company. So Colonel Fitzwilliam played the part he always played and entertained the lady while Darcy silently looked on, with the subtlest look of enjoyment. Darcy ventured so far as to inquire about Miss Elizabeth's health three times, and about her family's health even more often, yet he added little to the conversation. But no matter who was speaking, his eyes rested on Miss Elizabeth. Afterward, Darcy made no mention of the visit or Miss Elizabeth, but Richard knew his cousin well enough. He was besotted.

Darcy's sudden interest in walking the grounds of Rosings in solitude every morning, coupled with their frequent visits to see the ladies of the parsonage and several occasions in Miss Elizabeth's company in which his cousin was nearly *smiling*, made the colonel quite sure his cousin was finally ready to offer marriage.

But there had been no smiling face this morning. Instead, Darcy's eyes had been dark and distant, tired and pained. It was a very curious situation indeed. Something must have happened. And if taciturn Darcy wasn't going to reveal it, maybe he was could get the lively, enchanting Miss Elizabeth to divulge a hint.

*****

The colonel knocked on the door of the parsonage and brushed a few drops of rain from his shoulders and examined his boots for mud. For having just walked through the rain, he looked presentable enough.

The door opened, and the same servant who delivered the message led him into the sitting room where several things assaulted him at once. The room was stifling hot. Mrs. Collins was standing by the window, waving a fan across her face—a face which showed much relief at seeing him. Then he looked down at the chaise and saw what was likely the cause of Mrs. Collin's fears.

"Good God! Miss Elizabeth! What happened?"

Elizabeth started muttering incoherently. "Darcy . . . I did not know . . . I must write."

Colonel Fitzwilliam turned to Mrs. Collins. "What is wrong with her?"

"I do not know. I have already sent for the apothecary, but he is delayed with an emergency in Brenton."

"What happened to her?" he asked. "How long has she been like this?"

"All I know is that she took a walk this morning and was gone for several hours. I went looking for her when the rain started, and this is how I found her. She keeps talking about a letter to her sister Jane and how *you* must be the one to deliver it. I think she will get no rest until she gives it to you. That is why I sent for you."

The colonel walked around to the other side of the chaise and looked at Elizabeth. He pressed a hand to her clammy hot face and thought for a moment. She seemed as ill as any man he had seen in battle. "She looks absolutely dire." He gently took off the blanket and asked Charlotte for a cool washcloth.

"Of course," Charlotte replied. She pressed her hand to her own head and left the room to fetch one.

Colonel Fitzwilliam walked across the room to open the two windows. As he moved from one window to the next, he passed the writing desk, and couldn't help but notice the letter to Jane that Elizabeth was so worried about. He was startled to see the name *Wickham*.

Darcy had been so sure that she would not reveal Georgiana's near elopement, but a quick scan of the letter made it clear that she was discussing it in detail. But she wrote as if Jane already knew. And she apologized repeatedly throughout the letter. It was also clear that her sister Jane was somehow connected to Mr. Bingley. Richard glanced over his shoulder to check if he was still alone, then he moved the letter slightly so he could read it from the beginning.

Dear Mr. Darcy,

I have not the words to describe the onslaught of emotions, many of them most humbling, which have run the course of my body since reading your revealing letter. Please know that the most prevalent of feelings is one of regret for refusing you yesterday. Not because I wish to marry you, but because I was so unbelievably insulting and rude. Forgive me.

Colonel Fitzwilliam could hear Mrs. Collins discussing something outside the room, and he quickly gathered the letter and folded it into his vest. This was most definitely not a letter for Jane Bennet. As the servant came in, he took a few steps toward her and reached his hand out for the cloth. “Allow me.”

He began wiping Elizabeth’s cheeks and brushing the hair from her sweaty face. She seemed to toss her head towards the cool cloth with every swipe of the brow. “There now, Miss Elizabeth. Just sleep. I have done this for many men in battle, and you need not worry. You are in good hands.”

She opened her eyes to the voice, and her hand weakly reached out to him, but it wavered helplessly mid-air. “Colonel, I truly did not know . . .” she stammered. “The poor man! His eyes . . . they haunt me.” She started wildly rambling, whispering things that confirmed his suspicions and raised new ones.

She was clearly delirious, and it would have been foolish to pay heed to her. But Richard had seen Darcy’s eyes this morning. Her words were true, for Darcy’s eyes haunted him as well. And from the little he understood from the letter, Darcy had good reason for the pain and hurt that dripped from him like ice melting in the summer sun.

He wiped her brow once more and lowered his voice so Mrs. Collins in the doorway could not hear. “I have the letter,” he assured her.

"Do not worry. I will give it to Darcy." He then quietly added, "After he does a bit of explaining."

CHAPTER 2

"We need to talk," Colonel Fitzwilliam ordered with an air of authority.

"I am busy right now, Fitzwilliam, and I have no desire to discuss anything but these estate books. They are in such disarray that I shall be hard-pressed to balance them before our morning departure." Darcy had been trying his hardest to focus, but it was for naught. His mind and heart were a quarter mile away at the parsonage.

"Yes, about that. Perhaps we should delay our departure for a few more days, Darcy."

"As much as I enjoy listening to Aunt Catherine's dictations on the subjects of my future nuptials, Anne's imaginary talents, and the cost of the chimneys at Rosings, I must leave as planned."

"Really? How interesting that none of that stopped us from postponing our departure twice already this visit." Darcy made no reply. "Darcy, listen to me. You need to go to the parsonage. Miss Elizabeth is ill, and she is asking for you."

Darcy's lead broke as a pressure infused his hand and body at those words. He took a shallow breath and tried to suppress the desire to ask about her. He had told his cousin that he did not want to discuss her. "I am sorry to hear that. Please send my condolences." He took out the knife and started to mend his pencil. When his hands began to quiver, he nonchalantly turned his back on Richard and leaned over the wastebasket to hide the shaking. Silence fell on the room, and the whittling noises echoed loudly.

What did Richard mean that she was ill? Ill like one of those headaches ladies employ when they want to be left alone? Yes, surely that was it. *"The last man in the world . . ."* He had to distance himself emotionally from anything that had to do with Miss Elizabeth. He had no choice. He could ill afford to demonstrate any interest in her welfare. Even if he were still desperately interested. More than anything, he wanted to know whether his letter had helped to refute the two accusations she had spat at him yesterday. But was there really any hope of that? No. There was no hope; not for Mr. Darcy.

But just as he wore away at the pencil, the man standing behind him was wearing him down with that blasted patient silence. He tried to calm himself. Mending a pencil took steady hands and clear eyes. He could not afford any tears now with Richard just standing there as if it were only a matter of time until Darcy broke down.

Minutes passed. The pencil was as sharp as he could get it, and he reluctantly returned to the desk and attempted to again assess this particular tenant's supposed expenses and earnings. *A new plow horse?* Hadn't he seen another tenant claim the same thing? He flipped the estate book back a few pages, eyes scanning for the entry that seemed familiar, when Richard silently reached over and shut the book.

"Look at me, man. I said that Miss Elizabeth was ill."

Darcy let out the breath he hadn't realized he was holding and looked up at Colonel Fitzwilliam. "Have they sent for the apothecary?"

"Yes."

"Then what else is there to do? I cannot make her well by simply calling on her or extending my stay. What would it look like?"

Richard's upper lip turned up slightly. "Yes, what would it look like?"

"What is that supposed to mean?"

"Well, despite the lack of any verbal confirmation on the situation, anyone with eyes can already see what things *look* like."

Darcy could see that there would be little peace on the matter until he disclosed the facts. "Sit down, Richard."

The colonel sat down. Darcy took the pencil and twirled it between his fingers, rolling it from one finger to the next and finally to the thumb, and back again. It was a nervous habit, but one that helped buy time as he formed his thoughts. It wasn't that he hadn't thought about what to say to his cousin—he knew what he would say by heart now. He knew exactly which speech would appease him, and with his carefully worded statement, Richard would back down and let the issue drop.

Or so he hoped.

"As you know, I met Miss Elizabeth in Hertfordshire, where I was my usual self. How is it you put it? Ah yes, as warm and inviting as a wintery midnight in Nova Scotia. Soon after, Miss Elizabeth met Mr. Wickham, who was stationed there as a militia officer. Given Miss Elizabeth's poor first impression of me, she fell easily into the lies and deceits of that man. I think she may have even taken a fancy to him.

"I could not allow a nice lady like Miss Elizabeth to find herself in a compromising position," Darcy continued, "so, in order to protect her and her sisters, I disclosed in a very private manner the story of how Wickham had used his charms to manipulate my sweet Georgiana into thinking she was in love. And since she does not hold me in very high regard, I offered your testimony as corroboration. I assume that is why she summoned you. But as I said before, I care little for her opinions. Now, may I have Aunt Catherine's estate book back? I was very busy with an issue that needs my attention."

Darcy took a deep breath and prayed that it did not sound too rehearsed. He looked at his cousin, who gave him the disapproving look he saved for his insubordinate officers. He had not fooled him one bit. There was no satisfying that man.

Colonel Fitzwilliam walked over to the front of the desk and eyed Darcy's hand, which he hadn't realized was firmly gripping the corner of the desk. Darcy quickly moved it, but Richard eyes locked onto him. Darcy felt his conscious prick him as he remembered his father's counsel—*"Deceit of any form is the devil's snare, Fitzwilliam. As soon as one abandons the path of truth, one gets lost in a world where up is down and down is up."* But he reasoned that he hadn't actually lied; he had simply left out some of the more private parts of the story. Meanwhile, the colonel leaned back against the edge of the desk and patiently crossed his ankles.

After a few irritating and uncomfortable moments of silence, the colonel offered, "Since you will not ask, she is feverish and quite delusional. I only talked with her for a few minutes before returning here.

She rambled and murmured about things that seemed impossible. Irrational, in fact. Do you care to hear what she had to say?"

"No." It was the truth. "The mutterings of a feverish person should not be heeded. One never knows why they say the things they do." Darcy continued to nervously pass the pencil from finger to finger mindlessly. "No doubt you found something amusing in her words."

"Well, she said nothing of Wickham. But *you* were mentioned." A smug look came upon the colonel's face when he saw that Darcy had flinched.

"I suppose many people mention me in conversation every day. What makes Miss Elizabeth so special?"

His cousin grinned widely. "Yes, what does make Miss Elizabeth so special? Perhaps we should discuss this fascinating topic."

"Perhaps not," Darcy countered. "Now, please give me the estate book, unless you plan to take up the duties of an estate manager. I would be happy to hand over Rosings to you. Pemberley keeps me plenty busy."

"So busy that your two-week visit to Hertfordshire last autumn turned into two months? Very peculiar if you ask me."

Darcy was a little nervous with this line of questioning. "I do not recall anyone asking you. And in my letter, I explained my concerns. I felt it was unwise to leave Bingley alone in the neighborhood."

"Yes, something about matchmaking mothers, if I recall," Richard chuckled. "But Bingley is a grown man. If he fancied himself in love, then what does it matter that the mother wanted the match? Was the family really as disagreeable as all that?"

Darcy fidgeted in his seat and heard his own words to Elizabeth from yesterday. *"Could you expect me to rejoice in the inferiority of your connections?—to congratulate myself on the hope of relations, whose conditions in life were so decidedly beneath my own?"* Had he really said such a thing during a proposal? For the first time, he saw how truly brutal his words were. Honest or not, they must have wounded Elizabeth greatly.

"I say many things that are not necessarily of importance," Darcy remarked dryly. He stood and poured himself another drink.

Colonel Fitzwilliam walked up to his cousin, took the glass, and swallowed the entire contents. Then he slammed the glass on the table. "I will not do this, Darcy. I follow you to Rosings so that you can stomach the company of our aunt. I make excuses for you in London so you can leave parties early. I even watched over Georgiana when you insisted on traveling to the continent to look into that trade investment after you left Hertfordshire. But I am not a blind man. We *will* go see Miss Elizabeth," he commanded. "I have already informed Aunt Catherine that we will be staying three more days. And I have told Poole to unpack your trunk. We will go see her now, and we will not even wait until Poole shaves you. No more estate books, no more mending pencils, no more drinks. You, me, the parsonage, *now*!"

Darcy felt an inkling of guilt at the colonel's words. If Miss Elizabeth were feverish, she might not even remember that he came to see her. He could simply pay his respects, satisfy his cousin, and be done with it.

He nodded and took his great coat off the desk chair. He could do this. If she was ill, he could pay his respects. And as much as his heart ached to see her again, he would try not to get his hopes up. He was probably the last man on the earth that she wanted to see. In fact, he knew he was. He had heard it from her very lips yesterday.

*****

Elizabeth struggled to make sense of her surroundings. She had never been in such a place. She was standing in a garden, surrounded by beautiful exotic flowers and plants. The rainbow of colors was spectacular! Even the greens came in every shade imaginable. Deep, dark, nearly black, emerald moss grew on the bark of the trees. And spiky ferns near the foot of the trees were a cool jade-green. Bright lime-green bushes bordered the path. She reached her hand out to touch their feather-soft, fuzzy leaves.

Everything was bigger, brighter, and more captivating. She was amazed—not merely by the greens of the trees and the flowers in shades she had never seen before—but by the smells, the feel of the leaves, and the rocks underfoot. There were no distinct paths to follow. The garden had a jungle paradise feel to it, almost oriental in its exotic array of colors, shapes, and textures. She moved ahead, ducking beneath a beautiful fruit tree that was heavily-laden with something tiny and bright yellow, which she presumed was a small yellow plum. The morning sun had just risen in this paradise, and she saw patches of sunbeams radiating through the trees and flowers.

Something made her want to see the sun desperately.

She wound her way around a flowering iris patch beside a beautiful, stone-bedded stream that was making the most relaxing sound. The trickle was mesmerizing, and she bent down to put her hand into the crystal-clear water. Its chill was refreshing and wonderful. But she could not stop and admire the water. The sun called.

She stepped across the narrow stream to head east. Her nose was overcome with the scent of some flower in full bloom and, sure enough, as she followed the scent around the tree, she found a pink-and-white flower stretching its face towards the sun respectfully.

The sun. She wanted to see the sun.

Its pull was almost indescribable. She didn't know why she needed to see the sun, but she did. There was so much beauty around her, but she could not help but feel her heart race as she looked eastward, propelling her feet one step at a time.

A beautiful rose-colored path, a swirl of pink and mauve pebbles, suddenly came into view. She stepped onto it and looked westward, into the shadows. The path that way curved several times before it disappeared into the trees and flowers.

But she knew that wasn't where she wanted to go. She looked the other way, back towards the sun, and saw a very straight path. And although trees lined each side of it, there were no shadows because the sun lay directly overhead. The path would take her right to it. She felt the warmth of its rays penetrate deep into her. As she stood there, engulfed by the sun's warmth, she was seized again with an overwhelming desire to reach it.

In her happiest dreams, she'd never imagined such peace. The birds were singing beautiful, joyful songs, and she couldn't help but feel that love was in the air, a measurable influence. It was a tangible thing. The trees spoke of it as the wind whistled through them. The flowers reached up to the sun in love. The leaves reflected it. This place, wherever she was, was special. It was magical. It was heavenly.

She was suddenly aware of a companion by her side. She dared not look at him, but she was engulfed by his lemon-and-sandalwood scent. She kept her eyes fixed on the sun. The silence as they walked was enough; in fact, it spoke volumes. She could sense that he loved her. It was impossible not to feel the love all around in this garden, but the companion by her side *radiated* it. He seemed content to keep whatever pace she set. They walked silently down the narrow, straight, rose-colored pebbled path for some time. With the sun still as her goal, she pressed on.

*****

Darcy took off his hat and handed it to the servant. He followed his cousin into the parsonage sitting room, the very room where he had spent so many mornings admiring Elizabeth. This afternoon it felt different. This time she knew how he felt about her, and he was painfully aware of how she felt about him. He watched as his cousin greeted Mrs. Collins.

"Good afternoon. Is she any better?" Colonel Fitzwilliam asked.

Mrs. Collins shook her head and glanced at Mr. Darcy. "She keeps talking about you, sir. I have never seen her so confused." Just then, a maid announced that the cook had some questions for Mrs. Collins in the kitchen. "Please excuse me," Mrs. Collins apologized to the gentlemen.

Darcy bowed as she exited past him. Elizabeth was talking about him? His heart started to race in fear. Had she disclosed his proposal? Had she said anything about his sister and Wickham?

Without realizing his feet were moving, he found himself moving towards the chaise. The curls that always fell to the sides of her face were wet and plastered to her head with sweat. Her breathing was quickened. She shouldn't have, but she looked beautiful. He knelt beside her and just looked at her. He was too afraid to touch her or to speak. Even though she was ill, she had never looked more beautiful. She had a peace about her that he could not explain.

Colonel Fitzwilliam cleared his throat and scooted a chair towards his cousin. "Darcy, can I convince you to be seated? If she wakes up and sees you kneeling beside her, she might think you are repeating yesterday's offer."

Darcy looked up and gave him an expression of disapproval. But before he could reply, Elizabeth stirred and put her arm up by her face.

"Mr. Darcy?" she mumbled.

Now was the moment of truth. How would she react to his presence? "Yes, Miss Elizabeth, I am here," he soothed.

Her eyes fluttered open. She looked around, but her eyes seemed unable to focus. "Where are we?"

*****

Elizabeth knew it was him. Without any words, she slowed her pace along the rose-colored pebbled path towards the sun. She took a deep breath. She had so many questions.

"Mr. Darcy?"

"Yes, Miss Elizabeth. I am here."

"Where are we?" She couldn't help but look briefly away from the sun to look at him. He was so ruggedly handsome. His face showed such compassion and love. How someone so strong could look so patient and gentle, she did not know.

"Shh," he murmured. "Everything will be all right, Elizabeth."

She paused, astonished that he had just used her Christian name. But she didn't mind. His deep baritone voice spoke her name as if she were the only thing that mattered in his life, and it seemed only right in this paradise. She was important to him, although she was not entirely sure why. She pressed on in silence for a while. The warmth that surrounded her was coming from the sun, wasn't it? Or was it from him?

"It is so beautiful here, Mr. Darcy," she ventured. "Do you not agree?"

"Yes, indeed it is."

"Have you ever been here before?"

"Yes, several times."

"I seem to meet you everywhere I go," she marveled. "Incredible. Where did you go after you left Hertfordshire?"

"I went to the continent for a few weeks. I needed to clear my head."

"You were troubled?"

"Yes, quite troubled."

Elizabeth considered this information and took a deep breath. The slightly humid air felt good in her lungs. "I am sorry to hear that," she replied. Normally she would have been curious about such a guarded reply from him, but for some reason, there was no animosity or irritation or concern in this paradise. All she could feel was the sun's warmth. She wanted to get closer to it.

"Miss Elizabeth?"

"Yes, Mr. Darcy?"

"Please do not worry about me being troubled."

"I care a *great deal* about you being troubled, but I sense none of it now. We seem to understand each other better, do you not think so? I feel only happiness in this place," she smiled. "Is that why you came?"

He paused briefly before responding. "I came here for you, Miss Elizabeth," he whispered. "I am sorry to hear I have worried you. That was not my intention. I never meant to trouble you . . . All I want is to make you happy."

They walked in silence again. He offered her his hand as she progressed toward the sun, and she had no hesitation in taking it.

*****

Darcy slipped his hand into hers just as her eyes closed peacefully. Colonel Fitzwilliam handed him a cool washcloth, and Darcy wiped her brow with it again and again. After a few minutes, her breathing slowed, and it was clear she had fallen asleep.

Darcy took a deep breath. These last moments with her had been the most pleasant interaction he had ever had with her. She was confused and feverish, but she had been kind and concerned about him. And for the first time, he had been honest and open with her. He had nearly forgotten anyone else was in the room.

Just then, as if determined to not be forgotten, Colonel Fitzwilliam loudly cleared his throat and curiously eyed Darcy's hand clasping Elizabeth's. The expression on his face spoke silent volumes. Darcy suspected that his cousin knew the whole truth now, and that irritated him somewhat. But that was Richard's way. He investigated and searched out answers much like a lawyer who twisted and turned his witnesses until the truth burst forthwith in an onslaught. Yes, Richard wanted him to lay his cards out on the table. But this wasn't any card game. His very heart was lying on a chaise, with new beads of sweat on her brow, gently reaching out to him with her tiny limp hand. He didn't have time to explain himself to Richard.

He wiped her brow again and rubbed the cloth along her forearms down to the hand that he held. Every brush of the cloth seemed to calm her. She gently squeezed his hand. Whatever was ailing her, she seemed to find comfort with him there holding her hand. He could do that much. He would be happy to do whatever she desired. With a pang of anxiety, he paused with the cloth and wondered just how delirious she was. Was he taking liberties with her? Her words from yesterday still stung . . . *"the last man in the world I could ever be prevailed upon to marry."* He heard Mrs. Collins pass by on her way to the front door, welcoming the apothecary. He leaned down and kissed the back of her hand and then folded her arm against her chest and reluctantly left it there.

Ever so quietly, he heard Elizabeth whispering in her sleep, "Mr. Darcy, do not leave me . . ."

CHAPTER 3

Darcy glanced at his cousin—who was now openly grinning at him—and shot him a warning look. He hurried back to Elizabeth's side and whispered, "I will always be here for you, for as long as you need me." He kissed her limp hand once more, and she smiled and quickly fell asleep again. He then stood up just as the apothecary and Mrs. Collins came in. They were deep in discussion, and he was relieved that they hadn't seemed to notice him kneeling next to the chaise. He casually turned to face them, fully ignoring his cousin's smirk.

Mrs. Collins started retelling the story in detail. "She leaves every morning and walks around the grounds but is usually back by the morning repast. Today she was gone much longer. I expected she would return when the storm began. But another hour passed, and she still did not return. By then, I was very worried and went looking for her. I found her feverish and mumbling. She seemed determined to write a letter to her sister Jane, and even more determined that Colonel Fitzwilliam should deliver it."

Darcy curiously turned to his cousin, who sobered quickly under everyone's eyes. Richard patted his vest pocket and informed them, "I have the letter, and I will deliver it as soon as I possibly can." Colonel Fitzwilliam then straightened his stance and began to fidget slightly, betraying a slight nervousness that he could not entirely conceal from his cousin.

Mrs. Collins continued, "She seems to be dizzy, and she has reached her hand on her neck several times. She has been sleeping for the last hour or so,"—Colonel Fitzwilliam peered at Darcy, but neither of the Rosings nephews corrected Mrs. Collins—"but other than that, I do not know what else to tell you."

The man looked at Elizabeth and then to the two gentlemen standing in the room. "I assume you are Colonel Fitzwilliam?"

His cousin bowed. "At your service."

The man looked at Darcy and asked, "And you are?"

"Forgive me, I am Fitzwilliam Darcy. Our aunt is Lady Catherine de Bourgh of Rosings Park, and we were visiting Miss Elizabeth this afternoon when she took ill." Again, Darcy's words were not entirely true, but hopefully they would satisfy the man. The apothecary looked back at Elizabeth and then back to the two men. Darcy felt he wanted a bit more explanation. He motioned with his hands to Elizabeth and said, "Miss Elizabeth, Mrs. Collins, and I are acquainted from my recent stay in Hertfordshire. Miss Elizabeth and . . . I . . . she . . ." He cleared his throat a bit, and thankfully his cousin saved him from further embarrassment.

"Naturally we are concerned for her and would like to offer our assistance," Colonel Fitzwilliam interjected. "She has become a favorite of ours, and a favorite of Lady Catherine's as well."

"A favorite of Lady Catherine's? Well, I will give her my upmost attention and care. Lady Catherine funds a great deal of my research. My name is Mr. Osborn. My specialty is mysterious illnesses, especially ones like this, where the patient cannot provide any clues. I find it fascinating to study a subject and look at it from all sides. Take for example my last three patients. They all died, unfortunately—although I am sure that will not happen to Miss Elizabeth! But the last one in particular was most interesting. He had so many symptoms that I had to start writing them down!" He pulled a notepad out of his satchel and started listing them. "Red raised rash on arms and trunk, fever, sore throat the week before, swelling in the legs, fatigue, and malaise—that simply means being tired. Anyway, he also had swollen tonsils, red blotchy cheeks, glassy pink eyes—"

Oh dear Lord! Another Mr. Collins? Darcy interrupted him with as much civility as he could muster, "Fascinating. But perhaps you should examine this patient?"

Mr. Osborn closed his book and replied, "You are correct to redirect my attention. I commend you for your intuitiveness and insightfulness. But of course, I would expect any nephew of Lady

Catherine to do nothing less." He put his book away and walked over to the patient and started to feel her forehead and open her eyes and perform other ministrations.

Colonel Fitzwilliam's words startled Darcy out of his scrutiny of this obvious nut-of-a-man: "Would you like us to step out while you examine her, Mr. Osborn?"

"Actually, we would prefer to stay with the patient," Darcy declared, glaring at his cousin in frustration. *How could he suggest leaving her in the care of such an imbecile?* He gave his cousin a subtle shake of the head and then flicked his head towards the man hunched over Elizabeth. His cousin just smiled politely, completely ignoring Darcy's attempt to refute his offer.

Mr. Osborn looked up slightly and scratched his balding head. "I will not need to expose her in any way, so I see no reason why you cannot remain here to observe. Lady Catherine is always present when I examine her daughter Lady Anne."

Darcy smiled, thinking for a moment that the man might exhibit just a sliver of sense after all.

"Wonderful!" Colonel Fitzwilliam replied. He firmly seized Darcy's elbow and led him over to the corner. "Then we will just stand here, Mr. Osborn, observing your fine skills." He murmured to his cousin, "What are you doing?"

"I told Miss Elizabeth I would not leave her," Darcy muttered. "I am merely keeping my word."

"Ah, I see, just *keeping your word*," he teased. "Of course! How could *anyone* construe your behavior as anything but honorable?" Darcy frowned slightly, but otherwise ignored the comment. "Very well, cousin, enlighten me. How exactly do you plan on keeping your word for more than a few hours? As soon as the sun sets, you will have to return to Rosings."

"Then I will be back at first light. I do not trust that man. Does he have any training? Or any patients who have lived to see the morrow?"

"Darcy, be reasonable. She seems much improved since we arrived. A little overly-chatty on certain private subjects perhaps—" Darcy shot him another look to kill, and Richard grinned in reply. "But I believe she is in good hands. Osborn is a man of science. He is a researcher."

"Then he will not object to me *researching* his credentials," Darcy argued.

They both turned away from each other and watched silently as Mr. Osborn began his examination, opening her mouth and peeking inside. He turned her head to the left and then the right. When he tucked her chin down to her chest, she let out a small moan and Darcy stepped forward protectively. Colonel Fitzwilliam restrained him and shot him a warning look.

Darcy returned the look with one he had mastered over the years. All it did was make his cousin grin and hold back a chuckle.

"Darcy, you fool, I am only trying to help you!" the colonel whispered. "You must show at least *some* restraint! I can hardly believe *I* am lecturing *you* on decorum. Unbelievable!"

Darcy ignored his cousin and returned to watching the apothecary poke and prod Elizabeth. How could he have changed so drastically in such a short time? Half an hour ago he did not think he could even bear to hear about her; it hurt too much. And now he had committed himself to stay by her side as long as she wished? But her miniscule request had changed something deep inside him. He felt needed. He felt useful. She wanted him by her side. She had even squeezed his hand.

For the first time since the proposal, he took a deep breath and sighed. She must have read his letter. There was no other explanation for it.

She believed him.

He was grateful Mr. Osborn stepped to the side a bit to write a few things down because then he could fully examine her beauty without scrutiny.

Elizabeth started mumbling again. "Where are you? You said you would not leave me."

*****

Elizabeth had felt alone for a brief moment. But no sooner had she called out for Mr. Darcy, than he was right beside her again, his hand in hers again.

"Do not fret, Elizabeth," he whispered. "I am here."

Elizabeth opened her eyes and looked to her left, and sure enough, he was there. Her gaze returned to the sun. "This is such a beautiful place. I believe I could stay here forever. Do you ever stay here for long periods of time?"

"No, not usually. But I will stay if you wish."

Elizabeth was sure she already knew that. This place seemed to effectively communicate things with accuracy; she felt privileged to partake of it. She could hear things without ears. She observed without seeing. Without speaking, she was able to say exactly what she meant. Her heart spoke for her, yet she never felt her lips move, although they might have out of habit. Her only limitation in communicating in this garden was her ability to describe it.

There were simply no words.

She had no explanation for how it was possible, but she didn't doubt this knowledge. It was as if it was familiar, like a memory, and that she had always communicated with her heart and spirit but simply hadn't done so for a very long time.

Yes, she knew he would stay if she wished it. "I think I would like that," she confessed.

"Then I will stay. You have my word as a gentleman."

Elizabeth gave his hand a squeeze, and he returned it with a gentle one of his own. His hand sent tingles up her arm. There was something different about him. She couldn't quite say what it was. It tickled her brain, and she tried to remember what was so altered. She glanced at him. He was still handsome even though he hadn't shaved. She had the strongest urge to touch his face. She stopped walking towards the sun for a moment, and so did he. She paused in hesitation. It certainly wasn't proper to touch a man's face, but this paradise had a different set of rules. For some reason, she knew he wouldn't mind. There was some sort of unspoken language between them. She reached out her free hand and murmured, "May I touch your face?"

In a very hoarse voice, he replied, "You may."

Her arm felt heavy in its attempt, and he seemed to know it, so he reached for her hand and placed it on his jaw. She could feel the strength of his constitution. She could feel his integrity. She could feel his compassion and devotion. And she could feel his love. All with a simple touch. If it wasn't for the warmth of the sun on her back, she might have felt scared by these sensations, for surely they did not have that kind of relationship yet. But instead of feeling scared, she felt a renewal of her desire to continue walking towards the sun. She turned to go, but he held her hand to his face a little longer. In that small moment, she could feel a surge of his compassion for her. He was worried about her.

"Why are you worried, Mr. Darcy?"

"I want you to rest."

"But I want to reach the sun. I must go there."

"The sun will come up again tomorrow. Please rest, Miss Elizabeth."

He was right. She was tired. She nodded and just then, the sun started to go down. All this time she had thought it was morning. But she realized the light had never moved above the horizon.

Even though the sun's warmth was beginning to recede, she still felt warm and comfortable. She realized the warmth was coming from him now. He led her to a bench.

He gently said, "We can talk all day tomorrow if you would like."

They sat down together on the bench. The stone should have felt cold, but it was warm to the touch. The peace of the garden washed over her again, and although she had never been here before, she instantly felt at home.

"Are you comfortable?" he asked.

"Yes. I feel safe with you. Somehow I know you will protect me. I am not sure how I know it, but I do."

The silence was filled with the unspoken language that seemed to pass between them. She leaned into his shoulder slightly, and he placed his arm around her. It was as if they had known each other for decades.

"Why do you like lemon in your tea?" Elizabeth inquired after a few moments.

"How did you know I like lemon in my tea?" Mr. Darcy asked, surprised.

"You always smell of lemon. But it is more than that. Somehow I knew it as soon I as touched your face. I suppose a better hostess would have noticed how you take your tea, but this place communicates differently, or maybe it communicates more accurately, I do not know. It was like you told me all about yourself as soon as I touched your jaw." Elizabeth looked up at him, and he smiled briefly.

"My father always put lemon in his tea," he admitted. Her eyes started to drift closed, but she was fighting hard to stay awake. "I know you are weary, Elizabeth," he murmured. "Please try to rest."

"I am tired, so very tired. Do you promise we will walk to the sun tomorrow?"

"If you are feeling better, I promise we will. I would like nothing better than to walk in the sun with you."

Elizabeth felt confused. Something he had said wasn't right . . . "No, not *in* the sun. I want to walk *to* the sun. That light right there at the end of the path. The sun wants me."

"What do you mean? Why does the sun want you?"

"I do not know. I feel its light and warmth and love. It makes me feel safe. But you make me feel all those things too."

"Let us talk about the sun another time. For now, will you promise me something?"

She could hear his fear again. She closed her eyes. The sun was completely gone now, but she still felt warm with his arm around her. "Yes."

"Do not go to the sun without me."

"Why?"

"Trust me. I need you to stay with me."

She was silent for a while. She contemplated what he was asking of her. The sun was a good thing. She knew it in her heart. "But the sun wants me."

"I want you too," he whispered into her ear, and then he gave her shoulder a gentle squeeze.

"I know." She did not know how she knew, but she knew she was loved. She was desired. She was cherished. But she was so very, very tired. "Goodnight, Mr. Darcy."

"I will be right here when you wake up. Do not go to the sun without me."

*****

Elizabeth eyes closed, and her breathing became deep and slow. He could tell she had fallen asleep again. Darcy gently lowered her back down onto the chaise. He reluctantly looked up from Elizabeth's face and saw, for the first time, the expressions of everyone else in the room. They had all just witnessed every word uttered between Elizabeth and himself. Not only that, but they had seen her touch his face. They had witnessed him putting his arm around her shoulders.

To say the room was shocked was an understatement. Mrs. Collins's mouth hung open, and she had her hand on her lower abdomen. Mr. Osborn was seated at the desk, speechless, pen frozen in mid-sentence. Darcy willed himself not to, but he unconsciously looked to his cousin. Colonel Fitzwilliam was trying hard to adopt an appropriate look of disapproval to mask his obvious glee at the situation.

Darcy stood up and addressed the room briefly. "I realize my behavior just now was highly irregular. I do not make a habit of holding ladies in such a manner. But she was too weak sit up, and it seemed only gentlemanly to offer her my support." The corners of Mrs. Collins's mouth started to rise as he continued to try to explain away what just happened. "One must do what one can to assist the ill," he added, clearing his throat.

"Yes, of course, Mr. Darcy," Mrs. Collins agreed with a hint of a smile. "It is my understanding—and correct me if I am wrong, Mr. Osborn—that we should all do everything we can to support Elizabeth and make her comfortable, even if her requests may seem . . . irregular, as Mr. Darcy put it."

Colonel Fitzwilliam quickly caught on and began nodding his approval.

"Lady Catherine would insist upon it, I believe," Charlotte ventured. "Do you not think so, Mr. Osborn?"

The doctor lowered his pencil and notepad and seemed to gather his thoughts. "But are you not the nephew who is engaged to Lady Anne?"

Darcy could see the man's loyalty slipping away. But he could not allow the moment to pass him by. "While I certainly admire Lady Anne, I have never offered for her. And I am not sure she has the constitution at present to marry and bear children." When that seemed to offer only a small amount of satisfaction, he added, "Lady Catherine and I have discussed the need for an heir, and she fully understands." It was true that they had discussed the issue two days ago. But Darcy had, once again, failed to mention the fact he held no plans to ever marry Anne.

Devil's snare, Fitzwilliam. Darcy ignored the recollection and peered hopefully at the doctor. After a moment, Osborn leaned back in his chair, and nodded in satisfaction.

"I must admit I am relieved to hear it, Mr. Darcy," the doctor conceded with a hint of relief. "I do not think Miss Anne has the physical stamina to withstand childbirth."

Now it was Darcy who tried not to show his own relief too much. "Indeed not, and I would never risk her life in that way. But rest assured that she will always be well taken care of. I will manage her finances, and you, my good sir, will manage her health. And I feel very confident that you will do a fine job." With all his years of business negotiations experience, Darcy knew how useful flattery could be. The doctor blushed and nodded.

Darcy felt it was safe to move on to another subject. "What can you tell me about Miss Elizabeth's condition?" he asked. "Why does she think the sun wants her?"

Mr. Osborn opened his notepad again and studied his notes briefly. "It may just simply be the confusion from the fever. Or . . ."

Colonel Fitzwilliam had been content to silently observe what was happening, but now he stepped forward. "Or what?"

"Yes, or what?" Darcy echoed.

Mr. Osborn seemed to shift in his seat a little uncomfortably. "There are tales of people, patients very near death, who see things and hear things that cannot be explained. In fact, they all tell the same story, with remarkably few variations."

"What happens to them?" all three said in unison.

"They speak to the sun . . ."

CHAPTER 4

It was a long walk back to Rosings, and thankfully, Mrs. Collins had lent them a lantern. The night was quite dark now. Colonel Fitzwilliam kept the pace that Darcy set, which was painfully slow.

Much had happened in the last few hours. They had stayed as late as possible, but Miss Elizabeth had become increasingly disoriented as her fever increased. She hadn't talked any more of the sun, only mumbled anxiously of misunderstandings and her own poor judgment. Still, each time she stirred, Darcy was there to attend to her. At the sound of his voice, she slowed her breathing and quickly relaxed. His very touch, as he would reach for her hand, seemed to dissolve her anxiety almost instantly and she would rest again.

As they walked home, Colonel Fitzwilliam reviewed the day's evidence. It was blatantly obvious that Darcy was in love with Elizabeth. Of this he no longer speculated. Darcy's compassion, concern, and looks of admiration were transparent even to Mrs. Collins, although Richard was still unsure of where her loyalties lay. He could only pray that she would keep her suspicions from her husband.

It was also obvious that something had changed in Darcy with this visit. Aside from Darcy's interaction with Georgiana, the colonel had never seen his cousin attentive or caring to a lady. Let alone doting. At Miss Elizabeth's slightest movement, he was right back at her side whispering things that even the colonel was embarrassed to hear. It was as if Darcy's entire emotional wall had been broken down in the matter of an hour. He no longer lurked in the corner, instead he caressed and cooed. He no longer admired silently from afar, instead he stated very clearly his affection and devotion. And, then, when Mr. Osborn finally admitted what he believed was happening to Elizabeth, Colonel Fitzwilliam saw Darcy cry tears for the first time since his father died.

He shed them silently, only asking a few questions of clarification, but near the end, Darcy was finally forced to stand up and pace the perimeter of the room to dispel his anxiety.

As they slowly walked back to Rosings, Darcy spoke quietly next to him. "Do you really think she almost died? Do you really think she saw what Mr. Osborn thinks she saw?"

"I do not know, Cousin. It seems too fantastical to believe. Mind-boggling, even."

Darcy slowed his pace even further. "But to see heaven and to live to tell about it? She will live, do you not think so?"

Reassurance was what Darcy needed. "She will," Richard assured him. "If anyone can come through such an illness, it is Miss Elizabeth."

"But heaven? As in angels and halos and clouds?" Doubt was evident in his voice.

"Mr. Osborn did not describe it that way. And *you* were there—does that make you are her angel?" Richard teased.

"It could have just been a delusion from the fever," Darcy mused. A silent pause ensued, and then Darcy stopped walking altogether. Since he held the lantern, Colonel Fitzwilliam was forced to stop as well.

Darcy opened his mouth to speak, then closed it. He brought his free hand up and raked it through his hair.

It took a great deal of patience to watch the man struggle to speak his mind. Colonel Fitzwilliam endured the cool breeze that chilled his cheeks and watched the lantern flicker a few times. After several minutes of watching Darcy wrestle with himself, the colonel finally exclaimed, "Dear Lord! Just say it, man! What is on your mind?"

Darcy took a deep breath. "It is nothing at all," he muttered and resumed walking.

The colonel grabbed his arm. "Now see here, we both know you have been harboring more secrets than Napoleon on the run from His Majesty's navy. You promised to tell me what was going on if I went to the parsonage for you. I acted as your scout, just like you wanted. And it is time to keep your side of the bargain. I can start the conversation if you would like me to. How about we start with the fact that Miss Elizabeth refused you?"

Darcy whipped around and glared at him. "How did you know that?"

"Or should I start with the fact that you separated Bingley from her favorite sister? I imagine that is at least *part* of the conflict between you two. Really, Darcy, how could you?"

Darcy stepped back a little and put his hand out to brace himself against a tree trunk. "It was not like that. I did not think Miss Bennet loved Bingley, and I could not let a matchmaking mother use a sweet girl like Miss Bennet to catch my friend in the parson's mousetrap. Bingley loves people so deeply. He is such a devoted and loyal friend, I only wanted him to have someone who would return that same level of love and respect. Until Elizabeth told me so yesterday, I did not believe that Miss Bennet's heart had been touched. I was wrong. I was wrong about a lot of things."

His voice faltered briefly but he continued. "Elizabeth did indeed refuse my offer of marriage. And for good reason. I made quite the impression on her and, with the help of George Wickham, she was fully convinced that I was the last man in the world she could be prevailed upon to marry. Those were her very words. I know because they have been permanently etched into my heart. The last man, Richard. Last. Not even close to last. Last." He leaned his back against the tree and slid to the ground. He put his hand to his head and started massaging his forehead.

Colonel Fitzwilliam squatted down and took the lantern from Darcy's hand. He held it up to his face and squeezed Darcy's shoulder. "Love makes fools of us all, cousin."

"Richard, I had no idea she would refuse me. So many women try to trap me into marriage. I just assumed all ladies want to be Mrs. Darcy. I was terrible to her. I started out well. I told her how ardently I loved and admired her. Not such a bad way to start a proposal, is it?"

"No, Darcy, it sounds pretty good to me."

"But it all went downhill from there. The things I said . . ." Darcy shook his head. "I told her I struggled in my decision to offer marriage to her. I told her what a degradation it would be to align myself with her and her family. I used that word, *degradation*. I was deplorable. In my pride, I hardly considered that she would refuse me, so what did it matter how or what I said?"

"Then what happened? What did she say?"

"Do you remember that conversation we had the day you met her? Do you remember how you described her eyes? I called them fine, but you described them as full of fire. As she looked at me in that moment, I saw the fire you spoke of. She detested me, and yet as civilly as she could, she thanked me for the proposal and said a normal lady would be flattered, or something along that line. It was around this time that I started getting angry, and you know how I get when I am angry."

"Appalling."

"Exactly. I accused her of being uncivil. She deflected the same accusation back at me. Then she told me why she had every reason to not only be indifferent, but rather quite decided against me. Separating Bingley from her sister Jane was the first reason. How she deducted that, I still do not know."

Colonel Fitzwilliam cleared his throat. "Well, in the spirit of honesty, some of this mess may be my fault. Without knowing what lady you spoke of, or that Miss Elizabeth was at all familiar with Bingley's lady in question, I mentioned that you were somewhat proud of your intervention on his behalf. I am so sorry."

"It is no matter," Darcy sighed. "She had other reasons to refuse me. I still do not know what lies Wickham told her about me, but I am fairly sure they presented me as the backside of a horse. At least in this accusation, I am assured of no wrong doing."

"That is why you told her about Georgiana's near elopement?" Darcy grimaced and nodded. Richard joined Darcy at the tree, and they both leaned back, mesmerized by the flicker of the lantern and the night stars.

"I am surprised she even took that letter from you," Richard said after a while. "But I am impressed that you had the courage to attempt it. I know many decorated war heroes who would shy away from risking their heart a second time. Why did you write to her? Why not let her refusal be the last of your interactions?"

Darcy looked thoughtful in the lantern light. A long, telling moment stretched into well over a minute. He took a deep breath and glanced up at the moon, which had just shown its face from behind a cloud. "I suppose I knew she could not admire me any less. I had nothing else to lose. I was the last man she could ever be prevailed upon to marry. She even said as much. I believe her words were, 'You could not have made the offer of your hand in any possible way that would have tempted me to accept it'. After her telling me I was arrogant and that I had a selfish disdain for the feelings of others, I left. So, you see, I had nothing to lose."

"But everything to gain." Colonel Fitzwilliam was beginning to understand the depth of his cousin's sorrow.

"Yes. I suppose I had the slightest hope that she would reconsider," Darcy muttered. "I suppose that when you are at the bottom, when you are the last man—hope is the only thing left."

Richard knew it was time. He reached into his vest pocket for Miss Elizabeth's letter. "I have kept this from you long enough," he announced. "She wrote you back, Darcy." He handed Elizabeth's letter to Darcy. "I found this on the desk at the parsonage. I know nothing of its contents but the first few lines. It is yours to read. Good night. The moon is out now, and I can make my way to Rosings without the lantern."

*****

Darcy's hand had reached out with a will of its own to take the letter. He could feel his anxiety building as he watched his cousin walk away. The lantern lit up the folded pages and made them glow. He stared for the longest time at the cream-colored pages. They had small flecks of brown and green, evidence that this was paper used for special letters, not everyday business correspondence. Out of curiosity, he put it up to his nose and smelled it, hoping to catch a whiff of her lavender scent. But he smelled only pressed paper.

He sighed and reminded himself that it was just a letter. *Try not to get your hopes up*. But he failed at that miserably.

He quickly opened it. An initial review revealed she must have written it very quickly, for her handwriting was quite poor. He saw his name on the first page and brushed his fingers over the words. It felt surreal to be holding an unread letter that he knew, regardless of its contents, he would cherish for the rest of his life. He began to read.

Dear Mr. Darcy,

I have not the words to describe the onslaught of emotions, many of them most humbling, which have run the course of my body since reading your revealing letter. Please know that the most prevalent of feelings is one of regret for refusing you yesterday. Not because I wish to marry you, but because I was so unbelievably insulting and rude. Forgive me.

I have just a few moments before Charlotte attempts again to make me lie down, so I must be quick. I am afraid I do not feel well. My neck and shoulders ache terribly and are incredibly stiff. I do not know whether I am getting ill or whether it is my mortification that makes me feel so poorly, for I never knew myself until I read your letter. I admit I have always prided myself on my insight into a person's character. But I am ashamed to say that I was incredibly quick to paint your character. Your letter has enlightened and humbled me greatly. But I said that already. I do apologize. The pen is shaking in my hand, and I am having a hard time focusing.

You come from a long line of connections and wealth. I am simply a country gentleman's daughter with no connections and certainly little wealth. I suppose when I first saw you at the Meryton Assembly, you must have been suffering greatly with the weight of what had just happened with Georgiana and had no disposition to be social. And poor, unsuspecting Mr. Bingley suggested you dance with me. Yes, I heard you say that I was not handsome enough to tempt you. Pay it little mind. I thought I had ignored the insult, but now I see that it was the brush that painted the rest of my interactions with you. You were so rich; I was not. You were so poised; I was impertinent. Oh, I am just rambling. I need to get to the point.

I do thank you, this time in earnest, for your proposal. It was not my first horrid proposal, and I confess it was not the worst either. You may now look at Mr. Collins with pride. Pride, you ask? Yes, for I turned him down first. Therefore I must admit I lied to you. You are not the last man I could be prevailed upon to marry. Mr. Collins is.

I am noticing my handwriting is ill placed and can only beg you do not judge me for it. I will try to focus and inform you that I had no idea that there were men out there like Mr. Wickham who prey on innocent women. Poor Georgiana! I was very wrong in my judgment of him.

I see now clearly—even though, as you can surely tell from this letter, I am somewhat unfocused—that your intentions in separating Jane and Mr. Bingley stemmed from a loyal friend's heart. I hope he does not suffer as Jane does. If you truly believed that Jane's heart was not touched, then I cannot fault you for protecting your friend.

Oh dear, I must go now. I will end my letter as you ended yours. It was so tender. So kind. After all I said to you in anger, you still signed it:

God bless you,
Elizabeth Bennet

P. S. I am so sorry I misjudged you. I could have been much kinder in my refusal if my pride had not been hurt so long ago at the Meryton Assembly. Forever your faithful friend, Lizzy

Darcy sat back and relaxed a bit. It was a good letter; it offered him a bit of peace. There was much to be thankful for. He folded the letter and took the lantern and stood up. As he walked to Rosings, his step had a bounce to it. His eyes saw all the many paths that he and Elizabeth had walked over the last few weeks. Each moment that he had found her on her walk, he had never once imagined that she thought ill of him. But she did. At least back then. He smiled slightly. But perhaps she felt differently now.

He reminded himself that she was feverish and confused, and that her kindness and civility towards him might not represent how she truly felt. But the letter still affected him, even more powerfully than holding her limp hand or cradling her sleepy head on his shoulder.

For the first time since yesterday, he felt hope.

*****

Charlotte purred over the sleeping Elizabeth, wiping her brow and her arms. "There now, Elizabeth, it looks like you have some explaining to do. All those times when we spoke of Mr. Darcy, you were very convincing of your dislike of the man. I never doubted your opinion of him in the slightest, until now. So tell me, has he proposed yet? The familiarity between you two was quite a surprise. I can only suspect you have some sort of secret understanding with him." Elizabeth seemed to smile in her sleep, which made Charlotte giggle. She leaned down and kissed her friend's hand.

"I wish you could have seen his eyes as he looked at you," Charlotte sighed. "If only I felt those eyes from my husband. But you know me; I made my choice in Mr. Collins, and although there are times when I question that choice, ultimately I am content. I suspect that with time I might have what the two of you have. One is so different when one is feverish. It is as if all the social customs, rules, regulations, and restrictions seem to fall by the wayside. I admit I feel a little of that myself being in the family way."

It felt strange to say it out loud. Nobody knew yet, not even Mr. Collins. "Yes, Lizzy," Charlotte whispered, "I am with child. I cannot say I would recommend it. It has been only four months since I married, and Mr. Collins grates on my nerves more and more each week. I suspect he irritates me now even more than he ever irritated you. I think it is the baby that is affecting me so. No matter. Mr. Collins is seldom around anymore. I am grateful he was away today, for if he were witness to your familiarity with Mr. Darcy, I believe Lady Catherine would be quite displeased."

Charlotte adjusted the pillow under her friend's head and brought the blanket up to Elizabeth's shoulders and carefully brought each arm out above it. Right before she blew out the candle she said, "Yes, quite displeased. Now rest, Lizzy. Your Mr. Darcy will be here at first light."

Charlotte walked out of her sitting room and nearly ran into the maidservant. "Christine, I was just coming to give you your instructions. It will be a long night for you, I am afraid. Simply keep wiping down her face and arms until the fever breaks. Mr. Osborn believes the next twenty-four hours will be critical. Mr. Darcy and Colonel Fitzwilliam will be here again at first light. And if for any reason you feel she has worsened, please wake me."

"Yes, madam. But in your condition, I think your rest is just as important."

Charlotte stiffened slightly. "My condition?"

Even in the poor light, Christine's blush was evident. "I am sorry, Mrs. Collins. I couldn't help but hear you say you were with child. But I ain't never told nobody's secret before. You can trust me for sure."

Charlotte felt her insides flip, and she recalled all she said to Elizabeth. More than one secret had been discussed. Her mouth suddenly felt dry. "Christine, there can be nothing more important than you keeping to yourself what you heard tonight. Nothing you heard must ever leave your mouth. Not if Mr. Collins asks you, not even Lady Catherine––no one. Do you understand?"

"Oh yes! And I did not hear much. Just that Mr. Darcy proposed to that poor girl."

Full blown panic rose in her throat. She grabbed Christine's arm and pulled her into the sitting room and closed the door. She lowered her voice and said as calmly as possible, "No. You did not hear even that. Do you understand? You heard *nothing*. If I hear any rumors at all about what you may or may not have heard, I will know exactly the source. And you, your husband, and your mother will never work in this town again. No references. No pay. No forgiveness. No second chances. Do I make myself clear?"

Christine gaped at her mistress in shock. "Yes'm, perfectly clear. I ain't heard nothin'," she promised.

"I repeat, nothing. Do you understand?"

"Nothin'. The same as what will come out of my mouth. I swear to you, you can trust me."

"It is not about trust, Christine, it is about lives that could be ruined. Mine, Miss Elizabeth's, Mr. Darcy's, all of them could be ruined if you say anything." Charlotte saw the fear of God in the maid's eyes as Christine nodded. "Good," Charlotte sighed. "And for the record, I am saving the news of my condition for Mr. Collins's return next week, so please keep that secret as well. Wake me just before dawn. I will assist you in helping Miss Elizabeth into a new gown. She needs to look more presentable."

Christine smiled slightly, "Indeed, she does. Leave it to me, ma'am. I will have her hair looking beautiful too, but for no particular reason and for no specific gentleman who will be here at first light."

Charlotte let out a sigh of relief. "Thank you." She turned and opened the door, and with one more look at Christine, she left the sitting room and went to her room.

CHAPTER 5

"Darcy! I was just informed that you are on your way to the parsonage!" Lady Catherine exclaimed in shock from the hallway the next morning. Still blurry-eyed but full of indignation, she strode toward Darcy's open dressing room door. "What is of such great importance that it cannot wait until an appropriate hour? Paying a call in the wee hours of the morning demonstrates a serious lack of manners, Nephew, and I know your mother would not have approved. Surely no one but the servants are awake! What could you possibly have to do with any of them? Besides, you can hardly be presentable at this hour," Lady Catherine insisted, with her hair still in curling pins.

Her worries seemed humorous, for Darcy was confident he was much more presentable now than he had been yesterday. He took one last look in the mirror and thanked his valet, Poole, for the shave and bath. Then he straightened his cravat, laughed at the new-style knot his valet had tied, and turned to his aunt, who had, by this time, waltzed right on into his bedroom. But even Aunt Catherine could not dampen his mood this morning. He gently guided her out of his chambers and closed the door behind them.

As he escorted her back to her suite, he explained, in his most reassuring voice, the plan that he and colonel had devised: "It is not *I* that am requesting their company. I have been *summoned.* As you know, Mr. Collins is out of town on the business at your request. Mrs. Collins is requesting my experience and expertise in a matter of finance. I hope that by tackling the matter early, I may be finished in time to have noon meal with you and Cousin Anne. Mrs. Collins was kind enough to oblige my request, for she knows how much I treasure my time with the two of you."

"But why must Fitzwilliam accompany you? He has no experience in balancing ledgers. If you need assistance, *I* should be the one to accompany you. Mrs. Collins is entirely inept at managing her household, you know, and I am quite the proficient in these things." Darcy struggled to keep a straight face at such a bold lie.

"Oh no," he replied, "I could not let her impose on you that way, Aunt Catherine. And I so enjoy estate planning. In fact," Darcy gently reminded her, "I believe it has been many years since you have handled any estate business for Rosings." He was not about to let his aunt come to the parsonage with them.

"Yes, but I only save the work for you because you take such *pleasure* in it and so that you and Anne can have this time together each year. If I were to handle the planning, I would be quite skillful at it."

He tried not to betray any hint of a smile. "I am sure that is precisely how you feel. I do enjoy helping you and will continue to do so for as long as you or Anne need my assistance."

Lady Catherine stopped walking and turned to Darcy. "But I still do not understand why Colonel Fitzwilliam must go with you. He despises the rigorous calculations you speak of."

Darcy hadn't thought too much on this issue and stammered a little until he saw his cousin entering the hall, prepped and ready to go. He prayed his cousin would have a ready answer to that question. "Colonel Fitzwilliam, please tell our aunt why you must accompany me to the parsonage."

Without skipping a beat, he smiled and said joyfully, "As a chaperone, of course! Why, it would be scandalous to have Darcy spend hours upon end with the ladies of the parsonage without Mr. Collins present! I am surprised you did not see the need yourself, Aunt Catherine."

She looked startled for a moment and quickly replied, "Yes, of course. I would have it no other way. Perhaps I should send a maid with you as well?" Seeing Colonel Fitzwilliam's disapproving face she faltered, "Well, no, perhaps not. But you will be back for the noon meal?"

Devil's snare, Fitzwilliam, pestered a voice in head. Darcy ignored it and brought his aunt's hand to his lips. "I shall do my very best," he promised.

*****

"There now, Elizabeth, with that new gown on and your hair done up just right, we shall hope that today goes just as smoothly as last night," Charlotte soothed. She reached her hand out to touch her friend's cheek again, eager to feel how much cooler Elizabeth was. The fever seemed to have partially broken. Then Charlotte turned to Christine and asked, "Now, tell me again how you were able to get her hair into a plaited bun while she was laying down."

"'Twas easy, Mrs. Collins! I just turned her on her side! She was sleeping so soundly she didn't stir a bit, not even when I started combing. And her natural curls are so beautiful! Honestly, soon I was trying all sorts of hair styles simply to keep myself awake," Christine giggled. "It was fine entertainment! And she looks absolutely angelic now. Don't you think so, ma'am?"

"Yes, she does," Charlotte agreed. She smiled and felt for the first time in many weeks the calmness that had always accompanied her—that is, until she became with child. It was exciting and energizing to think that her dear Elizabeth could have found such a great match. Christine reported that she had said very little during the night, but it was obvious from their little display yesterday that there were mutual feelings between the two.

She looked again at Elizabeth in her pale-yellow day dress with her hair pulled up on top of her head, and she couldn't help but smile.

But just to make sure, she asked again. "Now, tell me again. What exactly did she say about Mr. Darcy?"

Christine fidgeted a bit and straightened Elizabeth's dress for the fourth time. "It was not much, madam. Just mumbles really. About flowers and trees and how bright the sun was. She kept saying she was waiting on Mr. Darcy. That's all. But I won't tell no one, I swear."

Charlotte took a deep breath and prayed that was the truth. “Thank you, Christine. I appreciate all you did for her last night. Now make sure you get some rest today.”

Just then there was a faint, but distinct, knock on the front door, just loud enough for them to hear from the sitting room.

“Yes, ma’am. As soon as I answer the door, I’ll shut my eyes for a few hours. But I shan’t sleep long. I want to be available if you or Miss Elizabeth needs me.” With a bounce in her step, Christine bobbed a quick curtsy then went and answered the door.

A few moments later Mr. Darcy entered with his hat in his hands, followed closely by Colonel Fitzwilliam. They hovered in the door of the sitting room until Charlotte motioned them in. “Come in. I believe she is a bit better. The fever has almost broken. And she drank a bit of aspen bark tea during the night.” She saw hesitation coupled with relief in Mr. Darcy’s face, and yet he still hadn’t moved. “Truly, she is better. Come see for yourself.”

Darcy inched forward. It was clear when he caught sight of her because his shoulders relaxed and he let out a deep breath he must have been holding. He slowly walked toward the chaise and gazed down at her. Then he looked up at Charlotte and gave a half smile.

“She does indeed look much improved,” Darcy replied. “How did the night go? Did she . . . did she need anything or . . . or ask for anyone?”

The poor man is besotted! Seldom did Charlotte feel an inclination towards romance, but she couldn’t help feeling glad that Elizabeth had found the love match that she so wanted. She realized she hadn’t answered him yet. “She remained very confused throughout the night. But she did mention that she was waiting for you, sir.”

Hope lit up his eyes momentarily, but he quickly put on a stone face. “I see. Thank you.” He put down his hat down on a side table. Then he then looked back at Charlotte. “I feel I must give you some sort of explanation for the familiarity between Miss Elizabeth and myself yesterday. I have considered the topic at length. But I am afraid that although you may desire, as well as deserve, an explanation, I am unable to offer one. Not until Miss Elizabeth is well.”

Charlotte could see in an instant that Mr. Darcy had his Hertfordshire mask on. Whatever progress Elizabeth had made with him in Kent was being well hidden. And this displeased Charlotte greatly. For not only did being with child make her nerves fragile and her mood irritable, it also made her somewhat wistful for the tender words and touches of couples in love. She had to admit that watching the two of them together yesterday had been like a dose of opium for her heart. It seemed to pull romantic notions out of her that made her nearly giddy. It was a pleasant relief from the constant anxiety she usually felt.

She wanted to make one thing clear, and now was as good a time as ever. "Mr. Darcy, if I may be so bold, I saw nothing exhibited yesterday but kindness. If you expect that I will separate the two of you or chaperone your every moment, then you are sorely mistaken. Besides, I am already much too busy to even attend to all of Elizabeth's needs. If it is not too much of a burden, would you be so kind as to sit by her and notify me if her condition worsens?" Her words had the intended effect, for a wonderful smile graced his lips and pulled ever so slightly at his firmly set jaw.

"I am at your service, madam," he replied. Then he looked down at Elizabeth again for a few moments. "I brought a few sprigs of lavender from Rosings. I saw how much she admired the plant every day on our walks. What I mean is . . . when our paths crossed, which seemed to be often . . ." He cleared his throat before finishing, "I have noticed that Miss Elizabeth is quite fond of lavender."

Charlotte couldn't help but laugh at the man in front of her as he stumbled on his words. He very nearly admitted that he and Elizabeth had been having secret rendezvous every morning while in Kent! She knew it was just as she thought—they had a secret understanding. "Yes, she is quite fond of lavender. She likes to dry the sprigs for sachets, which she keeps in her wardrobe. Its scent always reminds me of her. That was very thoughtful."

Colonel Fitzwilliam chuckled into his fist and then cleared his throat. "Yes, Mr. Darcy is *well known* for his thoughtfulness. Why, the last time we were in Devonshire, he presented an entire nunnery with bluebells!" He grinned at Darcy and then bowed slightly to Charlotte. "Mrs. Collins, I believe we are here to look over your ledgers, or at least

I believe that is my aunt's understanding of the reason for our visit. I would rather not divulge what may have led her to that impression, but if you would be so kind as to retrieve them and place them over there on the writing desk, then I can honestly report that we looked at them. It would not suit to deceive Aunt Catherine in any way."

Darcy looked up from staring intently at Elizabeth and colored slightly. "Yes, if you please, Mrs. Collins. I would make me feel much better if I at least knew the color of the leather."

Charlotte nodded with a knowing smile. "Well then, gentlemen, I shall gather my ledgers. Colonel Fitzwilliam, perhaps you might assist me, for they are numerous and quite heavy. Please excuse us, Mr. Darcy. We may be some time, for I fear I also need a second opinion on the cook's new scone recipe. I would appreciate it if you would be so good as to attend to Elizabeth in my absence."

"I would be happy to be of assistance, Mrs. Collins," Colonel Fitzwilliam answered. "Darcy, do see that Miss Elizabeth is comfortable while we are gone," he murmured with another deep chuckle.

The grin on Darcy's face could not be suppressed. He pulled up a chair and quietly replied, "I shall do my best."

Mr. Darcy slipped his cool hand into her warm petite one.

*****

Elizabeth could sense she wasn't alone again. The lemon-and-sandalwood scent alerted her to her companion. She opened her eyes and turned to him. It felt so good to hear his deep voice again, but his words made no sense.

"Mr. Darcy, why shall you do your best? I imagine you are meticulous in everything you do. Would that not qualify as doing your best?"

"You are too kind, Miss Elizabeth. May I ask how you are doing? You certainly look better this morning."

"I felt much better for a while. Could we begin walking again? You promised we would walk to the sun today."

"Indeed I did. And you promised not to go without me," he replied. "Tell me more about the sun."

"It is like nothing I have ever seen before! At times I think I feel it more than see it."

"What do you mean? Is it warm on your skin?"

"Oh yes, it is certainly warm, but it is so much more than that. It calls to me. It fills my entire soul with peace and happiness. It is as if there is nowhere else I want to go. It is the feeling of coming home after a long difficult journey and sitting by the fire. And someone holding my hand so that I know I am not alone."

Mr. Darcy replied, "You are never alone. I hope it is all right if I hold your hand like this."

"I suppose so. But it is distracting." They were walking, or more like floating, very quickly now towards the sun. There was urgency in their pursuit. "We must hurry."

"Why?" he asked. His voice seemed too calm, considering the speed at which they were walking.

She felt his other hand rest on the one he already held. It slipped onto hers ever so gently, and she felt the tingle go up her arm. "I am not sure. I just feel time is running out."

She walked in silence for a little while, and she listened closely to the birds and felt the gentle breeze on her skin sending shivers up and down her spine. At least she thought it was from the wind. The colors were beginning to blur.

"Is something wrong? Are you chilled?"

"I do not know. . . Mr. Darcy, may I ask you a question?"

"Certainly."

"Where exactly are we?" She looked around, and the trees were passing by too quickly to see leaves on them. It was making her dizzy.

"I believe we are exactly where we are supposed to be. Together. Is that not what matters?" Mr. Darcy said.

It all felt so right. Being here, in the garden, with the bright sun, and with Mr. Darcy. It was amazing. She tried to describe the feeling to him, but she couldn't find any words. "Can you feel it too?" she asked in awe.

"Yes. I have never felt so happy as I do right now, holding your hand and talking so pleasantly with you. I want this moment to never end."

"Do you see the sun? Did it speak to you too?" They kept walking, rushing onward, hand in hand. She began to feel increasingly dizzy from the speed. It was taking her breath away a bit. Darcy made no reply, and she sensed his anxiety. "Did I say something wrong, sir?"

He gave her hand a squeeze and brought it to his mouth and kissed it gently. "Not at all. The sun spoke to you?"

"Yes, but not with words. It was more of a feeling. Of being welcomed home. As if I had made it to my final destination after a long journey. And then I heard you. I could not see you, but you spoke to me, very clearly. I knew you were not there, but I heard you. The words were very clear."

"What did I say?" he asked in surprise.

"Your voice was so sad. You were almost pleading with me. Oh goodness! Look at that sun! We have nearly arrived!"

"What did I say?" he said with some urgency.

"Yes, just like that. Your speech was distinct and very sincere. It was sad, almost as if you were saying goodbye. I suppose you were saying goodbye."

"Dearest, can you tell me what I said?" his voice was somewhat panicked.

"Do you not remember?"

"I am afraid not. Please tell me what I said."

"You said, 'Elizabeth, your family still needs you. You have a mission left on Earth.'" He brought her hand to his lips again, and she felt tears drop onto her hand. She shivered again involuntarily from head to toe.

How strange! This was all so strange! In the speed it takes for a candle to go out, they seemed to have reached the sun. She could see nothing but the brightest of whites now, but very faintly she heard Mr. Darcy's voice calling to her. He kept saying the same thing over and over again. But the light was so bright.

She was home. Her heart had never felt such love and peace.

As her eyes adjusted to the light, she could see Him then.

The Son. It wasn't the *sun* after all, it was the Son.

CHAPTER 6

"Elizabeth! Come back! Your family still needs you! You have a mission left on Earth! Do not leave me!" Darcy yelled. "Richard! Mrs. Collins! Come quickly! Help me!"

Elizabeth's body was shaking violently, and her head twisted unnaturally to the side. He could hear her labored breaths, if they could be called that. Her jaw was clenched, and she was biting her lip quite forcefully.

He had heard of this sort of episode, but he did not know what to do for her. He tried to straighten her head, but her muscles were trembling and shaking too forcefully. His heart was shaking just as forcefully, for he could not help but fear she had gone into the sun without him.

He yelled out again for help and then lifted her shoulders into his arms and cradled her head in his chest while she shook. For what seemed like minutes, he watched her helplessly. Finally, Colonel Fitzwilliam came rushing in.

"What is wrong, Darcy? Oh, dear Lord! She is convulsing! Lay her on her side!"

Darcy did as he was told. Her breathing was getting more labored. He wasn't sure if she was getting any air at all. "Do not leave me, Elizabeth! Your family still needs you! You have a mission left on Earth! Walk away from the sun! Walk away! Turn your back on it, and come back! You can do this, Elizabeth! Make the choice and come back to me! You have a mission left on Earth, and your family still needs you! Damn it! Richard, is she even breathing? Look at her color!"

Colonel Fitzwilliam was trying to restrain her shaking arms while Darcy cradled her neck. "I see it, Darcy. I see it. Do not worry, these things do not last."

"But look at her!" Foam had started coming out of Elizabeth's mouth. "Sweetest Elizabeth, do not dare go to the sun! Your family still needs you! You have a mission left on earth! Fight! I will not lose you. Not now. I will never stop fighting for you!"

Mrs. Collins put her palm on Elizabeth's shaking forehead. "Her fever is back. It is too high," she muttered. The she pulled out her handkerchief and started wiping Elizabeth's lip, which had started to bleed. "Mr. Darcy, please, try to be calm. It will be over soon."

At that moment, Darcy could feel her burning neck and head relax slightly and the force at which she had her head turned lessened. For the first time in what seemed like decades, she took a gasping breath. "That is right, Elizabeth, come back. I need you. Your family needs you. And who the hell knows what mission you have left on Earth, but if that is what you need to hear, then you have a mission left on Earth! Breathe!"

Colonel Fitzwilliam looked at him oddly. "Why do you keep saying that?" he puzzled.

"I do not know!" Darcy yelled. "She told me I said that to her. It is my only hope!"

"Look, it is over now. Her color is coming back, do you not see?" Mrs. Collins said.

Darcy couldn't even verbalize the fear in his heart. He watched as her breathing returned to normal and her body relaxed. He caressed her face, his own just mere inches from hers, and contemplated everything that happened in the last ten minutes, their conversation running through his head over and over again. As his cousin and Mrs. Collins busied themselves around the room, he vaguely heard one of them speak to a servant to summon Mr. Osborn. Someone's hands were adjusting Elizabeth's gown where it had been dislodged by the shaking.

He traced his fingers over her bleeding lip. It had already begun to swell. He took out his handkerchief and gently dabbed the wound. Colonel Fitzwilliam offered him a wet cloth, and Darcy numbly took it and wiped the last of the blood away. Her eyes seemed to flutter slightly.

In his heart of hearts, he prayed most fervently. He couldn't chance letting his eyes close in respect for the prayer, but surely God heard prayers like the one he was making now. *Save her. You cannot take her now. I know I have no right to tell you what to do, God, but I beg you with everything I have: bring her back to me.*

Despite being the Master of Pemberley, he felt quite powerless at the moment. His blurry eyes made it difficult to assess her condition. He blinked the tears away. He had to be strong. He had to be ready to help her when she woke.

Her eyes fluttered again, and she reached a hand up to her face. He gently caressed her cheek. For the first time in his entire life, he felt completely and utterly powerless. He did not know how to help. He did not know what to do for her. But he needed her. Every fiber of his being needed her. She was everything to him. Without her in his life, he simply had no hope.

Elizabeth had been right all along. His pride and his conceit had directed his every choice up until now. But now his vision had finally cleared. Not because the tears abated, but because he could see what a selfish creature he had been.

Even now, even when she was so ill, he was doing exactly what he wanted with her. If he wanted to hold her hand, he did. If he wanted to hold her in his arms, he did. Even now, as he traced his fingers around her cheek and down to her chin, he did so without restraint. He wanted to. And he took great pleasure in doing these things, even though in his heart, he knew that she would be appalled by his actions if she weren't so gravely ill.

But at least, he consoled himself, he was not the *last* man she could be prevailed upon to marry. Perhaps second to last, but not the last. Why such fragments of hope buoyed him up, he did not know. But he took comfort that nonetheless. So much had changed in the last eighteen hours.

Elizabeth began to rub her head and squirm. She let out a cough that was forceful, and she attempted to sit up a bit, but Darcy, in his refusal to let her go just yet, held her gently down in his lap. "You will be well, dearest Elizabeth, I am here."

Her eyes sprang wide open and quickly scanned the room, dancing from Darcy, to Mrs. Collins, to Colonel Fitzwilliam, and back to Darcy.

She blinked quickly and said with some distress while swatting away Mr. Darcy's hand, "What in the world? Unhand me!" She tried again to sit up, but it was obvious she was still dizzy, and Mr. Darcy instinctively reached out to steady her shoulders. She immediately shook him off.

"Mr. Darcy!" Elizabeth exclaimed. "I do not know what has made you think I am the sort of lady you can take liberties with, but I assure you, I am not!" She turned to Mrs. Collins who was rapidly approaching her.

"Lizzy, dear, Mr. Darcy is here to help."

"And how is compromising me supposed to help?"

Darcy thought he had been sufficiently humbled when he had nearly lost her to the sun, but her words stung like alcohol on a fresh wound. He stood up quickly and adjusted his vest. "My apologies, Miss Elizabeth, I can explain." Could he? Could he explain his behavior?

Mrs. Collins looked slightly confused but then said, "Lizzy, it is just Mr. Darcy. Surely the fact that he offered you support during this difficult time is not so disturbing. I know at one time it would have been, but you must admit that you have not been totally open with me about your attachment. The last day has been revealing, to say the least."

Elizabeth quickly stood up but then swayed slightly and took a seat as far as possibly from Mr. Darcy. She looked at Charlotte with wide eyes. "My attachment? To Mr. Darcy? Goodness, Charlotte, someone had better start explaining what is going on around here!"

Colonel Fitzwilliam made eye contact with Darcy, and there was the deepest compassion in the look. But it was clear that Elizabeth recalled nothing of the time they had spent together in her illness.

His wounds stung even further. To make it worse, he had no good explanation as to why he continued to stare at her.

"Miss Elizabeth, Darcy here has been quite attentive to you in your illness," Colonel Fitzwilliam offered.

"My illness?"

Darcy wanted to speak, but he simply hurt too much. Every touch, every word they shared was just swept away and discarded. These moments that he cherished and had played over and over in his head were not shared moments, as he once thought. He saw them now as they really were: stolen moments.

Darcy cleared his throat. He retrieved his hat, bowed silently, and left the room. All without a word.

He could hear his cousin making apologies, but Darcy paid it no mind. It was time to leave. It was still early enough to set out for London. As he walked back to Rosings, his stride had purpose, his mind forming plans with each step. He could not see the disdain in her eyes one more day, not after feeling that glimmer of hope from her letter. He must leave, and he must leave today.

CHAPTER 7

Elizabeth felt her head start to spin as she watched Mr. Darcy walk quickly out the door. She put her hand out to steady herself but found little to grasp onto. She faintly heard Charlotte next to her and felt herself being guided back to the chaise. It all was such a blur. Shapes, sounds, even the feel of the chaise under her, all seemed to fade away.

She could hear the colonel talking quietly. Something about going after him. Going after whom? Charlotte was asking for his help. Help to do what? She felt an arm under her neck and another arm under her knees, and suddenly she was floating. She knew she was being carried, but where? Things were very confusing. She felt a sense of dread and panic. A man's voice was speaking to her.

"Shhh, do not worry, Miss Elizabeth," he soothed. "Mrs. Collins asked me to take you to your room. You have been very ill these last few days. Try to relax. We are nearly there."

"Colonel Fitzwilliam?"

"Yes, Miss Elizabeth?"

"Where did Mr. Darcy go?" She heard her own words, and they sounded as if she had been dosed with laudanum. They were slurred and painfully slow.

There was a pause before he answered her. She looked up at him—his face was drawn tight with concern. "He left, Miss Elizabeth," he replied.

Left? Why? She felt so dizzy. Nothing made sense.

"Close your eyes," the colonel added. "Try to be calm."

She did as she was told, and as soon as she closed her eyes, waves of lemon and sandalwood assaulted her. Her eyes snapped open again in surprise. A part of her knew she was still being carried by Colonel Fitzwilliam up to her room, but in her mind, she was back in the garden again. That beautiful place she had dreamed about. She searched frantically for Mr. Darcy, but he was not there. Neither was the Son. She felt her eyes fill up with tears. She whispered, "But he promised he would not leave me."

There was no answer. This garden was not nearly as beautiful without Mr. Darcy. He was supposed to be here. There was no pull toward the Son. There was no peace like before. Her hand felt remarkably empty. Her heart, indescribably cold. She looked down the rose-colored pebbled path in the direction of where the Son had been. Somewhere in her experience, in this garden, she had made a choice. She had made a choice to turn away from the Son, to turn away from His sweet welcome home. The garden she was in was no longer where she wanted to be.

The choice had been an easy one to make when she had heard Darcy's words. She knew he was right. And although she knew she had a mission left on Earth and her family still needed her, that was not why she chose to turn back. She had turned from the Son to be with him, Mr. Darcy. And now he was gone.

She let her tears fall. His scent still lingered in the air. The lemon was calming. The sandalwood was soothing. Deep in her heart, she knew the Son loved her and would wait until it was her time to see Him again. But He could not help her find her way back.

Colors began to fade. Trees were not so lush. Flowers showed signs of their age. The trickle of the spring was disappearing.

This time it was the shadows, the unknown, that beckoned her. He had left. Mr. Darcy was gone. She had given up this paradise to be with him.

Would she ever return to this place? She hoped so. But it didn't matter, it was worth the risk. She embraced her choice and knew it would be a long, lonely walk back.

It was time to find Mr. Darcy. All she had left was her hope.

*****

Poole was attempting to hide his ire. Darcy couldn't blame him. As of two days ago, they were to leave yesterday. As of yesterday, they were staying another three days. As of ten minutes ago, they were leaving in an hour. Darcy was rarely so impulsive, but he could not help it.

Love did strange things to a man. In the last twenty-four hours, he had loved, lost love, hoped for love, embraced love, and finally lost love again.

It had been painful enough the first time. But nothing could describe how it felt to lose it again.

Hope hurt. He would never again allow himself that luxury.

Losing patience with his valet, Poole, he started packing his belongings himself. He pulled out his greatcoat, the one he had worn the morning of their discussion of French literature. She had mentioned how nice it looked on him. Shaking off the thought, he folded it quickly and put it on the bed. He knew Poole too well to try to pack it himself. Reaching into the wardrobe once again he pulled out the stained cravat that held the tea drops that he had sputtered when Elizabeth asked if he had seen Jane in London these last few months. He never even showed Poole the stains. It now was some sort of proof of his arrogance and conceit.

Would she have ever accepted him if he hadn't separated Bingley and Jane? If she'd never met Wickham? If he hadn't said those idiotic words at the Meryton Assembly? No, that was not a thought he had the freedom to consider. She had said no. It was over. If only they hadn't shared those moments in her delirium. If only . . .

"Darcy!" Colonel Fitzwilliam stormed in, nearly stumbling over the kneeling Poole. "Poole, forgive me. Please give us some privacy."

Darcy was quite sure he did not want to have this conversation. "Stay," he instructed Poole very forcefully.

Poole looked torn. He looked from his master to Colonel Fitzwilliam and back again to Darcy. "But I must look in the Great Room for the book you were reading the other night."

"No, Poole, stay. I insist."

His cousin stepped around the small valet and walked right up to Darcy and gave him a fierce scowl. "Do you really want to do this in front of the servants?"

"I do not intend to do *this* at all. I suggest you direct your attention to the servant that is packing your trunks if you want someone to yell at, for I will have none of it today. Please exit my chambers. I will meet you at the carriage in an hour. That should give you plenty of time." He stood as tall as he could. When his cousin did not move, he tried to push him out of the way and step around him, but his cousin quickly reciprocated a not-so-gentle push to Darcy's shoulder.

His manners vanished. Darcy whipped his head around to Richard, gave him a shove back, and yelled, "Leave me be! I care little for your opinion! She despises me! She thinks I compromised her!"

"Deuces, Darcy! Listen to yourself! Of course she does! You must see how inappropriate it was to do and say those things without an understanding! How did you expect this would end?" Fitzwilliam snapped his head back at Poole and barked, "I said leave!"

Poole did not wait for an opposing command from his master. He dropped the breeches he was folding and left immediately, quickly closing the door behind him.

Darcy rubbed his shoulder with his left hand, and then he pulled back his right arm and swung as hard as he could, only to be blocked by Richard's forearm. In a matter of half a second, Richard had Darcy's arm twisted tightly behind his back. Darcy pulled and pushed and made no progress. He was no match for Richard's military training. But this realization did not deter him. He jerked forward, forcing Richard to take a step to maintain his balance, but all that did was wrench his arm even further. They took turns pushing and pulling, grunting in exertion, but Darcy was immobilized. He could not move.

"Checkmate, Darcy," the colonel said breathlessly. "Give up."

"Break my arm if you must, Richard. But I will not stay here. I am leaving."

Colonel Fitzwilliam dropped both arms and pushed him away. Darcy stumbled forward and righted himself, then turned towards his cousin. They stared at each other, catching their breaths. "You are a coward," Fitzwilliam sneered.

"She wants me gone. She *refused* me!" Darcy remembered the look of repulsion in her eyes. He had seen that look before. *Had you behaved in a more gentleman-like manner* . . . "There is no hope left for me."

"Then fight for her!" Richard bellowed. "Make your own hope! Do not shake your head at me, Darcy. I am already sorely tempted to knock some sense into that thick skull of yours."

They stood silently for a few moments. Then Darcy quietly returned to the wardrobe and began pulling out more clothes. "I am leaving in fifty minutes, Richard," Darcy announced. "If you would like to join me, I suggest you start packing. This signals the end of our conversation. Kindly send Poole in."

"You are a proud man," Richard fumed. "A proud, cowardly man."

"So I have heard—and from a much prettier face than yours."

*****

Charlotte whispered, "Are you finally awake?"

Elizabeth slowly blinked several times. "I feel like I have been drugged," she groaned.

"Mr. Osborn gave you several doses of laudanum to help you rest."

"Who?"

"The apothecary. You have been quite ill. How is your neck?"

"Fine. Just tired." Elizabeth looked around her room. It took her a few minutes to realize she was still at the parsonage. "How long have I been sleeping?"

"A few days. I have been so worried about you, my dear. You have been delirious and crying and very upset. That is why I had Mr. Osborn administer the laudanum. Your fever came back twice, but I believe it is gone now. At least you did not convulse again. You very nearly sent Mr. Darcy into fits himself."

Elizabeth startled a bit and tried to sit up. *Darcy was here? It wasn't just a dream?*

She took a deep breath through her nose, but there was no lemon and sandalwood in the air. The only bright light came from the window.

From what she could tell, it was the middle of the morning. She felt her stomach seize up, and she quickly sat up and put her hand to her mouth.

Charlotte seemed to know exactly what to do, and she brought the basin to her face while Elizabeth tried to suppress the urge to empty her stomach. It was some time before she sat back, relieved that she did not actually cast up her accounts.

"Your retching stopped yesterday. Do you still feel nauseous?" Charlotte asked.

Elizabeth nodded. She looked around the room and saw she was in her nightclothes. "Please tell me that I was not dressed like this when Mr. Darcy was here. Or casting up my accounts in front of him."

Charlotte patted her hand. "Definitely not," she assured her. "But I think we are due for a little tệte-á-tệte about that gentleman. Fevers have a way of making one quite—how should I put it?—*talkative*."

Elizabeth remembered the tender words and touches of Mr. Darcy in her dream and groaned. "Exactly how talkative was I?" she grimaced.

"Lizzy, what has happened between you and Mr. Darcy? You have been muttering deliriously of nothing else for a week! I will read you Mr. Collins's sermons all afternoon if you do not comply," she threatened.

Elizabeth looked at Charlotte's suspicious but curious eyes and said, "I can hardly tell what is real and what is not. How long have I been sick?"

"Do not deflect the question. Do you have a secret understanding with the man?"

"No! Of course not!"

Charlotte got up from the side of the bed and went to the bookshelf. She opened a book and took out a few pieces of paper that looked quite familiar.

"If there is no understanding, why then is he writing you? Now, do not fret, I have not read it. I only noticed the masculine handwriting and looked to see who it was from. What on earth has happened between you two?"

Elizabeth leaned her head back against the headboard and closed her eyes. She then looked up and reached her hand out for the letter.

Charlotte gave it to her. Simply having it on her person seemed to calm her enough to begin the story. "I suppose you are shocked that I accepted a letter from a man I have no understanding with, a man whom I loathed until I read this letter, no less. But apparently, Mr. Darcy has long admired me. He enjoyed all our little rows. So much so that when I claimed a headache and missed that dinner at Rosings, he came here to see me."

"That was the day before you got sick. I cannot believe he did that. He knew there was no one else but you here." Charlotte gasped.

"My thoughts exactly. I was so shocked to see him, but even more shocked to hear what he had to say. He declared that he ardently loved and admired me against his will, against his reason, and against his character. Then he asked me to be his wife."

The shock on Charlotte's face was so humorous that Elizabeth started giggling. Finally, Charlotte exclaimed, "I cannot believe it! And I thought it was bad when Mr. Collins proposed by saying, 'Miss Lucas, although I do not currently find you pleasing to the eye, I am sure that in time, I will grow accustomed to you. I insist that we marry quickly.'" Elizabeth's giggles exploded into laughter. "I did not realize until later that he had not even asked me," Charlotte added. "He had just assumed!"

"Yes, Mr. Collins and Mr. Darcy both fell into that trap. He was *quite* sure I would accept his offer. Oh, Charlotte, I was so cruel in my refusal—"

"You refused him? But—"

Elizabeth peered at Charlotte in disapproval and silenced her with an arched eyebrow before continuing. "I said many things, most of which I do not wish to repeat. Suffice it to say, I was enraged and insulted, and I hid it ill." Memories of his pained expression and his eyes flinching at each word engulfed her once again.

"He must have taken it very poorly," Charlotte murmured.

Elizabeth sighed. "His eyes still haunt me. I gave little consideration to the fact that he really did love me. I slept very poorly that night and woke early to seek him out. We had met accidently many mornings on the grounds of Rosings, and I wanted to apologize. I felt ill over my treatment of him. We found each other in the gazebo in the orchard. But there was no opportunity to apologize. He only said, 'I have been walking in the orchard for some time in the hope of meeting you. Will you do me the honor of reading that letter?' And then he was gone."

"So you took the letter from him. Then what?"

"I felt dizzy and feverish, so I sat down and read the letter right away. My neck began to ache, and the pit of regret in my stomach grew and grew, and for the first time, I saw how wrong I had been. Everything between us had been a misunderstanding. Oh, Charlotte!" Elizabeth sighed. She involuntarily yawned, feeling all the strain of the conversation in her neck and shoulders.

"I have kept you from getting your rest," Charlotte apologized. "You still need your sleep."

"I believe you are right. But you never answered my question. How long have I been ill?"

"For eight days."

"And did anyone else fall ill? Colonel Fitzwilliam perhaps? . . . Or Mr. Darcy?" she stammered, blushing.

Charlotte reached for her hand and gently squeezed. "My dear, Mr. Darcy and Colonel Fitzwilliam left Rosings the day you had your convulsion."

"What?" Elizabeth tried to mask her disappointment. "He left me?" A part of her seemed to already know this.

"I am afraid so." Charlotte squeezed her hand again and kissed her forehead. "Right after you accused him of compromising you."

Elizabeth eyes widened, "I did what? Oh dear! How I must have hurt him!"

"I am afraid so. I have never seen such confusion, sadness, and pain in a man's eyes," Charlotte admitted. "But, let me get you some tea, Lizzy. You look so tired. We can discuss this later when you are more rested."

Elizabeth's eyes filled with tears, and she quickly glanced away from her friend to look out the window. "Oh dear, Charlotte! I have made such a mess of everything. How can I ever fix things?"

Charlotte smiled widely and then winked at her. "I was hoping you would say that."

CHAPTER 8

Colonel Fitzwilliam swirled the brandy in his glass and looked up at Darcy. "I received a letter from Rosings today."

Darcy sensed danger in his tone. *He is going to bring up Elizabeth again.* Since they left Rosings two weeks ago, his cousin had mentioned her more times than he could count. It was not helping his resolve to put Elizabeth out of his mind.

Nothing was helping. Not fencing for hours a day. Not attending balls and dinner parties every night. But even if he couldn't stop thinking about her, Darcy was determined not to get into another brawl over her. He was still chastising himself for his outburst two weeks ago. He was generally a private man, yet right in front of Poole, he had blurted out that he had compromised Elizabeth. Such lack of control was weak. And Darcy had no intention of making the same mistake twice.

New knots formed in his stomach as he remembered his actions at the parsonage. His lack of control with his cousin paled in comparison to the liberties he had taken with Elizabeth. What was the matter with him? Why, upon seeing her so ill, had he become so unguarded? He had asked himself the question many times, but there was no satisfying answer.

He knew that if his actions became widely known, her reputation would be in ruins. What if Mrs. Collins or Mr. Osborn insisted on him honoring her reputation? What would he do? He knew he still loved her, but he was painfully aware of her wishes. He was, after all, the second-to-last man she could "ever be prevailed upon to marry." He knew it was selfish—a personal trait he had been blind to before, but now recognized at every turn—but maybe if he married her, she would somehow learn to love him.

For a brief moment, memories of her soft touch and lavender smell stirred him to close his eyes and savor each moment they had shared. Her hand, so soft and small. Her nails, neatly trimmed. Her hair, delicately and temptingly curled. Her shoulders, petite but strong. The memory of how she had cradled her head on his shoulder and the feeling of her breath on his neck sent new shivers up his spine.

"Are you not going to ask me what the letter said?"

Darcy had little interest in Aunt Catherine's missives today. They were usually filled with pages of flattery for Darcy and urges to not make "dear Anne wait too much longer". He had received three such letters in the last two weeks, and they were still unopened on his desk. He usually responded quickly, as his aunt's letters sometimes mentioned estate issues that needed to be addressed in a timely manner, but he could not chance hearing about Elizabeth.

And once again, his thoughts turned to the pale ivory skin he had wiped with a cool washcloth over and over again. She had been so very ill. But he could not think about her. He struggled in vain to put some distance between everything they shared while she was ill and the onslaught of emotions that left a trail of pain in its wake.

"Come now, Darcy! I will not mention Miss Elizabeth if you do not wish it. I will omit telling you that she is finally well enough to return to her family, a full week after she was able to get out of bed. Ah ha! I see you are calculating it out in your head! Yes! She was quite ill for several days after we left. Anyway, she reports that Miss Elizabeth departed for London yesterday. It seems she plans to stay with her aunt and uncle for a month."

London? Darcy looked at the three letters from his aunt on his desk, his finger running the length of the grain of the wood beside them. He would have to answer them sometime. He took up his pen and attempted to write a response to the dinner invitation that he did not really want to attend. His mind wandered to the delirious letter Elizabeth had written him. The letter that he had stowed away in a locked drawer that even his steward did not have a key to. The letter that offered a hope that had been snatched away the next day.

"And since we are not discussing Miss Elizabeth, I will *not* attempt to mention that she sends her warm wishes for your birthday coming up."

"What did you say?"

"Miss Elizabeth wishes you a happy birthday, but that is exactly the type of information you instructed me *not* to tell you, so I apologize. My manners are in sore need of refinement. Blame it on the uniform. Would you like a drink, Darcy? You seem a little flushed."

Darcy looked at the smirk on his cousin's face and knew he had fallen into his trap. He started twirling his pen from finger to finger and back again. *What does it mean that she sends her warm wishes?* The agony of this thought left him nearly speechless but not completely void of sense. "That was very polite of her."

"Yes, it was. The letter was quite insistent that I relay Miss Elizabeth's sentiments." Colonel Fitzwilliam stood and poured himself more brandy and then poured another glass and handed it to Darcy.

"Thank you," Darcy muttered.

"In fact, since Miss Elizabeth is here in London, perhaps we should pay a call on her. It would look impolite if we knew of her being here in London and did not at least enquire after her health."

His heart started beating rapidly, and he took a hefty swallow of the drink. "It would look impolite," he repeated.

"Indeed. The letter even recommended it."

Darcy was beginning to be suspicious of all this information that supposedly came from their aunt. "The letter from Rosings?"

"Yes."

"I see."

"Do you?"

"I see that you are playing on my sympathies for the lady, and you have never had an aversion to bending the truth when it suits you."

"Believe what you wish. That should be the motto on the Darcy crest." Fitzwilliam replied sarcastically. "'Believe what you wish'. What a marvelous phrase! Take Miss Elizabeth's reaction when she woke up, for instance. You could believe that her anger was genuine. Or you could believe what you wish—that it was a moment of fever-induced delirium. You could have noticed how she was so dizzy she could hardly even hold her head steady as she said it. You could have stayed just a moment longer and watched her collapse in fatigue and have carried her to bed as I did. You could even have heard her ask why you had left when you had promised her you would not—"

"Enough already! I know what she said, and I saw it in her eyes. She despises me!"

"Believe what you—"

"Get out!"

Colonel Fitzwilliam set down his glass very deliberately. "If you are seeking a bit of hope, Darcy, I just gave it to you," he continued. "Believe it . . . if you wish." And without another word he turned to leave.

"Wait," Darcy called out after him. "Forgive me. I did not intend to lose my temper. Lately it seems that all my emotions are heightened. If I am nervous, nothing brings me peace. If I am angry, my temper is unrestrained."

The colonel nodded slowly. "And if you are in love?" he prodded.

He let out a sigh. "If I am in love, it seems I am passionate without any thought to the repercussions."

"Go see her, Darcy," Fitzwilliam urged. "See whether she truly despises you. I will wager your annual income that you will see something else."

Darcy considered the idea and drummed his fingers on the desk. "You are wrong about one thing, Fitzwilliam. You imply that I wish to believe that Elizabeth despises me. I actually, very deeply, hope to believe something else."

"Then believe what you wish."

He couldn't help but grin slightly. It was not lost on him that it was his first smile in two weeks. "Perhaps I shall. London, you say?"

"Yes, right here in London." The colonel smiled widely at him. "Mrs. Collins will be so pleased to hear her letter did some good."

Darcy looked over at Richard with a confused look on his face. "Mrs. Collins?" he asked.

"Yes. My letter from Rosings. From the parsonage. Oh, did you think I meant Aunt Catherine?" he grinned. Colonel Fitzwilliam chuckled as he left the room.

Darcy stood for many minutes staring after him. Colonel Fitzwilliam was a genius. A tenacious, obnoxious, irritating genius. Darcy took a deep breath and started forming his plan. If he remembered correctly, Elizabeth's aunt and uncle lived in Cheapside. Who they were or where they lived in Cheapside, he did not know. But he knew a certain lady who did. He let out a groan and finished his brandy. It would be a dangerous endeavor for sure.

*****

Jane looked at her favorite sister and smiled. "I am so glad you are here, Lizzy! Aunt and Uncle Gardiner and I were all so worried when we heard you were ill."

"I was anxious to see you again," Elizabeth replied, "and the journey was not too far. Although my neck is still quite sore." She paused before enquiring further. "And you have heard nothing of Mr. Bingley?"

"Oh no. As I said in my letter, his sister made it very clear that she wished to cut all ties with me. It seems to be Mr. Bingley's wish as well. I do not hold any particular feelings for him anymore. No truly, I do not. It is a difficult situation to be in, for sure, but I know in time the sadness will abate." Her eyes glanced away, and she stood to move to the window. "I would sit in this window for many hours each morning, eagerly awaiting their call. I simply do not know how I could have misread him so terribly. I have not had too many suitors to compare him to, but I was at least confident that he admired me."

"I am *very* confident that he admired you. I believe he still does. We just need to have faith in him."

"Oh, Lizzy, you are too kind. No, he will not return to Netherfield. I am resolved to put him behind me."

Elizabeth wanted so badly to share the information from Mr. Darcy's letter with her sister, but that would require a great deal of explanation. And she was not quite ready to divulge all of what had happened in Kent. Furthermore, it had been several months since the Netherfield ball. It was clear that Bingley had been very attached at one time, but what did he feel now? If he were to see Jane again, with no regard for her, Jane would be devastated. Elizabeth felt trapped in her knowledge and wished that she could reassure her sister more definitively.

Just then, their bedroom door flung open, and their young cousins came rushing in. "Lizzy! Avelina got butterfly, and she no give it me! She say it her prince!" Four-year-old Nathan was a spoiled little boy—he was the youngest and quite happy to be so—but Elizabeth and Jane couldn't resist his smile. His brother, Wesley, was a few years older and a bit more self-controlled. But it was Edward that had grown the most since Elizabeth had last seen her cousins.

Edward warned, "Nathan, Wesley, you must behave, or Nanna will tell Momma. I am sorry, Cousin Jane and Lizzy. We do not often see butterflies, and Avelina is beside herself."

"Well, let us go celebrate with your sister!" Elizabeth cried. "I know she is most intrigued with butterflies!"

Jane scooped up Nathan in her arms and kissed his cheek. He quickly wiped it off and yelled, "Ew, Janey! Put me down! I a big boy!" She giggled and put him down.

It was then Elizabeth's turn to laugh as her twelve-year-old cousin offered his arm to her and bowed. She curtsied in return and said, "You are becoming quite the gentleman, Edward."

"Papa says he will send me to the Worthington's School for Boys in a few months so I can learn to be a gentleman. All the landowners' sons go there."

"Indeed they do. You must work hard to get good marks. But here is a little lesson for you. You should probably have offered your arm to my eldest sister."

Edward smiled and said, "But you are the one in greater need. I know you have been ill. How do you feel today?"

She patted his arm. "I am getting much better, thank you. Now let us go see Avelina and her butterfly."

The entire group went outside. Elizabeth looked on as her oldest cousin, Avelina, was examining intently the specimen in front of her. She was getting very mature. She still had a young woman's slim hips and petite shoulders, but her tiny waist hinted at her maturity. Many other fourteen-year-olds did not look quite so feminine. Elizabeth knew Avelina's height made people assume she was older than she was. But despite her feminine form, her interests were far from ribbons and lace. Asking her to choose between shopping for a new bonnet and polishing her new rock left one feeling foolish for asking—for Avelina would always choose the rock.

She had a thirst for nature like Elizabeth, which endeared her to Elizabeth even more, for her young cousin was always willing to go on long walks. But while Elizabeth simply enjoyed her surroundings and the fresh air and sunshine, Avelina was quite a talented naturalist, diligently studying each rock and insect along the path and illustrating her finds in chalk and pencils.

But above all, Avelina was tenderhearted and kind. If Elizabeth were to compare her young cousin to anyone else in the family, she would say that Avelina was very much like her sister Jane, so the young girl held a special place in Elizabeth's heart. She had been so glad last night to learn that Avelina was to come on a tour of the Lake District with Elizabeth and Mr. and Mrs. Gardiner in two months' time.

Avelina was bent over looking into her glass jar, studying her new specimen intently. Elizabeth came up and placed a hand on her shoulder and said, "So, what kind is it?"

"It is a Painted Lady butterfly, a form of *Nymphadilae*. A male. You can tell from the markings."

"He looks like the one you already have," Jane said.

Avelina looked up and smiled. "He is! Now I have a male and a female. I have found a prince for my princess!"

Elizabeth and Jane took turns asking questions of the very knowledgeable Avelina while Edward tried to calm his two younger brothers. "Can they mate?" Elizabeth asked.

"Absolutely. That is what makes it so exciting! It is so romantic! Just think of it, Elizabeth, after turning down all the other ladies who tried to claim his notice, he has finally found his companion! Can you imagine how ardently he must love and admire her?"

Elizabeth was shocked by Avelina's wording. "Pardon me, I am fatigued," she stammered. She quickly turned and went inside. But distancing herself from her innocent cousin's words did not make them echo in her heart any less.

CHAPTER 9

The neighborhood of Mayfair was buzzing with carriages. Darcy was glad he had decided to walk to Bingley's townhouse. He had sent his calling card ahead and was hoping that he would be able to avoid Miss Bingley until he had a chance to talk with her brother. He was not looking forward to their conversation, but he knew it had to be done.

He rapped on the knocker and heard the crisp clink each time the metal hit metal. He took a deep breath and waited.

The butler opened the door and said, "Good morning, Mr. Darcy. Come in."

"Thank you, Wilder." He stepped in and handed Wilder his gloves and hat.

"I was told to show you right into his study. He is waiting for you."

Darcy nodded and followed the butler through the halls as quietly as possible, his eyes darting every which way, hoping to avoid Miss Bingley's notice. He chuckled slightly when he thought that he was more nervous to ask a question of Miss Bingley than to confess his sins to her brother! He sobered quickly as the door was opened to reveal Bingley setting up the billiards table.

Bingley's study was quite different from Darcy's. Darcy had a large desk covered with tomes and bookshelves lining every wall. Priceless pieces of artwork were displayed in every available inch of space. And his desk was turned away from the window so that he would not be distracted by the street life. Bingley's desk, on the other hand, was directly facing the window. And instead of ancient pieces of artwork, there was a billiards table and a card table and an entire bar devoted to fine wines and brandy. His friend never over-imbibed, but he had a taste for rare, and often illegal, French brandy.

Bingley finished setting up the balls and casually said, "Thank you, Wilder. How are you, Darcy? I did not expect to hear from you so early today. Did you not go to the Parkers' ball last night? But I must remind myself who I am talking to; of course you are up and about at an early hour."

Darcy looked Bingley over a bit. He noticed that although his words were polite, there was no real joy in his tone. Bingley stood leaning on his billiards table with a pleasant smile; however his eyes had no light or spark. Today was no different than the last several months. Bingley was still the same as he had ever been since the day Darcy first counseled him to forget Miss Bennet.

Darcy waited for Wilder to close the door, and then he replied, "Good morning. I might remind you that it is nearly afternoon, and I see I am not the only one who is up and about after the Parkers' ball. But if I am not mistaken, you did not stay long either."

"I do apologize. I find my heart is just not into dancing as it used to be. I used to love to meet new people, to be introduced to all sorts of ladies, but now I . . . that is to say, I have a great deal of things to do right now. My mind has been otherwise engaged. I am glad you are here, for I have come to a decision: I will give up Netherfield. My lease is not up until August, but if I were to find someone to take over the lease, I am sure that there would be no problem—"

"About Netherfield . . . Perhaps you should reconsider. There is something I must tell you before you give it up."

"No, there is nothing for me there. I shall start looking for a country estate somewhere else, perhaps Derbyshire."

This isn't going to be easy. Darcy nervously started drumming his fingers against his leg. "Certainly nothing would please me more than to have you settled with a fine lady near Pemberley."

Bingley winced slightly. "I do not mind being a bachelor. It is not as bad as I once made it out to be."

"We have not discussed ladies lately. Are there any that catch your eye?"

"Darcy," Bingley sighed, "you know very well why we have not discussed ladies lately. *None* of them catch my eye. None since Miss Bennet." He reached out a hand to the table at the mention of her and let out a breath. His other hand raked through his light-red hair, and he looked away from Darcy as if to avoid eye contact. "I am trying to forget her, I truly am. I go to even more balls and dinner parties than your cousin Colonel Fitzwilliam. Granted, I usually leave early, but I am confident that with time, her sweet smile will no longer haunt me."

Darcy took a deep breath. "Bingley, I have recently come to question the counsel I gave you, and I fear you have suffered from its ill effects. Let us play a game of 'what if'. *What if* Miss Jane Bennet were in London?"

Bingley's head snapped up, and he opened his mouth to speak, pausing briefly. "I imagine she would enjoy her time here. She was always most content in any environment."

"*What if* you knew where she was? Would you pay a call on her?"

Bingley hesitated uncharacteristically. "Yes, I believe I would," he replied. "Not that I wish to create an attachment, of course . . . but merely because it would be the right thing to do. We both agree she is a sweet girl, even if her heart was not touched. She tends to enjoy my company. The visit would merely be a formality . . . Oh, I do not know! What do you think? It would be the right thing to do, no?"

"Right as a matter of common courtesy?" Darcy queried. "Or right because you still admire her?"

Bingley looked toward the window and sighed. "Darcy, I sit at this desk for hours every day. And every time a blonde passes that window, my heart catches in my throat out of sheer desperate hope that it is *her*. I have searched every face in this city, looking for that angelic smile that enslaved me from our first dance at the Meryton Assembly." Bingley paused. "Yes, I admit that I still admire her very much. In fact, I am quite enamored with Miss Bennet. If she were here in London . . . Well, I would very selfishly pay a call just to see her again, and God willing, to behold that smile. Lord, I am such a lovestruck mooncalf!"

"Glad to hear it. Do you mind if I help myself to a drink?" He walked to the bar and deliberately took his time in his choice. To Bingley, it probably looked as if he were taking his time selecting a drink. And then, as he poured, it probably appeared that he was being careful with the priceless amber liquid. When he could delay the moment no longer, he faced Bingley again, who had a very curious expression on his face.

"I am rather surprised to hear you say that," Bingley admitted. "Darcy . . . what is it you have come here to tell me?"

Now it was Darcy's turn to wince. "I have something to confess. Something slightly embarrassing," Darcy groaned.

He watched Bingley raise an eyebrow at him and then quickly flip his coattails out from under him as he sat down. "Fitzwilliam Darcy of Pemberley embarrassed? This sounds like quite a good story."

Darcy then proceeded to tell him all—his attraction to Miss Elizabeth Bennet, how he had misjudged Jane's attachment, and how he had even conspired with Caroline to keep Bingley from seeing Jane in London. Bingley listened wide-eyed, clearly speechless. Darcy swallowed a bit of his liquid courage and then flatly told him that he knew for a fact that Jane had admired him last fall because in the course of offering marriage to Miss Elizabeth Bennet, she had brusquely corrected his misunderstanding of the situation.

"You fell in love with Elizabeth Bennet, proposed, and were refused because you separated Miss Bennet and me? Is that what I am hearing?" Bingley's tone was lively and excited rather than accusatory.

Darcy let out a breath. "Indeed. It appears I was *very* wrong about Miss Bennet's feelings for you. She cared for you a great deal. She very well still may, at least that is what I gathered from Elizab—Miss Elizabeth."

Bingley stood up and said, "Let us play this game once more. I believe your first question was, 'What if Miss Bennet were in London?' Ask me again."

Darcy smiled slightly as he watched Bingley's boyish energy truly infuse his entire body. "What if Miss Bennet were in London?"

"I would not let anything stop me from paying her a call! Ask me another question."

"What if she no longer cared for you?"

"It would not matter! If she loved me once, I can win her heart again! Ask another."

"But what if she rejects your suit?" Darcy remembered the look of disdain in Elizabeth's eyes. Could he face her again? *What if Colonel*

Fitzwilliam is wrong? What if she still despises me? I am not sure if I could bear it again.

"Darcy, I would fight for her until my very last breath. She is worth it."

"Indeed she is," Darcy muttered to himself. He shook his head in an attempt to clear his mind of thoughts of Elizabeth and tried to focus his thoughts to Bingley. "I am very happy for you, and I wish you the best. One more question though. What if your best friend had broken your trust? Could you ever forgive him?"

"Of course! Furthermore, I would insist that my rather-dimwitted friend come with me to see a certain other young lady!"

Bingley clapped him on the shoulder and smiled at Darcy's forlorn expression. "Come on, old friend," he coaxed. "It has been all misunderstandings between us and the Bennet sisters. But we must not give up on them—not until our very last breath." Then he jumped up, called for his coat and hat, and grinned. "Let us go immediately! For once, I will have the advantage of a clearer mind, although I cannot guarantee it will make me any more rational!"

Darcy smiled at his exuberant friend but then peered at him with a strange look in his eye. "But what if you did not know where in London they were?"

Bingley stopped short in his excited fidgeting and looked directly at Darcy. "Pardon me?"

"I do not know *where* in London they are. Only that they are staying in Cheapside with their uncle. I do not know even know his name."

"You are in earnest? You have me nearly giddy with excitement, ready to put on my hat and go this very instant, and now you tell me you know not how to find her?" Bingley slumped down into the chair again.

"Unfortunately so. But I know someone who does."

"Darcy, are you suggesting *I* know where this mystery relative lives? Let me assure you I do not. Why are you looking at me like that? You seem to have another secret for me."

Darcy groaned again and took a deep breath. "Is Miss Bingley home?" he winced.

Bingley's glorious laughter filled the room. It was a sound that Darcy hadn't realized he had sorely missed. "Ah, I see! We must appeal to your co-conspirator for the address. Ha! Well, I suppose that will be your penance for misleading me," Bingley chuckled. "Fitzwilliam Darcy is requesting to speak with my sister. I will never hear the end of this—all these years I have called her delusional, for she insists you admire her and are waiting for just the right moment to make her mistress of all of Pemberley."

"Delusional, truly delusional." Darcy laughed, for although Miss Bingley displayed no symptoms of fever, she too might have a near-death experience in a few moments when she learned who was requesting to see her. "But desperate times call for desperate measures, I suppose."

Together they walked out into the foyer in search of the butler. "Wilder," Bingley requested, "will you please inform Miss Bingley that Mr. Darcy has requested to see her? He and I have been discussing a very delicate matter, and he is eager to ask her something as soon as possible."

Darcy glared at his friend in disapproval, but Bingley could only grin and shrug his shoulders in response. The stoic butler tried to conceal his surprise before obediently turning and walking upstairs to Caroline's parlor. The two gentlemen watched him go.

"Was that truly necessary, Bingley?" Darcy whispered.

Bingley clapped him on the shoulder and smirked. "You were the one who involved Caroline," he laughed. "I would say this makes us about even! Now, she will be reluctant to share the address if she knows why we want it. Do we have time to inform me of your plan of attack, or should I just blindly follow?"

Just then they heard a feminine squeal from the upstairs quarters, and Darcy shook his head, "I think you will have to just blindly follow."

CHAPTER 10

Caroline Bingley had no time for more than a simple bun. Her curls from the Parkers' ball the night before were still acceptable. She quickly reviewed her reflection in the mirror as her lady's maid adjusted the dainty shoulder straps of the evening dress—it was somewhat ostentatious for morning tea, but what was too fine for Mr. Darcy?

"That will do, Eliza. I must not keep Mr. Darcy waiting. Just spray me once more with the perfume."

"But, madam, I already sprayed your neck and wrists. I worry that any more would be overwhelming," her new lady's maid ventured.

Caroline glared at the young girl in the reflection and pressed her lips together in a firm line, a look that she had perfected over the years. "You *worry*? Well, how fortunate for you that *I* am the mistress and *you* are merely the maid. Must I really remind you again, Eliza?"

"Yes, madam." Eliza bowed her head and sprayed her mistress several times.

"Dismissed," Caroline commanded with a sigh. It was so exhausting to train hired help. They all seemed to believe that they deserved her notice and that their opinions mattered. She couldn't imagine why. Accepting the advice of a servant was *unthinkable*. Such people clearly lacked the morals and breeding of proper ladies and gentlemen. If they had even a fraction of the education and refinement she possessed, they might be considered tolerable. But the truth of the matter is, when generations are bred with no education, no culture, and no moral guidelines, ignorance cannot help but be perpetuated.

She gathered her skirts and tucked a handkerchief into her pocket and pressed her hand to her stomach. Now was not the time to lament about the servants. They did not deserve her notice, not on a day like today. She lifted her chin and examined her profile in the mirror. Yes, today would be a wonderful day. She practiced her most dignified shy smile, which she knew would come in handy as Mr. Darcy proposed. She could see him being so overcome by such a look that he would ask her if they could marry quickly.

For a brief moment, she considered what she would say if he really did request an expedited engagement. Normally she would agree with anything that Mr. Darcy suggested. But she would need time to arrange the wedding. The entire *ton* would be invited. Her dress would be of the finest silk, with lace imported from Italy, and these things cannot be rushed. And after the wedding in London, they would, of course, need to host a celebratory ball at Pemberley. Her debut to Derbyshire society would be nothing less than magnificent!

A knock at the door interrupted her reverie. "Enter," she called.

Mr. Wilder bowed slightly. "I was instructed to inform you that Mr. Darcy and Mr. Bingley are still awaiting you in the parlor," he announced. "Shall I say that you are prepared to receive them?"

"Yes. I will go there straight away. Tell me once again what Mr. Darcy said."

He cleared his throat. "I believe it was Mr. Bingley that said he had been discussing a delicate matter with him and now Mr. Darcy desires to see you." He cleared his throat. "Ah, and that he had a question to ask."

Caroline smiled. "And how was his mood?"

"His mood? I would say he was in good spirits."

So it was indeed as she suspected! Mr. Darcy was to propose today, and her brother, Charles, had already given his blessing! "I see. Please send for some fresh tea, and make sure there is lemon on the tray for Mr. Darcy."

She stood and walked past him towards the parlor. She paused to pinch her cheeks a bit and then paraded in. As expected, her brother and Mr. Darcy stood and bowed.

"Good day, Mr. Darcy. What a pleasure it is to host you today!" She gave him her most charming smile and a curtsy that could only have been described as perfection.

Mr. Darcy cleared his throat and replied, "The pleasure is all mine. I apologize for intruding so early after the Parkers' ball."

"Think nothing of the hour, sir! I enjoy your company *so much*. Do sit down. Have you and Charles had a nice conversation?"

"Well, I . . . that is, Bingley and I—"

"—have been discussing a very delicate matter," Charles interjected. "One that required my immediate attention. Darcy was so eager that could not bear to delay even an hour."

"Indeed? Well, gossip, my dear sir, is highly frowned upon unless you share it with me." She smiled wickedly and batted her eyelashes at him. She could see it had its intended effect. He turned away in an obvious attempt to control his attraction.

Charles sat up and said, "Darcy was quite revealing in our discussion this morning. I believe more than one lady's name came up."

"Yes, Bingley," Darcy replied, "but I do not want to give Miss Bingley the wrong impression." He turned to Caroline and said, "I must admit we discussed several ladies, but I am not the sort of man to be fickle and give my heart to more than one lady. You know that about me by now, do you not?"

The blush on his face nearly gave her goose bumps! She demurely placed her hands on her lap and crossed her ankles. Just then, the tea was brought in.

She took her time pouring the cups. Her harshest teacher at the Hilliard School for Ladies could not fault her for her posture nor the care she took. Placing a slice of lemon in his cup, she stood and carried tea to Mr. Darcy. He took it from her, and as he did, her hands grazed his ever so gently. She heard him clear his throat a bit before he thanked her.

Speechless! "You are very welcome, Mr. Darcy," she purred in reply. "I hope you like the tea. I do try to meet your expectations, as any good hostess should. For it is an honor to have you in my home. I find the role of hostess is one of the most important roles a lady can take, and I flatter myself in my talent in the area."

He sipped it briefly. "Yes, the tea is wonderful. I must tell you, Miss Bingley, I had to confess a few things to Bingley this morning, something that involved you and a former acquaintance."

"Oh, I cannot imagine that you doing anything that merits an apology to Charles!" she laughed then threw a dark look to her brother. "Surely Charles is mistaken," she insisted. *But which acquaintance could he possibly mean?* She knew all his connections; she made it her goal in life to follow in the same circles.

"Well, Bingley has learned that Miss Bennet is in London. I came this morning to apologize for keeping that information from him. Such deceit was wrong," he confessed. "But I did share with him the kind gesture you made to help her feel welcome."

She studied Mr. Darcy and tried to examine his motivation for bringing up their little secret. Then she quickly glanced at her brother. He seemed to be smiling and cheerful as usual.

She remembered clearly the day she told Mr. Darcy about Jane's visit. When she had asked his counsel on whether or not to return Miss Bennet's call, Darcy had encouraged her to make it clear she intended to cut all ties, and to not say a word to Charles. It had been so thrilling to engage in a conspiracy with him! To work together clandestinely! After delaying for several weeks, she had paid the briefest of visits and made it clear that she would not be returning anytime in the future. She might have even mentioned that her brother was enchanted with an heiress; a falsehood, of course, but it had been necessary to ensure that Miss Bennet understood that any future relationship was impossible.

But today, Darcy's description of the visit, not to mention Charles's reaction, was slightly confusing, for Darcy was calling it a *kind* gesture and Charles was as calm as she had seen him. "Yes, I paid a call on her," Caroline replied cautiously. "When I heard she was in town, it seemed only right."

Darcy smiled and responded, "Of course. It was most kind of you to visit her in Cheapside. It must have been difficult for you to find the street she lived on. What was it again? George Street? Grove Street?"

She felt some relief in his comment. At least he seemed to still disapprove of the Bennet's relations, which was encouraging. "Gracechurch Street," she replied. "A truly hideous place. How anyone can bear to live between a milliners shop and a Rose and Crown Inn is beyond me! With all the comings and goings of commoners, it felt a degradation just to walk the same cobblestones! A bath was sorely desired upon my return."

"It sounds like you truly condescended, Caroline," Bingley replied. "How awful you make it sound! Darcy, have you been to

Gracechurch Street? Is it truly as bad as she makes it sound? For surely Miss Bennet's aunt and uncle—what was the uncle's name again, Caroline?"

"Gardiner," Caroline shuddered. "A *tradesman*."

"Yes," Darcy clucked sympathetically. "You surely outdid yourself, Miss Bingley. And I am sure that it was obvious they were in trade by the appearance of their house," Darcy speculated with a small smile on his face.

Caroline thought he was being most charming this afternoon. It made her feel more confident in her deduction that today would indeed be the day she would claim the title as future mistress of Pemberley.

"Oh, I flatter myself in my ability to see fashionable colors and trends, but their sad little red brick home had the dullest of brown trim on the windows. Someone had tried to brighten the place up with some potted geraniums next to a terribly old garden bench, but honestly, it hardly made a difference! Who puts a garden bench in front of their house? A tradesman, that is who!"

She continued to pour tea for Charles and brought it over to him. He seemed to be in especially good spirits. It was surprising to see his eyes bright and smiling again. She was feeling fairly confident in the opinions she gave, opinions that she was sure Darcy shared and Charles seemed to find acceptable, but Charles seemed to be at peace with knowing Miss Bennet had been in London. This piece of knowledge was surprising, to say the least, for she had been sure he was still questioning his decision not to return to Netherfield.

Darcy stood up and placed his cup on the tray and bowed. "I thank you for the excellent tea, Miss Bingley; but I just recalled an urgent matter that requires my attention. Bingley, would you do me the honor of accompanying me?"

"I would be happy to assist you. Caroline, you have been most entertaining. Thank you."

Such flattery was welcomed anytime; however, Mr. Darcy could not leave just yet! "Mr. Darcy, could I not interest you in a stroll along the Mayfair neighborhood? It is so delightful at this hour!"

"A walk does sound enticing; however, Mayfair does not hold my interest currently. Perhaps another day. But please let me say, I have never appreciated your conversation as much as I have these last ten minutes. Thank you so much. Good day."

She couldn't help but wonder at the sudden departure. Charles seemed to nearly jump out of his seat. He hadn't even taken a sip of tea. But her worries were dismissed quickly as she basked in the splendid compliment Darcy had bestowed on her. *"Excellent tea", "Perhaps another day",* and especially the last: *"I have never appreciated your conversation as much . . ."*

Pemberley would have to wait for its mistress, it seemed, for its master's expertise was sorely required in so many matters—the urgent business that had dragged him away only proved it. She smiled at the thought. The best things were worth waiting for.

Mrs. Caroline Darcy of Pemberley! How splendid that sounded!

CHAPTER 11

Elizabeth was easily fatigued these days. She reminded herself that the last two weeks had been very difficult. As her tired body stirred from a lovely nap, she growled at the afternoon sun coming in through the west window.

All she wanted to do was return to her dream that she wished she could understand—a dream that she knew she needed to make sense of. It replayed in her mind every time she closed her eyes. It felt more real than any experience she had ever had, so perhaps *dream* wasn't the right word. But what else could she call it? Charlotte had hinted that it may not have been a dream at all. Charlotte's description of what had happened in the parlor with Mr. Darcy during Elizabeth's fever sounded oddly familiar, and paralleled the same conversation she experienced in her dreamlike state. How much of it had been real?

She rolled over and continued her examination of the events in the garden. It been some kind of heaven, that much she knew. She couldn't imagine her concept of heaven being anything but a beautiful garden to be endlessly explored. The emotions she had experienced there were still overwhelming at times—an all-encompassing love, the sense of being welcomed home, an indescribable peace, and the ability to communicate without speaking. But had it truly happened? Or was it merely the delirious result of a fever?

And why was Darcy there? *He* had not been feverish. It had been *her* heaven, not his. She once cared little for his opinion and even less for his horridly conceited proposal. But she had to admit that reading his letter had altered her view of him. Not so much that she felt for him what she had felt in the dream, of course. Not feelings of . . . What did she feel for the man? Admiration? Love? Respect? Yes, definitely respect. She could at least admit that.

She marveled that there had been no contention or animosity whatsoever in the garden. As if unkind feelings were simply not allowed. While in the heavenly garden, she had remembered his behavior in Hertfordshire, or at least that they had not always understood each other, but not his hurtful proposal that had occurred the day before. She had not harbored any ill feelings for him in her "heaven". And the only feeling she had felt from him was companionship and kindness, not the distain and judgment she usually associated with his intense looks. In fact, his presence amplified the peace and love that existed in the garden. He had been so attentive and caring and deeply passionate. She found herself pondering those last words she used to describe him. Attentive. Caring. Deeply passionate.

The entire thing left her quite confused. And whether or not she wanted to admit it, the experience had changed her feelings for the man quite drastically. She knew now that she had misunderstood him. Each touch and each kind word testified what a pure, honest, and loving man he was. He was exactly the kind of man she could fall in love with.

But then he had left; even after promising not to. She had been left alone. Her heart ached momentarily with a powerful sense of loss.

Perhaps someday she could find another Mr. Darcy. She understood now that she had refused a man that could have made her happy. Every other gentleman of her acquaintance was now weighed against him—she asked herself, "Is he a Mr. Darcy? Does he have the love, compassion, and strength of constitution that Mr. Darcy had?"

The answer was always "no".

Her heart lurched a little at the thought. Every now and then a small idea danced across her mind that perhaps she need not find his equal or locate a duplicate; perhaps she could hope for Mr. Darcy himself . . . But her mind struggled against the notion. After all, such a hope seemed rather bleak at the moment. According to Charlotte, Elizabeth had accused him of compromising her.

Stretching, she pulled back the covers and looked at the clock. It was a quarter past two in the afternoon, which meant she had slept for three hours and missed the noon luncheon. Although her appetite had not returned, she knew she should eat something. She slipped on her house slippers and checked her hair in the mirror. Her bun had fallen out a bit.

She did nothing more than replace a few pins, for there was no one to impress at her aunt and uncle Gardiner's house. She brushed away the stray hairs with wet fingers and sighed.

As she made her way downstairs to the kitchen, she was alerted to the fact that Mrs. Gardiner must be entertaining guests. She took the servant's staircase, carefully avoiding the sitting room. She took her time, for her nap lethargy still lingered.

Upon reaching the kitchen, she said, "Good afternoon, Judith Ann. Might there be a bit of bread I can attempt to eat?"

The cook smiled sweetly and rubbed her wet hands on her apron. Mrs. Gardiner's cook, Judith Ann, was as pure and kind as any woman she ever knew. "Indeed," she replied. "I was going to bring you a bit of vegetable broth as well. It will help that sallow look under your eyes."

"Thank you, that sounds heavenly. Do you know who is visiting Mrs. Gardiner?"

Judith Ann spooned out some broth into a bowl. "Yes, ma'am. It is two gentlemen who are acquainted with you and Miss Bennet. I believe it is the man that your sister was so devastated about."

"Mr. Bingley? Mr. Bingley is here?" Suddenly her heart started beating rapidly in her chest, and she felt warm, just like in her dream. If Mr. Bingley were here with another gentleman, the most logical conclusion was that Mr. Darcy had accompanied him.

Judith Ann handed the bowl of broth to her, but Elizabeth shook her head. "Excuse me, I . . . I must return to my chambers." With what little stamina she could muster, she quickly retreated to the servant's staircase and rushed into her room.

Quite short of breath and bracing herself against her vanity, she tried to make sense of it. Had Charlotte's plan worked after all? Elizabeth started unpinning her hair and took extra care with her new bun. Her eyes really did look sallow. But there was no time to dwell on that. She desperately wanted to see Mr. Darcy and knew she must hurry. There was a pull she could not explain. The very thought of him made her nervous, yet, strangely enough, calm at the same time.

She heard a quiet knock on her door, and Avelina came in. "Elizabeth, I am so glad to see you are awake! You have visitors downstairs. Let me help you with those pins." Avelina took the pins from her trembling hands and started to place them strategically in the right places. After a minute or two she said, "There! You look wonderful."

"Thank you, Avelina. I heard that Mr. Bingley was here. Do you know who the other gentleman is?"

"It is a Mr. Darcy." She noticed the look on Elizabeth's face and said, "You are acquainted with him, correct? Is there something wrong?"

She knew him all right. She felt she knew him better than any man she had ever met.

"No, dear, nothing is wrong, but I should probably go down and greet them."

"I am glad to hear it, because he has asked about you several times. Jane appears most uncomfortable. Is this the Mr. Bingley that she was in love with?"

"Indeed. We shall have to tell you all about it when they leave. How long have they been here?"

"A good half hour, I think."

"Oh dear. I must hurry if I want to see them." She followed Avelina down the stairs and stopped briefly before rounding the corner. She could hear Mr. Bingley conversing with someone, probably Jane, but she could not hear Mr. Darcy.

She took a deep breath and felt a sense of peace as she detected the faint smell of lemon and sandalwood. A flash of vivid memory engulfed her. She remembered his sweet words and tender touches. She had felt so endeared to him, so protected by him. So loved and cherished. They had been so content together in the enchanting garden. There had been no awkward lulls in conversation. Although they had spoken to each other, most of their communication had been unspoken. He had made her feel how much he desired her, that he wanted her to stay with him.

She heard her name mentioned and knew it was time to greet her guests. She entered the room and both gentlemen stood and bowed.

Her attempt to be composed in his presence was thwarted as she saw the man of her dreams standing before her. He had no particular expression on his face but seemed to be searching hers.

They stared at each other for a moment before she recalled herself and said, "Good afternoon, Mr. Darcy."

He bowed again. "Miss Elizabeth." He looked away a few seconds later.

She felt saddened by the loss of eye contact, but as he turned she was able to admire his strong jaw. She flushed as she recalled the moment in her dream when she had reached out and touched it. As if it had just happened, she felt his love and compassion again and his strength of constitution. She entered and took a seat opposite the windows. Mr. Darcy sat down across from her. Because he was silhouetted by the bright light coming in behind him, she was unable to decipher his facial expressions. This frustrated her immensely, and she frowned. For how was she to know if he still admired her if she could not see his face?

*****

24 April 1812

Dear Mrs. Collins,

I was very pleased to receive your letter yesterday. As a colonel in His Majesty's army, I have been well-trained in observation, and I agree wholeheartedly with your assessment. Anyone with even one good eye can see that Miss Elizabeth and Darcy need a little help. The information you sent me, although somewhat cryptic, was clearly understood.

But because Darcy is as stubborn as a mule waist-deep in frozen mud, I was forced to expand upon your excellent plan of attack. Please let Miss Elizabeth know that she sent warm wishes for his birthday in your letter. It may also be prudent to inform her that he, in fact, has a birthday next week, on May 1st.

I must confess that I have never before told so many falsehoods in my life as I have told these last two weeks. If these two lovebirds require much more assistance, I may begin to fear for my soul. But God is love, as St. John says. I will hold out hope that He therefore views my dishonesty with mercy.

Once I won Darcy's attention with Miss Elizabeth's counterfeit warm wishes, he was like a dog to a bone. It is my understanding that he set out at once to apologize to Bingley about his misguided interference regarding Miss Bennet. In fact, he fled so quickly from my presence that I quite forgot to give him the Gardiner's address that you had so wisely included. But I understand they are both at the Gardiners' this very hour. Apparently a dog with a bone can be quite ingenious when information is desired!

I am relieved to hear that Miss Elizabeth suffers only fatigue and lack of appetite. It is rather singular that she has some memories of her delirium. Has she disclosed to you what happened? I would never ask you to break her confidence, but I find I cannot stop thinking of it. Do you believe Miss Elizabeth had a near-death experience as Mr. Osborn suggested? If so, I would be most curious to hear about it. If she really went to heaven and saw God, then why was Darcy there?

Forgive my ramblings. It is just that I have never heard of these experiences before, and it amazes me that it could be possible to see God and live to tell about it. Perhaps in time I will hear the full story. For now I will close this letter.

Also of note, I believe I am to wish you joy! Mr. Collins did not hesitate to tell Aunt Catherine, who then informed me. It seems you were blessed very quickly in your marriage. I pray that you and the baby are well. I am sorry to hear that Mr. Collins took ill so soon after Miss Elizabeth recovered. I hope he has improved. Please send my sympathies.

Your servant and willing cohort,
Colonel Richard Fitzwilliam

Colonel Fitzwilliam signed his name and sealed it. He then called Darcy's butler and had him mail the letter as an express. He was under the impression that Mrs. Collins was anxious for news and was a bit emotionally invested in seeing Miss Elizabeth and Darcy together. Darcy wouldn't mind the extra expense, he was sure.

If Darcy was indeed at the Gardiners' at this very moment, he couldn't help but wonder at the duration of the visit. Things must be going very well.

*****

Darcy was feeling quite warm with the sun on his back. He tried not to fidget. He sorely wanted to take off his topcoat, but that would be inappropriate. And he was committed to thinking, behaving, and speaking within all possible bounds of propriety. He could not risk another error. He had to show Elizabeth that he had never meant to compromise her and that she could trust him to behave honorably. More importantly, he desperately wanted to observe her behavior towards him.

He listened quietly to the conversation progress from the weather to the Gardiners' summer travel plans, but it was not until he heard his home county of Derbyshire mentioned by Mrs. Gardiner that his thoughts on Miss Elizabeth were redirected.

"Elizabeth," Mrs. Gardiner announced, "this morning Mr. Gardiner learned of a critical shipment coming into town during our planned holiday to the Lake District, so I regret to tell you that our journey will now only take us as far as Derbyshire. I did not wish to wake you to give you such bad news."

Elizabeth's face seemed disappointed. She stole a quick glance at Darcy, and she seemed to look at him with narrowed eyes as she responded. "I am sorry to hear that." The sun on her face revealed the pale color of her cheeks. He reminded himself that she had only recently been gravely ill. It was wonderful just to see her well enough to receive visitors. Nevertheless, he couldn't help but feel saddened by her comment. Her disappointment that she must travel to Derbyshire only confirmed her original opinion; she did not wish for his presence.

But he was a selfish man—as she had so charmingly informed him. So selfish that he could not bring himself to leave. He just needed more time with her, regardless of her indifference.

He tried to hide the disappointment in his voice. "Miss Elizabeth, Derbyshire is wonderful country. It offers a great deal. Perhaps not all that the Lake District offers, but there is still a variety of things to see. I have lived my whole life there, and there is no other place I wish to call home. I am sure that with your love of walking, you will find a great deal of satisfaction with its rugged and varied terrain."

Her eyes met his as he spoke, and she seemed terribly fatigued, but there was a small polite smile on her face as she said, "I do not doubt that, and I meant no slight on Derbyshire. It is simply that I had my heart set on seeing the Lake District with my aunt and uncle and my cousin Avelina."

He perceived her polite smile as simply a gesture in civility, and he was determined to be civil in return. He addressed Mrs. Gardiner next. "Where in Derbyshire will you be going, ma'am?"

"Lambton, my home town. It is a small town just north of—"

"Me," he interrupted. "Just north of me. Lambton is a mere five miles from Pemberley." He stole a glance at Elizabeth, who seemed to catch his eye. Her expression was difficult to read. He could not tell if she was pleased by this information.

"Yes, I am actually acquainted with Pemberley," Mrs. Gardiner replied. "My father helped rebuild the shelves in the library when I was young, and we made it a semiannual event to tour the estate. My father was very proud of the work he did."

Darcy was surprised at this connection, however indirect, to his favorite room of the estate. "Rightly so. It was excellent craftsmanship." He tried not to look directly at Elizabeth but instead turned to Avelina. "You should come and stay with us and be our guests. My sister, Georgiana, would be most pleased to have two young ladies and their family come to visit, and I personally would be happy to host the party. There is much to do on the estate for anyone interested. I never lack for entertainment."

Avelina, smiling widely, asked, "Do you have many butterflies?"

"Indeed we do, and I shall show you the very meadow where Georgiana was most successful in catching them." This made Avelina burst with joy. It seemed he could charm the aunt and cousin but not the lady in question. He was acutely aware that Elizabeth had said very little. He was trying to look for any indication that her opinion had changed but found little reassurance in this area.

He again attempted to engage her in conversation. "Miss Elizabeth, I assure you that my staff is quite accustomed to visitors, and it would be an honor to share my home for as long as you desire."

She tucked her chin, and a charming blush infused her cheeks. She looked up briefly and said, "It is not my decision to make. I am at the mercy of my aunt and uncle."

Mrs. Gardiner smiled and said, "I must confer with Mr. Gardiner, but it is a very tempting offer. How much notice would you need?"

He forced himself to look away and to not interpret what Elizabeth said as evidence that she did not wish to be his guest. All he needed was some indication of how she felt about him. He was coming up with nothing more than common courtesy and polite smiles. It was quite frustrating.

Out of the corner of his eye, he saw her stand and walk over to her aunt. She had her back turned to him and realized he had not answered Mrs. Gardiner. "I need no notice at all. We keep many rooms in constant state of readiness. I truly insist, if it is acceptable to you and your party. Please be our guests. My sister has heard much of my friends and acquaintances from Hertfordshire, and she would be more than delighted to actually meet one of them." He hesitantly turned his focus back to Elizabeth, who was now walking towards him with a cup of tea.

Elizabeth walked slowly and carefully, as if it took a great deal of effort to cross the room, and stopped right in front of him. "I saw that your tea was empty. Would you like another?" Elizabeth said with a small smile on her sweet lips. Her eyes, although still shadowed with dark circles under them, were kind and bright.

He exchanged cups with her and responded, "Thank you." He looked down and saw a lemon floating in his tea.

"I . . . added a lemon. I remember you once told me that you like lemon in your tea because your father drank it that way," she added breathlessly, almost in a whisper.

He looked at her in surprise and suppressed an even greater smile. She had admitted in her delirium that she had never noticed how he took his tea, but somehow touching his face told her that is what he preferred.

An overwhelming sense of relief filled him.

She remembered.

She remembered their conversation during her fever, that his father had liked lemon in his tea. And she had taken an extra step to please him. He had never enjoyed tea as well as he did at that moment. For all the searching he had been doing in her facial expressions and words, it was this simple peace offering that she performed that made his heart bounce with glee. She remembered. Perhaps there was hope after all. He looked up and repeated himself, "Thank you."

She tilted her head casually and curtsied. "It is my pleasure, I assure you."

He sipped it and felt warmth fill his entire soul. The sun may have warmed his back, but the warm gesture of the tea burned his soul with gratitude.

He turned his attention to Bingley, who had been having his own conversation with Miss Bennet. It had been some time since either of them had contributed to the general conversation of the room. Darcy examined Miss Bennet's appearance and manners towards Bingley with new eyes. Her smile was genuine, not forced. The flirtatious tilt of her head was ever so slight, but it was there. She looked down at her hands with every comment he made to her, but she always returned her gaze to his and met it briefly before she responded. These were not signs of indifference.

He stood and walked over to Bingley. "Miss Bennet, we noticed a park across the street. Could we interest the ladies of the house in a stroll?"

Miss Bennet brushed a curl away from her face and glanced at her sister briefly before responding. "I am not sure my sister is up to it."

From behind him, he heard Elizabeth speak up, "I am unfortunately too fatigued for walking, however we could sit and enjoy the sun. I adore the warmth of the sun. It is a pleasure I especially appreciate lately."

Darcy looked at her and bowed. "I cannot imagine a greater pleasure." Then he gave her a sly smile and added, "Would you like to walk to the sun with me?"

Elizabeth smiled genuinely and raised her eyebrow slightly. "I would very much like to walk to the sun with you, Mr. Darcy." Then, in the softest of whispers she added, "Again."

It was more than he hoped for. It was more than he deserved.

She remembered.

CHAPTER 12

Three days later, after many long discussions between Elizabeth and Jane about the gentlemen's call to Gracechurch Street, Elizabeth concluded that she needed to make three disclosures to her sister. The first was the contents of Darcy's letter—which necessitated Elizabeth informing Jane about Darcy's proposal. But Jane needed to know that Bingley loved her and always had. It was a lengthy conversation, one that nearly exhausted Elizabeth.

Jane's only question at the end was a poignant one: "So, you regret refusing him now?"

Elizabeth did not know how to answer.

The second disclosure was what Elizabeth remembered from the heavenly garden and her interactions with Darcy. She explained that Charlotte had been witness to most of it and it all correlated to what she remembered. Elizabeth tried to explain what had happened when she walked to the Son but found she was still at a loss to fully understand it.

The third disclosure was how Charlotte had written to Colonel Fitzwilliam, cryptically trying to express Elizabeth's improved opinion of Darcy. Elizabeth had only dared to hope that she would be able to see Darcy once again and renew their acquaintance.

Jane looked surprised and kindly asked, "So, you think Mr. Darcy only seeks to renew your acquaintance?"

Elizabeth simply replied that she hoped so. And if their visit the other day was any indication, the answer was clear regarding Bingley, but Darcy was still somewhat of an enigma. He had been polite, even offering to host them at Pemberley, but the openness she remembered from her dream had not been there. He asked about her health more than once as they sat together in the sun, but he seemed very reserved, even tentative.

Avelina, although much too young to understand these private conversations, still enjoyed feeling grown up. As such, Elizabeth and Jane spent a great deal of time with her. They understood that she was at an impressionable age and just as her mother, Mrs. Gardiner, had done for Jane and Elizabeth, the two sisters nurtured their cousin's spirit.

Today, as the rain fell in sheets outside, the three of them were huddled together in Jane's bedroom listening to the steady raindrops coming down.

Avelina climbed onto the chaise next to Elizabeth and snuggled under her arm. "Tell it to me again. It is just so romantic!"

Elizabeth laughed softly. She looked to Jane, who smiled sweetly back at her and was nodding her encouragement. "Where do you want me to start?"

"Start where the handsome prince entered the ball with his friend."

"From the beginning?" Elizabeth asked. "Very well." She took a deep breath and started. "There once were two poor sisters who were very close. The eldest was the fairest one—"

Jane piped up, "That is not true."

"It is my story, let me tell it," Elizabeth teased. Jane rolled her eyes and smiled back at her. "As I was saying, the eldest was the fairest one, the youngest was only known for her wit and intelligence. Both dearly wished to find handsome princes who cared for them, but they lived in a small town where gentlemen were scarce. One day the entire town assembled to dance. It had been rumored that a handsome prince had moved into the town and would be in attendance, and many young ladies were hoping he would notice them. But all of the ladies but one were disappointed that night. The new neighbor did indeed come, but he seemed to notice only the fairest sister. In fact, he asked her to dance *two* dances with him. He was most amiable. But he had not come alone. He had brought with him a gentleman friend."

Avelina added, "A *rich* friend."

"They both were rich," Jane explained, "but that does not matter. This is a love story."

"Yes, a love story that has yet to have the ending written." Elizabeth winked at Jane. "The friend was rumored to be worth ten thousand a year. But unlike the neighbor prince who was amiable, this man seemed to refrain from polite conversation and chose instead to look at the poor townsfolk and their country manners with contempt. It did not take long for the town to see the striking difference between the two men.

"The younger, yet wiser, sister was sitting out a dance and observing all around her. She was pleased to see her sister happy, but as the dance was nearing an end, the neighbor prince came and asked his wealthy friend why he was not dancing. Although she should not have been eavesdropping, the younger sister listened closely, for she dearly wished to hear his response. The friend replied, 'You are dancing with the only handsome lady in the room'. From this comment, the neighbor prince laughed and offered a suggestion. He said, 'Why not dance with her sister? She is right over there.' To which the rich friend replied—"

Avelina giggled. "Let me say this part," she insisted. "'She is tolerable, but not handsome enough to tempt me.' Did I get it right?"

"You are quite correct," Jane replied. "It was very wrong of him to say such a thing, but remember that we cannot judge him too harshly."

"Why not?"

Elizabeth then said, "Because, Avelina, the man was very sad about his sister and felt he did not want to dance at all, no matter who the lady was."

"Had his sister died?"

"No, but she had been nearly captured by an evil villain. The rich friend was too sad to tell the neighbor prince why he did not wish to dance. So instead, he pretended the younger sister was not handsome enough to tempt him. The younger sister, with her charm and wit, did not take offence at first to such a slight; however, this did not stop her from telling the story to her friends. She laughed about it all evening. And soon, deep down, she reached a conclusion about the man who slighted her. She judged him to be the proudest man she had ever met. Her opinion was so decided that she convinced herself she saw nothing but disdain in his face."

Jane added, "Even though many in the neighborhood saw good in the friend. It was only logical that the neighbor prince, who was so well liked, would not align himself with such a disagreeable man."

"Jane, this is my story. He was a proud man, and nobody but the fair sister and the neighbor could tolerate him."

Avelina looked up at Elizabeth and giggled. "One could say that he was handsome, but not tolerable enough to tempt anyone!"

"Yes, indeed! And then, to make matters worse, the rich friend did a dreadful thing. He disapproved of the sisters' family, so he convinced the neighbor prince to travel far away—"

"Lizzy, that is hardly fair. He did it because he thought the fair sister did not love his friend. He was trying to help—"

"Shh, Jane!" Avelina insisted. "You are ruining the most dramatic part! Jump ahead to where he proposed, Lizzy."

Jane rolled her eyes at the Avelina's dramatic flair and smiled at Elizabeth. "Well," Elizabeth began, "many months later, the rich friend and the younger sister met again in a distant land. Quite unexpectedly, the rich friend declared that he most ardently loved and admired her."

Avelina squealed. "That is so romantic! But she refused him, right? Because he had separated her sister and the neighbor prince?"

"That she did. And she did it in the most offensive and cruel of ways. She even said he was the last man in the world she could ever be prevailed upon to marry."

She heard Avelina gasp in shock. "And this is when she fell ill?"

"Yes, she became very ill. So ill that she was very unaware of what she said or did. But the rich friend came back after her cruel refusal. He was kind and helpful while she was ill."

Jane broke in, "It takes a good man to return after being so wounded and hopeless. One must admit that he was quite humble to risk her disapproval again."

"So maybe he was not so proud after all?" Avelina said hopefully.

Elizabeth smiled and said, "No, he was not as proud as she once thought. In fact, she learned a great deal about him while she was ill. She learned that he was kind and respectful. She learned that he was the best of men." She could hear the sadness in her own voice, and she closed her eyes and said again, "The best of men."

"And they lived happily ever after?"

Jane said, "Avelina, we told you this was a story that has not been finished yet. The end has not been written. You must be patient and wait to see how it will end."

"But what about the fair sister and her prince?"

"Somehow the prince found her again," Elizabeth smiled. "And his love for the fair sister was so clear that no one could doubt that he would make her an offer *very soon*."

Jane blushed brightly and said, "Oh, Lizzy! We do not know if that is how the story will unfold." Jane paused and looked down at her hands before admitting, "Although I would very much like that ending very much."

Avelina sat up and said brightly, "Two best friends fall in love with two sisters at the same time! They could have a double wedding! Oh, please tell me that is how it will end!"

Elizabeth clasped Jane's hand. The sisters both declared in unison, "I would like that very much." All three burst out in giggles.

*****

Darcy glanced at the morning post while his cousin read a book. There were two bills, a thick envelope from his steward that was probably the quarterly summary of his holdings, three dinner invitations, an invitation to Fosters' annual spring ball, and another two letters from his aunt, one of which was sent by way of express, which wasn't too unusual.

He knew he should probably address the letters from his aunt soon. If he didn't, she would continue writing every day until she exhausted all the ink in Kent.

He broke the seal, read the first two lines, and gasped in shock. "Richard," he stammered, "Mr. Collins is dead!"

Colonel Fitzwilliam put down his book. "Good God! Mrs. Collins told me he took ill after Miss Elizabeth left, but it sounded like merely a cold of some sort."

"Apparently not," Darcy replied. He continued to read. "And Mrs. Collins is with child. A widow with a fatherless child."

"What a terrible blow!" Fitzwilliam murmured. He closed his book and placed it on the table. "He will be sorely missed, although I must admit not by me. I have often wondered why such an engaging lady ever aligned herself with such an insipid man." Darcy nodded in grim assent.

". . . unless she was mercenary," Fitzwilliam mused quietly. "And I can hardly imagine that someone so honorable . . ."

"What does it matter now?" Darcy sighed. He walked over to his liquor cabinet and poured a drink for himself and his cousin. "What will happen to Mrs. Collins? And to Longbourn? He was to inherit the Bennets' estate."

"Hopefully the child will be a boy," Fitzwilliam commented.

Darcy stared at his cousin coldly. "No matter the sex of the baby, it will grow up without a father. How can you be so insensitive?"

"I meant no disrespect to the child nor Mrs. Collins. You know I enjoy Mrs. Collins immensely. I only meant that if her baby is male, then he will inherit Longbourn, which may be able to provide some small security for Mrs. Collins."

"And when Mr. Bennet dies, I suppose he can take advantage of that *security* by pushing the family out as soon as he pleases," Darcy snapped.

"Lord, Darcy, why must you get so defensive? It is not my fault or Mrs. Collin's fault or her unborn child's fault the estate was entailed away. Would you rather Longbourn were passed to a complete stranger, some relation even more distantly related?" Colonel Fitzwilliam glared at his cousin and downed the rest of his drink.

"I am sorry," Darcy apologized. "I think it is the weather. I have never appreciated the rain. Especially when it keeps me indoors."

Fitzwilliam chuckled. "You mean away from Miss Elizabeth."

Darcy slumped back into his chair and tossed the letter on his desk. "You are probably correct. I would like to see her again, but the rain has been nonstop the last few days. Do you think it too late to go see her right now?"

"I think news like this should be delivered immediately, regardless of the weather. And I am sure Bingley would like to pay his respects. Why do we not pay a visit to his place?"

Darcy grimaced. He could not bear the idea of seeing Caroline again. He cringed remembering how she had batted her eyes at him. “I cannot go to Bingley’s.”

“Still afraid of his sister, are you? Then let me fetch him. It is but a few blocks. I will be back shortly. Then we can go to the Gardiners’ together and offer our sympathies.”

CHAPTER 13

Elizabeth sat with Avelina's head in her lap as she traced the shape of her tiny ear. Before falling asleep, Avelina had asked once again to hear the story of the two wealthy princes. This time she had asked if the rest of the story would ever be written.

Elizabeth remembered Jane's promise: *Someday it will be.* It was a comforting thought.

She rested her hand on Avelina's shoulder and closed her eyes briefly. Today was the first day since she took ill that she had not napped after luncheon. She wanted to get back into a normal routine, and her fatigue was getting better each day. But she was regretting her choice now. Avelina's steady breathing was nearly hypnotic. With her eyes closed, she felt herself drift off once again into memories of the beautiful enchanted garden. The peace and love she had felt there with Mr. Darcy quickly rushed back. Even the fact that he had not come these last five days did not diminish her comfort as she thought of the man.

Their conversation a few days ago had been amiable and reassured her that he at least desired to further their friendship. Friendship; yes. They were friends now. Perhaps it wasn't entirely encompassing of her true feelings, but she could at least say he was a friend. Perhaps there would be more between them someday. And like Jane had said, perhaps someday the end of the story would be written. Of course, how she wanted it to end was still unclear. Did she wish him to renew his addresses? The thought brought butterflies to her stomach, and she knew she did not dare answer that question. Did she dare hope for Mr. Darcy?

The knock on the front door made both Avelina and Elizabeth jump out of their drowsy states. Elizabeth reached up and rubbed her neck a little. She must have drifted off to sleep because now she had a most painful kink in her neck. She rolled her head from side to side and tried to work out the tension.

Avelina pushed herself to a sitting position and asked, "Who is at the door?"

"I do not know. Should we go see?" Avelina sat up and tried to straighten the wrinkles in her dress. Elizabeth reassured her. "Do not worry, dear, you look wonderful." Elizabeth continued to rub her neck.

"Is your neck stiff again?" Avelina asked.

"No, I just fell asleep with it in the wrong position."

"Would you like me to rub it for a few minutes?"

"You are so sweet. Your offer earns you the title of my favorite cousin."

Avelina laughed. "Is that all it takes? If so, then you shall get a neck rub every day!"

"I am only teasing," Elizabeth said, and then with a wink she added, "You may claim the title anytime you want."

They both heard the commotion at the front door and listened closely. It was clear that they had several visitors. With umbrellas in hand, Jane had taken the youngest on a much needed walk to work out their youthful boyish energy, and Mrs. Gardiner was paying a call to a friend. As the deep voices started to become apparent, her heart began to pick up speed and the lethargy of her short nap quickly fled.

The housekeeper, Mrs. Brown, escorted the three gentlemen in and announced them unnecessarily since Elizabeth was quite familiar with all of them. "Mr. Darcy, Mr. Bingley, and Colonel Fitzwilliam. Should I send a servant for Miss Bennet and Mrs. Gardiner?"

Elizabeth stood and smiled at the gentlemen—perhaps she smiled at one of them more than the others. His eyes were dark and handsome this afternoon. "Mrs. Gardiner is not necessary, but if you would please send for Jane, she will be anxious to see our guests. I believe she went toward the creek."

Colonel Fitzwilliam stepped forward, took off his hat, and held it across his chest. "Miss Elizabeth, perhaps you should summon Mrs. Gardiner. I am afraid we bring bad news."

She looked at him closely. And as always with Colonel Fitzwilliam, she instinctively knew she could believe him. She instructed the housekeeper to send for Mrs. Gardiner as well. She watched as Mrs. Brown took the hats from the gentlemen and they stood fixed in their positions by the door.

"Forgive me, please come in. Sit down. What is this news that requires three gentlemen for its delivery?"

Darcy walked across the room and bowed to Elizabeth and then sat in the chair next to her. She felt Avelina sit up straighter beside her, her eyes bouncing around each of the somber faces in the room. Bingley and Colonel Fitzwilliam sat down stiffly on the edge of their seats. No one seemed relaxed in any way, and it was discomforting.

Elizabeth turned her attention to Darcy as he cleared his throat ready to speak. But suddenly they heard another knock on the door. Her worry was building, for Mr. Darcy was more serious in his manners than she had ever seen, and that was saying something.

"Mr. Darcy, has something happened?"

In an instant, Darcy's face had a sweet, familiar compassion emanating from it, and he said, "Has Mrs. Collins written to you recently?"

"I received a letter two days ago."

"What news did she have?"

Elizabeth blushed slightly as she was reminded of all the probing questions Charlotte had written regarding Mr. Darcy. Charlotte had been most curious to know whether their plan to elicit Colonel Fitzwilliam's help had succeeded. Elizabeth knew that this was not the type of information that would leave three gentlemen so serious looking.

"It was the usual letter. She hoped I had arrived safely and that I had improved since leaving the parsonage. Why do you ask?" She was starting to feel a sense of dread.

Bingley asked, "Did she mention Mr. Collins?"

Before she could answer, she was interrupted by Mrs. Brown bringing her what appeared to be a letter.

Mrs. Brown said, "Forgive me, Miss Elizabeth, but this just arrived by express for you."

She took it and looked down and saw Charlotte's familiar handwriting. More to herself than to anyone in the room, she said, "It is from Charlotte." She looked over to Mr. Darcy, and he placed his hand on hers.

"I am afraid we arrived just in time. I am sure you will find in that letter the same information that I received this afternoon from my aunt. Would you like some privacy? It may be distressing." Darcy said kindly.

She could feel his considerate gesture, but if she were to receive bad news, she very much would like Mr. Darcy beside her. He brought with him the peace she felt in the garden. "That will not be necessary." She opened the letter and could feel Avelina leaning in and reading it next to her.

Dear Elizabeth,

Since I wrote to you last, several things have occurred. Perhaps I should start from the beginning. I tell you, my mind simply is not my own since I became with child.

When you left last week, you might remember that Mr. Collins felt out of sorts and kept to his room. He exhibited symptoms similar to yours, but they came on slower and so mildly that I did not associate them with the seriousness of your illness. I thought it was only a cold. But the day after you left, he developed a terrible headache. On Sunday night, he became quite confused, feverish, and delirious. It was not until then that I realized he was seriously ill.

I am grieved to tell you that he lost consciousness early yesterday morning and passed away a few hours later.

I am now a widow at the age of eight-and-twenty. I am faced with some terrible decisions to make in the next weeks. How will I care for my child? What will become of us?

The funeral will be Saturday. I would dearly love to have my best friend return to help me make the necessary arrangements. Please tell me you can return to Kent to help me.

I have many letters to write, but your response is the one I will most eagerly await. I am terribly distraught. I cannot find the words to describe how I feel. Please say you will come. I anxiously await your response.

Charlotte Collins

Elizabeth lowered the letter and heard Avelina crying next to her. She put her arm around the tenderhearted girl and whispered to her, "This is very sad indeed."

Bingley stood and offered his handkerchief to Avelina. "Do you know Mrs. Collins well, Miss Gardiner?"

Avelina sniffled slightly and wiped her eyes and said, "No, but I am close to her sister, Maria. She and I are just a year apart. Every time I visit Longbourn, we make time to see each other, and we write to each other often. She had much to tell me about her last visit with Elizabeth to Rosings."

Elizabeth felt a hand on her shoulder and turned to see Darcy, who was handing her a handkerchief. She hadn't even realized that she was crying. She gave him a weak smile and thanked him.

"Can I get you anything?" Darcy said softly. "A glass of wine? Mr. Gardiner? News like this is so devastating. I wish to help in any way possible."

The tears started pouring out, and her shoulders started to shake. Darcy scooted his chair closer to her and placed both her hands in his. So many emotions were flowing through her that she did not know which one dominated; her grief for Charlotte's loss, the tenderness she felt from Mr. Darcy, the fear for the baby, or the guilt she felt in thinking that at least only Mr. Collins had died and not anyone else.

The last weighed heavily on her. She never liked the man, not when she first met him, not when he proposed (if that is what you would call it), not when he became so overbearing and controlling to Charlotte when they married, and not when he would lecture her about her behavior. But he was her cousin after all. Shouldn't she feel some grief over his untimely death?

She looked up and saw Jane walk in the room, and her tearful state must have shocked her immensely.

Jane rushed over to her, and seeing that Avelina was crying too, she asked, "What is the matter, Lizzy?" Elizabeth simply started crying harder.

Bingley then tried to explain. "Miss Elizabeth just got word that your cousin, Mr. Collins, has died."

"Oh no!" she whispered breathlessly. "Poor Charlotte!" Jane cried.

Elizabeth found her voice then and said, "She is with child. Her last letter told me she had just felt it move. It had made her so happy. Oh, Jane! Now she will have nothing! And the baby will grow up without a father!"

Jane wrapped her arms around her, which forced Darcy to remove his hands from hers. Jane opened her arms up to include Avelina who had laid her head on Elizabeth's shoulder. The three of them held each other silently for many minutes with the ever-steadfast Jane whispering in their ears. "Charlotte is strong. She and the baby will do just fine. You watch; that baby will never want for anything. She is so levelheaded that we are probably showing more fear for her wellbeing than she worries for herself. And she has enough love and devotion to provide everything the child will need."

Bingley concurred. "Miss Bennet is correct. Mrs. Collins is everything she described and more."

Elizabeth heard Colonel Fitzwilliam voice his agreement and looked at his kind face. "Miss Elizabeth, Miss Bennet, Miss Gardiner, have no fear for Mrs. Collins. We will all support her. Please tell us how we can be of assistance."

Jane loosened her embrace on Elizabeth and Avelina. "But what is there to do?"

Avelina sniffled and said, "She is asking for Elizabeth to go to Kent and help her with the arrangements and the funeral on Saturday."

Darcy said, "I think that is a fine idea. Would you like to do that, Elizabeth?"

She turned her gaze back to Darcy and smiled at him. He had used her Christian name, and it felt so right coming from him. "I most certainly would."

Colonel Fitzwilliam smiled brightly and said, "Bingley! Have you seen Rosings this time of year? Why, Aunt Catherine's cherry orchard is in full bloom, and you can smell the blossoms from a good half mile away. How would you like to escort these fine ladies to Kent and pay your respects to Mrs. Collins?"

"Well, I was planning on returning to Netherfield soon, and Kent is not too far out of the way. If your aunt will have me, I would be happy to offer my carriage."

Of course, Kent was actually quite out of the way, but that only showed how much Bingley was willing to help. Elizabeth noticed that Jane and Bingley exchanged meaningful looks. It had not seemed surprising to Jane that Bingley would be returning to Netherfield. Seeing them gaze at each other made her heart lighter, and her thoughts were returned to the man next to her.

Darcy looked puzzled for a brief moment and then said, "We will need two carriages, and I am happy to offer one as well. I admit I owe my aunt an apology for my hasty departure. And I may be able to negotiate more time for Mrs. Collins to stay at the parsonage."

Elizabeth could feel that compassion again from him and the strength that radiated out of his eyes. "I do not know what Charlotte's plans are, but she would probably appreciate someone negotiating on her behalf with Lady Catherine. Thank you. Jane and I both would love to go to Kent and be there for her during this difficult time." She reached her hand out to Darcy's and squeezed it. He placed his other hand on top of hers and held it there.

"What about me?" Avelina asked. "I know I am only fourteen, but I love Charlotte too and want to help. I know I could be of assistance. I promise I will not be a burden in any way. Please, please say I can come. Mother was going to let me go back to Hertfordshire with you anyway until our trip to the Lake District. This would simply be a few weeks early. I know my mother would let me."

Mrs. Gardiner had entered the room and heard the plea. "What will I let you do?"

Mr. Darcy dropped Elizabeth's hand and stood and bowed. He seemed suddenly anxious, as if he was caught doing something wrong. "Mrs. Gardiner," he stammered, "I was informed this afternoon by my aunt, Lady Catherine de Bourgh, that Mr. Collins took ill and passed away yesterday. The funeral will be Saturday, and Mrs. Collins has requested Miss Elizabeth's assistance. I would like to convey Miss Elizabeth to Kent as soon as possible. That is to say, my cousin, Colonel Fitzwilliam, Mr. Bingley and I . . . and Miss Bennet and young Miss Gardiner. . . with your permission, of course—"

Elizabeth tried not to giggle at the obvious anxiety in Darcy's voice as he attempted to convince Mrs. Gardiner to let three single men escort two of her favorite nieces to Kent. She listened to him a minute more as he rambled on in his attempts to convince her aunt to agree to such a scheme. Finally she reached a hand out to Darcy, and he paused in his speech to look at her. She gave him a smile, and his posture relaxed a little. Her gesture had its intended effect, and he calmed even more.

"Aunt Gardiner, I do believe you have made the Master of Pemberley nervous." Elizabeth winked at her and gave a small smile.

Mrs. Gardiner's eyes smiled, yet her face was quite fixed. "Avelina, is the Master of Pemberley correct? Would you like to accompany them to Kent?"

"Yes, Mother! Oh, please let me go! You are always telling me how grown up I am, and I would so like to help Charlotte. I will help, I promise."

Mrs. Gardiner took a seat as if she was already exhausted from hearing the story. "What a terrible turn of events! I admit I can hardly think of anything but Charlotte's difficulties." Mrs. Gardiner's eyes filled with tears, and Elizabeth and Jane and Avelina rushed over to comfort her.

Elizabeth sat by her aunt and related the full story from Charlotte's letter. "If it is acceptable to you, Aunt, I would like to leave as soon as possible and stay until her plans are set. It may be a week or two. I am still very weak and would so appreciate Jane there as well. Avelina would not be in the way. I think she would be quite useful."

Mrs. Gardiner patted Elizabeth's knee and smiled. "Of course you may go. I only wish I could help in some way too. I would accompany you myself but Mr. Gardiner has a pressing business matter this week, so I appreciate Mr. Darcy's offer." She turned her head and looked at Mr. Darcy, who still hadn't sat back down and whose hands were nervously clenched in small fists. "When are you planning to leave?"

Darcy noticeably relaxed. "Tomorrow, if you approve, madam. I will make arrangements for myself, Mr. Bingley, and Colonel Fitzwilliam to stay at Rosings while Miss Elizabeth, Miss Bennet, and Miss Gardiner stay with Mrs. Collins. Is that acceptable?"

Mrs. Gardiner nodded and promised she would send word after discussing it with her husband. All three men stood and bowed. Colonel Fitzwilliam was the first to depart. Bingley hung back, giving his condolences to Jane, and Elizabeth offered to walk Darcy out.

"I appreciate your offer to take us. You are a good man." Elizabeth tried not to blush at her forward words.

Darcy took her arm and silently wrapped it around his, placing his hand on it in the most gentle and comforting of ways. He rubbed his thumb gently along the back of her hand. Their pace was slow and deliberate, both of them relishing being in each other's company.

Finally Darcy took her hand and brought it to his lips as they stopped a few feet from the door. He turned to her and said, "I will do anything for you. Forgive me for being so presumptuous, but as much as I sympathize for Mrs. Collins, I find myself elated to have an excuse to spend more time in your company."

Elizabeth found herself speechless, dumbly frozen in place. It was more than she had hoped for.

"I have never looked forward to a funeral before," he continued. "I tend to avoid them. When my mother passed, I was just barely twelve and my father thought it was appropriate for me to attend. I cannot say I have fond memories. When it was time to bury my father, those feelings resurfaced. Yet along with the anxiety and sadness of losing the last parent I had, I was in charge of the arrangements. I still remember how helpful my housekeeper, Mrs. Reynolds, was. She anticipated every need and oversaw every detail.

"Now I hope to be that person for Mrs. Collins. Whatever she wants, no matter what it is, or how expensive, I will cover the costs. If she wants him buried in a tomb in Jerusalem, I will break my back to get him there. Do not hesitate to ask me for anything for your friend. I know my aunt well, and she will put up some resistance to certain things, but I can handle her."

She looked into his eyes and examined the deep brown orbs they were. His genuine honesty in disclosing his memories of his parents' funerals reminded her of their conversations, both verbal and nonverbal, while in the garden. She realized that even in Hertfordshire, he had never been less than completely honest with her. Perhaps his honesty in the garden wasn't just because it was impossible to tell a falsehood in her heaven. Perhaps that was just the way he was.

She wanted to thank him, but words simply just did not express it well enough.

She reached her hand up to his jaw and cupped it in her hand, like she had done once before.

He leaned his face into her touch, then turned his face slightly and kissed the inside of her hand.

Sometimes there is no need for words.

CHAPTER 14

The day was bright and warm. All three gentlemen had chosen to ride, leaving Darcy's carriage for the ladies. Bingley's carriage traveled behind carrying no one but Poole, Darcy's eccentric valet. Darcy didn't want to be without his valet for such a length of time. He had chosen to ride so that he could discuss a few things with Bingley and Colonel Fitzwilliam. They had much to discuss regarding what would occur in the next several weeks. Netherfield would be opened again soon, and Bingley was as confident as ever that his angel was the most perfect being on the earth. Darcy had argued a bit with him but all in jest.

They briefly discussed Mr. Collins, and Colonel Fitzwilliam again asked why such a charming, intelligent woman had ever aligned herself with a man who was so completely devoid of both sense and tact.

Darcy tried to explain. "I asked Elizabeth that same question once on one of our walks—although perhaps with a little more finesse, Fitzwilliam. She said that Mrs. Collins had all but lost hope of having a home of her own. She was nearly eight-and-twenty and had never had a suitor when Mr. Collins proposed. She had no romantic inclinations about the match; she just hoped to be an independent, respectable woman. In a way, Mr. Collin's offer was an opportunity to have that dream fulfilled. Elizabeth mentioned that Collins was eager to do Aunt Catherine's bidding and therefore traveled a great deal. Although she did not say it directly, I gathered the frequent travel pleased Mrs. Collins very much."

Colonel Fitzwilliam looked pensive and then said, "But was she happy? I cannot imagine that being able to run your own house would be enough enticement to sacrifice any future hope of companionship or intelligent conversations."

Bingley said, "We will never know. She is now in a much worse situation than if she had never married."

Both men murmured their agreement.

*****

Charlotte had never felt such a tangible weight lifted as when she answered the door. The gentlemen delivered the ladies to the parsonage and stayed long enough to express their condolences. Darcy had asked to speak with her privately before he left. Charlotte listened as he detailed his wish to do everything and anything she needed. The heaviness seemed to lift further the more he expressed how he wished to be an advocate for her with his aunt. He then bowed and finally mentioned that he knew this was a difficult time, but that the pain that seemed so acute now would lessen over time. His kind words brought fresh tears to her eyes.

Elizabeth was a very lucky woman to have earned the respect and love of a man like Mr. Darcy. She vowed she would voice that very thought as soon as possible.

She entered the parlor and gave a weak smile to her dear friends. "Thank you so much for coming. It means so much to me."

Elizabeth came and gave her the sweetest embrace and rubbed her back. "Charlotte, I would do anything for you. What is most pressing on your mind? Let us use all our energy and make the necessary decisions. Where are we with the funeral?"

"The curate, Mr. Cress, has agreed to officiate. He will do a fine job. He has also agreed to step into Mr. Collins's place until a new rector can be found. Lady Catherine has already begun her search and has asked my staff to keep the house in its finest condition so that it might be shown to potential candidates."

"Before Mr. Collins is even buried?" Jane asked incredulously.

"I am hardly surprised, Jane. She is as callous as she is officious," Elizabeth retorted.

Charlotte felt the need to defend Lady Catherine. "She is simply efficient, not officious. But to tell you the truth, I do not wish to stay here any longer than necessary. Yes, it has been my home these last four months and I have wonderful memories here. The experience of running my own home has been beyond my wildest imagination. But I do not wish to delay the inevitable change of my position any longer."

Avelina asked, "But where will you go?"

Charlotte pulled out her handkerchief and looked at the dress that she had dyed black. It was her favorite day dress, the finest she owned. She didn't know how to voice the feelings she had been having since her husband died. At first she was shocked. Then, as she felt the baby move inside her, she felt a great deal of relief.

It had been a long four months of marriage to a man who seemed only a simpleton, but behind closed doors, had turned into something quite different. To say he had not been kind was an understatement. To say he was controlling and demanding was too mild of terms.

He disapproved of everything she did. Her every choice was questioned and ridiculed in the most verbose and effective way. If he intended to make her feel less important than he was, he most definitely succeeded. Her confidence had been shaken to the core. Never had she thought a man who could carry a conversation for ten minutes about the chimney at Rosings—or the interesting way fabric is woven into bed sheets for that matter—no, never had she thought he could ever raise his hand to a woman; but he had. She still had bruises on her ribs to prove it.

Elizabeth reached for her hand, "Charlotte? Are you well?"

Elizabeth's voice startled her from her darker thoughts, and she offered a small smile. "I am sorry. What was the question?"

"Avelina asked where you will go."

"I suspect that I will return to live with my mother and father. I do not have any other options right now." Although returning to Lucas Lodge would be unpleasant, it would be better than staying a moment longer in this house—where she had never felt anything but anxiety and fear. Once Elizabeth and Maria had arrived, Mr. Collins had returned to the garrulous and loquacious man that everyone thought he was. It was hard to hit a woman when her cries could be heard from across the hall.

With that decided, they then discussed the plans for the day of the funeral. Of course, the women would not attend the funeral itself, but they were required to host a reception afterwards at the parsonage. Lady Catherine had graciously offered her own home, but Charlotte declined.

She hoped that holding it at the parsonage would discourage the guests who wished only to earn Lady Catherine's favor.

So the rest of the day was spent organizing the food preparations and trying to create the perfect engraving to go on the headstone. Charlotte was completely at her wit's end by the time they came up with one she felt she could live with. She penned a quick note for the stonemason.

William Collins
12 December 1780 – 28 April 1812
Rector
May 1811 – April 1812

She didn't want to put "husband" or "father" on it any more than she wanted to explain her reasoning. She then looked up at the calendar and gasped.

"What is it?" Elizabeth asked.

"Tomorrow is Mr. Darcy's birthday! I was supposed to inform you of it."

Elizabeth furrowed her brow slightly. "Why are you smiling, Charlotte?"

The ease of it all came out very quickly. "Apparently my plan to enlist Colonel Fitzwilliam's assistance with Mr. Darcy was not entirely successful by itself. Colonel Fitzwilliam had to improvise somewhat. When it looked like Mr. Darcy was continuing to be stubborn, he mentioned that you wanted to wish him greetings for his upcoming birthday. His improvisation must have worked because he set off to search you out that very day!"

Charlotte scrambled to find the letter and then smiled widely when she found what she was looking for. "Yes, here it is. He described Darcy as a dog with a bone. Nothing could dissuade him." Somehow focusing on her matchmaking of Darcy and Elizabeth made many of her burdens lighter.

Elizabeth blushed and briefly looked at Avelina, who looked confused. "I cannot imagine why Mr. Darcy would become so determined after hearing my supposed warm wishes," Elizabeth stammered.

Charlotte noticed the quick glance at Avelina, who now had an even more confused look on her face. It was obvious that Avelina was unaware of Darcy's affection for Elizabeth. She tried to remedy the mistake. "Well . . . I expect your birthday greeting signaled to Mr. Darcy that you consider him a good friend. He was then naturally anxious to see you well again."

Jane smiled a little and then said, "Yes, I believe that accounts for it." Avelina looked slightly less perplexed.

Attempting to change the topic to something less strained—as the last few hours had been filled with nothing but strain—Charlotte stood and turned her profile to the side and placed her hand on her lower abdomen. "What do you think, Avelina, do I look like I am in the family way yet?"

Avelina blushed. "I do not know the proper response to that question," she hesitated. "I do not wish to say the wrong thing. You have a fine figure, Mrs. Collins. The swelling is most becoming."

They all laughed briefly, and Charlotte sighed. She could never have done this without these ladies. They continued to discuss the arrival of the few guests she knew were coming. Her father and mother and sister would be here tomorrow afternoon. She had a cousin coming tomorrow night who had known Mr. Collins when they were in school together. Charlotte reluctantly admitted she did not have enough room for all the guests. And she knew from their previous visit that her parents would be much more comfortable at Rosings. Elizabeth added it to the list of the things she would address with Mr. Darcy.

After a long discussion and multiple refusals, Charlotte had finally acquiesced to let Darcy cover the costs of the box and the headstone. After further persuasion, Charlotte conceded that it would also be helpful to hire a few extra cooks and servants to handle the many visitors after the service. Elizabeth assured her that Darcy could handle seeking the necessary help.

It all seemed like so much to decide in such a short amount of time. How she wished she understood her financial situation better. The paltry sum that Mr. Collins relinquished to her each month for household expenses left little to spare. He had never discussed with her if there was any other money or holdings in any other area. Jane suggested that Darcy look at the ledgers tomorrow and try to make sense of them for her. Charlotte couldn't help but see the irony. Here she was, handing over her ledgers to Darcy—just like they had pretended to do during Elizabeth's illness.

She felt some relief in these decisions, and her confidence began building. There were many more things that needed to be done to prepare for the funeral, but for now, all she wanted to do was sit with her dear friends.

*****

Darcy had come and received his instructions shortly after three. He was pleased that it was Elizabeth who offered to meet with him. He took the opportunity to take a short walk in the afternoon sun with her while she relayed Charlotte's needs. He usually had no need to write anything down, but listening to Elizabeth's sweet melodic voice making such requests and hearing her express her gratitude for his willingness to help was somewhat distracting. Praise of any kind from Elizabeth was highly motivating. He was anxious to exceed her expectations and accomplish the tasks immediately.

He followed her to the parsonage to retrieve the ledgers and the inscription Charlotte wanted on the stone, but before they entered the front door, he took her hand in his, and she turned her beautiful brown eyes on him. They were bright and encouraging. He took a step closer and whispered, "Thank you for letting me help your friend. I know it must have been hard to convince Mrs. Collins."

Elizabeth smiled sweetly and said, "I did have to do a bit of convincing. I believe I could have made you blush with the praise I associated with your name."

He chuckled slightly and said, "Gentlemen do not blush."

"I assure you, if I desired to, I could make you blush."

"Is that a challenge?"

She raised her eyebrow in the way that he adored, and his heart started to speed up as he looked at her full lips that were turned up so temptingly. "You, sir, will blush within a week. I assure you."

"Even though I know you will not succeed, I look forward to your attempt with my entire being." She then squeezed his hand right before dropping it to allow him to open the front door for her. He quickly took the ledgers and imagined the moment when she made good on her promise. He would dearly love to see Elizabeth try to make him blush.

When he arrived at Rosings, he immediately brought the ledgers to the study and sent a rider to the stonemason with the inscription. He knew the stone was not usually placed at the time of the funeral; however, he would double the fees to have it ready by tomorrow. From the sounds of it, Charlotte did not want to linger at the parsonage, even though he was ready to negotiate on her behalf. So, it was that much more important that the stone be placed quickly.

He then found his aunt and discussed the need to open her guest rooms to Charlotte's visitors. The extra servants Mrs. Collins required could easily be obtained from Rosings. There was no reason why Aunt Catherine's three cooks and abundant chambermaids could not assist the parsonage for the next few days. Without even asking his aunt, he picked out the best she had and gave them instructions to report to the parsonage at seven o'clock tomorrow morning. If his aunt had any concerns over his instructions, he would simply pay a bit more attention to Anne.

He turned to head back to the study and intended to engross himself in the ledgers when he was accosted by Colonel Fitzwilliam and Bingley.

"How is Mrs. Collins?" Colonel Fitzwilliam asked.

"I believe as good as can be expected. I only spoke with her briefly. I got most of my instructions and updates from Miss Elizabeth."

Bingley asked, "And the ladies? Are they all well?"

"Miss Bennet was in good spirits. She and Miss Gardiner were making a list of things needed for tomorrow's luncheon. I believe they were intending to head into town shortly. Perhaps they would like a ride in your carriage?"

Bingley smiled widely. "I shall offer it. Excuse me, gentlemen." He turned to leave.

Darcy continued to head into the study and realized his cousin had followed him. "Did you need something, Fitzwilliam?"

His cousin seemed to fidget a little and looked down at his boots, which had somehow garnered a great deal of attention. When he finally looked up, Darcy saw something in his eyes that he had never seen before. Fear. Here was a man who had been to battle many times. His courage and ingenious knack for outmaneuvering the enemy was what earned him his rank as a colonel. He was a gifted soldier. But he was anxious about something.

"Richard, what is it?"

"Are you sure she is well? I only ask in case there was something I could do to help. I heard you giving the instructions to Aunt Catherine and have already heard her complain about losing two of her cooks and several servants for two days . . . I just wondered if there was anything I could do to help Mrs. Collins." Colonel Fitzwilliam took a deep breath and seemed to be holding it in for some reason.

Darcy felt like he was missing something in this conversation. "I have several ledgers to review. I could give you the one associated with the church funds. That should not be too difficult. Mrs. Collins was left quite in the dark regarding finances and has no idea what kind of situation she may be in. I have a sense that she has only limited household funds at this time."

"I would be happy to help. It may seem like I care little for numbers, but I did oversee my brother's ledgers for an entire year when he went off to the continent. I rather enjoyed it."

Darcy then searched two or three ledgers until he found one marked *The Church of England, Parish at Rosings Park.* He handed it to Fitzwilliam and watched him pull up a chair and sit on the opposite side of the desk. Richard pulled out a pencil and buried his nose in the book. It was interesting to Darcy to see him so attentive to Mrs. Collins's finances. Fitzwilliam consistently avoided any involvement with their aunt's finances.

Darcy placed the ledgers in the right chronological order and decided he would start with the most recent one and work his way back as needed. As he studied, he kept glancing up at Fitzwilliam, who was working so hard and fast that his childhood habit showed: whenever

Fitzwilliam was deeply engrossed in concentration—which wasn't often—he had a habit of unconsciously sticking his tongue out and rhythmically licking his top lip. Darcy returned to the ledger in front of him and shook off the nagging suspicion that his cousin was behaving most singularly.

*****

The day of the funeral came quickly. All three gentlemen had stopped at the parsonage multiple times Friday to ensure everything was going smoothly. The Lucases were very pleased to be staying at Rosings. Darcy realized that if Mr. Collins's praise of his aunt had been difficult to endure, Mr. and Mrs. Lucas were beyond anything he could have imagined. Here was their daughter, an expectant widow, and they couldn't drag themselves away from the knees of his aunt to give Charlotte the time of day. This pleased his aunt, as it always did when people gave her more attention and respect than she deserved. But it also served Darcy's own purposes well since that left him free to see Elizabeth several times without his aunt's watchful eyes.

Poole was putting the finishing touches on his cravat when Fitzwilliam came in unannounced. "Oh, splendid," the colonel announced. "You are ready. I thought we could check in once more at the parsonage before we head to the church."

"My thoughts exactly. Is Bingley ready?"

"He has been ready longer than I have. That man needs no more encouragement to see his *angel*! I think he might be more besotted than you!"

Darcy just smiled back. It simply wasn't possible to be more besotted than he was. He thanked Poole and they met up with Bingley, who seemed to have been pacing for some time at the front door. Darcy did not need to even motion towards the door, for Bingley was two steps ahead of him.

As they were let in to the parsonage, all the ladies stood and Darcy forced himself to address Mrs. Collins first. He then walked to the window where Elizabeth was standing and stood silently next to her. Her lavender smell permeated around her person, and he struggled to keep his physical reaction to such an enticing fragrance under control.

Mr. Darcy said, "Thank you again for the birthday present. I hope you know I have never received flowers from a lady before. The lavender was quite beautiful."

Elizabeth turned her face to him, and he couldn't resist looking into her eyes, which seemed to be full of mirth.

"Is that so? And how many ladies have you *given* flowers to?"

He felt his face flush slightly. "I did not mean to imply . . . I have never given flowers, nor have I received them . . . unless you count my mother or Georgiana. I suppose I gave Mrs. Reynolds a handful of wildflowers once when I was ten, but what young boy does not have an infatuation with the only lady in his life besides his mother? Not that I have an improper relationship with my housekeeper. Certainly not." He felt the embarrassment reach his ears. "I treat her with the utmost respect. She is more of a mother to me. In which case, perhaps I *should* be giving flowers to her—"

He paused briefly. "Good God! You did it!"

She grinned and put the back of her hand against his face. "Yes, sir, you blushed in less than two days."

He watched her walk away and wrap her arm around Charlotte, who had grown tearful again while speaking with Colonel Fitzwilliam. Elizabeth glanced back at him and smiled genuinely with a smug look on her face.

Oh, how I am going to love these next few weeks with her.

CHAPTER 15

Darcy truly did hate attending funerals. It brought back too many memories of his parents' untimely deaths. But his heart was quite light at this particular one. The difference, of course, was Elizabeth. Her ability to alter him so wholly was remarkable. He had once thought he simply wanted to marry her. Now he wanted to do much more than that—he wanted to fulfill her every need. He wanted to be her lifelong companion.

At that horrid moment when she accused him of being prideful and having a selfish disdain for the feeling of others, he had been angry. Undeniably so. But now he felt nothing but gratitude for her words, for they had sparked an irrevocable change in him. She had made him want to be better than he was. He was determined now to identify the rest of his flaws and turn them into strengths. Never had he examined himself so thoroughly. He realized he had a great deal to work on.

He saw Mr. Osborn heading his direction and forced his thoughts to return to Mr. Collins's funeral. Darcy tipped his hat and bowed. "Mr. Osborn, it is so good of you to come."

"Not at all. I admit it is always hard for me to attend a funeral of one of my patients. Death is never easy, but a patient's death . . . Well, it is especially hard."

Mr. Darcy put his hand on his shoulder. "I saw what you did for Miss Elizabeth, and I sincerely thank you. Mrs. Collins said you were just as faithful in her husband's care. Do you know what illness befell them? I confess I have never seen anything like it."

Mr. Osborn knit his eyebrows and slowly shook his head. "Nor I," he admitted. "I am conferring with a few colleagues to see if they have any insight on the matter. But why Miss Elizabeth was able to survive the same illness and Mr. Collins was not, I fear I shall never know. And I wish that I knew more about Miss Elizabeth's near-death experience!"

Darcy's interest was piqued. He and Elizabeth hadn't discussed her illness, but he knew he would never forget the image of her convulsing in his arms as he tried to will her to live. "What has she told you of it?" he asked.

"Not much. She seems reluctant to discuss it with me. She did admit to seeing the same light the others have mentioned. Then she said she heard a voice telling her she had a mission left on Earth and that her family still needed her, so she came back. Actually, her exact words were, she came back *alone*. She seemed quite distressed on that point and would say nothing more. I am not sure what to make of it."

Darcy could see that the service was about to begin, so he thanked Mr. Osborn again and sat down with Bingley and Colonel Fitzwilliam.

His mind replayed Mr. Osborn's words again and again. *She came back alone*. He had not been there. His heart lurched at the pain his departure must have caused her. He had vowed not to leave her, yet he had done just that. He would have to find some way to bring it up so he could apologize.

Fitzwilliam leaned over and whispered, "It sounds like Miss Elizabeth has quite the story to tell." Darcy nodded but did not have time to respond as the music ended and the curate stood and approached the pulpit.

Mr. Cress, an elderly man who had worked for his aunt as long as Darcy could remember, lifted his hands. The crowd's whispers died down. "We gather together to celebrate the life of Mr. William Collins, the man who preached from this very pulpit. I am humbled to officiate at these services. He was taken so young and so quickly. He served the people daily, giving of himself in every way."

Darcy let out a small sigh. He hoped it would not be another one of those funerals that exaggerated the deceased as if they were an angel walking on Earth. He simply could not handle it.

Mr. Cress continued, "I could expand on the merits of the deceased as so many funeral services do. But when such a tragedy strikes, I feel it is not the deceased's life that we should examine, but rather our own lives. I like to think that it is at times like these when I feel Jesus Christ tapping me on the shoulder to let me know He is there, as He always is. Life is fragile and precious, and because of that, we must recognize what a blessing each day is.

"Therefore, instead of praising Mr. Collins, I would like to impart some of the lessons God has patiently taught me through my many years of study. After all, I believe I am the oldest person here today. And I think it is safe to say I have listened to the most funeral sermons. An occupational hazard," he chuckled.

Mr. Cress continued, "In many ways, being human is like living in a dark room. Saint Paul writes that 'we see through a glass darkly.' Our mortal eyes perceive only glimpses of God. There is so much we cannot see. Imagine, for a moment, being in a dark room and hearing a baby cry. You know no one else hears the child but you. What would you do? Well, I would like to believe every one of us would search out that baby. But in the darkness, our path would be very difficult and even dangerous.

"What then would you do to combat the darkness? Well, you would light a candle, of course. We need *light*. And Jesus Christ is the light of the world. If we seek out His light, He will offer us vision and perspective. He is the bright sunshine beaming down on us. Without Him, we stumble in the darkness." Mr. Osborn's words stirred something in Darcy.

Something about Jesus Christ and sunshine and what Elizabeth had said in her delirium. She had said she needed to walk to the sun—that it was calling to her, that it filled her with warmth and peace and a feeling of being welcomed home. But had he misunderstood? Was she talking about walking to the sun, or walking to the Son?

Darcy felt light and warmth in his chest. He suddenly knew in his heart that Elizabeth had caught a glimpse of heaven. It had been real. But why had she been allowed to return and live? The whirlwind of questions in Darcy's mind was making him dizzy. He struggled to focus on what Mr. Cress was saying.

"My sight is leaving me ever so slowly. Ironically, this makes me value what little sight I retain more than ever. I can no longer read the good book or write letters to my dear loved ones," Mr. Cress admitted.

"Take it from an old man. Sight is invaluable. Light is everything in this world. However, even as my physical sight leaves me, my spiritual sight continues to grow bright."

Mr. Cress pulled out a large candelabrum and started lighting it. "Consider a candle in a dark room. What does it represent? I suggest to you that it represents hope. By lighting the candle, do we actually find that crying baby in the dark? No, but we *hope* to find it. With that hope, we can summon our own faith to step forward. And that choice to have faith—to put our hope into action, to move, to do something—is more important than any of us realize. If we do not progress, we get nowhere fast."

Colonel Fitzwilliam leaned over to Darcy and whispered, "Sounds like good advice. When I get home, I am writing that down. 'If we do not progress, we get nowhere fast.' I could use that mantra with my regiment."

Darcy nodded.

"So, we take that first step," Mr. Cress explained. "We choose to progress. And with each step we take, the candle will light the path a little further—but only so far as we carry it with us. If we leave the candle on the table and go in search of the child, it will be of little use. We must not leave Christ in the church pew or in the Bible or in the graveyard. We must carry Him with us. We must let Him be our constant companion. If we wish for vision and perspective, we must draw close to our Savior.

"Then with each choice, each step we take, the light of Christ will enlighten our path just far enough to help us to see the next step. The responsibility lies with us to continue to step forward, one foot after another.

"Let us pause a moment and look at how powerful our choices are. Each of us has to make decisions daily, even hourly. What will you do with the decisions God has given you? Will you choose to help the widow, build a friendship, and express your devotion?"

Mr. Darcy felt his heart pound. He had helped the widow and built a friendship with Elizabeth's London relations, but he had yet to express his devotion for her. She behaved quite differently towards him now. Her flirtations and smiles and the frequency of her seeking his company was not something he could ignore. He was hesitant to say her feelings were ones of admiration, but they had definitely changed. But had they changed enough? Would she ever reconsider her refusal?

His breath caught in his throat at the thought. He prayed she would. One thing he knew was he needed to let her know that *his* feelings had not changed and that his offer still stood. He would find a way to tell her.

He tried to return his attention to Mr. Cress's sermon. "As we see from the death of William Collins," Mr. Cress explained, "the body is weak. Death is a non-negotiable part of life. Each one of us will pass through that portal. We must live in such a way that we will be proud to meet our Maker when our time comes. We must turn our weaknesses into strengths. We must overcome our sins.

"Ultimately, it is up to each of us to decide whether we will make the choices of life by the light of His grace, or in spiritual blindness," Mr. Cress continued. "To reject Christ's light, to live without hope, to stay in that dark room, is very grave indeed. Our Savior wants all of us to have hope. He grieves when we turn away from Him. Have you ever been completely without hope?"

Darcy felt like Mr. Cress was speaking directly to him. He had been without hope. It had indeed been a dark place. He thought of the letter Elizabeth had written him, of reading it by lantern light under a tree.

He remembered when Fitzwilliam had told him Elizabeth was in London—*If you are seeking a bit of hope, I just gave it to you.*

And he remembered seeing her again in London—desperately searching for a sign, a clue, anything, that indicated Elizabeth's feelings had changed—and her handing him a cup of tea with lemon.

Each time, hope had ignited something deep inside him, something intoxicating and overwhelming, like a sudden rush of light into a dark room.

"Each of us has faced sorrow and felt despair. There may have been times when we felt as that child, alone, crying in the night. As Christ has given each of us hope, we must endeavor to give hope to others. Be the light in someone's life. Reach out to your fellowmen.

"I leave you with the wandering thoughts of a nearly-blind old man. Let Jesus Christ be your light as you make choices. Let Him be your hope. Share His hope with others. May each of us live more worthily of that hope He has mercifully offered us." Mr. Cress blew out the candles on the candelabrum and cautiously made his way back to his seat.

Colonel Fitzwilliam startled him out of his enlightened state. "Darcy, are you well, man?"

Darcy hadn't realized that everyone was making their way to the gravesite as he sat contemplating how precious hope was. Nor had he noticed that his eyes were wet. He blinked them away and reassured his cousin. "I am well. Indeed, I am well."

*****

Jane looked at the peaceful scene in front of her. Avelina had insisted that Elizabeth lay down while the men were at the funeral. The last few days had been so busy and emotionally trying that Elizabeth collapsed into bed every night. Avelina had begged her to rest, but Elizabeth refused until Avelina offered to lay down with her.

Now the two of them were lying together on the small bed facing each other with their hands clasped. Avelina absolutely loved to fall asleep holding someone's hand. Even as a tiny girl, she would ask for a story and snuggle up close, holding your hand and sucking her other thumb, and just like some sort of favorite blanket, she would fall asleep immediately.

Jane put her hand on her sister's shoulder. "Elizabeth, I believe the men will be arriving soon."

Elizabeth stirred and stretched. She leaned over to Avelina and kissed her cheek. "Avelina, it is time to wake up." She rubbed her cousin's shoulder and kissed her cheek again then pulled back the blanket and stood up.

Jane offered, "Let me fix your hair, the bun is loose."

Elizabeth sat and allowed Jane to rearrange her hair, something that they had done many times.

"Do you feel better, Elizabeth?" Avelina asked.

"I do. Thank you. How is Charlotte, Jane? Is everything ready for the luncheon?"

"Yes, everything is in place." Jane frowned slightly. "I think Charlotte is doing well. Her mother has offered to take her back with them tomorrow, but I think she wants to spend a few more days here."

"Has Mr. Darcy or Mr. Bingley indicated when they wish to go to Hertfordshire?" Avelina asked.

"No," Elizabeth said, "but I am sure they would be willing to stay a few more days. We could escort Charlotte to Hertfordshire next week if she wishes it."

Charlotte knocked on the door. "I am sorry. I did not mean to overhear. Do you really think I could come with you?"

Elizabeth stood and looked her right in the eye. "Without a doubt. When would you like to leave?"

"Next week sometime. Much of what I have accumulated will need to be given away, but it will take time to sift through it for the sentimental things."

"Then we shall leave for Hertfordshire next Saturday."

*****

The guests started trickling in around noon. Each one addressed Charlotte as they entered. Elizabeth stood fixed to her friend's side. Charlotte, although tearful, was holding up remarkably well. She simply nodded at each of their comments that eventually all sounded alike.

"Such a tragedy."

"So sorry for your loss."

"Our prayers are with you."

"My thoughts have not strayed far from how hard this must be for you."

"I wish to give my condolences."

"He was a good man."

"Life is short, and this makes me simply want to cry for you."

"I would have never suspected a stout man like that could die so suddenly. Life is fragile."

"I wish I could have known him better, but now I will never have that chance."

"I cannot imagine the pain you are going through right now."

"You poor thing."

Charlotte turned to Elizabeth, and with a weak smile, she asked, "Lizzy, could you get me another handkerchief? They are in my dresser upstairs."

Elizabeth put her hand on her arm and gave it a gentle squeeze. "Absolutely."

Elizabeth left her side just as Darcy and the other gentlemen were returning. She caught his kind eyes as she left to retrieve the handkerchief. She had just started going up the stairs when she heard a servant whispering one floor above. She had almost rounded the corner when she heard something shocking.

"It is true. Mr. Collins would hit her until she begged him to stop. I heard her screams night after night."

Elizabeth froze on the stairs.

Another voice said, "But he was a rector! He would not hit his wife."

A third voice said, "I ain't supposed to say anything, but now that he's gone, I suppose it's all right. Whenever I helped Mrs. Collins dress, I saw bruises all over on her chest and arms. She kept saying she was clumsy and had fallen down. But that is a lot of falling if you ask me. I say good riddance to the man. He was no more a servant of God than I am a titled lady."

Elizabeth was so shocked she couldn't make herself move. Had her cousin been striking his pregnant wife? No wonder she does not wish to stay here until the baby is born. This had not been a home, it had been a hell! Her heart ached for her. She started searching her mind for evidence of such behavior.

Admittedly Charlotte had changed since her wedding. Once very rational and levelheaded, Charlotte had become anxious and fidgety. Her insistence that Elizabeth do everything according to the dictates of Mr. Collins and Lady Catherine had seemed uncharacteristically submissive. But Elizabeth had reasoned that Charlotte was simply trying to be a dutiful wife in respecting her husband's wishes. And although Elizabeth hadn't been intimidated by Lady Catherine, she had been surprised that Charlotte took such great care to please her.

Oh, poor Charlotte! She took a deep breath and ascended the rest of the stairs.

All the servants but Christine had dispersed. The maid who had been such a constant companion to Elizabeth during her illness quickly turned to leave, but Elizabeth called after her. "Christine, would you be so kind as to show me where Mrs. Collins keeps her handkerchiefs?"

Christine's cheeks flushed, and she bowed her head. "Yes, miss. Of course."

Elizabeth followed her into Charlotte's room and closed the door behind them. The noise obviously startled Christine. "Forgive me," Elizabeth began. "I never got the chance to thank you for helping me while I was ill. I understand you helped a great deal."

Her head was still bowed as she said, "It is no great thing. You are so sweet. I loved hearing you talk about the garden you saw."

"Did I tell you about the garden?"

"Not 'xactly. It was while you was still feverish. You mumbled in your sleep many nights."

Elizabeth pondered this. Christine had never discussed this before with her. She tried to place which servant's voice had said what a moment ago. She now was sure that Christine was the third voice which had confirmed Charlotte's bruises. "May I ask you a question?"

She seemed to squirm a little but nodded.

"Do you really think that Mr. Collins was striking his wife?"

Christine took a deep breath. "I do not like to talk about the dead in such ways."

"But that did not stop you a moment ago. What harm is there in telling her closest friend?"

Christine grimaced and bit her lip. Then it all came out in a rush: "He was not a good man, Miss Elizabeth. Not like your Mr. Darcy. He was a different person behind closed doors. Mrs. Collins did not deserve it. If you look, you will see the signs. She always wears long sleeves, even in the evening, even in this warm weather . . . But I should say no more. Here are the handkerchiefs." She handed them to her, bobbed a quick curtsy, and fled.

Elizabeth sat on the side of the bed and thought about what Christine had said. Charlotte had most likely suffered a great deal for many months. She remembered a conversation she had with her yesterday.

"Sometimes God intervenes even when we do not realize we need it," Charlotte had said.

Elizabeth had thought she was talking about Darcy being willing to help her in her needs. "Yes," she had agreed, "help is always offered. We just have to accept it when it comes."

Charlotte admitted, "It has been somewhat of a relief."

"I am sure it feels that way. I am pleased you can find gratitude and peace at such a hard time."

"Yes. Peace is long overdue."

Elizabeth remembered feeling confused at the statement. It had only been three days since the death and to find peace so soon was quite fast.

Now remembering the conversation, put in perspective, she realized she hadn't been talking about Darcy at all. She was expressing the relief that Mr. Collins had died and that she was now free from his abuse.

Her heart again ached for Charlotte. She would be there for her in any way possible. It was a promise that was vital that she keep. No matter what, she would help her and the baby.

CHAPTER 16

Darcy couldn't imagine where Elizabeth was. He had caught a glimpse of her smiling face as she was leaving to go upstairs, but it had been over fifteen minutes now. Between Mr. Osborn's questions about her near-death experience and Mr. Cress's sermon on hope, he had so much he wished to discuss with her.

Colonel Fitzwilliam was making the rounds of the room and ended up by his side. "Where is your lady?"

"She is not *my* lady."

"Perhaps not *yet*."

"No, not yet." He couldn't help but smile at the thought.

After a minute or two, Colonel Fitzwilliam repeated, "So where is your lady?"

Just then he smelled lavender behind him, and he turned to see her with a cup of tea. "Miss Elizabeth." He bowed deeply to her and gave her a soft smile.

She returned a curtsy with a smile and said, "I thought you might like some tea."

Colonel Fitzwilliam excused himself and went and stood near Bingley and Jane. Darcy took the cup and, with pleasure, he could see she had placed a lemon slice in his tea. It was balm to his heart. "Thank you. You are so kind."

"It is you that is kind. I know I have said this before, but Charlotte is so grateful for your help. You were under no obligation to assist, which makes your actions even more appreciated."

"If you will thank me," he replied, "let it be for yourself alone. That the wish to give happiness to you might add force to the other inducements which led me on, I shall not deny. But Mrs. Collins owes me nothing. As much as I respect her, I believe I thought only of you."

"I see. Is this why Colonel Fitzwilliam called me your lady?" She smiled and raised an eyebrow at him temptingly.

"Forgive his manners. He is aware of my . . . my . . . I admit I do not know what to say." He lowered his voice and said, "He is aware that I offered for you."

She leaned into him and whispered with the slyest of grins on her face, "I believe your words then were that you ardently admired and loved me. Why hesitate to say so now, Mr. Darcy? Has something changed?"

She was teasing him and he knew it, but Darcy was shocked that she would bring it up so openly. He looked around and realized they were quite secluded in the corner. The closest couple was sitting on the chaise deep in conversation about five feet away.

Perhaps this discussion should be done in private. He placed his cup down and offered his arm to her silently. She nodded and placed her tiny hand on his arm, and he led her towards the gardens.

What should his response be? If felt good to walk with her so casually. They were putting quite a bit of distance between them and the parsonage, but he knew he needed to respond to her.

He decided to spar with her—a favorite pastime. "Miss Bennet, what is it about funerals that compels you to very nearly declare yourself to me?" He saw the surprised look on her face and tried not to grin himself.

"I did not intend to . . . I did not say anything . . ." she stammered.

"Ah, but you did."

"I only reminded you what you said, sir."

"And you asked me if I still felt the same."

"And yet *your* feelings were the topic of discussion. You can hardly accuse me of *declaring* myself."

"I am no blind man. Proud, perhaps, but not blind."

"And what exactly do you so confidently see?" Although she was not looking at him, he could hear her voice tremble.

"I see your eyes light up when you see me." She blushed becomingly. "And I see your rosy cheeks flush each moment we are together."

"It was warm in the parsonage, sir."

"So, now you wish to discuss the weather?"

"No," she whispered. Her reticence only encouraged him.

"Why did you so openly remind me of my feelings for you?" She made no reply. "Come now, Miss Elizabeth. I was quite at a loss as what to say a few moments ago, but with your help, I find myself more at ease. Is there something you wish to discuss?"

She blushed even deeper before stammering, "I find myself hesitant to discuss the topic you seem confident to bring up."

"I did not bring it up. It was you, dearest Elizabeth."

"Sir, I beg of you, this conversation is making me most uncomfortable."

"And do you assume it is easy for me? I was refused the last time we discussed these things."

"Do not remind me."

"Again, I did not bring it up."

"Mr. Darcy, do you truly intend to make me say it? Very well, I believe you are trying to make me admit that I admire you and wish you to renew your addresses."

"Am I, now?"

"Yes, sir."

"Now that I know my task is defined, I suppose I could just plainly ask, or . . ."

She let out a small gasp which pleased him greatly. "Or what?" She breathlessly asked with a tantalizing smile on those lush lips. It only encouraged him further.

He leaned closer and said, "Or you could listen instead of battling me."

Although he had been avoiding looking at him this whole time, he had seen her pink cheeks moving from pink to scarlet depending on what had been said. He watched her brush her curls away from her face with her free hand, stop walking, and turn to him, thus making eye contact for the first time since leaving the parsonage. He could see her take a noticeably deeper breath.

She very nearly whispered, "I am listening, dear sir."

He wanted so much to make her at ease, but this time was no easier than the first time. Perhaps even harder. But he had to let her know that his offer still stood. He stepped closer to her and took the hand that was on his arm and brought it up to his mouth and brushed it gently against his lips, softly kissing each knuckle. He then opened her hand and with his finger traced the creases in the palm. He wasn't sure how exactly to do this. Obviously his prior instincts had been all wrong.

He took a breath and said, "These wrinkles in your hands are adorable." He reached one hand up to the corners of her eyes, and with his thumb, he lightly grazed the smooth pink skin. "I hope one day to know you so well and for so long that when wrinkles reach this area right here, I will be the only one to still recognize you. It is my deepest wish to place so many grins and smiles on your face that your eyes will forever express the same joy and happiness that I feel when I look at you.

"It may be difficult to believe, but I love you more than a man should love a woman. For the greatest commandment is to love thy God with all thy heart. But I must admit that I have sinned. For I believe my heart loves you even more. I have made you my idol. So I have committed two sins. Not only do I love you more than I do God, but I worship you—and make no excuses for doing so."

As he looked at her and watched her eyes fill with tears, he still did not know how she felt about him. He had laid his heart out for the second time in four weeks.

She took her free hand that was not still being held by him and cupped his jaw. She then said, "Somehow I knew that already."

He looked deep into her eyes, and he saw her answer to the question he had yet to ask. "I love you, dearest Elizabeth, and I want to grow old with you. I want to share my good and bad days with you. I want to hear every detail of what happens to you, and I want to pull every thought from your head. I want to fulfill your every need. I will always love you, no matter how you answer me, but please consent to marry me. I am entirely altered by knowing you, and there simply is no hope for this man if you refuse him again."

She smiled, "So you are saying there is no hope for Mr. Darcy?"

"None at all unless you say yes."

She at first started giggling then started laughing without restraint, dropping her hand from his face and holding her middle. She put her fist to her mouth and tried to stifle it but burst out anew. He was perplexed at her reaction but could tell he was not being refused.

"Do tell me what it is about my proposals that first enraged you and now lead you to hysterics."

She giggled harder and pulled him to a nearby bench, where she sat down to catch her breath. "Sir, I apologize for my reaction. It is just that after I woke from being ill, I had an entirely altered view of you. And I feared I had lost my chance. I am the one who felt there was no hope. I can hardly believe this is happening."

"So, is there any hope for either of us? Do I dare hope you have consented to be my wife?"

He kneeled down in front of her so that he was at eye level. He wanted to see every expression as she said it. Sure enough, she smiled brightly and blinked back tears. "Yes. I have every hope we will be very, very happy together."

He could see her love, and it made him react without thinking. He took her face in his hands and gently pulled it to him. Pausing inches away from her lips, he inhaled her sweet lavender scent and yet somehow he had the control to remember never to assume her affirmative answer again. "May I kiss you, my sweet, wonderful intended?"

"If you do not, I am afraid you will have a very disappointed woman on your hands." Her cheeks were pink, and he could see she was holding her breath.

He inched his way towards what he had dreamed of and placed the briefest of kisses on her lips.

It was too much, yet not enough.

He pulled away and looked into her eyes once again which had a dazzling look of desire in them. It was all the incentive he needed, and he kissed her again.

This time he lingered and felt her lips move with his ministrations. Each moment his lips met with hers was like igniting a fire deep in his chest. After a minute or so he leaned his forehead against hers and took a moment to regain composure.

He then stood up and in one smooth motion pulled her to a standing position and embraced her, wrapping his arms around the small of her back and holding her to him. She leaned into him and wrapped her arms around his neck. His head could rest on the top of her chocolate curls and she seemed to have fit perfectly in his arms. He gently rocked her back and forth as if there were music being played. They danced there in the sun, and he couldn't have been more content.

She had accepted him! He would never be able to put to words the feelings he was having, for truly it was priceless, but somehow she managed to find the words.

With her head on his chest, Elizabeth said, "I love holding you like this. I cannot imagine a better feeling."

*****

Elizabeth simply let him caress her back and kiss her hair. There was so much to say, but they had been gone long enough. She needed to be there for Charlotte.

She lifted her chin and was rewarded with a few gentle kisses. She closed her eyes to savor the powerful emotions she was feeling. Her entire insides felt like they were melting, and truly they had been melting from the very moment he took her arm and walked outside. She had not expected him to renew his addresses so soon.

When he suggested that his feelings had not changed, her heart had begun to pound in her chest. But each word he said only hinted at his intentions. She had tried to protect her heart from truly letting go. For what if she admitted her love for him and he never offered again? She had not dared hope for his love in return.

As his lips caressed hers, she was suddenly reminded of Charlotte's bruises and the cruelty that Mr. Collins must have inflicted. She pulled away quickly.

Mr. Darcy grinned and allowed her to pull away slightly but didn't let go of her entirely. "Is there something wrong? I am sorry if I got carried away. I find I have a weakness for your lips; a knowledge that I have just become aware of, so you must not censure me in any way.

But you may if you wish to. A proud man must be humbled frequently, I believe."

"Is that a challenge? Must I always keep your pride in check?"

"Always, without a doubt, for I am a very, very proud man." He was grinning widely, making his sweet dimples show. "Truly, what is bothering you?"

"I am sorry. It is just that I heard some upsetting news today." Elizabeth then told him what she had overheard at the base of the stairs and what Christine had confirmed. She watched his eyes grow distant and cold. As she described the anxiety that Charlotte exhibited since becoming married, his jaw became set and she felt him stiffen slightly. He was holding back a great deal of emotion.

"It is my impression that the parsonage does not hold good memories for her," Elizabeth reasoned. "She desires to leave it as soon as possible. Her parents have offered to take her tomorrow, but she will not be ready by then. I hope you do not mind, but I offered transportation with us. She thinks she could be ready by next Saturday."

"I find it hard to digest this information. How a man could ever raise his hand to his wife, let alone one that was carrying his child, is beyond my comprehension. I truly am speechless. No wonder she did not put anything more personal on the headstone."

"I think you may be correct," she sighed. They each considered the unsettling information in silence for a few moments.

"Please let her know Saturday will be fine. Bingley and I will be quite ready by then. Colonel Fitzwilliam has asked to continue to Hertfordshire with us and that will offer him a good four weeks before he is required to return to his regiment."

She was still worried about something, and she knew he could tell. "Mr. Darcy—"

"Please call me Fitzwilliam." His eyes smiled as he said it.

She could feel the heat in her cheeks as she contemplated using his Christian name. He had already used hers several times, and it was wonderful and felt somewhat intimate. Surely she could call him by his Christian name now that they had kissed. He would soon be her husband, after all.

"If you do not feel comfortable calling me Fitzwilliam, I will understand." He had misinterpreted her hesitation and seemed to be growing more worried by the minute.

"I admit it feels quite intimate," she said with a smile, trying to put him at ease. "But I only hesitate because I think of Colonel Fitzwilliam when I hear that name. Are there any other names that you use?"

He chuckled. "I certainly do not want you thinking of my cousin while we are alone together. That will not do. What do you say to William or Will?"

She smiled back at him. It was nice to see his sense of humor. She was more convinced than ever that he was the only man she could ever be prevailed upon to marry. She decided he needed to know that. "I like both of them, Will, but I have a confession to make."

"Should I be worried?" He grinned.

She took a deep breath and looked down at her hands. This was not easy for her. "I said such terrible things to you the last time. I said you were the last man in the world that I could ever be prevailed upon to marry. I was so cruel to you, and I feel so awful, I—"

Her words made his grin soften and his eyes grow serious. He closed the gap between them and he embraced her so tenderly. She could only imagine the sadness he must have felt when she so cruelly refused him. She reached her arms up to his hair and let her fingers run through the curls at the back of his neck. "I am so sorry, Will," she whispered. He then reached up and removed her hands and reverently kissed them in that special way he had.

His voice was hoarse and his eyes were glassy, but he managed to say, "Think only of the past as its remembrance gives you pleasure, my dear. There is nothing to forgive. But I am afraid if you continue running your hands through my hair, I will simply claim ownership of your mouth once again. You do not know the affect it has on me. I am committed to being the gentleman you deserve."

What was it about him that made her cheeks flush so constantly? She was reminded of their walk in the garden when she knew somehow that he desired her. There was no mistaking his desire now.

"Well then, Will, I do believe we have been gone long enough." He offered his arm, and she was pleased and proud to take it.

"Dearest Elizabeth, how I love you."

"And I love you." She could hear her voice quiver and knew he deserved to hear it said with less hesitation.

CHAPTER 17

Mr. Darcy could sense that Elizabeth was desirous to return to Mrs. Collins. She had been distant ever since she had revealed Mr. Collins's abuse. Even when she told him she loved him, it felt somehow strained. He was most delighted that Elizabeth had accepted his hand and that someday, hopefully soon, she would be his wife, but he could sense her uneasiness. As they walked back toward the parsonage, he was content to keep the pace she set. He noticed she seemed to slow slightly as they neared it.

"Elizabeth, is there something on your mind?"

"I am surprised you noticed. I shall count being observant as another of your virtues."

He tried to lighten her mood. "I have virtues now? Not merely a 'selfish disdain for the feelings of others'?"

She smiled slightly. "You know you do. And although I am very pleased that we have come to an understanding, this is still a very difficult day for Charlotte. I feel sharing our good news might be . . ."

"Insensitive?" he prodded.

"Precisely. She just lost her husband. Even though we know he was not good to her, she does not know that we know that, and I think we should wait until . . ."

He could feel his heart lurch in fear. "Until she tells you about Mr. Collins's abuse? Pride is not entirely monopolized by me, my dear. That may be quite some time. "

"Oh, no! I did not mean that at all. Charlotte will confide in me if and when she wants to. I simply would like to wait until she is settled in Hertfordshire. Would you mind too terribly if we allowed Charlotte the attention she deserves?"

He could see her pleading eyes and smiled at her. They were close enough to the parsonage that he could not kiss her, but he did place his hand over her hand as it rested on his arm. It was such a powerful sensation to be so near her, and to have kissed her so recently, but yet restrain himself. He would do anything she desired of him.

"Of course. But you should know that my acquiescence also stems from an entirely different reason. You are aware, no doubt, that my aunt intends for me to marry Anne," Darcy sighed. "I have never expressed any such inclination, but—"

"—But your aunt believes she possesses sufficient inclination for all participants." Elizabeth grinned.

"Precisely. I fear my passiveness on the subject will now present unpleasant repercussions for both me and you. If she learns of our understanding while you are still in Rosings, or even still in Kent, your entire party will be subject to her wrath. I would prefer for you to be safe at Longbourn when that happens. I will try to prepare her the best I can, but she will not take it well."

Elizabeth giggled at the stern look on Darcy's face. "I would be delighted to leave that particular announcement to your expertise, my dear," she laughed.

"Thank you, my dear. But may I ask a favor?"

"Certainly."

"May I tell Colonel Fitzwilliam and Bingley?"

She smiled at him and nodded. "As long as you do not mind my mentioning it to Jane. Even her generous disposition would be put out if I kept such wonderful news to myself. I hope you realize you have secured for yourself the less charitable of the two eldest Bennet sisters."

"For the record, I dispute that opinion entirely."

*****

Charlotte had only narrowly escaped the latest group of well-wishers. Hidden in the dark of her kitchen pantry, she felt her lip start to tremble again.

Breathe, she commanded herself. *In and out.* They simply did not know him. And that was how it would always be. She was not about to sully the name he had created for himself. It would only reflect poorly on her, after all, for she had been fool enough to marry him.

She had been able to mask her emotions thus far today, but she was beginning to feel herself slip. Her anxiety and anger was building with each pat on the arm from husbands who had only ever touched their wives with tenderness—and worse yet, the looks of pity from the women who knew what it was like to be loved.

She did not think she could bear to go out there again and see all their faces drenched in compassion. But she knew she needed to do so soon. She had seen a scarlet-cheeked Elizabeth walk out with a grinning Mr. Darcy. They had been gone some time now. And not long after that, she had ordered the servants from the kitchen and absconded to the pantry. Her absence was probably already apparent.

But before she returned, she would allow herself this moment of privacy to weep. With that thought, her tears quickly started flowing, as if they knew she was in a rush to be rid of them. She had never been so afflicted with conflicting emotions. She was relieved that her nights would contain rest. But she also felt guilt at not truly mourning the loss of the father of her child. She finally let go and wept like she hadn't allowed herself to weep since he had passed.

Her tears and the sound of her own crying prevented her from seeing or hearing that she was not alone.

*****

"Mrs. Collins, please do not be alarmed." Colonel Fitzwilliam whispered quietly. His gentleness was not enough to prevent her from jumping in surprise. "I am terribly sorry to have startled you. I saw you leave, and when you did not return, I feared I might find you like this. Please, take my handkerchief." He handed it to her and she took it.

"I am so sorry. I was unprepared to handle the emotions that his followers would elicit."

She wiped her eyes and stared absently out the window. Clearly she was trying to avoid looking at him, and he suddenly felt the awkwardness of his presence. *Why the blazes did I come looking for her?*

He should never have left his post at the mantel near Bingley, whose attention was completely occupied by Miss Bennet. He had felt he was in their way as their whispers got lower and lower. The lovebirds may not have noticed Darcy and Miss Elizabeth leaving, but he most definitely did. Because it meant that Miss Gardiner and the Lucases—the latter seemed to not even notice their daughter's difficulty—were the only remaining support left for Mrs. Collins.

He had fought the urge for a good ten minutes to go stand by her side. What would that look like? Out of any in that room, he—a bachelor of no relation—was the least appropriate candidate to be offering comfort. Yet he could not help but desire to assist her in some way. He kept his distance, yet his watchful eyes drifted often to her. He was close enough to hear her stiff tokens of appreciation to each of the many visitors. Her voice was controlled, but her emotions were betrayed by her eyes. He knew it was only a matter of time until she found a way to leave the never-ending flow of neighbors.

After he watched her leave, he paced by the window. Almost immediately an influx of servants had begun to circulate in the room. Used dishes were gathered and stacked neatly, and cups were filled with more tea, whether it was asked for or not. He had checked his pocket watch. Fifteen minutes passed and the room was still buzzing with the servants and visitors. Even he needed a reprieve.

That was when he went to the kitchen and heard her sobbing. There was no mistaking the pain she was going through, and with no one in the room, and having entered without any attempts to be quiet, he knew his presence would be noticed soon. At that moment, he had made the decision to address her and offer his handkerchief.

But he was here now, and there was nothing he could do about that. He turned away and looked out the window to offer some privacy while she struggled to regain composure.

"I am so sorry," she said, looking down at her lap.

He continued to look out the window but shook his head. "There is nothing to apologize for. Is there anything I can do? I know we have spent very little time together, but I hope you know that I would like to help you in any way I can. You are not alone, Mrs. Collins."

She stood and smoothed her skirts. "Thank you," she sniffed. "I believe I am recovered." He could see out of the corner of his eye that she had lifted her chin bravely to look out the window. Neither one knew what to say, so instead they simply stood side by side, each of them conducting a thorough examination of the garden.

Fitzwilliam felt he should say something. He usually did not struggle with conversation, but something was holding him tongue-tied. He focused his attention further into the garden, and he looked as far as he could see. It was then that he spotted Elizabeth's purple dress and white petticoat. Darcy was kneeling in front of her. He nearly missed Darcy altogether as his green topcoat blended in with the surroundings, but then he saw Darcy's hands reaching for Elizabeth's face and he realized he was about to witness them kissing. He turned away at the same time as Mrs. Collins. He saw in an instant that she had seen it too.

"I had not noticed them out there until just now," Mrs. Collins explained as a blush started to color her cheeks. Her voice was soft, but the pain he had heard in it earlier was lessened.

"Nor I. It appears they need no more help from us."

Mrs. Collins genuinely smiled back at him. It was a most engaging smile. "Indeed not." She took a deep breath and wiped the last of her tears away. "If you will excuse me, I must return to my post."

She turned to leave but only got a few steps away when she turned around again, paused, and said, "Thank you."

"Not at all. My pleasure, ma'am."

*****

Elizabeth had suggested that she first enter the parsonage alone, so as not to raise suspicion that they had been together. Mr. Darcy waited the allotted five minutes in a happy reverie, reviewing all that had occurred in the last half hour with Elizabeth. He was pleased his boldness had proved so beneficial. He truly had not meant to propose again so soon, but every blush and every word she spoke only spurred him on.

But he endeavored to remind himself that his happiness was occurring at the same time as Mrs. Collins's mourning. He vowed to add sensitivity to his virtues.

He entered the parsonage and greeted a few of his aunt's neighbors. It was uncomfortable for him to discuss Mr. Collins's virtues after what he had just learned about the man. He looked around the room and observed Miss Gardiner conversing with Miss Lucas in one corner, Jane and Bingley on the chaise with smiles on their faces that resembled his inner feelings, and his cousin standing next to Elizabeth and Mrs. Collins. He took a moment and examined his future wife.

Her hair had been swept up into an elegant bun with small ringlets at the nape of her neck. Her delicate chin was resting comfortably on top of her long feminine neck. Her gown was conservative and a simple shade of deep purple that had a silver ribbon bow on each of the gathered sleeves. Her thin waist looked tiny compared to Mrs. Collins's, who did not have as light and pleasing a figure, especially in her current condition. Elizabeth's hands were expressing themselves with great animation, and he immediately found his thoughts veering to the moment when she ran her fingers through the hair at the back of his neck. With delight, he relived the moment, while attempting not to make a spectacle of himself in front of the crowd.

Colonel Fitzwilliam caught his eye and was coming towards him purposefully. He had something very important to discuss it would seem. "Fitzwilliam, I hope everything is well."

His cousin motioned with his head to follow him, and when they reached the far corner of the room, the colonel murmured, "It would be wise to be more cautious, Darcy. Aunt Catherine has just arrived. Mrs. Collins and I may not have been the only ones who witnessed your private interlude in the gardens."

The pleasure he felt in remembering Elizabeth's fingers in his hair was immediately replaced with dread. They had walked a great distance away from the parsonage and had been surrounded by lush greenery. He had thought they were well out of sight. Once again his impulses had got the better of him when it came to propriety.

He avoided looking at his cousin but said, "Duly noted. I seem to be powerless at times. Well, at certain times, with certain people. But I will attempt to do better." He focused on the people in the room, none of which seemed to be noticing them together in the corner.

Colonel Fitzwilliam put his hand on his shoulder, and Darcy looked at him. He had the subtlest of grins on his face. "I should hope so. Now, if I am not mistaken, I believe you owe me your annual income."

Darcy's brows furrowed slightly. "Pardon me?"

"When I told you about the letter from Rosings, I bet you your annual income that a certain lady's feelings were not as disdainful as you feared," the colonel explained. "Do not tell me you do not recall this conversation! I was rather banking on such wealth to free myself to marry whomever I wish! It may be a small fortune, but a fortune nonetheless."

Darcy couldn't help but chuckle at his cousin's teasing, and he walked away shaking his head.

*****

Elizabeth caught Darcy's eyes for a brief moment and felt her cheeks flush. She quickly glanced away only to be met with Charlotte's questioning look.

Elizabeth tried to redirect her thoughts away from the kisses they had shared. His hands had been so gentle as he had pulled her face towards his, pausing only to ask permission. She smiled just thinking of it until she heard Charlotte trying to extricate herself from the current grieving neighbor. The mourner was gushing over Mr. Collins's skill and exuberance at the pulpit. When Elizabeth noticed Lady Catherine behind the man, she understood all too well why he was so excessively flagrant in his praise.

Lady Catherine cleared her throat, and the man turned his attention to her presence, which he was undoubtedly already aware of. With false surprise in his voice, he bowed and proclaimed that he had little doubt that the Mistress of Rosings Park would find a most suitable replacement.

The Mistress of Rosings Park just eyed him up and down haughtily and stepped around him to address Charlotte. "Mrs. Collins, I only have a moment, as Anne's health did not permit her to accompany me."

Charlotte said, "I am sorry to hear that. I hope Lady Anne feels better soon."

"Merely a precaution, Mrs. Collins. It would be unwise to have her here where two people have fallen ill in the last month," she replied. "As I said before, I can only stay briefly. I hope we can settle his affairs before you leave."

"Yes, I hope so as well. I was just discussing it with Colonel Fitzwilliam. He and Mr. Darcy have been working very hard on the ledgers. They assure me they are making progress."

"I certainly hope so! When they are not here, they are sequestered in my study with their noses in those books! It is most displeasing." Lady Catherine turned to Elizabeth and said with her nose in the air, "I see you are feeling improved."

"Indeed, I am," Elizabeth replied. "Thank you for asking." It occurred to Elizabeth that Lady Catherine hadn't actually asked about her health, she had only commented on it. Without saying another word, Lady Catherine left them.

Jane had made her way over to them. She asked quietly, "Was that Lady Catherine? Did she offer any condolences?"

Elizabeth just shook her head briefly. The surprise on Jane's face was brief but detectable. Jane was a master at suppressing her inner thoughts.

Elizabeth stayed by Charlotte's side for the rest of the luncheon, but she was always aware of where Mr. Darcy was. She tried not to make eye contact with him too often, but every time their eyes met, she smiled and her heart started racing. How could she be so lucky to have earned his love?

She could somehow detect his lemon-and-sandalwood scent from across the room, and her ears were quite attuned to his deep baritone voice. He said very little and was brief in his responses, but his voice was smooth and sent chills up her spine. She found herself daydreaming of what it would sound like right next to her ear. Suddenly she was quite flushed. Charlotte seemed to have noticed, and Elizabeth gave her a small apologetic smile.

Little by little, all the visitors started to take their leave. Charlotte's heart was blessed many times as if it was the only thing to offer in each visitor's farewell.

"Bless you, child."

"Bless your heart."

"May God bless you."

"You are a special soul. Bless you."

"You must write to us and tell us how you fare. God has a plan for your special heart."

Finally the last of the neighbors left, and only Lady Catherine, the Lucases, and the three gentlemen were left. Elizabeth didn't quite understand why Lady Catherine had stayed at the parsonage, as she had said twice that she only had a moment to stay when she first arrived. The servants were busy removing the food and dishes, and all the remaining guests took a seat. Elizabeth realized it was probably the first time Charlotte had sat down since the luncheon began. Her heart went out to her on so many levels.

Colonel Fitzwilliam broke the silence, "Aunt Catherine, may I assist you back to Rosings?"

Lady Catherine glanced at Elizabeth for some reason before answering. "Not yet." Another awkward silence fell on the group. "This house is too warm," Lady Catherine announced. "Open a window, Miss Bennet."

Jane stood to do as she was told, but Lady Catherine interrupted, "Sit, Miss Jane Bennet. I meant for Miss *Elizabeth* Bennet to open the windows. Do go upstairs and open the windows to properly air out this stuffy house. I simply insist."

Elizabeth felt the desire to say something cheeky, but she did not want to make trouble for Charlotte. "Yes, ma'am."

She stood and went to the upstairs rooms and opened the windows in all three guest bedrooms, then went to Charlotte's room and opened the window there. It was the second time in two hours that she had been in this room. She noticed that the door to Mr. Collins's room was open, and, out of curiosity, she peeked inside.

The servants had cleaned it recently, that much was obvious. His bed coverlet had crisp folds down the center. The room smelled of alcohol and medicine. The curtains had been closed, giving the room an almost sterilized, cold feel to it, but Lady Catherine was correct in that the house was warm. She went to the window and pulled back the curtains and, in doing so, a large book tumbled from the ledge. She tried not to cry out when the corner landed right on her slippered foot. It fell open as it landed.

Elizabeth picked it up and she saw that it was a ledger. She was going to close it when she noticed a sum of £6,742 on the bottom of the page. *What an extraordinary sum!* she marveled. Curiously, she turned a few pages. She had seen her father balance his books many times and had often helped him when something didn't add up correctly. She knew most ledgers had one column for debits and another for credits, but this one seemed to only have credits.

She closed the book and examined the front. It looked like all the other ledgers they had found in Mr. Collins's study two days ago. But why then was it hidden behind a curtain in his room?

Her curiosity was piqued further. She recognized the handwriting; she was confident that the ledger belonged to her deceased cousin. She opened the book at the beginning.

The first entry was less than three hundred pounds and was dated four years ago. She quickly flipped the pages. Almost halfway through, she came across a folded piece of paper. On that exact page, a large credit was applied of four thousand pounds. Most other entries were small amounts—less than fifty pounds—but the book was nearly entirely comprised of credits. What could it be? She flipped all the way to the last entry and saw a staggering number that made her knees weak: another credit of another £4,000, making the grand total £11,354.

Eleven thousand three hundred fifty-four pounds! What was this ledger tracking? And why would Mr. Collins be managing such a large sum of money? She heard a commotion downstairs and felt conscious that she was probably being missed. She stashed the ledger in her own bedroom. It would need to be handed over to Mr. Darcy but certainly not in front of Lady Catherine, whose demanding tones were easily decipherable above the growing din of voices coming from downstairs.

CHAPTER 18

Maria Lucas had asked that Avelina spend the night at Rosings with her. The young Miss Gardiner had developed quite a fear of Lady Catherine, but at Elizabeth's urging, Avelina had agreed to go.

Late that evening, with all the guests gone, Elizabeth sat back and listened to the whole story of what had happened while she was opening the windows upstairs.

"It was very shocking!" Jane exclaimed. "As soon as you had left, Lady Catherine started saying how disrespectful you were that you were not in black!"

Elizabeth said, "But he was just a distant cousin. I do not have to go into mourning. And did she not notice that you were not in black either?"

"Apparently not. Her ire was aimed at you and you only. She ranted about how impertinent you were. Then she tried to get Mr. Darcy to agree with her. She went on and on about how 'country upstarts raised without a governess' could never offer a respectable man anything in the way of connections or fortune. She abused you most wretchedly. I am afraid she thinks you quite conceited. She even used the word *wild*!"

Charlotte agreed with Jane. "She certainly did. She said you roam the gardens with such little concern for propriety that your cheeks take on a wild pinkness that only farmers should possess."

"I am hardly surprised that she holds such a low opinion of me," Elizabeth laughed, "but what compelled her to voice it at her rector's funeral, of all places, and in front of everyone? It was very bad form. Did not Sir William say anything?"

Elizabeth saw a look of compassion on Jane's face. "Well, I am sure he would have defended you, but—" Jane began.

"—But my parents would never openly disagree with the great Lady Catherine de Bourgh of Rosings Park," Charlotte sighed. "It is kind of you to defend them Jane, but their behavior was unconscionable. However," she smiled, "my parents were not the only ones in the room. Both of her nephews quickly came to your defense. I have never heard Mr. Darcy speak so forcefully. He actually called her disrespectful for not showing compassion during such a difficult time. But she would not be silenced. She actually raised her voice and started shaking her finger at Mr. Darcy. That was when her nephews escorted her back to Rosings."

Elizabeth sat back befuddled and looked out the window. She wished she had been able to speak with Will before he left. "But why would she get so irate?" she asked. "I did not do anything!"

There was a long silent pause. Elizabeth turned back to the ladies. Jane appeared confused and showed true empathy.

But Charlotte had a small smile on her face. "I would not say you did not do *anything*, Lizzy. I am confident that such an intelligent lady as yourself can deduce the reason if you put your mind to it." Charlotte reached her hand out and placed it on Elizabeth's. "Do you have some news to share, my dear?"

Elizabeth tried to read the tones infused in Charlotte's voice. It was not accusing. It was not judgmental, nor was it reproachful. "Oh, no! Charlotte! Are you telling me that you already know? Oh dear! Does Lady Catherine know as well?"

Charlotte giggled. "No. The colonel and I saw you in the garden. We were not trying to spy, honestly. In fact, truth be told, it was somewhat awkward when we realized what we had seen. And I can see from the great confusion on Jane's face that even she is not yet privy to the information. I believe Lady Catherine would have done more than shout and wag her finger if she had seen you and Mr. Darcy—"

"What! Oh my goodness! Lizzy!" Jane interjected. "What happened in the garden?"

"You will have to ask Lizzy!" Charlotte replied with a carefree laugh and belied her still red-rimmed eyes. "I saw only a brief moment, but I suspect congratulations are in order," Charlotte said with a satisfied smile.

Elizabeth could see real joy in Charlotte's eyes for the first time since they had written to Colonel Fitzwilliam. She remembered her saying then that being with child seemed to make her nostalgic and romantic. "Charlotte, I did not want to say anything today, of all days, when such sadness surrounds you."

Charlotte put her hand on Elizabeth's and squeezed it. "Seeing you two in the garden is what pulled me through. Your happiness is my happiness."

"Lizzy!" Jane demanded, "What happened? Did he propose?" Elizabeth smiled widely and nodded. "Oh, I am so thrilled! How exciting! You must tell me all of it, every moment!"

Elizabeth glanced at Charlotte, who laughed and whispered to Jane, "It may not be proper for her to tell you *all* of it."

Jane gasped. And Elizabeth and Charlotte giggled even more.

After gathering her wits, Elizabeth looked at Jane's blushing face and said, "Do not think the worst of me, dear sweet Jane. He simply asked to kiss me."

"Before or after the proposal?" Jane asked.

"After, of course!" Elizabeth flushed deeply and cheekily said, "I did not use my arts and allurements to solicit a second proposal!"

"Well then, Sister, I think you must tell all you are allowed to tell, for I do not think I shall sleep a wink until you do!"

Elizabeth smiled and glanced again at Charlotte, who seemed to truly be enjoying herself. Not only were her eyes bright, but her very body language spoke of her desire to hear the story as well. "Charlotte, are you sure I am not infringing on a day that should be focused on Mr. Collins? I want to be sensitive to your needs."

Charlotte smiled and leaned back in her chair. She only took a moment and then very confidently stated, "I have spent a great deal of time today paying respects to my late husband. I will not say it was easy, nor will this coming year of mourning be easy. But I will not deny myself the small tender mercies that God sends my way to comfort me.

"And for now, believing in the kind of love that you and Mr. Darcy share is definitely a tender mercy. It is being offered on a day when I most needed to be lifted. It has offered me something to hope for.

One can never undervalue hope. So if the world wishes to chastise me for being happy for my friend, then let them do it."

Suddenly Charlotte must have felt a little flutter move across her belly. She gasped in excitement. "There! I felt the baby move again!" Charlotte waved her friends over and Jane and Elizabeth rushed to her side, placing their hands tenderly on her belly. Tears filled Charlotte's eyes.

"Oh, Charlotte!" Elizabeth cried, "I am so sorry! How could I have been so insensitive? I know you say you are happy for me, but—"

"No, no! You have mistaken the source of my tears, Lizzy. I am very, very happy at this moment. You know I have never been romantic. But being with child has stirred feelings of love that I never dreamed were possible. I know you both think you love your suitors, but wait until you feel a baby move inside you. Listen to my monologue about being a mother! And I have hardly begun! But this love, here in my heart, is stronger than anything I have ever experienced.

"And I find myself, for the first time in my life, hoping for my own Mr. Darcy. I know that may sound heartless coming from a wife whose husband has only just been buried, but someday I hope to feel love like that from a man. Do not think for one minute that I will deny myself to share in your joy. It is a tender mercy on a day like today. So, if you please, start from the beginning."

*****

Mr. Darcy was accosted by Colonel Fitzwilliam at the top of the stairs. He gently pulled him into one of the rooms. "I see you are up early this morning. Might I have a word?"

"Of course, Fitzwilliam." Mr. Darcy could hear the concern in his voice. There was no doubt whom this conversation would be about.

The colonel closed the door behind them and said, "I breakfasted early, as I can see that is your plan as well, but Aunt Catherine is already waiting for you. She was asking the most probing questions, and even I, someone who has considerably less difficulty bending the truth than you do, was struggling to satisfy her. I believe she knows enough to cause problems."

Mr. Darcy suspected as much from her attack on Elizabeth's character yesterday. "How much do you think she knows?"

"Well, for starters, she thinks Miss Elizabeth somehow lured you into admiring her. She asked me how you behaved toward her when we called at the parsonage. I think she suspects that you have been disillusioned into believing that she is more suitable than Anne."

Mr. Darcy rubbed his chin a little. He looked to his cousin and decided they needed an ally. "I think I shall see if Anne is able to take a stroll with me for a moment. We might need her cooperation."

"Are you sure you will not be hurting Anne in telling her your feelings for Miss Elizabeth?"

"Quite sure, but I need to speak with her alone. Can you manage Aunt Catherine for the next fifteen minutes?"

Richard scoffed. "I can confidently say I will give you thirty! But any more would be pushing my luck."

"Thank you." Darcy left the room and headed away from the dining room where he could hear his aunt. He gave one last look back at his cousin, who had taken a daunting task onto his broad shoulders.

Darcy went down the servants' staircase and found Mrs. Jenkinson sewing near the entry to the kitchen. He motioned with his head that he wished to speak with her. As expected, she put down her sewing, apparently shocked that Darcy would come down to the kitchen with the servants, let alone wishing to speak with her. He felt a pang of guilt for not giving her the respect that she deserved. Once again he realized how his pride had directed even the smallest of relationships. All those people in Hertfordshire had been correct: he *had* felt he was too good for them. It was time to set things right.

"Mrs. Jenkinson, I wish to speak with Anne privately as soon as possible. Do you know where she is? May I attend to her?"

As her companion, Mrs. Jenkinson was very familiar with the whereabouts of her charge. "Of course, Mr. Darcy. She is alone in the East Parlor, writing in her journal at present." Mrs. Jenkinson hesitated before continuing, "To be truthful, sir, Lady Catherine does not approve of me leaving Lady Anne unattended, but my lady enjoys her morning solitude so much. I hope you will be so good as to not mention it to Lady Catherine . . ."

"Of course, Mrs. Jenkinson. You can count on my discretion. Thank you."

He left and went up the stairs to the East Parlor. He found Anne at the writing desk, looking up at him in surprise. Her brow rose slightly as he entered.

He bowed, "Anne, I come to solicit your help. I have very little time, and so I will be brief. Each minute I waste is another minute Fitzwilliam is adding to the things I owe him. So far I owe him my annual income. Do not ask. May I sit?"

Anne stood and put down her pen and closed the book. She walked to the chaise and sat on the far end of it, motioning for him to sit as well. "You have never sought my advice or assistance before. But you shall receive it all the same."

"Thank you." Darcy was not quite sure how to start. "Do you remember our conversation a few years ago about what each of us wanted in a marriage?"

"Yes. I said I wanted a man who would be loyal and encouraging, whose temper was trustworthy, and who cared little for my money. You desired an intelligent lady who you could respect and who would not bend to your every wish. One who challenged you and stirred a passion in you that resembled what your parents had."

Lady Anne paused and smiled. "And does Miss Elizabeth Bennet meet all these requirements?" He nodded and she smiled widely. "I confess I am quite pleased to hear that, although I am not unaware of my mother's opinion on the topic. How can I help?"

He took a deep breath. "As you are aware, I help your mother with the estate issues. So I know that the estate was bequeathed to you on your twenty-sixth birthday. And, even though your mother still makes all the decisions, she is not the legal owner of the estate anymore. Your father was a good man and made sure to offer you a way to be free from her. Let us be honest for a moment, for a moment is all I have—he made sure you would have a way to be free from her dictatorial control over your life."

"I think I see."

"Do you?"

"I do. Perhaps it is time to have the Dower House aired out, no?"

Relief spilled over him, and he let out a sigh. He reached over and placed his hand on hers. "I am deeply sorry that you have not found your loyal and encouraging man yet, but you will. I will follow your lead. If all you wish to do is threaten her, then do so, but if you need my help enforcing the legalities of actually putting her there, you know I will do everything I can."

"Yes, of course. But, just to be clear, why exactly am I threatening her with the Dower House? What do you hope to see happen?"

"I just want to give Elizabeth a chance to succeed as mistress of Pemberley. There will be plenty of people who will question my choice of a connectionless, poor, country lady; they need no encouragement from my aunt. Elizabeth is strong and she will try to laugh it off, but I do not want her reputation tarnished simply because Aunt Catherine thinks I will reconsider if the appropriate pressure is applied."

Anne let out a small laugh, which made her cough. Concern resurfaced in Darcy's mind. She took a deep breath and assured him, "I shall be fine. I do not even need the medicine anymore. My lungs are much improved. Truly."

"How long have you had that cough?"

The look on Anne's face was telling. Darcy stood and offered his arm to her, and they both walked slowly but silently towards the dining room.

*****

Colonel Fitzwilliam was ready to deck Darcy for sending him back to the front lines. He was using any and all tactics to delay their aunt from seeking Darcy out and demanding he marry Anne. He had coddled, flattered, agreed, argued, negotiated, and flat out manipulated her to stay in the dining room, but he was now at his wit's end. He finally heard Anne's thick barking cough behind him.

Lady Catherine had long since left her chair. In fact, he had bodily prevented her from leaving at one point. But when Darcy and Anne came in arm in arm, she wordlessly took a step back in shock. It was rather surprising for the colonel as well, since Darcy never walked with Anne arm in arm. Darcy was always very careful not to give rise to any of the rumors started by their aunt, and yet there he was, comforting Anne so tenderly. Colonel Fitzwilliam pulled out a chair for Anne, and sat down but did not relax into the chair.

Anne coughed once into her handkerchief and then took the tea that Darcy offered her. She did not, however, drink it. She turned to her shocked mother and said, "Mr. Darcy and I have an announcement."

Lady Catherine nearly fainted in shock. Colonel Fitzwilliam did not know who to help first; his aunt, who was stumbling to find her chair, or Anne, whose dry raspy cough had started again. He opted for his aunt and guided her to a chair.

Lady Catherine said, "Finally! The union can now be announced! Oh, dear Lord! I thought it would never happen!"

Darcy said, "I assure you, it will happen." Darcy took the chance while their aunt had her hand to her forehead to wink at Colonel Fitzwilliam.

"I have been saying it for many years," Lady Catherine gasped, "and there were nay-sayers, who did not believe me, but I knew you would find a way to offer for her!" Darcy's aunt took out her handkerchief and blotted her forehead with it. She had gotten very worked up in the previous twenty minutes.

As Anne's coughing subsided, she said, "I believe Mr. Darcy will be quite happy in his choice of wife. We have discussed what he desires in a marriage partner many times."

"You have? Why have you not discussed this with me? I could have helped you all this time."

Anne smiled sweetly. "I know, Mother, but it is a private matter, after all. I am afraid that nothing you do or say will have any effect whatsoever on the union."

"Nonsense, Anne! Do not speak so ridiculously! I am sure Darcy will not look kindly on such impertinence from his future wife."

Colonel Fitzwilliam felt like he needed to add something. "On the contrary, Aunt Catherine—Darcy admires impertinence. He is fond of ladies who are witty and intelligent. He most definitely knows what he wants."

"Oh, shush, Fitzwilliam! Darcy is engaged! And to my Anne! Lord, you had me doubting it would ever happen!"

Darcy then smiled slyly and said, "I fear I must correct you, madam."

"Well, if it is my permission you are waiting for, Anne is certainly of age to make these kinds of decisions! No need to wait for me to grant my blessing!"

Anne said, "Your blessing on Darcy's union is exactly what I am asking, Mother."

"Well, you shall have it!"

Darcy smiled wider and said, "I thank you. Miss Elizabeth thanks you as well."

"Miss Elizabeth? Why must that woman thank me? All I ever did for her was educate her on how a proper young lady should act and behave."

Anne calmly said, "Mr. Darcy has proposed, and he is to be married."

"Of course he is! I am no dimwit! I can see a man crossed in love when he grins so widely before me!"

"Then we have your blessing, Aunt Catherine?"

"Oh, you can call me Mother now."

"No. I cannot. Not now, not ever." Darcy said stepping away from Anne and standing taller.

Colonel Fitzwilliam could sense something change in his aunt's demeanor. The chill she emitted was palpable. As Darcy said those words, she seemed to understand a few things. As quickly as her delight had turned, so did her temper. The colonel unwittingly stepped back, as if the teakettle had begun to screech its readiness to blow.

Aunt Catherine pushed her chair back and stood, but at the same time, so did Anne. They looked at each other long and hard. He had never seen Anne look so determined in her life. Aunt Catherine took a step towards Darcy, but Anne stepped into her path. When it looked like Aunt Catherine was going to strike her own frail child, Colonel Fitzwilliam grabbed his aunt's arm to restrain her. She quickly tried to shake off his grip, and he instinctively reached out and restrained her other arm as well. All of this happened in seconds that felt like minutes.

Colonel Fitzwilliam was being careful, but he could not allow his aunt to harm Anne. The shock alone that Anne would try to stand up to her verbally, let alone physically, was astounding! "Aunt Catherine," he murmured, "let us be rational. Darcy was never going to marry Anne. You yourself said you doubted it would ever happen."

Aunt Catherine struggled to shake free. When she stopped writhing, he let her go but remained where he was. It was a strange position they found themselves in now, all of them standing in a line, as if at a ball—Anne having stepped between Aunt Catherine and Darcy, and Colonel Fitzwilliam having stepped between Aunt Catherine and Anne.

It was too good to hope that Lady Catherine was rendered speechless, for she finally opened her mouth and started ranting, but she did not get far before Darcy stepped around Anne and faced his aunt directly.

"That is quite enough, Aunt," he ordered. "I will marry whom I please. Anne knows I could never make her happy, and there is only one woman whom I could ever be prevailed upon to marry. Miss Elizabeth Bennet has agreed to be my wife, and I shall expect your full blessing."

"Well, you shall never get it!" Lady Catherine screeched. "I will make sure that thing you call a daughter of a gentleman will never be accepted into the *ton*!"

Anne very coldly said, "No, Mother, you will do everything you can to ensure she is brought into the finest circles. You will be very vocal in your praise and admiration of the nameless country lady who was able to secure the most eligible bachelor in Derbyshire."

Aunt Catherine raised her voice and leaned forward imposingly. "I most certainly will not!" she shrieked.

Anne casually picked up the teacup and sipped it carefully. She then turned to Darcy and said, "I had hoped the Dower House would not need airing out so soon. I am afraid to ask, Cousin, but how long has it been since it has been used and refinished?"

"In all my years of living, it has only been used to board the extra servants. I have never seen anything in the ledgers to indicate it was being used by guests."

"I shall let the servants know to air it out immediately. What kind of budget are we looking at to get it suitable for my mother?"

Colonel Fitzwilliam tried to keep a straight face as he said, "I hear the chimney could cost upwards of eight hundred pounds."

Darcy upper lip twitched at the comment, but he quickly recovered and said, "I am not sure the estate can spare eight hundred pounds. But there is no need to replace the chimney. It only has one crack, and it does not go all the way to the top. We may be able to make it suitable for Aunt Catherine and a few servants without much expense. There are certainly no funds to refurnish it; I am most certain of that."

All three cousins turned to watch a red-faced, yet silent woman stomp out of the room. Just as she was leaving, she said with her nose in the air, "Congratulations, Darcy. I shall look forward to seeing her in town on my many visits. She will need some guidance for her manners lack—"

Darcy cleared his throat loudly, and Anne said, "Mother, I shall not warn you again. Not one more time. I have taken the liberty of inviting the whole parsonage party to dine with us tomorrow. My decision to air out the Dower House will depend heavily upon your behavior towards Miss Elizabeth."

"I am not the one raised without a governess. I know how to behave!" She turned and left, leaving three breathless people standing in the room.

Colonel Fitzwilliam and Darcy both rushed to Anne's side and helped her sit down as she immediately started coughing and gentle tears started flowing.

Darcy said, "I can never thank you enough, Anne. What you did for me was amazing and courageous."

Colonel Fitzwilliam said, "Indeed, you could have outmaneuvered the entire army of France with such strength. I know it was not easy to threaten her."

Anne took another sip of tea and shook her head in disbelief. She looked up at her cousins and murmured, "You do not know how long I have wanted to do that. The timing was quite fortuitous." She then turned to Darcy and smiled. "Just promise me that you will have every happiness your parents had."

Darcy grinned. "Elizabeth has already made me the happiest of men. I want nothing else in life but to see that she is happy. She has altered me so drastically that I hardly know the man standing before you. A man who has no regrets, but simply possesses a hopeful heart. Thank you."

"No, it is I who should be thanking you. I should have had the Dower House aired and cleaned a long time ago. And as much as I hope she will not force my hand, we all know my mother. She will never truly submit to anyone's rule, and I do not intend to fight her at every meal. She will most likely have to leave. You have forever changed me."

Darcy said, "A lot of change has been going on around here."

Colonel Fitzwilliam could not agree more. Both of his cousins were smiling, and their futures were brighter than they had ever been.

He finally let out his breath and slumped into his chair. Eight hours of battle in the harshest of winters had failed to prepare him for this morning's skirmish.

Anne coughed once and then added, "I believe this was my first sound investment in the management of Rosings Park. Do you not think so, Darcy?"

Chuckling, he said, "By far the soundest investment made in years."

CHAPTER 19

"May I walk you back to the parsonage, Miss Bennet?" Bingley eagerly asked.

"I would like that very much."

This offer was extended by all of the gentlemen, and Colonel Fitzwilliam was kind enough to make Avelina feel special by offering his arm to her. This made Elizabeth very happy. Avelina truly was growing up and had been so helpful during this time. Dinner had gone surprisingly well at Rosings, and when the handsome gentleman beside her pressed his hand on the small of her back so gently, she looked up and smiled back at him.

"It was a good evening," Elizabeth said. "Perhaps the most enjoyable one I have ever spent at Rosings."

Mr. Darcy chuckled slightly. "Yes, my aunt seems to have been on her best behavior."

Elizabeth wrapped her arm around his and, in the fading light of the evening, she felt very close to him. "I suppose you had something to do with it?"

"No, not entirely, it was really all Lady Anne."

"Lady Anne?"

They slowed their pace a little, and Darcy explained to her how the previous morning had gone. "It is incredible that, even as frail as she is, she was so quick to step between me and her mother."

"Oh my!" Elizabeth exclaimed. "I am very glad no one was hurt."

"As am I. It is very fortunate Colonel Fitzwilliam was there."

The colonel in question now offered his other arm to Charlotte, who seemed to take it cautiously. Sure enough, almost as soon as she took it, she dropped it and proceeded to walk alone. There was a curious look exchanged between the colonel and Charlotte that Elizabeth couldn't make out. It was odd. Charlotte had never been awkward or uncomfortable around him before.

Elizabeth looked up at Darcy, who seemed to have noticed as well. He had a most serious scowl on his face. Elizabeth thought she would distract him. "I found a ledger hidden in Mr. Collins's room yesterday."

"Really?" Darcy asked. "Where was it hidden?"

"Behind a curtain. I would have given it to you tonight only I did not want Lady Catherine to see it. It has only credits, and some of them are quite substantial. I do hope you will be able to make sense of it soon. It is most confusing."

"What is confusing about it?" Darcy asked.

"For one, I understand a rector does not make much money. Enough to support a family and a home, but no more than a thousand pounds a year."

Darcy's brows furrowed. "Very few make more than fifteen hundred pounds. Am I to assume that there was a substantial amount of money in the ledger?"

"The earliest entry, dated four years ago, was only a few hundred pounds. But the last entry was made the week I was ill. It was a credit of four thousand pounds."

Darcy stopped walking and turned to Elizabeth. "Are you saying that Mr. Collins made four thousand pounds in four years?"

"No, it was a *credit* of four thousand pounds. The balance was over eleven thousand."

Darcy looked perplexed for a moment. "I most definitely want to see this ledger. Are you sure it was his?"

"Well, it was hidden in his room and written in his handwriting."

"I will make of it what I can. But in the meantime, I cannot help but notice that we have lost our party. It seems you walk at a remarkably slow pace. Are you trying to get me alone, Elizabeth?" he asked with a flirtatious smile.

"Sir, you are the one who stopped walking a moment ago. And now you are steering me in a most peculiar direction. I cannot imagine how one could fully appreciate a cherry grove at night, when the blossoms are covered in darkness." Elizabeth felt her heart start beating wildly as he pulled her into his arms.

The night had been tense as they ate at Rosings. On at least two occasions, Elizabeth could have sworn that Anne silenced her mother with a kick under the table.

But none of that mattered as she felt herself melt into his strong arms. She let him cradle her head, and she placed it on his shoulder. Her face was perfectly positioned to rise and fall with his breathing, which seemed slightly quickened. She wrapped her arms around him and tilted her head up to him and felt his deep penetrating gaze that pierced her with the realization of how fast her opinion of him had changed.

She said, "I never desired your good opinion, Will, but I most certainly appreciate it now."

He released one arm and grasped her hand and brought it to his lips, careful to kiss each knuckle, effectively making her catch her breath. Each touch, each graze of his fingers as they passed the food at dinner had been thrilling. She didn't know how he had arranged it, but she had been most pleasantly surprised to discover that they were seated next to each other, as far away as possible from Lady Catherine. Even Avelina had sat closer to Lady Catherine than they did. At one point, Mr. Darcy had allowed his knee to brush up against hers under the table. She had applied the same pressure back, welcoming the sensation.

"My dearest," he whispered, "you have made me so happy. I wish to marry quickly, and I do not think I can wait until Saturday to ask your father's permission. Hertfordshire is merely fifty miles from here. What would you say to me riding out tomorrow? Lady Catherine is no longer a concern, so the only person who has any say in my happiness is your father." His eyes were pleading with her.

She reached her hand up to his face, cupped his jaw and rubbed her thumb along his cheek. "I should probably go with you. My father is still under the impression that we do not like each other. Avelina would make a fine chaperone, and Jane can stay and attend to Charlotte."

"Then it is settled. Tomorrow we will travel to Hertfordshire. We will return the next day to finish helping Mrs. Collins." He placed his hand over hers that was on his face and brought it to his lips.

She closed her eyes, relishing in the divine sensation coursing through her body. Before she could open them, she felt the slightest brush of his lips against hers sending new tingles up and down her spine. He leaned in further and placed a few feather-light kisses on the lips, and then she felt him ever so slowly move his lips up her cheek near her ear where he whispered, “My love, my life. The love of my life.” His deep baritone voice was smooth as silk in her ears, and she savored each warm breath as he said it. Goosebumps formed unbidden, but most definitely not unpleasant.

She couldn’t help herself, and she allowed him to kiss her neck just below the ear as he continued to whisper between kisses, “My love, my life. The love of my life.”

She finally found her voice and with great effort was able to tell him in return, “I love you, Will. I do.”

He lifted his head and looked longingly into her eyes. His eyes were full of passion and desire. “Say it again, my love, my life.”

“I love you, Will.” She knew this was the first time she had said it with full feeling and no reservations. It was like saying aloud for the first time. In truth, it probably felt that way to him.

“I am afraid you have little knowledge of the power you have over me. I am entirely at your disposal. Ask and you shall receive.”

She smiled at him and looked briefly to see if they were alone.

“What is it?” Darcy’s corners of his mouth pulled up and his dimples showed ever so slowly. They were too charmingly handsome. In the moonlight, he seemed to glow.

“May I kiss you?” she asked with a raise of the eyebrow.

“I believe it is my turn to say that if you do not, you shall have a very disappointed man on your hands.” He then leaned into her and placed his lips upon hers with a pressure that was not firm, but spoke of his impatience. He slowly wrapped his hands around the small of her back and pulled her toward him. Their lips did not part for some time, each being unwilling to separate without being satisfied.

*****

The carriage left early in the morning. Elizabeth and Miss Gardiner sat on one side of the carriage, and Mr. Darcy sat on the other. They had been traveling and chatting for a good hour when he finally broke the silence and asked the question he had been dying to ask.

"Miss Elizabeth, what is the weather in Hertfordshire like this time of year? I wonder if you have any firsthand knowledge of walking to the sun that you might be willing to share with me."

Miss Gardiner giggled and said, "You do not need to be sly with me around, Mr. Darcy. She and Jane told me all about her experience in the garden."

Darcy looked at Elizabeth, who was blushing becomingly. "Is that so? Well enlighten me, Miss Gardiner. She has yet to tell me about her walk."

Miss Gardiner sat up and started explaining, "She was very ill, so ill that those who took care of her were deathly afraid that she would die!"

"Deathly afraid? I can only imagine." Darcy said with a straight face. It was obvious that Elizabeth had not informed Miss Gardner of his involvement. Whatever the reason for the omission, he decided to play along.

"Oh yes," Avelina continued. "But before she lost consciousness, she did something that you must not censure her for, because it was very romantic and it had to be done."

Elizabeth laughed. "Yes, because as long as it is romantic, the rules of propriety do not matter!"

"Oh, Lizzy! Ignore her, Mr. Darcy. She is just embarrassed. She wrote a letter to a man, a man she was not engaged to! I see your shock, but I assure you she did. He wrote first, you see, because there was a big misunderstanding, and so after getting his letter, she felt a strong urge to write back to him and apologize and tell him she had been wrong. Anyway, she fell into a deep sleep and had the most amazing experience of a beautiful place, like a vivid dream. It was a place full of hope and peace. Elizabeth calls it her heaven."

Darcy asked, a little more seriously, "*Her* heaven?"

Elizabeth explained, "Yes, for it was a beautiful exotic garden, full of all sorts of flowers and trees. There were colors I cannot even describe and plants I have never seen. It was my heaven. I cannot imagine heaven being anything other than a beautiful garden."

"Like a Garden of Eden." Darcy smiled at her, and Elizabeth nodded.

"But the garden was not the most important part!" Avelina interjected. "For someone else was there too!"

Darcy turned his attention back to Miss Gardiner. "Who was there?" he asked with a look of feigned curiosity.

"Her prince!" Avelina put her hands to her heart and leaned back in the carriage and sighed.

He couldn't help but grin. He surreptitiously glanced over at Elizabeth and saw that her cheeks and ears were already nearly crimson. He tried not to add to her embarrassment.

"Am I safe to assume this prince is the man she wrote the letter to?" he asked Avelina.

"Yes! And they walked and walked, arm in arm. She even held his hand! He talked so kindly to her and stayed beside her. But Elizabeth felt like she needed to walk to the sun. Mr. Darcy, you will not believe me, but things were not as they seemed in Elizabeth's heaven. For the bright light they were walking to was not the sun at all!"

"What was it?" Darcy asked.

Elizabeth cleared her throat and interrupted them. "Avelina, it will be a long ride. Why do you not get some rest? I will finish telling Mr. Darcy about this later. Some things are too sacred to talk about so lightly."

"You are so right, Elizabeth. I am so sorry I was not treating it with the respect it deserved. I did not even ask you if it was appropriate to tell Mr. Darcy. But it is such a beautiful story!"

"Do not worry, darling. Mr. Darcy and I are good friends, and I have no problem telling him about my walk in the garden. I think he will understand. Now lay your head on my lap and go to sleep. When you wake, we should be at Longbourn." Elizabeth guided her head to her lap and started playing with the hair around her ears. It was such a motherly thing to do that Mr. Darcy had to look away briefly to regain composure.

When Mr. Darcy looked back at the two a few minutes later, Elizabeth was holding Miss Gardiner's hand and adjusting the blanket around her shoulders. The carriage rocked slightly, and Elizabeth held her closely. It was not long until Miss Gardiner was soundly sleeping. A good half hour passed before he could work up the courage to speak again.

"You will make a fine mother someday." She blushed slightly and turned her head away. "I did not mean to make you uncomfortable," he added.

"You did not. But I admit you caught me considering such a thing." She paused before adding, "I cannot imagine a better father than you. I remember all those letters you wrote to Georgiana while at Netherfield. I believe you wrote every day. What could you possibly have to say that you had not said the day before?"

Mr. Darcy shrugged his shoulders and smiled. "I write her when I am troubled. It helps me make sense of things. And I found I was quite disturbed that week by a certain pair of fine brown eyes that sparred with me at every turn. Everything about you confused me. Feelings emerged inside me that I had never felt before."

"You wrote to her about me?" she marveled.

"Yes and no. I may have mentioned that you had a refreshing impertinence and pleasing figure." He grinned at her when she gasped.

"Will!" she exclaimed, her cheeks scarlet and her brows furrowed in displeasure.

He laughed. "I am sorry, I could not resist teasing you. I did not write anything of the sort. Rest assured that I only mentioned you in passing, my dear. My interest in you prompted questions that I was not prepared to answer. I could hardly admit it to myself, let alone to Georgiana. It took me many months to come to peace with how vital you were to my happiness. You are my love, my life. "

"Thank you, Will. I love you so very much."

Darcy smiled back at her from across the carriage. They sat in silence for a few moments, but he couldn't shake the question out of his head. "Will you not tell me what happened in the garden?" he asked. "If you would rather not speak of it, I understand. Mr. Osborn told me you were reticent, but I would dearly like to hear about it."

She nodded slightly and looked at her hand that was holding Miss Gardiner's. He noticed she gave it a slight squeeze before releasing it.

"It was a beautiful place," she began, looking up at him with bright, shiny eyes. "Not just because of the garden, but more importantly because of the feelings I felt there. There was a sense of peace, unconditional love, and serenity that I had never felt before. I could feel things being communicated to me in a nonverbal way. I somehow just knew it was a place of healing and love. I felt welcomed home and completely at peace with what was happening."

She continued, "I could sense there was a bright light that I needed to walk to. I described it to you as the sun, but, in reality, it was much more than that. It was like a magnetic pull. And it was not really a light, but rather a compilation of a glow of happiness, a brightness of spirit, and pure unconditional love. It was Jesus Christ. He was there in the garden, in my heaven, and he was welcoming me home." As she spoke, he was spellbound and in utter amazement.

"I have never felt so loved as I did in that garden. It was so beautiful. But as we got closer to the Son of God, everything sped up. Things began moving so fast they started to blur. When I got close enough to actually see His face, I could see great compassion there in His eyes. He was so glad to see me; the feeling is indescribable. But that is when I heard you behind me and realized that you had not come to the Son with me. I knew I would have to choose. At one point God looked at me and, without words, He nodded his understanding. He knew me so well that He knew what I would do. You kept saying the same thing over and over again."

Darcy choked out the words, "You have a mission left on Earth, and your family still needs you."

Gentle tears ran down her face, and she sobbed, "Yes, that is exactly what you said." He handed her his handkerchief and let her cry. He leaned forward and caressed her wet cheeks. She continued, "I have often asked myself since then why it was not Jane or my father or someone else there with me. Why would God send you to be my companion during such an experience? Why would you be in my heaven?"

"I do not know."

"And what is my mission left on Earth?"

Miss Gardiner stirred on Elizabeth's lap and sat up. "Lizzy? Are you well? You are crying."

Mr. Darcy gave her a moment to compose herself. "She was just telling me how her prince told her that she had a mission left on Earth and that her family still needed her. She does not understand."

"Oh, well I do," Miss Gardiner said confidently. Both Mr. Darcy and Elizabeth looked confused. Miss Gardiner sat up quickly and explained. "It is so simple! Elizabeth needs to marry the prince from the garden. The prince loves her so much that he simply could not live without her. *He* is the family that still needs her. See? When they marry, *he* will be her family. God knew he was going to reenter your life again, Lizzy. That is why He put him in the garden with you. She is his life, Mr. Darcy, his true love. Nothing can stop true love. And he did come back! Elizabeth told me she saw him in London! But then Charlotte's husband died, and we had to come here."

Darcy smiled at the innocence and yet profound insight of youth. "I believe you might be right. For nothing less than the prince's pure, unconditional love could be strong enough to pull her away from the Son. I imagine he would do anything for her, follow her anywhere, hoping, against all hope, that she would be his." He smiled at Elizabeth, whose tears had stopped. They gazed deeply into each other's eyes until Avelina looked up. Elizabeth quickly glanced out the window.

Darcy could see her cheeks growing warm again. He made another attempt to distract the young woman: "But Miss Gardiner, what is her mission left on Earth?"

Avelina looked thoughtful. She glanced at Elizabeth and took a deep breath. "A mission could be defined as a single task or a lifelong goal. I imagine this mission it is a little bit of both. My father says Elizabeth has a great deal of that 'something special'."

"That she does," Darcy agreed, smiling at Elizabeth.

"My father says when someone has that 'something special', they must share it with others. This is God's way of spreading his love to his children. He uses people like Elizabeth to help people. She will share God's love with people her entire life. I think that is her mission."

Elizabeth obviously could not help herself and embraced Miss Gardiner tightly. "Avelina, you are remarkable! I have been trying to make sense of the garden for weeks without any luck! I talked to Jane, Charlotte, and your mother, but you, who are but fourteen, have offered insight that none of those others were able to! How did you become so mature?"

She giggled, "Years of practice! And because my father says I have that 'something special' too!"

Darcy looked at Elizabeth and asked, "Have you told Miss Gardiner who this prince is?"

Elizabeth smiled and looked at Miss Gardiner. "Would you like to know? It might surprise you."

"Oh, please! Please tell me!"

"You said I was his life. You said he would follow me anywhere."

"Yes, I did."

Darcy said, "And I said the prince would do anything to make her his. Even risk rejection."

"Yes." Miss Gardiner's excitement was not easily contained. She was squirming in her seat looking from Darcy to Elizabeth. A moment ago she seemed mature for her age, and now she seemed to have all the excitement of a schoolgirl.

Elizabeth looked deeply at Miss Gardiner, and then suddenly Miss Gardiner turned her head to Mr. Darcy and an enormous smile infused her face. She gasped and then exclaimed, "But you are not proud, Mr. Darcy!"

The entire carriage rocked with the laughter in seeing her joy. Avelina wrapped her arms around Elizabeth and started crying. "Are you happy with how this fairy tale has played out?" Elizabeth asked. "Do you like the ending?"

"Is that why we are going to Longbourn? Is Mr. Darcy going to ask Uncle Bennet for permission to marry you?"

Mr. Darcy said, "Indeed I am."

More understanding graced her face as she said, "That means that Mr. Bingley loves Jane!"

"Indeed he does." Elizabeth and Darcy said in unison.

"I could not be happier with your prince!"
Elizabeth turned her gaze to Mr. Darcy and said, "Nor could I."

CHAPTER 20

The carriage pulled up to Longbourn. Mr. Darcy helped Avelina down and then turned to offer his hand to Elizabeth. As he helped her down, she could feel an extra little squeeze that she quickly returned.

Avelina had run on ahead, eager to see Kitty and Lydia again. Elizabeth took this time to ask, "Are you ready for this? I know my family is difficult to bear." She knew this would not be easy for him.

Mr. Darcy took her hand and kissed it just as Mrs. Bennet came out, which caused her to blush.

"Lizzy! I did not think you were coming until Saturday! Why did you not write to tell us you were coming? Is Charlotte well? Oh my, you are quite flushed, you must sit down. I imagine the carriage ride was unpleasant, considering the company. Mr. Darcy, you needn't have felt obligated. Bingley could have easily offered his carriage. "

Mr. Darcy bowed to her mother. "It was no trouble at all. I rather enjoyed our time together."

"Well, I hope Lizzy was not trouble. She does like to make trouble, that girl!" Mrs. Bennet peered at him, expecting him to take his leave, but Darcy remained where he was. "I suppose you have business here in town," she hinted.

Elizabeth wrapped her arm around Mr. Darcy's and said, "Mamma, Mr. Darcy has had a long carriage ride. Perhaps we should invite him in and offer him some refreshment." Elizabeth tried not to smile as Mrs. Bennet looked in puzzlement at Elizabeth's close proximity to Mr. Darcy.

Mrs. Bennet shook her head slightly as if an unwelcome thought had come into her mind. "Well then, I suppose you should come in. I cannot say we have hosted many gentlemen lately. The militia have left town, and Mr. Bingley has not returned. But he wrote the housekeeper last week, and Netherfield is ready to receive him. You can tell him I said so. Lydia is off in Brighton with Colonel Forster and his wife. She was asked to be Mrs. Forster's particular friend in Brighton while the militia is stationed there! Such an honor for my dear Lydia!"

Kitty had come out then and, overhearing the last thing said, she piped up, "Mamma, I should have liked to be her particular friend! Mrs. Forster is my friend too!"

"Oh hush, Kitty! You were not invited! Now go in and tell Hill that Mr. Darcy is here." Kitty stomped her foot and turned away.

Mr. Darcy guided Elizabeth into the house, and Hill rushed forward to take all their outerwear. Elizabeth thanked her, and Mr. Darcy bowed respectfully. Elizabeth could hear Mary attempting a piece on the piano. It was difficult to identify the tune through all the mistakes as the piece, whatever it was, was certainly beyond Mary's skill. Elizabeth then blushed to hear her mother growling at Mary to put the piano music away and come help entertain "that unfriendly Mr. Darcy".

They walked into the sitting room and all sat down. Mr. Darcy stood when Mary entered, carrying her music with her. "Miss Mary, your talent on the piano shows great improvement. I see you have been practicing."

"Yes, sir. My sisters do not see the value of diligent practice, but I believe it is the only way to improve one's skill," Mary replied.

Mr. Darcy nodded and continued, "My sister, Georgiana, says the same thing. She sets out to master the hardest part first, as it will get the most attention and therefore will be the most moving when performed."

"That is exactly what I do," Mary nodded. Then blushing slightly, she added "Although I am sure Miss Darcy is much more proficient than I am."

"Perhaps only because she has had masters to learn from. I cannot say she shares your level of determination."

Elizabeth couldn't help but be amazed at how well Will was handling Mary. Even her mother seemed to have noticed. Mrs. Bennet kept looking from Elizabeth to Mr. Darcy and back again. The tea was brought in, and Elizabeth motioned to the servant to place it in front of her. As Elizabeth began to pour the tea, Mr. Darcy began to talk to Mary about the piano again when Mrs. Bennet interrupted.

"Mr. Darcy, what exactly is the nature of your visit to Hertfordshire today?"

Darcy cleared his throat. "Well, it is a matter of both business and pleasure," he replied. "I am considering a merger in the next few weeks and have come to seek advice and counsel from a few friends."

Mrs. Bennet looked skeptical. "A merger? What kind of merger?"

Elizabeth handed him his tea and offered an encouraging smile. "I am seeking a partner to help me build a new group," he said carefully. "Someone who could fit into the finest circles with finesse."

Elizabeth couldn't help but smile at the sly way he was discussing their marriage plans right in front of her matchmaking mother. Elizabeth handed a cup of tea to her mother, who only briefly tore her eyes from Mr. Darcy before saying, "Yes, but what kind of group? We dine with four-and-twenty families, you know, and I am an excellent judge of character. I may be able to suggest a candidate."

Elizabeth couldn't wait to hear how Darcy was going to answer this one. But he surprised her once again. "Thank you, Mrs. Bennet. I would appreciate your advice. This person would have to be willing and able to travel a great deal, offer sound counsel, and speak to me as an equal. The partner would spend a great deal of time entertaining of my friends and family, as well as helping with daily tasks at Pemberley."

"Do you not already have a steward?"

"Oh, yes, and a competent housekeeper too, but it is a large estate with few landed gentry around. It can get lonely at times."

"You are not trying to split Pemberley are you?"

Elizabeth could tell he was getting uncomfortable, but he once again answered the probing questions. "Not exactly. Mrs. Bennet. May I ask where Mr. Bennet is? I would like to counsel with him on the matter."

"Oh, do not be silly, Mr. Darcy! He is right behind you!"

Elizabeth tried not to giggle as she saw Mr. Darcy turn bright red and slowly turn to look at her father. "Papa, you remember Mr. Darcy, do you not?" Elizabeth began.

Mr. Bennet looked stern. "A merger? For business and pleasure? I cannot imagine why I would have much to say on the matter." Elizabeth gave him a stern look. "Very well, why do you not join me in my study, Mr. Darcy?"

Mr. Darcy put his tea down and gave one last glance at Elizabeth. His eyes showed every bit of the anxiety that she expected.

*****

Mr. Bennet led the way and Darcy followed. Mr. Bennet was not ignorant. He knew he was about to discover why his favorite daughter was escorted home by a bachelor who, at one point in the past, had declared she was not handsome enough to tempt him. From the many looks and flushed cheeks he saw on Elizabeth's face while listening to the nonsense Mr. Darcy was spouting to his wife, he had a good suspicion of what this "merger" entailed.

He showed Mr. Darcy a chair and then took the one behind the desk. "So tell me, Mr. Darcy, how can I help you find a partner to help you run Pemberley in this mysterious merger you described to my wife? I must say, it does not sound like a very sound investment. What man would wish to spend his life working on a property that he would have no rights to?"

Mr. Darcy squirmed slightly. "I admit it does not sound promising to certain men. However I did not say that there would be no rights to Pemberley."

"Ah, so you *are* going to split Pemberley."

"No, sir. Neither am I looking for a man. I actually already have a candidate in mind. A candidate with every skill necessary to be my partner."

Mr. Bennet was enjoying himself. He stood and poured himself a brandy and looked directly at Mr. Darcy who had begun to perspire slightly. "You seem warm, Mr. Darcy. Would you like me to open a window? Oh, forgive my manners, I should have offered you a drink."

"Thank you, sir. I would love one."

Mr. Bennet took his time and poured a full three fingers of brandy and offered it to Darcy, who took it eagerly. "So you have a candidate in mind, and this person seems to meet your expectations. Would you say they are a tempting candidate?"

"Ah, I would say so."

"And would you say the candidate is handsome?"

Mr. Darcy's face flushed. "Yes, many think the candidate is."

"But I do not care what *many* think, Mr. Darcy, I care what you think. Would you say this person is handsome enough to tempt you?" But Mr. Bennet couldn't quite keep a straight face as he said it.

Darcy had clearly caught onto the game. He smiled widely and took a hefty swallow. "Most handsome. Most tempting."

Mr. Bennet wondered who was playing with whom now. The tables had turned quite quickly, and Mr. Bennet was now the one uncomfortable. "Well, enough about the candidate. Let's talk about the merger. What needs to happen, and how can I avoid all the hassle of being a part of it?"

"I am afraid that it is too late now," Darcy said with a serious look on his face.

Too late now? What has happened? The remains of a smile vanished from Mr. Bennet's face. Mr. Bennet reached a hand out to brace himself. He made his way to the chair and sat down. He downed the rest of his brandy and felt the burn reach his stomach and heat him through and through.

His poor Lizzy! Doomed to marry a man she detests! This man, sitting right from him, must have pushed himself on his favorite daughter. And now there was no hope for her!

"Mr. Bennet? Are you well?" Darcy asked with concern.

Mr. Bennet shook his head. "I see. So all this talk about groups being formed . . . you mean to tell me that a baby is coming soon."

Darcy's face paled, and he nearly dropped the brandy glass in his hand. "Excuse me, sir?"

Mr. Bennet rarely let his temper get the better of him, but the audacity of this man tested his patience. "You said you are an honest gentleman, Mr. Darcy. If you want my blessing, you must tell me the truth. How did you trap Elizabeth into being compromised?"

Mr. Darcy turned bright red. "Sir! I have done nothing but what a newly accepted man might ask of his betrothed!" Darcy stammered in a shaky voice.

"So, she is not ruined?" Mr. Bennet demanded.

"Certainly not!" Darcy quaked. The two men stared at each other with puzzled looks. Then Darcy started laughing, which only confused Mr. Bennet even more. After what seemed an eternity, Mr. Darcy sighed, "This is a wretched beginning indeed! I am sure nobody else will believe me if you do you not! Am I so detestable that you think I lack the ability to woo your daughter as a gentleman, Mr. Bennet?"

Mr. Bennet breathed a sigh of relief and downed the remainder of his brandy. He laughed nervously, glad to hear Elizabeth was out of harm's way, but still somewhat confused. "Then why on earth would she want to marry *you*? I mean no offence, sir, it is just that I am quite sure she detests you. I know she is not mercenary. She will not marry you solely to become the mistress of Pemberley—or your partner, or whatever title you want to give it. Has she really accepted your offer? The Lizzy I know will only marry someone she loves."

Darcy smiled and his eyes softened. "She *does* love me. And I love her very much. I can assure you of that. This is what I have been trying to tell you. I will take good care of her," he vowed.

Mr. Bennet took a moment to digest this information. "So all this she being 'not handsome enough to tempt me' and her promising 'never to dance with him', it was just a facade? You truly love each other?" It was hard to believe, but the grin on Mr. Darcy's face declared it to be the truth.

"Well, in that case, Mr. Darcy, please accept my apologies and my blessing." He stood and walked over to him and shook his hand. "Welcome to the family."

"Thank you, sir." Just then they heard a loud, all-too-familiar scream from outside the study door.

"It seems that Elizabeth has shared the news with her mother. You might find a difficult situation just outside that door, sir. Would you like me to clear a path, or would you prefer to tell your future mother-in-law about your merger plans yourself?"

Darcy straightened his shoulders. "I am quite equal to the task, I assure you."

*****

Elizabeth, confident that Will could handle her mother's flutterings and quiverings, left Mrs. Bennet in his care to go in search of her father, who still had not come out of the study.

He was sitting at his desk, with his head in his hands. "Papa? Are you well?"

He looked up and smiled. He motioned for her to come to him. "Yes, child. I am just realizing how grown up you are. It seems it was just yesterday that you were scaring off boys with garden snakes, and now you are catching them! It is a hard thing to know I will not be the only man in your life. But I see now what you see in him. He is charming and quick. He had me thinking there for a minute that he had compromised you. I am most relieved that he has not."

"No, Papa, he has not. He has been quite the gentleman. He only kisses me when I ask him."

He put his hands up to silence her. "No, please, do not talk about kissing him. I barely can imagine you loving him, let alone doing such things." Mr. Bennet sighed, "Oh, Lizzybell! I feel like I have lost you already. We have been so close over the years and now I must share you. You will move all the way to Derbyshire! I will never see you!"

Her heart ached for her father. "I understand Pemberley has a very large library. And Mr. Darcy plays an excellent game of chess. You could visit us during the *peak season.*"

She heard him laugh as she mentioned their code word for her mother's bouts of anxiety. They had always escaped to the study when their mother ranted and raved about the latest gossip. Whenever it got so bad that she asked for her smelling salts, her father would slyly remark, "It must be the peak season."

"Indeed. But your mother will insist on accompanying me! And that means two and a half days of travel with her effusions! Listen to her out there with Mr. Darcy. Her first tiny glimpse of Pemberley and his ten thousand a year will send her into raptures, my dear," he sighed. "And there will be no retreat to escape to in such a small carriage."

"Well, you do what you think is best. But know that you will always be welcome at Pemberley. I will always be your Lizzybell. May I ask you a question, Papa?"

"Certainly, child."

"Are you sure that Lydia should have gone to Brighton? You know how she is."

"Oh, Lizzy! Lydia will never be easy until she has exposed herself in some public place or other, and we can never expect her to do it with so little expense or inconvenience to her family as under the present circumstances."

"But she is unguarded and imprudent. I fear she will put us all in shame."

"Oh, you need not worry. You have your match—unless your mother manages to cool Mr. Darcy's affection for you—so what injury could there be? There is no harm to you, and with you so well matched, I daresay your mother has the right of it: your sisters will be thrown in the path of other rich men."

"Call her back, Papa. Please. Write to her immediately and tell her she is needed at home for her sister's wedding. Promise her a new gown, if you must, but do not let her stay in Brighton one more day."

Mr. Bennet rolled his eyes and sighed in exasperation. "Very well, Lizzybell, if you insist. It shall be called your wedding present. Now be off on your way and make me hear no more of it."

She stood and stared at him until he picked up his pen to begin the letter. "Would you like to write it yourself, or do you trust me to do as I have been so clearly instructed? Even though I am impertinent, I believe I can be trusted to keep my word. Off with you, child." He paused a moment. "No," he corrected himself, "for you are no longer a child. You will be a wife soon. Lord, help me!"

Elizabeth went and kissed her father's forehead and said, "I love you, Papa. You will always be the first man who captured my heart."

CHAPTER 21

Notwithstanding Mrs. Bennet, Darcy would have gladly spent the rest of the day at Longbourn by Elizabeth's side. But he had promised to relay some instructions from Bingley to the Netherfield housekeeper, so he took his leave, promising to return for dinner. Not surprisingly, this vow sent Mrs. Bennet into fits of hysterics all over again. He smiled knowingly at Elizabeth, who, as she endeavored once again to calm her mother, returned his smile with a giggle. Then he set off for Netherfield.

After discharging his duty, he sat in Bingley's study and investigated the mysterious ledger that Elizabeth had found. He had glanced through it only briefly when Elizabeth gave it to him that morning in the carriage.

Elizabeth was correct in that all it contained was credits. As he flipped through the pages, he found a paper folded into thirds. He peered at the paper, mindlessly rolling a pencil from little finger to forefinger and back again. It seemed to be a letter of some sort, but the outside markings and address were missing. He studied it a little and could see it was written on very fine paper, of the highest professional quality. The top was engraved with a seal, an embellishment of the name "P & S". He also noticed that the letter had been placed in the exact page where a four-thousand-pound credit had been added. He opened it up and read:

12 August 1808
P&S
London

Mr. Collins,

As per your instructions, £4,000 has been applied to your account. The funds are immediately available. All remaining funds were spent refinishing the deck of the Horizon's Challenge, *just as Captain Blackhurst suggested.*

We have addressed your concerns regarding Captain Dixon, and are confident it has been dealt with to your liking. I have placed an advertisement in the London Times *for potential candidates and have several very promising prospects. Enclosed are Captain Conrad Jersey and Captain Frank Farthington's credentials.*

I, myself, would recommend Captain Jersey, as he seems to have the most experience with vessels of this size. Although a little older than most, I think he is capable of running the crew. I will confer with Captain Blackhurst on the matter as soon as the Winter's Night *returns to port and will forward his opinion as well as any other available news.*

I would like to thank you for your business. My brother and I appreciate working with such a fine man. If you have any other needs, please do not hesitate to ask. We are at your bidding.

C. W. Pastel

Darcy took a pencil and started underlining the names of the ships and their captains. The four thousand pounds in the letter clearly corresponded with the entry in the ledger. Whoever this C. W. Pastel was, perhaps he could explain what this ledger meant. Why would Mr. Collins be directing the hiring and firing of ship captains? And what kind of company was P&S? "P" could be a name, perhaps "Pastel". And "S" could indicate the name of a partner. Was it an accounting firm? A bank? A solicitor's office?

Darcy tried to think who he could ask in London. His solicitor perhaps. But when would he be able to go to London? He did not want to leave Elizabeth so soon, and they still had to return to Kent tomorrow to transport the rest of the party to Hertfordshire.

He closed the ledger and looked at his pocket watch. He could not be late to Mrs. Bennet's dinner, of that he was confident. Some people wore no disguises. At least he did not have to puzzle her out.

*****

That evening, Mr. Darcy was not allowed to return to Netherfield until Mrs. Bennet had fed him a full five courses at dinner. However, this was convenient to his purposes, as any time spent with Elizabeth was welcomed. He hoped he would get a chance to speak with her about the mysterious ledger.

But first, Mr. Darcy had to listen to Mrs. Bennet's effusions about Pemberley. She asked how many windows it had, how many servants it took to manage it on a daily basis, and if the mistress suite had been refurnished lately.

"No. To be honest, I doubt anyone but the chambermaids have gone inside for several years."

Mrs. Bennet threw her hands up excitedly. "Well then, Lizzy, I should think you should have a great deal of say on the refurbishment! And you will need my help, of course!"

"Mother, I am sure Pemberley will suit me just fine. There is no need to redecorate anything."

Mrs. Bennet waved her hand dismissively and squealed, "Nonsense! Of course it will need to be redecorated! He just admitted it! Mr. Darcy, tell her you will let her redo the mistress's suite! Tell her! She simply does not know what it takes to run an estate of that magnitude! Not that she could not manage the estate, no, sir, she most definitely could! Of all my daughters, my dear sweet Elizabeth is the one who is the most talented in these things! Why, she even helps her father balance the ledgers. Yes, Elizabeth is going to make you a fine wife, to be sure."

Mr. Darcy tried not to smile at her ramblings and instead put down his spoon and assessed the whole table. Miss Kitty was leaning over her plate with a saddened look on her face. He had heard her several times lament over not going to Brighton. Miss Mary's head was looking at Mr. Darcy as if she was awaiting his response to something. Mr. Bennet had a book to the side of his plate that had drawn most of his attention during the meal, but at the moment, something must have struck him humorous because he closed his book and looked expectantly at Mr. Darcy. Elizabeth was pink in her cheeks from obvious embarrassment.

Mr. Darcy placed his hand on Elizabeth's under the table and gave it a gentle reassuring squeeze. "Mrs. Bennet, I could not agree with you more. I think the mistress's suite is still decorated in the pale-green color that my mother favored, and I know Miss Elizabeth favors yellow. She will most definitely need to refurbish it." His hand felt Elizabeth squeeze his back, and then, daring even further than he did, she slipped her foot next to his, making their legs touch from ankle to knee. His mind went foggy slightly as he relished in the sensation.

Weeks, not months. I must convince her to marry quickly.

He chanced a glance away from Mrs. Bennet and caught a sweet look from Elizabeth, who was looking up from her eyelashes at him slyly. He cleared his throat and redirected his gaze only to catch Mr. Bennet's furrowed brows looking at Mr. Darcy's hand under the table. He gave Elizabeth's hand one last caress with his fingers, released her, and proceeded to reach for more pudding, even though he had truly eaten more than enough already. He would have to watch himself around Mr. Bennet; Elizabeth's father was clearly much more observant than her mother.

Mr. Bennet scooted his chair back and said to Miss Kitty, "Catherine, do tell me, what did Lydia's letter this morning say? Was there anything other than silly talk of ribbons, balls, and red coats?"

Darcy did not fail to notice that Miss Kitty looked up startled at her father's question. She stammered a bit in her response. All in all, Miss Kitty gave no answer at all.

Mr. Bennet put up a hand to stop her. "Never you mind, Catherine, I should know better than to ask. I simply was surprised that she wrote. Lydia never was a good correspondent."

Miss Kitty's cheeks turned pink, and she concentrated on the pudding in front of her. Darcy noticed she was not really eating it.

Conversation continued and Darcy responded when appropriate, however, he continued to watch Miss Kitty with some concern. She had seemed bored earlier, maybe even sad and disappointed that she hadn't gone to Brighton, but now she was undeniably nervous. She seemed eager to leave the table. At one point she put her napkin down and tried to excuse herself, but Mrs. Bennet gave her a disapproving look. Darcy couldn't be sure, but he was fairly confident there was a kick under the table as well.

Darcy looked to Mr. Bennet, who had reopened his book. He did not seem to notice any of it. Mr. Darcy placed his napkin on the table and sat back, trying to indicate as respectfully as possible that he was satisfied. "Mrs. Bennet, that was a delightful meal. I commend you and your cook."

She blushed deeply and said, "Given such late notice of having company for dinner, the compliment is much appreciated. Are you sure you do not wish for more baked apples?"

Elizabeth interrupted and said, "Mother, he had two helpings. I am sure you will have other opportunities to feed Mr. Darcy. He is not going anywhere."

"I suppose you are correct. Mr. Bennet, do you not wish to offer your French brandy to Mr. Darcy?"

Mr. Bennet looked up from his book, took a deep breath, and sighed. Placing a bookmark on the page, he closed his book. Standing up and tucking it under his arm in the same movement, an obviously practiced mannerism, he said somewhat reluctantly, "I suppose my solitude after dinner must be put off to another date." Mr. Darcy stiffened slightly at the obligatory tones lacing his voice. "There now, do not take my word at face value, Mr. Darcy. I may seem disinterested, but I assure you, I observe a great deal. Why do we not discuss my observations in my study? Elizabeth, you will not mind parting with your intended for a bit, will you?"

"No, Papa. But do be on your best behavior. Mr. Darcy, if you find him difficult, you may wish to threaten to limit his access to Pemberley's library. I rather foolishly invited him already. Perhaps we should have held out for something of value in return."

Mr. Bennet chuckled. "Yes, a rather serious blunder, my dear. But you did stop short of stating whether the invitation included your mother."

Mrs. Bennet sucked in a ragged breath and screeched, "My dear Mr. Bennet! How can you say such a thing! Of course *I* am invited to Pemberley! *I* am her mother! And I certainly will not waste my time in the library! Did you not hear how many rooms it has? Mr. Darcy says it—"

"Papa, look what you have done!" Elizabeth whispered to her father. "It will take me a quarter of an hour to settle her again! If you do not leave immediately, I shall state you had malicious intent to throw me under the carriage!" Elizabeth stood up and went directly to her mother and started fanning her in a rhythmical way that only showed how practiced she was at the act.

Mr. Darcy wished he could have a moment to speak with Elizabeth, but she was clearly quite preoccupied with her mother's ranting and wailing about how Mr. Darcy would never exclude her on purpose. Mr. Bennet grinned and shook his head and waved at Darcy to follow.

He caught Elizabeth's exasperated expression and saw her roll her eyes in frustration. He turned and followed Mr. Bennet into the study.

Mr. Darcy asked, "Was that really necessary?"

Laughing, Mr. Bennet said, "Oh, I just did you a favor! She had been angling for an invitation all night with all her questions about Pemberley. You would have never been allowed to leave the table without inviting her. I believe she would have had the cook drum up three more courses if needed."

Mr. Bennet walked to his desk, opened a drawer, and withdrew a cigar box. "Never you mind about my wife and her nerves," he continued. "I guarantee that they are healthier now than they have ever been. You, sir, are a better match than Mr. Collins, or Mr. Goulding, or even Mr. Bingley! Why she could not be happier! I take that back, she *could* be happier if the invitation came directly from you. But now Elizabeth can do it for you and you will be rid of the bother."

"I see. Do you always prod her in this manner?"

"I see you disapprove." Mr. Bennet offered him a cigar.

"No, thank you. Let us just say that I do not yet fully appreciate Mrs. Bennet's enthusiasm for me. It seems rather sudden. I was always under the impression that your wife disliked me immensely. I believe I even heard her ask Miss Elizabeth at the Netherfield Ball,"—here Mr. Darcy raised his voice slightly before continuing— "'What is he to me? I care nothing for Mr. Darcy's disapproval. I would welcome his good opinion as much as he would welcome a mud bath with my pig!'"

This sent Mr. Bennet into hysterics and nearly choked on his cigar smoke.

"Forgive me, sir," Darcy apologized. "I should not have mocked your wife."

"Oh, if you only knew what joy that brought to me! I will be the first to admit I married a silly woman. I only hope that your honesty holds true. I do warn you that you will need to set limitations on her invitations to Pemberley; perhaps for the Christmas holidays one year and part of the summer another. I also warn you that once you and Elizabeth start a family, I imagine her focus on finding good matches for her daughters will be entirely shifted to spoiling her grandchildren. Grandchildren! Good Lord, how odd that sounds! I surely am too young to be a grandfather." Mr. Bennet got a faraway look in his eyes.

Mr. Darcy let Mr. Bennet smoke his cigar in silence. He stood and walked to the bottle of port on the side table and asked, "May I?" Mr. Bennet waved his hand, and Darcy went ahead and poured himself a glass. He walked the perimeter of the room and examined the books that lined the shelves, many of which he owned himself. If Mr. Bennet had this fine a library, they would get along nicely.

They talked briefly about his taste in books and shared opinions on one book in particular that Mr. Bennet claimed was one of Elizabeth's favorites. The book was about two sisters, vastly different in temperaments, but both hoping to find love. Darcy found that Mr. Bennet's take on the book was quite unique. Where many readers viewed the tale as an endorsement of the eldest's sense, Mr. Bennet argued that both the eldest's sense as well as the youngest's sensibility was of value. Each sister had to develop the other sister's strongest quality.

The conversation was very engaging, and Mr. Darcy was confident that, given any book in this entire room, Mr. Bennet could find deep life meanings, perhaps meanings hidden even from the author.

Mr. Darcy found that he was quickly counting Mr. Bennet as a friend, one he hoped to have for a great length of time. He appreciated the witty yet insightful comments he made. Clearly he was the source of Elizabeth's deep thoughts. No wonder he called the younger daughters silly, for he could not imagine them conversing like this.

Thinking of Elizabeth's two youngest sisters, he was reminded how anxious and uncomfortable Kitty had been at dinner upon mention of Lydia's letter. He decided to ask Mr. Bennet about it.

"Sir, I noticed something at dinner that concerns me."

Mr. Bennet looked up. "As did I," he replied, raising an eyebrow at him somewhat challengingly. Darcy could feel the heat rise under his cravat.

"I suppose you are referring to our hands under the table. My apologies, sir. I promise you I was only trying to reassure Miss Elizabeth. She seemed somewhat uncomfortable regarding your wife's energetic questions about my estate."

Mr. Bennet snuffed out the butt of his cigar, leaned back, and put his hands behind his head. "I am not going to lie and tell you it is easy to see my daughter in love, but I am pleased her feelings are reciprocated. I hope you know what you are getting into with Elizabeth. She is a special soul."

"I could not agree with you more." Darcy's mind wandered back to the first time he had seen her at the Meryton Assembly. Her natural laugh and the spark in her eyes had drawn him in like no one he had ever met. The strength of it had alarmed him, and he had tried to fight his feelings as much as possible. He looked up at Mr. Bennet. "A very special soul," he mused.

"But what I observed tonight at dinner did not involve Miss Elizabeth. It was Miss Kitty, when you asked about Miss Lydia's letter. I do not claim to know your daughters well, but I think something in that letter has made her very nervous."

Mr. Bennet leaned forward and furrowed his brow. "Are you saying that Kitty is hiding something? Something that is in Lydia's letter?"

"I cannot be sure, but I think Miss Lydia might be in some mischief. Miss Kitty seems to be close to her, and I imagine she is struggling with a confidence of some sort."

"I will ask her about it. Those two have a tendency to get into mischief and keep it between themselves. Once when Lydia was eight, she had convinced Kitty to climb a tree. Kitty was just barely ten at the time. Their plan was to haul wooden planks up to the highest part and create a fort of some sort. They pulled a few boards off the old shed and carried them up the tree, one holding the board, and the other scurrying up above to pull the board up to the next branch. After going up and down three or four times, they were quite fatigued. It only seemed logical to take a nap, so both girls fell asleep on the boards fifty feet above the ground.

"When Kitty woke, she got nervous and came down right away. But when it was time for dinner, Lydia was still nowhere to be seen. It was clear that Kitty knew where Lydia was, but she would not disclose it. Despite my best efforts, Kitty refused to budge. By this time it was dark outside, and I was considering drumming up a search party from the village. But I had an idea that if I dismissed Kitty and just followed her, she would lead me directly to Lydia. Which of course is what happened.

"I found Lydia crying at the top of a tree because she was too afraid to come down in the dark. The loyalty between those two is not entirely understood, but I have never underestimated it since then. Yes, I shall talk to Kitty straight away. Now, I am sure the ladies are missing us. Well, you, at least."

Mr. Darcy felt some relief. "I would very much like to spend some time with Miss Elizabeth before I return to Netherfield. Could I take her for a walk in the gardens?"

"I suppose that would be appropriate. I will have Mary go with you."

Mr. Darcy couldn't help but be disappointed. Of the two sisters, Mary would be the most vigilant in her role as chaperone. He stood and thanked Mr. Bennet. Mary or no Mary, he would at least be able to discuss the ledger with Elizabeth.

CHAPTER 22

Elizabeth heard the study door open, and she eagerly awaited Mr. Darcy's entrance. Both he and her father came out in good spirits. They had been sequestered in the study for some time now. Even her mother was getting nervous.

Elizabeth stood and walked over to Mr. Darcy and gave him her best smile. He had done so well all night with her family's eccentricities. Mary had tried to be a part of the conversation, but everything she said seemed to come out awkward and forced. But she couldn't blame Mary; Mr. Darcy had shown such kindness to her that no man had ever expressed.

Mr. Darcy came and took her hand and softly said, "I am sorry we were in his study so long. Would you like to walk outside for a minute?"

He offered his arm and she took it, just as her father was asking Mary to accompany them to the gardens. She heard Avelina ask if she could come as well. As they all put on their outerwear, she could hear her father ask for Kitty to come to his study. Elizabeth noticed a panicked look spread through Kitty's features and wondered to its import.

The four of them went to the gardens. Mary quickly, and very uncharacteristically, walked ahead of them with Avelina and went right to the bench by the roses. As they walked past them, Mary gave her a slight smile. It was very kind of her to offer them a moment to themselves. Knowing Mary, it was a token offered in trust. If Elizabeth ever wished a repeat of this gesture, Elizabeth would have to perform to Mary's standards. There was no doubt that her sister would be watching.

A few paces past Avelina and Mary, Elizabeth whispered, "Mr. Darcy, I do believe you have won my whole family over in a matter of a day."

"Will, Elizabeth. Call me Will."

"Forgive me," she said with a blush. "I did not mean to revert back to Mr. Darcy."

"I will forgive you for anything, for I am entirely at your leisure. Whatever you desire shall be granted."

Her blushed deepened, and she walked to a bench and sat down, patting the seat beside her. "Were you able to make anything of the ledger?"

He reached into his pocket and took out a paper. "I have a lead. This letter was on the same page as the large four-thousand-pound credit. Hopefully you will be able to see something I did not," he said handing it to her. "For me, it offered more questions than answers."

By the dim light coming from the window behind them, Elizabeth read the letter. It was a very curious, to be sure, and she could feel her excitement grow. It could only mean that Mr. Collins was either the manager or the owner of two vessels—which meant Charlotte could stand to inherit them. She grinned and looked up. "This looks promising."

"Yes, it may mean that Mrs. Collins has some assets, but the situation is very unclear. I have no idea who this C. W. Pastel is or how to find him."

"Of course you do."

"What do you mean?"

"The letter is dated. And Mr. Pastel said that he had placed an advertisement in the *London Times* for a captain. All you need to do is go to the conservatory and research old editions of the newspaper that ran around that time. Positions like a captain of a ship probably ran for several weeks. I am sure you would not have to look too far back past the date of the letter to find a contact address."

Darcy looked at her in amazement. "Brilliant! Since you are so clever, let me ask you what you make of the seal."

"The P&S? It could be his name, Pastel, but I am not sure . . . He mentions a brother. So maybe it is a family company. Perhaps C. W. Pastel is the 'S'."

"But 'Pastel' doesn't start with *s*."

"No, I mean, maybe it is 'Pastel & Sons'. Maybe C. W. Pastel is the 'Sons' part."

"You are remarkable, my dear! I will need to make a trip to London and contact my solicitor to be sure. I hate to leave you so soon, but I think I will leave as soon as Mrs. Collins returns to Hertfordshire. And I have another reason to go to London, Elizabeth; I am hoping to get a special license. We have not discussed when to marry, but it is my wish to marry as soon as I return. What are your thoughts?"

Elizabeth was very grateful that they felt the same way, but as she opened her mouth to answer him, she heard a commotion in the house. Her worry alerted Mr. Darcy, and he too stood and turned towards the house and, without even needing to be told, they hastened their return to the front door.

Upon entering, Elizabeth could hear her father's raised voice, endeavoring to make himself heard over Kitty's tearful demonstration: "Catherine Arlene Bennet, you will not see the inside of a ballroom for a year! No, for ten years! You should have alerted us of Lydia's plans immediately! I cannot fathom what possessed you to withhold such information! Think of your sisters! If you cannot think of them, think of yourself! What are your chances of finding a respectable husband now? Good God! Do you have any sense?"

Mrs. Bennet was slouched on the chaise with her hand at her forehead and was wailing, "My dear Lydia! My child! I will never see her again!"

Kitty was so tearful in her response that Elizabeth could hardly make out anything she said besides that Lydia had made her promise not to tell.

Elizabeth looked to Darcy, concerned, and asked, "Do you know what is going on?"

Before he could answer, Mr. Bennet started pacing and added, "You are very lucky, Mr. Darcy! A lucky man, indeed! For since the engagement has not been announced, you may walk away free from the scandal."

She heard her mother start wailing even louder, "Walk away? My salts! My salts! I have never had such tremblings and flutterings! I am sure to die this very moment! Oh, how could he have done such a thing? To run away with my sweet girl! She is but fifteen! Oh, Mr. Darcy! Please marry Elizabeth anyway! We can say you two were secretly engaged for some time. You must marry her! Surely you have compromised her in some way!"

Darcy boldly took a step forward and every bit of his tone spoke of his offense at such a statement. "I beg your pardon, madam, but the virtue of your daughter is assuredly intact."

Mr. Bennet threw up his hands and growled, "The virtue of *this* daughter anyway. Not that it matters now!"

Elizabeth did not know who she should comfort first. Her mother was still calling for her salts, Kitty had been thrown into a fit of coughing and was choking out sobs of her own, and poor, tenderhearted Avelina had now begun to wring her hands. As calmly as possible, Elizabeth asked, "What has happened to Lydia? What has she done this time?"

Mr. Bennet pointed at Kitty and said, "Kitty, here, thought it was appropriate to not disclose that Lydia ran away to Gretna Green with a lousy, low-life officer! Damn those red coats!"

Kitty hollered, "Mr. Wickham is a good man, he is not a low-life! And she is getting married! What is so wrong with that? Mamma, you should be happy for her!"

Elizabeth was beginning to piece the puzzle together. "Kitty, sit down. Avelina, go to the kitchen and fetch some wine for Kitty and my mother. Do not just ring the bell; bring it yourself. We do not need servants overhearing this. Mary, fetch Mamma's smelling salts. Papa, sit down and explain exactly what has happened and with whom. Am I to assume that Lydia eloped to Gretna Green with Mr. Wickham?"

Mr. Bennet waved a letter at her and continued pacing. "That is exactly what happened! Their plan was to leave this morning. It is too late to save her now."

Mr. Darcy shifted uncomfortably beside her. "And you have concluded," Elizabeth stammered, "that Mr. Wickham . . . has dishonorable intentions."

"Right again," Mr. Bennet huffed. He sat down and put his head in his hands. "I doubt very much that Gretna Green is their destination or that marriage is their goal."

Mr. Darcy took a deep breath and looked at Elizabeth. "I am quite familiar with Mr. Wickham," Darcy added. "As painful as it sounds, I fear you are correct, Mr. Bennet. He has all the form and manners of a gentleman, but propriety means little to him."

Mrs. Bennet burst out anew with her wailings. "So he *has* compromised her! I told you my Lydia would never do such a thing! My girls are ruined!"

Avelina came in and offered glasses of wine to Kitty and Mrs. Bennet. Mrs. Bennet instead took the smelling salts from Mary and dramatically waved them under her nose, scrunching up her face at the offensive odors. She let out a moan again.

Elizabeth asked, "Father, but if they did not go to Gretna Green, where are they?"

"My guess is London, where they can easily blend into the crowd. Seeking them there would be like finding one leaf in a forest."

Mr. Bennet announced he must write to Mr. Gardiner at once for his assistance, while Kitty burst out anew with tears and coughing, and Mrs. Bennet took another whiff of her smelling salts.

Darcy turned to Elizabeth and spoke softly so that only she could hear him. His tones were full of sorrow and sadness. "I am so sorry, Elizabeth, I should have disclosed Wickham's true nature and informed your father of the danger long ago. I do not know how you will ever forgive me. My pride in hiding Georgiana's near elopement with Wickham has now cost me my life, my love, the love of my life."

He took Elizabeth's hand and he kissed each knuckle and then opened her hand and kissed the palm tenderly, reverently. When he looked up at her, his eyes were full of large tears that threatened to escape, but he took a deep breath, bowed, and turned to leave.

Elizabeth was suddenly panicked. Where was he going? Why did it feel like he was saying goodbye?

She ran after Mr. Darcy and accosted him at the front door. She grabbed his arm and forced him to turn around and look at her. She did not care who could see them at the moment. She reached up, with both hands, and kissed him long and hard. She could sense he was holding back.

But she could not let him go. She simply kept her lips locked with his, letting them caress and soothe the pain and guilt she knew he was feeling. Slowly, their passion grew until he wrapped his arms around her tightly, pulling her into a loving embrace. His hands came to her neck and then his fingers pulled longingly at her shoulders.

She heard her father clear his throat in the next room, and Will tried to pull away, but she still would not let him go. She pressed further and finally she felt him relax. His kiss was no longer saying goodbye. It only communicated his love and compassion. She knew now that it was time to release him.

Sometimes there is no need for words.

She stepped back and smoothed her skirt and tried to adjust her hair. His face was soft and gently pleading with her. He opened his mouth to speak, but she put her finger to his lips and then slowly dragged her fingers across his cheek and cradled his jaw as she had done so many times. She did not chance looking to see who had witnessed such bold behavior. She had been forced to resort to drastic measures. For the first time, she felt completely powerless. Without a doubt, their entire family's reputation lay in the hands of Mr. Darcy.

She said it very plainly, so as not to be misunderstood: "I shall hope for Mr. Darcy. For there is no one I trust more than you, Will, to find Wickham and make things right. Do whatever it takes, and do it quickly, for I do not wish to stand alone at an altar at the end of May."

CHAPTER 23

Darcy gazed at the lady before him. Her eyes sparkled but spoke of her resiliency and unwavering commitment. He imagined how he would feel if their roles were reversed; he doubted that he could forgive anyone whose actions had brought harm to his sister. But Elizabeth had. His sweet, dearest Elizabeth had.

After she finally released him, he allowed her to pull him back into the room where her father stood unamused and quite shocked. He realized that everyone in the room had witnessed Elizabeth's bold kiss at the door, which also meant that they witnessed his weakened resolve as their bodies and lips simply melted together.

He cleared his throat. "I apologize, Mr. and Mrs. Bennet, for that display back there," he announced. "I promise it will not happen again."

The stern look on her father's face softened slightly, and the corner of Mr. Bennet's mouth turned up. "Be careful what you promise," he grumbled.

Mrs. Bennet had been rendered speechless but now found her voice quite readily: "Now you *must* marry Elizabeth! No matter what that Mr. Wickham has done to poor Lydia, I saw you! That was very clearly a compromising situation! I cannot have two daughters' reputations ruined! I am sorry, Mr. Darcy, but there is no backing out now."

He couldn't help but smile at Mrs. Bennet's attempt to manipulate him. After a kiss like that, he was putty in Elizabeth's hands. He would even allow her mother to believe that she had garnered his cooperation. "I agree, madam. I cannot deny that no man would want your Elizabeth after that . . ."

And then seeing Mrs. Bennet getting nervous, Mr. Bennet start to snicker, and feeling the elbow to the ribs from Elizabeth, he added,

"No man but me. She has agreed to marry me at the end of May. I am a man of honor."

Then looking at Elizabeth, he added, "And a man quite besotted. Have no worries about my intentions. I could never give Elizabeth up now." He turned and looked at Mrs. Bennet and couldn't resist one more jab. "Not after she has gone to such shocking lengths to seduce me." He felt Elizabeth stomp on his foot, and he bellowed his agony briefly before he started chuckling.

"You wicked man!" Elizabeth hissed.

"Do not forget—proud too!" He said between chuckles.

He took a calming breath and addressed Mr. Bennet. "Sir, on a more serious matter, I must ask for your forgiveness. I am to blame for Miss Lydia's elopement."

Kitty had been stunned as well but now found her voice "No," she argued, "it is all my fault, Mr. Darcy. I should have disclosed her plan before it was too late. How can you be to blame?"

Mr. Darcy led Elizabeth toward the chaise and sat down beside her. He took courage from her sweet reassuring smile, and he realized that he had never felt more humble. When Wickham had first come to Hertfordshire, Darcy had been tempted multiple times to expose him in some way. But each time, Darcy's pride had held him back. If he revealed Georgiana's near elopement, even if only to protect others from Wickham, his sister's reputation would be in ruins. The risk to their good name had been too great. And the longer he said nothing, the more firmly he believed he had made the right choice. So he had held his tongue and failed to privately warn Mr. Bennet or any of the fathers in town.

But he had changed since Elizabeth had refused him a few weeks ago. Indeed, examining the changes in himself left him astounded. Before meeting her, he had always abided by the strict societal rules that marked the bounds of propriety. Rules that he believed in, because gentlemen should not write letters to ladies they did not have understandings with. Nor hold hands. Nor cradle their heads in their laps. Nor caress their faces. Nor embrace them. But he had done all of that with Elizabeth. And he had revealed the whole of Georgiana's involvement with Wickham too—not only to Elizabeth, but to Bingley as well.

And now, here he was, about to reveal it to the Bennets and Miss Gardiner. All the faces around the room were looking at him expectantly. He swallowed his pride, the same pride that had held him back before. He would risk all he had to save Elizabeth's family. He would do anything for her, because in his mind, she was already his wife. Her family was his family. So the idea of protecting Georgiana, his blood relative, only to harm his married family seemed incongruent with this new self that had emerged over the last few weeks.

He looked around the room and briefly debated how he was to answer Kitty's question as to why he felt it was his fault. Mrs. Bennet was not one to hold her tongue on juicy gossip, of that he was sure. Even if he swore her to secrecy—which he assumed would only make it all the more tempting to say something—the risk was too great. How could he admit what had happened without hurting Georgiana? How could he say what he should have said months ago?

"Miss Kitty, it is a long story, one that Elizabeth is aware of. And when you hear it, I fear your new good opinion of me may falter." He swallowed hard and gathered his courage. "George Wickham once attempted to elope with an acquaintance of mine, a close friend of the family, who was only fifteen years of age. Even now, remembering the event causes me great anxiety. But despite what I knew of Wickham's history, my pride prevented me from exposing him."

Then, without disclosing her identity, he proceeded to tell the story of Georgiana's near elopement with Wickham: how Wickham had rejected the generous living provided for him in Darcy's father's will; how he blamed Darcy for his pecuniary circumstances; how his object had been Georgiana's thirty-thousand-pound dowry and revenge on Darcy; and how Darcy only learned of the planned elopement when he happened to spy Georgiana and Wickham together in a compromising situation.

Mr. Darcy squeezed Elizabeth's hand and explained, "I managed to convince the lady in question to think better of the elopement. Wickham, reverting to his unreservedly cruel manners, said the most dishonorable and ungentlemanly comments about her as he took his leave. I am told she kept to her room for a week. It was even longer before she could look a man in the eye. She was devastated. She lost her trust in men, in love, and in the goodness of people.

"I saw the pain she was in and also saw that it would be much worse if the story became widely known. So I promised her that I would never tell anyone about the incident. That promise kept me from disclosing his true character when I saw him in Meryton. I naively thought that perhaps he had changed his ways, since he was finally in a respectable profession."

Mr. Bennet took off his glasses and cleaned them. Without looking up at Darcy, he asked, "You said that the lady's dowry was a motivating factor for Wickham in that matter. But Lydia has no fortune. She has no connections, nothing to offer him. She has nothing to offer but her virtue."

Mr. Darcy was uncomfortable discussing such delicate topics but there was a certain necessity of it at this time. "Yes. I am afraid that without a dowry, he is very unlikely to marry your daughter, whatever he may have promised her. He can be very convincing. He is a practiced seducer. I promise you I will do everything necessary to find her. Sir, if by chance her virtue is intact, how do you want me to proceed?"

Mrs. Bennet had found some composure, but her hands shook in her lap, and she tightly wound her handkerchief anxiously. She turned her head to her husband. "Mr. Bennet? How should he proceed?"

Mr. Bennet stared off into the distance as he considered his response. "As of now, the only people aware of this elopement are the people in this room," he replied a few moments later. "I assume I will hear from Colonel Forster soon that she is missing, as she only left this morning. Let me handle him. I will tell him that she did not run off with Wickham unescorted, that I gave them my blessing. This will satisfy him long enough for us to find Lydia and decide what to do.

"Of course, if she has been compromised, I must insist that he marry her. It disgusts me that she would be bound to such a vile, conniving man, but that is how it is. Her behavior will impact the entire family. Jane, Kitty, and Mary will be branded. They will never be looked at seriously by any respectable gentleman again."

Kitty mumbled something under her breath. The whole room looked at her, and she spoke her mind more clearly: "Someday, Papa, the action of one person will not affect the whole family. The accountability of a single person's choice will one day fall on that one person alone, as it should. It may be another hundred years from now, but someday society will hold only the sinner in condemnation."

Mr. Bennet put his glasses on and looked at her perplexed. "I have never heard you express such sentiments, Catherine."

"I think a lot of things, Papa, but you never ask me about them. To you, I have always been just your silly daughter. But I think women should be able to vote and own property and testify in court. And not just gentlewomen—all men and women."

Mr. Bennet stood and walked to the fireplace and stirred the embers. Without looking behind him at the people in the room, he said, "Forgive me, Catherine. I shall not call you silly again."

After Kitty wiped the tears that had escaped at her father's tender words, the room grew silent. Mr. Bennet seemed to gather his thoughts again and returned to his seat. "Mr. Darcy, I feel that if I go to London now, any rumors that develop will be confirmed by my absence, regardless of my attempts to convince Colonel Forster that Lydia has not done the thing which she has done."

"You need not ask, sir. My purpose in leaving a moment ago was to depart for London. I feel all the responsibility of the situation and, therefore, feel all the weight of making it right. And since I know Wickham so well, I am more likely to have success. I will go to London immediately and seek them out. Perhaps, Mr. Bennet, you could provide me with a list of Wickham's debts here in Meryton. They are likely to be substantial. You will have to be discreet in case they are forced to marry."

"You think he has substantial debts? How will making a list of them help us?"

Mr. Darcy paused in his next statement. He understood that pride was difficult to maneuver around, and, right now, Mr. Bennet was about to be humbled in a way most respectable gentlemen hope to never be humbled. "Giving me a list of his debts may be the only way to avoid sending your daughter and potential son-in-law to debtors' prison," he suggested. He waited for the understanding to grace Mr. Bennet's features. "Perhaps you would like to speak in your study about the particulars?"

Mr. Bennet stood and, with a red face, said, "I most certainly would!"

Darcy followed him obediently and closed the door behind him.

Mr. Bennet said gruffly, "I will not have you pay for Wickham's expenses or my daughter's mistake. There will be no discussion on the matter."

Mr. Darcy was prepared to battle. "This is my mistake, and I will do everything necessary to correct it. I should have warned you and your daughters. Hell, I should have warned all of Meryton!"

"Any man would have done the same thing. No, I will pay Wickham's debts."

"No, you will not."

"I may not earn ten thousand a year, Mr. Darcy, but I will not be bowled over by you." Mr. Bennet peered at him. "You will not *buy* my permission to marry Elizabeth," he warned.

"I might remind you that I have already received your permission." Mr. Darcy then told Mr. Bennet the true identity of the close family acquaintance of his who nearly eloped with Wickham. When he learned that the young lady in question had been Georgiana Darcy, Mr. Bennet's face paled and he stumbled to a chair. "So you see now why it should be me who pays Wickham's debts," Darcy explained.

Darcy stood tall and broadened his shoulders. He knew it would be difficult for Mr. Bennet to pay Wickham's debts. Rumors were that he made less than three thousand a year, and with the size of the estate, he couldn't imagine him having a large cash reserve. "Do not make this about you, sir."

"This is every bit about me! How dare you come and flash your money as if you are better than all of us. A man has his—"

"—pride," Darcy finished for him. "Yes. I once told a very wise lady that where there was a superiority of mind, pride would always be under good regulation. And from our discussion after dinner, I am fully convinced that you have a superior mind."

Darcy took a deep breath and prepared to deliver a most painful blow. "However, I was wrong about pride," he continued. "It is a weakness. It blurs our judgment. It clouds our opinion of ourselves and of others. It shifts our concern from whether or not our actions are right to whether or not they will win the approval of others. Do not let it dictate your actions tonight, sir." Darcy waited and watched carefully. Mr. Bennet started pacing, rubbing his temples with both hands.

"You are sorely wrong to think this affair could have been prevented by you, Mr. Darcy," Mr. Bennet sighed. "The blame is entirely mine. I let Lydia's behavior go unchecked. I regarded her as silly. I allowed her to go to Brighton. Mr. Darcy, I should be the one to bear the responsibility. What would it look like if I let you do this?"

"Mr. Bennet, if you are still worried about winning the approval of others, perhaps you did not understand the full meaning of my advice."

Mr. Bennet stopped pacing and looked up at him. He looked defeated and dejected. It had been a trying day for him, and Darcy felt badly for handling him so firmly. But there was simply no negotiating on the matter.

Mr. Bennet's eyes were deeply troubled. "How could I ever repay you?"

Darcy knew that if Mr. Bennet had any money, he would have invested it in his daughters' dowries. "That will not be necessary. Give me the satisfaction of serving justice for what he did to my sister, sir." Darcy could sense that Mr. Bennet was softening to the idea. He watched Mr. Bennet walk to the side table and pour himself a glass of brandy.

After a hefty swallow and the grimace from the burn of it, Mr. Bennet walked to the window and looked out. There were many minutes of silence. Darcy waited patiently. He had pushed him hard, but Mr. Bennet was a smart man; Darcy knew he would come to his senses eventually. Darcy waited a few more minutes, poured himself a brandy and stood next to Mr. Bennet. Together they looked out the window into the darkness, knowing full well there was nothing to be seen.

Mr. Bennet put one hand on the window frame and leaned onto it with his head down. He gently shook his head for a moment and then stood up and dropped his arm. He turned to Darcy and said, "Good luck in London. I shall gather the information you requested."

"Thank you, sir." Mr. Bennet waved his hand dismissively.

It was clear the conversation was over. Darcy downed his brandy and said, "One more thing, sir. I promised to return Elizabeth to Mrs. Collins tomorrow, but I now must away to London. I do not think it would be wise to have the ladies travel unaccompanied directly to Kent from here. Could I convince you to allow Elizabeth and Miss Gardiner to come with me and stay at Darcy House tomorrow night? I assure you that I will be a gentleman, and I know my sister and her companion would be only delighted to receive them. After one night, I will send them in my carriage the last few miles back to Mrs. Collins."

"You ask a great deal of me today," Mr. Bennet grumbled. "First my daughter's hand and then Wickham's debts. And now, as soon I am sufficiently humbled, you ask me to allow my unmarried daughter and niece to follow you to London? But I do not think I can say no, not when I am so indebted to you. Very well, go to London. Save the family's reputation, make the whole world think that it was me who did it, and make my daughter fall more in love with you than ever. My father taught me that anything less than the truth is the devil's snare. So know that my agreement to this scheme of yours is most painful and humbling. Please go now. I need a moment to myself."

Darcy offered his hand and shook Mr. Bennet's. He then bowed deeply and said, "I assure you I understand how painful it is to be humbled. I was at the receiving end of a similar conversation a few weeks ago. Forgive me for having to be so direct and firm. But after Elizabeth wielded the humility sword so expertly at my first proposal, I can think of nothing else but how grateful I am that she was direct and firm. For if not, I doubt it would have been as successful."

"I assure you, your sword was just as sharp."

CHAPTER 24

The carriage pulled away from Longbourn bright and early. The conversation waxed and waned, but Elizabeth could not talk about what she most desperately wanted to discuss. Not in front of Avelina.

A few hours later, she could tell that they were entering the Mayfair neighborhood and would be arriving at Darcy House shortly. As the carriage rolled to a stop, she looked out the window at the impressive building in front of her.

It was of white alabaster stone with beautiful masonry work that spoke of elegance and fine taste. The carriage door was opened, and Darcy exited and was immediately welcomed by the footman. Darcy whispered something to him, and the footman hurried off to execute his master's orders. Then Darcy turned back to the carriage and handed Elizabeth and Avelina out.

"Welcome to Darcy House, ladies! Devon just assured me that Georgiana is at home and went to notify her of our arrival. Come, Miss Elizabeth, let me show you your future home." He offered his arm and Elizabeth took it readily, feeling the closeness and tenderness in his touch. He wore a proud and somewhat boyish smile on his lips that revealed his adorable dimples.

He then offered his other arm to Avelina, who placed her hand on his arm and said, "Thank you."

Elizabeth could not stop drinking in all that surrounded her. As she entered the vestibule, she was in complete astonishment at the black-and-white marble floor, the beautiful textured wallpaper, and the detailed carpentry work along the doors and floors. The simple but sophisticated furniture pieces that dotted the hall were beyond anything she could imagine. She looked at Darcy and said, "Mr. Darcy, this is most impressive! Of this I am to be mistress?"

"So you approve?" His grin widened and reached to his excited eyes.

"How could I not?" she marveled. She had known he was rich, but this . . . ! She wasn't sure what she had been expecting, but the house was stunning. And unlike Rosings, it was not gaudy or pretentious in any way. "You could not have impressed me more," she said. "I think I shall like to live here very much. It speaks a great deal of the owner." Just then Elizabeth heard soft footsteps behind her, and she turned around.

A tall blonde young lady was walking quite hurriedly towards them, and Darcy dropped Elizabeth and Avelina's arms carefully and embraced the lovely lady. There was no doubt that this was Georgiana. Elizabeth spied the same dark eyes and the same sweet dimples in their smiles.

Mr. Darcy released his sister and turned to Elizabeth and said proudly, "Georgiana, I would like to introduce you to the lady that you will soon call sister. This is Miss Elizabeth Bennet and her cousin, Miss Avelina Gardiner."

Georgiana looked surprised, but slowly and shyly she smiled and curtsied to both. "It is a pleasure, Miss Bennet. I have heard so much about—" She then quickly turned to her brother, who was grinning, and asked, "Wait, did you say 'sister'?"

Darcy nodded, and Georgiana put a hand to her mouth and giggled excitedly. "Oh, Fitzwilliam! She is lovely! Miss Bennet, I do not know what to say! Look how happy my brother is! I have never seen him beam so handsomely. I could just hug you right now!"

Elizabeth smiled and did something that she hoped would be well received. She stepped forward and embraced her new sister. "It is a pleasure to finally see the other woman in his life, Miss Darcy." Elizabeth could see Georgiana was surprised at the gesture, but her shock was short lived and soon Georgiana was embracing her in return.

"Please call me Georgiana. I cannot imagine using formal titles if we are to be sisters."

"Then call me Elizabeth or Lizzy. My family and friends use either one. Some shorten it to Eliza, but I do not fancy that much." They finally released each other, and when Elizabeth looked at Georgiana, she saw small tears break from her eyes. "Did I say something wrong?"

"Oh no! It is just that I am so happy! I have always wanted a sister. Forgive me for getting emotional. It has been difficult the last few weeks since Fitzwilliam came back from Rosings."

Elizabeth laughed, "Let me guess: he was taciturn, distracted, and short-tempered."

Georgiana looked confused briefly and then looked at her brother.

Darcy said, "I told you she was a little impertinent."

Elizabeth laughed merrily and said, "Do forgive me. My ways often get me in trouble."

"There is nothing to forgive," Georgiana assured her. "Shall I ring for tea, William?"

"Not for me, I am afraid. I must be going," Darcy replied. "I have a great deal of business to see to tonight. But before I leave, let us assist these fine ladies to their rooms. I will show Miss Elizabeth the Green Room, and I believe Miss Gardiner will be most happy in the Butterfly Room."

Avelina, who had been content to quietly observe up to this point, gasped. "You have a butterfly room?"

Georgiana smiled and took her arm and started leading her towards the winding staircase. "Yes. It has a mural of butterflies! My grandmother painted it in the last years of her life." Georgiana's voice trailed off as they departed.

Darcy turned to the butler, who had been observing all of this, and said to him, "Well, Franklin, have you nothing to say to the new mistress of the house? I suppose I should say soon-to-be-new mistress."

The butler bowed deeply. "My name is Nicholas Franklin, madam. Let me be the first to congratulate you. I agree with Miss Darcy in that I have never seen the master so happy, which speaks volumes of his choice in wife. May I take your things?"

She curtsied and removed her shawl and handed it to him. "Mr. Franklin, I expect I will need something from you in the near future."

"And what is that, Miss Bennet?"

"I will need an advocate to keep Mr. Darcy in line. I have done my best, but there is much more work to be done. How he has lived for so many years in such a prideful state is beyond me. I have yet to tweak his nose or box his ears, so I must appeal to your expertise. Which method would you recommend to keep him sufficiently humble?"

Mr. Franklin smiled and then schooled his features. The wrinkles in his brows grew deep, but it was clear he was playing along. "I have served here long enough to have seen his father box his ears. It did wonders back then, and I would be very pleased to see the tradition reestablished."

Darcy chuckled and shook his head. "Franklin! Ten minutes in her presence and you no longer respect your master?"

Elizabeth giggled too then. "The house just needed a woman's touch, my dear. Thank you, Mr. Franklin. I shall see what can be done about granting you a raise."

Franklin grinned and bowed. "Thank you, madam. I will alert Mrs. Franklin that there are guests. She will be most happy to hear of the master's engagement to such a fine lady." Franklin turned and left.

Once he had gone, she asked, "Mrs. Franklin?"

"The housekeeper, his wife. They have been running Darcy house for the last fifteen years. Their son and daughter grew up with Georgiana. Come, let me show you to your room. I will need to hurry if I am to find Wickham and your sister."

Darcy escorted her up the stairs and presented a beautiful room with all shades of green. As soon as she entered, she realized her mouth had dropped open, but she couldn't help herself. The room was three times as large as her room at Longbourn. It had a large vanity, with the most elegant antique mirror attached, but it wasn't the mirror that caught her eye, it was what she saw in its reflection.

She turned around. Above an enormous bed, along the entire wall, was a painting of a scene that was far too familiar.

She felt the tingle of tears fill her eyes, and she just stared at the painting. There were trees with all colors of greens, a bank of flowering irises, and a small, crystal-clear stream with rose-colored rocks. It was exactly the same as her dream. She stepped closer and reached her hand out to the painting, but then pulled away when she saw that the rose-colored path led to a bright sunset. It *was* her dream. And she relived every moment of it all over again. Tears flooded her eyes and the painting blurred.

Mr. Darcy wrapped his arms around her from behind and whispered in her ear, "What is it? Please tell me what is wrong."

"The painting . . . Who painted it?"

"My grandmother. Why?"

"Is it a place you know?"

Concern was evident in his voice. "Yes, dearest, that is the garden at Pemberley."

"Pemberley? Your home?"

"And it will soon be your home. Is there something wrong?"

"Will, I know this place—the flowers, the trees, the path—everything. Just beyond that bend, that rose-colored path is as straight as the street outside. And there is a yellow fruit tree, a small plum I believe, on the other side of that rock formation. There are some unique flowers behind that tree that smell of roses and peonies."

Darcy turned her around and looked at her. "Yes, there is. When did you visit Pemberley?"

The tears in her eyes spilled onto her cheeks. "This is the place I dreamed of," she whispered. "It is where we walked together to the Son. It seems Pemberley is my kind of heaven."

Darcy's face softened as if the words she uttered had melted his heart. He leaned forward and kissed her forehead. "I do not know what to say. There are no words."

"Sometimes things are understood without even saying them. I love you, Will."

His voice cracked as he answered her, "I love you too, Elizabeth. You are my love, my life."

CHAPTER 25

Colonel Fitzwilliam had received Darcy's express early that morning. After a brief stop by the Rosings parsonage to privately inform Miss Jane Bennet of her youngest sister's elopement, nothing delayed him from riding as swiftly as possible to London. If he travelled quickly enough, he might arrive in time to help Darcy search for that miserable rake. Darcy and Elizabeth, leaving from Hertfordshire, were closer to London than he was; but they were traveling by carriage, and he was on horseback. He was grateful the dry weather of the prior week had left the roads firm and he made good time.

Covered head to toe with a fine dust, he rode up to Darcy House a few hours later, dismounted, and stretched a bit. It had been a long ride, and he had stopped only to change horses along the way.

A footman welcomed him and led his mount to the stable. "Keep him saddled," Colonel Fitzwilliam directed. "I may be leaving again shortly."

"Yes, sir. But if you are looking for the master, he just left."

"Do you know where he went?"

"No, sir, but he always tells Mr. Franklin."

"Thank you, Devon."

Colonel Fitzwilliam never used the knocker at Darcy House; Darcy was so welcoming that it felt as much his house as Darcy's now. The colonel had lived there on-and-off for the last two years. Darcy never denied him a room, knowing full well that Fitzwilliam often needed to escape both the pressure to get married from his mother, Lady Matlock, and the boredom of being home alone in his bachelor's flat. As the colonel entered, he saw Franklin walking his way, offering him a letter.

"Mr. Darcy asked me to give you this as soon as you arrived."

He took the letter and thanked him. Without moving further into the house, he read it, which was nothing more than a brief note relaying Darcy's plan. "How long ago did he leave?"

"Less than a half hour ago, I believe," Franklin replied.

Colonel Fitzwilliam thanked him and was just turning to leave when he heard Georgiana's sweet giggle from the music room. "Is someone visiting Miss Georgiana?"

"Miss Bennet and Miss Gardiner, sir," Franklin replied with a smile. "It is a nice change to hear Miss Georgiana laughing again, sir," he added.

"Yes, I agree. It has been far too long. Good day, Franklin."

"Of course, sir. Will you be staying here tonight?"

"Yes, please prepare my rooms. I may be quite late."

*****

Darcy had no appointment, but his solicitor always received him, and today was no different. He was shown in and offered refreshment, but he declined. He hadn't eaten anything since early that morning, but he wasn't hungry. He only prayed that his solicitor could supply the lead he was hoping for.

Mr. Carter came in and Darcy stood to greet him. He was taller than Darcy, but the lawyer was far too lean. It even appeared that he had lost even more weight since Darcy's last visit.

"Good day, Mr. Darcy. How can I assist you? I assume you received the quarterly report I sent?"

"Yes, I did. I admit my time has been occupied lately, and I have not looked over the numbers quite yet. A friend's husband suddenly passed, and I have been assisting her with the funeral, among other things." Darcy said the last bit with a smile on his face.

Mr. Carter looked at him curiously. Darcy rarely shared his personal activities with his solicitor, and they both felt immediately awkward. Darcy shifted in his seat a little and removed his smile. "I come for several reasons. Perhaps you would like to make a list."

"Of course, sir." Mr. Carter put on his glasses and tapped his pen against the inkwell. "I am ready."

"First, I need an inventory of all the businesses that George Wickham held debts with last spring—the ones that we paid off. Especially any London businesses." Hopefully Wickham had returned to the same establishments. "As soon as possible, please."

"Certainly, sir. That information is in our archives. We keep them in a locked building a mile from here. But I can send a man now if you will excuse me."

Darcy nodded, and Mr. Carter stood and poked his head out the door, instructing one of his assistants to fetch Darcy's 1811 file. Then Carter walked back to his desk and announced, "I should have that for you in an hour or so. What else can I do for you, sir?"

"I need the last known address of Mrs. Younge. I believe it was somewhere in London."

"That I have right here." He opened Darcy's file and flipped the pages back to nearly the beginning of the ledger. "Here is the address." He handed it to Darcy.

Darcy looked at the address. "Port Angels Street?"

"Indeed, but . . . Ahem, might I suggest, sir, that if you require something from Mrs. Younge, you send a servant rather than going yourself? The area is renowned for transient sailors and widowed women who sell things that a gentleman like you would not wish to buy."

"I imagined it would be somewhere like that."

"Is there anything else?"

Darcy said, "Indeed. And I can tell you that it brings me far more pleasure to direct you in this next endeavor. I would like you to send the following announcement to a church in Meryton, as well as the parish in Kympton. 'I publish the banns of marriage between Mr. Fitzwilliam Darcy of the Parish of Kympton and Miss Elizabeth Bennet of the Parish of Longbourn. If any of you know cause or just impediment why these persons should not be joined together in Holy Matrimony, ye are to declare it.'"

A slow smile crept across Mr. Carter's otherwise impassive face as he finished writing. "My most sincere congratulations, sir. She must be an impressive woman to have caught the ever-evasive bachelor of Derbyshire."

Darcy couldn't help himself, and he chuckled slightly. "I suppose you could say she left quite an impression on me. This leads me to the last thing. I need you to draw up settlement papers immediately."

Returning to the paper in front of him, Mr. Carter asked, "Give me the details and it shall be done."

Darcy then took the next ten minutes detailing what Elizabeth would receive upon his death, her claim to Pemberley, and full rights to make any decisions in his place if he were incapable of doing so. He wanted to make sure that Elizabeth never wanted for anything. Just as he was finishing the instructions, there was a knock on the door.

Mr. Carter put down his pencil and apologized. "They are instructed not to disturb me when I am with a client," he explained. "This must be quite urgent." He went to the door and opened it.

Darcy could hear Colonel Fitzwilliam being shown in. He welcomed his cousin and said, "Thank you for coming so quickly, Fitzwilliam. Excuse me, Mr. Carter, I must take my leave." He stood up, glanced again at Mrs. Younge's address in hand, and started to walk out the door with Colonel Fitzwilliam trailing when Mr. Carter stopped him.

"Sir, I remember that many of George Wickham's debts were incurred near Port Angels Street. If you can wait a few more minutes, my man should be back with the list for you, so you will not need to go that way twice."

Darcy looked at his pocket watch. It would take him nearly half an hour to reach Port Angels Street, and it was nearing five in the afternoon already. He did not have time to simply wait, but nor did he have time to make two trips. "Thank you, Mr. Carter. We will wait outside then."

Once they were out of anyone's range of hearing, Darcy explained to his cousin, "I have a lead. Mrs. Younge's final check was mailed to this address. I fear it will be an unpleasant interaction."

Colonel Fitzwilliam looked at the address and whistled. "Port Angels Street. I know it well. I often have to deliver my officers to the inns there when they are well into their cups. I recommend emptying your pockets of anything valuable."

Darcy nodded and took a good look at his cousin. "You are covered in dust, man. Did you not get a chance to change?"

The colonel rolled his eyes. "No, Fitz, I came as fast I could. I did not even pack a bag. And since you left Poole at Rosings, I could hardly borrow any of your clothes. But it is no matter. I will blend in better looking like this than you will, I assure you. Now tell me what happened."

His cousin gave him a detailed account of Lydia's letter and Mr. Bennet's efforts to hold off Colonel Forster. He avoided the topic of the ledger for the time being, although he still was not sure why. If anything, he could use the colonel's help in finding C. W. Pastel. But something had made him hold back the information. Darcy merely added, "I am making progress on the household ledgers. It looks as if there might be some small holdings that could help Mrs. Collins in the next little while."

Adjusting his cravat, which had come lose and was quite dirty, Colonel Fitzwilliam smiled. "So there might be some hope Mrs. Collins will not be destitute! What a relief! She is a fine lady, and to find herself with child and a widow at the same time must have been devastating. She seems to be handling Bingley and Miss Bennet's big news quite well."

"Big news?" Darcy asked.

With a trace of bitterness in his voice, Fitzwilliam remarked, "Yes, love is in the air. Bingley hardly waited until your carriage had departed for Longbourn before he asked for a private audience. Everyone is getting married now it seems."

Darcy could sense his cousin was struggling with what should be happy news. He had never heard Fitzwilliam lament over someone's engagement before. "Did you have feelings for Miss Bennet yourself, Cousin?"

"Miss Bennet? Do not be absurd! She is Bingley's *angel.* I never once looked at her." With slightly false bravado, he quipped, "Besides, I plan to escape the parson's mousetrap for many more years to come. An eternal bachelor."

Darcy didn't know how to respond to Fitzwilliam's odd behavior. His cousin's words said one thing, but his tone and body language said something else. Hoping he wasn't overstepping the unspoken boundaries that existed between men, Darcy put his hand on his shoulder and said, "Your time will come."

Fitzwilliam cleared his throat and pretended to laugh, but it was forced at best. "Careful now, you are beginning to sound like my mother! She considers the life of a bachelor soldier to be very sad and lonesome indeed. Marriage is all fine and well for people of means, like you and Bingley. But my choices are admittedly more limited. And I have no plan to marry the nearest available heiress."

"Then what is your plan?" Darcy queried.

"To outlive my older brother and become the heir, of course! Then I will be able to marry anyone I like." Fitzwilliam's voice trailed off as if he lacked conviction in his words.

"Yes, of course," Darcy replied hesitantly. "It is an excellent plan." They sat together in silence.

Mr. Carter found them a few minutes later and presented Darcy with the list. They set off at once to Mrs. Younge's address.

*****

Half an hour later, they could smell the salty sea air of ships. They were approaching the docks. Colonel Fitzwilliam stopped his horse in front of a tavern. "I have an idea," he announced.

Darcy recognized the name of the establishment as one he had paid off for Wickham. "What are we doing here?" Darcy asked.

"Well, for starters, I need a drink," Fitzwilliam said with a grin. "Follow my lead," he added.

The colonel tugged his cravat loose and walked into the tavern with a limp as if his knee was troubling him. Darcy followed after him. Richard slurred his words and called out, "Two pints—damn strong pharaohs—please! My friend bet me I could not win his horse! Now I've got two! What's a man to do with two horses and no carriage?" Fitzwilliam turned a dizzy head to Darcy and said, "Hey, you got a carriage? Want to play double or nothing for it?"

The barkeeper put the pints of strong ale down in front of them and walked away.

After he was a good distance away, Fitzwilliam whispered, "Play drunk, man." Then he quickly picked up both drinks, drank one, and pretended to stumble into Darcy, spilling the other pint all over Darcy's cravat. "Blast it! A waste of a good pharaoh!" he bellowed. "Well, what's one more cravat, eh? You have entirely too many, even for someone as rich as you."

Darcy growled as best he could and gave Fitzwilliam a strong shove. Imitating the same slur Fitzwilliam was using, he yelled, "Now look what you did! My valet will never get that smell out! I suppose I will have to throw this one out too." Darcy fumbled with his cravat and loosened it, trying to pick up on what the colonel was getting at.

Fitzwilliam went over to the barkeeper and slurred, "My friend here thinks he is a card sharp. But I know his weaknesses. I just need the right partner. Know anyone looking for easy winnings?"

Darcy could finally see where he was going with it. He bellowed, "I challenge anyone here to beat me!" He took a step directly into a man's chair and stumbled, cursing as he fell, and spilled the rest of his drink. "Another pharaoh! That hooligan spilled mine!"

A young boy ran him out another pint of alcohol. While Darcy dribbled the drink down his chest, Fitzwilliam asked the barkeeper, "You seen George Wickham lately? He's exactly what I need for this. Look at 'im. He's as drunk as a skunk!"

The barkeeper peered at the colonel. "Wickham came in last night," he offered. "Should be round again tonight. But are you sure that guy'll last?"

"Ha! Don't worry about that! I'll keep 'im busy for a few more hours. Just let Wickham know we'll be back here tonight, eh?"

The barkeeper nodded. Fitzwilliam slapped the table and hooted. "Hot damn! I'm gonna win me a carriage tonight!" Then he hollered, "Drinks for everyone, mates! That guy is paying!"

The entire tavern roared to life, and the barkeeper was too busy filling orders to notice the two gentlemen leave, one with a miraculously absent limp.

"How did you know Wickham had been there?" Darcy asked.

Fitzwilliam put his finger to his lips and shushed him. This was Wickham's territory, and any of his friends and acquaintances could be around. The two men hurried to a nearby alley with their horses is tow. When they were out of sight from the bustle of the road, Fitzwilliam whispered, "The next street over is Port Angels, and this is the closest tavern. I was taking a gamble. I recognized the name as one of the merchants you paid off. Sorry about your cravat. I will buy you a new one."

"It is of no consequence."

"You were a little slow on the uptake back there. Did I not say to follow my lead?"

"Well, you could have been a little more forthcoming of your plan. What now?"

"Now we go see Mrs. Younge. My guess is she has seen him too." Fitzwilliam hoped this would work. "But we will be hard-pressed to pull one over on her."

*****

Georgiana had been having such a wonderful time with Elizabeth and Avelina that she hadn't noticed the time until the housekeeper, Mrs. Franklin, came in.

"Dinner awaits, mistress," she announced.

Georgiana looked at the clock and furrowed her brows. It seemed the sun had already set. "Oh, my! I had not noticed that how late it has become. Mrs. Franklin, I believe that we should wait a bit longer for my brother."

Elizabeth placed her hand on Georgiana's tenderly. "Georgiana, it may be a while yet. He had a great deal of business to do."

"But he said he would be back tonight."

Elizabeth tried to mask her own worry. "Yes, of course," she assured her. "It is just that Avelina and I have not eaten since luncheon at the roadside inn. It will be great fun to dine with just us ladies, would it not?"

"I suppose so." Georgiana stood and they followed her into the dining room.

Elizabeth was impressed by the large table that could easily serve twelve couples. She noticed that there were five places set. "Is someone else expected for supper, Mrs. Franklin?"

Mrs. Franklin, who had been directing the footmen in their duties, turned around and replied, “Yes, madam. Colonel Fitzwilliam arrived in town just after you did. He is with Mr. Darcy now.”

Elizabeth had not known that Colonel Fitzwilliam had come to London. This was slightly disconcerting as it confirmed the danger of the situation. Was Will concerned enough to have sent for Fitzwilliam? Was he worried he might need a second? Her heart suddenly lurched at the thought. Surely he wouldn’t challenge Wickham. The thought made her heart pound furiously in her chest. As the meal was being served, all she could think of was how badly she needed to know he was safe.

She pushed her food around the plate and commented when appropriate and responded to direct questions, but her mind and heart were with Will, somewhere out there in the dark, praying that he would be able to find a desperate man who had no scruples nor integrity. Wickham’s pleasing manners were still in her mind. She knew how convincing he could be. But regardless of all the heartache Wickham has caused her own family and Darcy’s, it had never occurred to her that Darcy was in danger. Had she been wrong to let him go?

Luckily Avelina carried the conversation easily. They talked a great deal about Pemberley, which should have interested her, as it was to be her new home; however she couldn’t pull her thoughts from the possibility—even the probability—that Will was in danger.

CHAPTER 26

Darcy was getting irritated. Mrs. Younge was clearly hiding something.

After sticking a foot in the door to keep it from slamming in their faces, they had pushed their way into a dismal foyer, where they were assaulted by dirt, grime, and filth. Mrs. Younge had certainly lowered her standards. Her face was red and puffy, and they could smell alcohol on her breath, but her expression was stern. She knew where Wickham was all right, but she wasn't about to budge. Not for the likes of them.

"Mrs. Younge, as I said before, we intend Wickham no harm," Colonel Fitzwilliam sighed. "Our only interest is the girl he has with him. She is but fifteen and under the impression that he is going to marry her."

Mrs. Younge laughed boldly.

"Yes," Fitzwilliam continued, "I think we all agree that a wedding is highly unlikely, which is why her family is so concerned for her. If you cooperate, we are willing to overlook the fact that you seem to be running an illegal bordello."

Mrs. Younge ignored Colonel Fitzwilliam and turned to Darcy. "Like I said, he is not here, *sir*," she sneered. "I run a respectable inn. It was the only option I had left. You left me with no references, no compensation, and no way to make a living."

"Compensation?" Darcy asked. "So this is what it is about? You should have said so an hour ago. Name your price. A lady's reputation is at stake, and time is of the essence."

Darcy watched as she eyed him suspiciously. After a lengthy pause, she answered, "For every detail I give you, I want one hundred pounds."

"Done."

She took a deep breath and said, "He came by last night with a girl."

"And where is he now?" Darcy asked.

"I was not here so they went to the inn down the road."

"What inn was that?" Colonel Fitzwilliam asked.

Mrs. Younge ignored Colonel Fitzwilliam but answered the question while looking at Darcy. "Ocean's Hallow."

"Was the girl safe?"

She smiled mischievously. "I did not see them, remember?"

"But you have seen them since then." Darcy was getting irritated again.

"Yes. They went shopping today."

"Shopping?" Colonel Fitzwilliam asked.

"The girl wanted to show off her wedding gown," Mrs. Younge snickered. "Naive little thing. Just Wickham's type."

Darcy pressed his lips together. Mrs. Younge's disinterest in the girl's welfare was disgusting. "Have you no pride, madam?"

She shrugged her shoulders. "It is not me who has *pride*, Mr. Darcy."

"What do you mean?"

"It means that girl has been more trouble than Wickham predicted. Quite a stubborn maiden."

Darcy considered what she was saying. "Are you saying they have not . . . ?"

"No, they have not. And it is frustrating Wickham. He is getting desperate."

"What are his plans?"

"I believe, Mr. Darcy, that we are now up to eight hundred pounds."

"Make it an even thousand and reveal the last that you know."

*****

Darcy and Colonel Fitzwilliam hurried back to Matlock House to change their clothes. Lord and Lady Matlock were fortuitously out of town, so they were spared having to offer any explanation for their sudden interest in the costume box in the attic. With the light of a single candle, Darcy and Colonel Fitzwilliam hastily rummaged through its contents. They didn't have much to choose from. But between the costumes and Lady Matlock's charity box, they managed to assemble two passably impoverished outfits, complete with outdated, torn hats. A dusty coal rag added the finishing touches. Taking a look at themselves, they both laughed.

"You could pass for a street urchin in those breeches!" Colonel Fitzwilliam laughed.

"Says the man who looks like he ran away with the circus. I never imagined I would be using Twelfth Night costumes to save a young lady from George Wickham. He may have even worn these once. But I suppose this is the best option available."

"I still say we could have bought the clothes off the homeless man for a few farthings."

"Yes, but I gave all my pocket change to the children on that street," Darcy replied. "I only wish I could have given them more." Darcy pulled his outdated and worn hat on tighter and said, "Shall we? I believe we are sufficiently disguised."

*****

George Wickham thought himself a patient man. And Lydia Bennet was pleasant enough. After all, he only had to pay her the slightest attention to reap huge rewards. She was always up for a little flirtation, and he loved that she allowed him to take in her ample bosom with his eyes as often as he pleased, even in polite society. Their excursions down to the river and the small liberties she allowed him in the seclusion of the trees had been . . . enjoyable. But he was done being patient. Tonight he would be satisfied.

It had not been hard to see that she was an easy mark. So obsessed with his regimentals! She wasn't the only lady who seemed pleased by his new profession. It was a little sad that he was done playing soldier, but he never did like the idea of being under anyone's thumb. Colonel Forster hadn't been too bad, only a little soft. It had been all too easy to convince him that his wife needed a companion, a "particular friend", while in Brighton. Wickham laughed, remembering how the conversation had played out. At the end, Colonel Forster had proudly declared, "What a capital idea! I am glad I thought of it!"

Lydia was vivacious, curvy, a little dim, and adventurous; just the way he liked his women. And she was so free with her flirtations that she had caught the attention of every rake in an eight-block radius. Yes, he had told a few lies to get her here. But how could he have been expected to pass up such easy pickings?

Truth be told, he told a lot of lies. More than a butcher desperate to sell old meat. Wickham didn't like to think of himself as desperate, but it had been a long two weeks since they arrived in Brighton. It took some time to cajole new women in a new city. Sometimes he got lucky and found a willing servant, but most women needed some courting.

Lydia apparently needed it in spades.

His usual *modus operandi* was fairly simple: tell her that you will marry her, and bam! Just like that, she gives it up. But this chit kept talking about marriage and how romantic it would be to elope to Gretna Green. She wanted all the pomp, the gifts, and what she called "romancing". The woman wanted to have an actual "moment".

So when they arrived in London yesterday, he took her shopping. Shopping! She thought they were actually eloping, and she wanted to get pretty new nightclothes before they got married! It was ludicrous. Wickham didn't understand it in the slightest, but a man does what he has to do to get what he wants. So they shopped, not only for new night clothes, but for an actual wedding gown. He was a little nervous that she wouldn't give in at all, that she would truly hold out for a wedding night. But underneath that stubborn streak, he felt Lydia's resistance slipping. She'd gotten her gown and her night clothes. It was time.

When they had arrived at the inn, she had addressed the innkeeper and said with all the authority and pride the statement could possess, "This is Mr. Wickham, and I am the soon-to-be Mrs. Wickham!" Wickham had inwardly groaned—now they would have to get two separate rooms or risk the innkeeper calling the authorities. So, as a gentleman, he put two rooms on credit, but only for two nights. Tonight was the night that she would let him into her bed. He could feel it.

He adjusted his cravat and examined the coins he had left. The gown maker insisted he pay in full for it instead of putting it on credit, which had greatly diminished his reserve. But he still had enough to meet his needs. If she wanted "romancing", she would get what she wanted, but . . . so would he.

Wickham tapped his hand on the bar to get the barkeeper's attention. "Sammy, a bottle of your best wine please." Considering the quality of the establishment, the "best wine" was probably just bottled, barely aged, and mostly water, but he had already seen how poorly Lydia handled her alcohol. One bottle would probably do it. Just to make sure, he added, "Make that two."

"Wickham, I ain't been Sammy for years. It is Samuel now," the barkeeper warned.

"Sorry, Samuel. I suppose I still think of you as the snotty-nose kid who wanted to tag along on my endeavors."

"Well, I ain't. I got me a good job, a job that pays money. Speaking of which, you left last night without paying your bill."

"Ah, come on, I always pay you, you know that! Remember two summers ago? I paid in full, every last penny and even gave you a bonus. That is what friends do."

Samuel grunted his disapproval. He wiped his hands on his apron and pulled out two bottles. "I ain't sayin' these are the best, but I suspect they'll serve for your purposes. You stayin' at Mrs. Younge's place?"

"No, she was out when we arrived, so I took a room at the Ocean's Hallow. Saw her today though. If I did not have a lady waiting, I might just get *reacquainted*, if you know what I mean. This wine is for another woman, quite curvy too."

"Always the same with you, Wickham, isn't it?" the barkeeper frowned. "Which reminds me, there was a man in here askin' about you today. Brought in a drunk gentleman with a real displeased look on his face. Of course, I'd be displeased be too if I had just lost my horse in a bet."

"A gentleman drunk *and* gambling? That happens to be my specialty, Sammy. Who brought the poor bastard in? Was it Johnny?"

"I told you. It's Samuel," the barkeeper scowled. "And I know who Johnny is, you bacon-brained idiot. If it was Johnny, I would have said it was Johnny who brought him in. Na, this guy was filthy. Tall, broad shoulders, walked with a limp. He had dark hair and grey eyes, one of which squinted at me like a pirate or somethin'. He wanted me to tell you that he was going to keep the gentleman good and juicy for tonight."

Good and juicy? A drunk gentleman willing to gamble away small fortunes was very tempting. But the bottles of wine in his hand made him stay focused. Money was not the only need he had right now, and he was close—too close to give this one up. "Well, if they come in again, just keep the drinks flowing. I will be back in a couple of hours. A man should never leave a lady waiting, but he should always leave the lady when his wait is over-! Ha! Am I right?"

Samuel shook his head in disgust. "Just give me my money you owe me, and I'll make sure they stick around."

Wickham slapped several coins down and said, "Keep the change. I feel lucky in more ways than one tonight!" Wickham turned and laughed at his own sick joke. He was too excited to see two grungy gentlemen stand and follow him out the door.

*****

Colonel Fitzwilliam pulled his hat down further as he exited past the barkeeper. Darcy tried to slouch as he walked, in an effort to hide his noticeable height. As they walked outside, they felt the breeze off the nearby Thames send chills down their back. Neither one needed to tell the other to stay quiet.

They followed Wickham from a distance. At one point, he stopped to talk to a woman—obviously a lady of the night. Both men leaned over the rail by the dock and examined the river casually. They continued their pursuit and, as they passed Mrs. Younge's establishment, they noticed that Wickham slowed down ahead of them. Wickham fished around in his pocket, threw a coin of some sort to a young lad at the door, who saluted him, and a faint "Yes, sir!" was heard.

Darcy turned down the nearest alley. Colonel Fitzwilliam followed. They stole glances from around the corner and saw that Wickham entered the building.

"We must follow him," Darcy whispered. "You heard him in the tavern. He is going to get her drunk. There is no time to lose."

"No, Darcy," Fitzwilliam hissed. "Timing is everything in a battle like this. If we go in now, before Wickham puts his plan into motion, Miss Lydia will see us only as unwanted intruders, and she might run again. We must wait. Mrs. Younge says she has been holding out against his persuasions for two days now. Let us give her ten minutes to see his intentions."

"Anything can happen in ten minutes, Fitzwilliam! If he forces himself on her, she will be ruined. How will we live with ourselves if we let that happen?" Darcy was beginning to feel nauseated from the anxiety. Elizabeth had put her faith in him, and he could not let her down.

"Easy, Fitz," the colonel urged. "Just a few more minutes. Wickham is all charms, not force. Trust me. Beguiling people is part of the game for him."

Darcy considered Fitzwilliam's warning. "I think I have an idea," he murmured. "Follow me."

Fitzwilliam followed him as Darcy walked up to the lad who was squatting by the door of Ocean's Hallow Inn.

Darcy said, "You look chilled, young man."

The boy couldn't be more than ten, and his hair was long and greasy. "What's it to you? It ain't nothin' that I ain't felt before."

Darcy reached into his pocket and pulled out a large coin and flipped it from little finger to first finger and back again. "I just thought you would enjoy a nice cup of tea, that is all. And maybe some cake."

The boy unconsciously licked his lips and eyed them suspiciously. "What do I gotta do?"

Darcy said, "For a warm blanket and a new set of clothes, tell me what that gentleman there paid you to do. I assume you have some task to perform."

"What makes ya' think I need new clothes? Mine're in better shape than yours, mister!"

Darcy had to laugh at the boldness and confidence of the young man. The lad was right. In his singed, dirty clothes, Darcy looked nearly homeless, certainly unrecognizable. But he also had to show the boy that he had some authority. "I am not here to play games with you, son. Agree to my terms or no warm blanket."

The boy hesitated a little and watched Darcy twirl the coin in his fingers. Darcy stopped twirling it and held it out to him. The urchin took it and said, "He just wanted me to keep an eye out for anyone that didn't belong 'round here."

Darcy pulled out another few coins and handed them to him. "Thank you. Do you know which room his lady is staying in?"

As he snatched the coins, the child eagerly said, "I can find out! What else can I do?"

"That is all for now, young man," Darcy replied. "But do not let him know we were asking about him."

"No problem, mister!" The lad left and was back in less than a minute. "She ain't in her room. She and the gentleman are in the dining room right now. But the innkeeper says her room is across from his on the second floor. They are the only two rooms on the second floor." He held out his hand expectantly.

Darcy placed another few coins in his hand and said, "Good work. Now go use that money and buy yourself something to eat and a warm blanket. Where is your mother?"

"She is, um, working right now . . . on the third floor." He looked a little uncomfortable for a brief minute.

"I do not understand. Is she a servant?" Darcy asked.

Colonel Fitzwilliam pulled on Darcy's arm and cleared his throat. "Leave it be, Darcy," he whispered. Then turning toward the boy, he asked "What is your name, son?"

"William, sir," he said proudly.

"Ah, a fine name! I know many good men out there with such a fine name. I am just going to ask one more thing of you. Where in the dining room are they sitting? Are they close to the entrance? By the window?" Colonel Fitzwilliam asked.

The boy looked confused. “There ain’t nowhere to sit besides by the window. It ain’t a big dining room, sir. But where they are sitting makes it hard to see the stairs. Is that what you were asking?”

Colonel Fitzwilliam pulled out a few coins and placed them in his expectant hands. “Precisely. Ever think about being a Bow Street runner?”

“No, sir. Ya think I’d be good at it?”

“I do, indeed. Now go get your tea and cake.”

“Thanks, mister.”

Darcy watched him run down the road and then he turned to his cousin. “Do you think his mother is upstairs . . .”

“Yes, Darcy. She and every other woman on this block. Come on. We can sneak up to Miss Lydia’s room while they are dining.”

They each pulled their hats down and, one by one, walked casually into the front entrance. No one was at the desk, so Darcy stole a brief look around while Fitzwilliam peeked into the dining room through the open doors. He turned to Darcy and muttered, “He is indeed there with a woman. I have never met Miss Lydia. You had better check if it is her.”

Darcy walked over to the dining room doors and saw Lydia dining with Wickham. He wasn’t sure what he had been expecting, but this certainly wasn’t it. Lydia was acting just as silly as ever, laughing and flirting with Wickham. Darcy stared at them for a minute, listening to their conversation.

She asked him why they could not stay at a better inn. Wickham replied that he had a special inn planned for their honeymoon that overlooked the beach. It was an old cottage that was turned into an inn, and he had reserved the entire thing.

Wickham then offered her more wine. Darcy noticed that Lydia giggled much the same as she did at the Netherfield Ball when she had taken too much wine.

Darcy whispered to Fitzwilliam, “That is her, all right. She looks good so far.”

“Then we wait upstairs.”

Just then they heard Wickham ask if he could at least see the new nightdress. Lydia paused slightly and replied, “I suppose so.”

"How about now, my dearest?" Wickham purred.

"But, George, I have not finished my wine!" she argued.

"Very well. But after you finish, can we not go upstairs? I just want to see you in that gown and hold what is most precious to me, my dearest. We will not do anything we have not already done by the river, I swear. I just want a taste of the happiness you will bring me."

Lydia hesitated. "It does sound so heavenly. But what if someone sees you come into my room?"

"You go up first, and then I will wait a few minutes so you can get dressed. When no one is watching, I will knock three times so you will know it is me."

Darcy heard Lydia push her chair out and stand, and Darcy and Colonel Fitzwilliam crept upstairs. The room on the right had Wickham's clothes thrown around, and his uniform was draped over in the corner. They hurried in and closed the door behind them.

From across the hall, they heard the other door open and close, but after that there was silence. After what seemed like ages, they heard footsteps in the hall, and they both held their breath. Would Wickham come to his own room or go directly to Lydia's? Then there were three knocks on the other door. It opened.

Wickham's voice was muffled, but they heard a somewhat filthy compliment come about how beautiful and irresistible she was, and then the door closed. They stood silently as the clock struck ten. It had been a quarter of an hour now, and Darcy's hair on the back of his neck was standing straight up.

"Remind me again why we should not just charge in there and take Lydia home?" Darcy groaned.

Colonel Fitzwilliam looked just as anxious. "She needs to know what kind of man he really is."

"Are we waiting for some kind of sign, then? How will we know when we hear it?"

"We will know it." Right then they heard voices being raised, one clearly Lydia's. The other was quieter.

"Now?" Darcy asked.

"Just a bit longer."

They heard breaking glass and a very distinct "Get out!"

Neither one doubted that they had their sign. Fitzwilliam was the first to reach the door, and once they were in the hall, they heard more of what was being said in Lydia's room.

"I told you already last night!" Lydia yelled. "Not until we are married!"

Colonel Fitzwilliam put a hand on Darcy. "Wait. Wait a little longer."

"No, Richard. No more waiting!" Darcy opened Lydia's door and rushed in to find Wickham had ahold of both her wrists and the gown on Lydia's shoulder had been ripped at the shoulder. "Unhand the lady, Wickham!"

Wickham whirled around and looked confused for a moment. "Darcy?"

Lydia pulled her hands free and stepped away and repeated the same sentiments. "Mr. Darcy?"

Wickham looked at Colonel Fitzwilliam, who had begun to take his coat off and was approaching Lydia. "Miss Lydia, I am Colonel Fitzwilliam, Darcy's cousin," the colonel assured her. "Take my coat and cover yourself." She did as she was told and then stepped into the far corner.

Darcy and the colonel stepped towards Wickham. "Very clever of you to promise marriage to an unsuspecting young lady, but not very creative," the colonel quipped. "Seems you have fallen back into old habits."

"Wickham, what do they mean?" Lydia asked with fear in her voice.

Fitzwilliam answered for him. "You are not the first lady he has promised to elope with. How many is this for you now?"

Wickham stayed silent.

Without taking his eyes off Wickham, Darcy said, "Miss Lydia, your family is very concerned about you. Are you well?"

"I am now."

"Am I to assume that this rake tried to force himself on you?" Colonel Fitzwilliam asked.

"Yes, sir." Her voice cracked as she uttered the words, and Darcy could tell she had begun to cry.

The surge of emotion running through Darcy was building. Wickham had tried and succeeded to hurt him in multiple ways and multiple times. He had beguiled Darcy's father, Georgiana, Elizabeth, and now Lydia. He was like a noxious weed that tried to smother all the happiness out of Darcy's life. No matter how many times Darcy cut him down, Wickham always turned up again.

"Fitzwilliam, please escort Miss Lydia and a set of clothes to the room across the hall. Stand guard at the door and let her get dressed. And then inform the innkeeper to send for the magistrate. I believe Wickham and I need to have a chat."

"Of course, Darcy," the colonel replied, picking up Lydia's dress from the floor and handing it to her. "Miss Lydia, your sister Elizabeth is waiting for you at Darcy House," he gently explained. "I would be happy to escort you there as soon as you are dressed. Darcy will gather the rest of your belongings for you."

The very silent Wickham finally opened his mouth. "Congratulations, Darcy! You and your brave tin soldier have beaten me again. What a bore you all are!" he laughed. "Well, it was fun while it lasted, Lydia, but I do not think we are such a good match after all. If only you were not such an insufferable prude, darling. Ha! What gentleman wants a woman who acts like a lady even when her parents are not around?" he snickered.

Lydia gasped and moved to approach Wickham. Darcy quickly put a restraining arm out to her. But she merely pushed Darcy's arm away and walked straight up to Wickham and hissed, "How is this for ladylike?" Then she clenched her fist and swung, hitting Wickham squarely in the jaw. She must have hit him with all she had, because he stumbled backwards and tripped, hitting his head on the coffee table.

Wickham was out cold.

CHAPTER 27

"Bravo, Miss Lydia!" Colonel Fitzwilliam cheered.

Darcy was too busy calming his heart to consider cheering. Wickham was subdued for now, but he could wake at any time. "Miss Lydia, do you have something to tie his hands? Some ribbon or such?"

"Why are you here, Mr. Darcy? And what are you wearing?"

"The ribbon, Miss Lydia," Darcy reminded her urgently.

Lydia went to her trunk and pulled out several and handed them to Darcy. Darcy and Colonel Fitzwilliam both started tying Wickham's hands and feet. When they were finished, they turned around and saw that Lydia was gone.

Panic rose in Darcy's chest. "Lydia?" he called out. "Where are you?"

A muffled sound came from outside the room. Colonel Fitzwilliam said, "Go see to her. I will watch him."

Darcy saw that Wickham's door was closed, and he knocked on it. "Miss Lydia, are you in there?"

"Yes. I am almost done getting dressed," she replied.

Darcy looked at his watch and saw it was nearing ten-thirty. He went to check on Wickham.

"Are you sure you can handle him?" Darcy asked.

Colonel Fitzwilliam nodded. "If I can subdue our Aunt Catherine for a half hour, I am confident I can keep this scoundrel in line for a few minutes."

"Then I will call for the magistrate."

*****

Elizabeth found Georgiana to be kind and sweet. Although it was clear she was shy, she had an innocent, trusting glow about her. Just thinking about the poor girl being manipulated by Wickham broke Elizabeth's heart. Georgiana was a genuine soul. One who was quite thoughtful in her responses. It took Elizabeth a good half hour to convince Georgiana that she should retire. As for herself, Elizabeth was determined to wait up to make sure that Darcy returned safely.

Georgiana looked confused upon hearing Elizabeth's plan. "But why are you waiting up?" she asked. "Should I be worried about him? Is he in danger?"

Elizabeth just looked at her for a moment and tried to decide what to say. She wanted their relationship to be open and honest. She wanted her new sister to trust her. Elizabeth explained, "Probably not. He is simply meeting an old acquaintance at my request. But he has been gone for five hours. I confess I had hoped he would be back by now."

Georgiana replied, "I will make sure Avelina is settled. Then, if you do not mind, I will stay awake with you."

After seeing to Avelina, the ladies talked for a bit, hoping to distract one another from their worries. In time, they both turned to their reading. A few hours later, as the clock struck its quarter hour past twelve, Elizabeth watched Georgiana's eyes start to drift closed.

"Georgiana, would you like to go to bed now?"

Georgiana stretched. Elizabeth could see the fatigue in her eyes. Even without knowing what the business was or who it involved, Georgiana was deeply worried. Their relationship was more tender than most brother-and-sister relationships.

"Oh dear! I fear I am losing this battle," Georgiana said with a yawn. "If I had not slept so poorly last night, perhaps I would have fared better."

"If you like, I can send your brother to your chambers as soon as he returns," Elizabeth offered.

"Very well. Ask him to wake me the minute he walks in."

"I will, my dear. And, Georgiana, I just wanted you to know that I have thoroughly enjoyed our time together today. I shall look forward to calling you my sister."

A genuine smile crossed her lips, and she walked over to where Elizabeth was sitting and leaned in for a tender embrace. "I feel the same way. I am most pleased with my brother's choice. Goodnight, Elizabeth."

Elizabeth said goodnight and returned to her book. It was only another half hour before she heard a commotion at the front door. She closed her book and hurried to the library door to look out into the hall.

Lydia was standing there with Will, and he was giving instructions to a servant to direct Lydia to the Red Room in the family wing. Will's clothes were singed and dirty, and they were not the same ones he had left in, but Lydia seemed unharmed.

Elizabeth didn't know who she was happier to see. She couldn't help herself and ran and threw her arms around both of them. Her eyes tingled with the pricks of tears that she had wanted to shed all evening. She felt Will release her and Lydia's arms wrapped fully around her. She looked around and saw that the servant had left them.

"Oh, Lydia! I am so glad you are safe!"

"Lizzy! I had no idea that Wickham could be so devious! To think I almost married him!"

"Are you all right? Did he hurt you in any way?"

"La! You should be asking that of him!" Lydia laughed.

Could it be? Could she truly not have been fully compromised? She looked to Will, and he gave a subtle shake of the head. Relief surged through Elizabeth's body, and she hugged Lydia again, crying more happy tears.

"Come, Lydia, I will show to you the Red Room myself," Elizabeth announced, wrapping Lydia's arm around hers.

"Oh, good Lord, Lizzy! I'm deadly tired!"

Elizabeth smiled, then she turned back to say, "Mr. Darcy, I am under strict obligation to order you to Georgiana's room. She says you are to wake her immediately and let her know you are safe. She would never forgive me if I delayed you any further. But I am afraid I left my book in your library. I will need to retrieve it after I see to my sister."

He raised his eyebrow slightly and said with a half-smile, "I highly recommend you do, Miss Bennet."

*****

Elizabeth was anxious to hold Will in her arms. She was confident he had gotten her message about meeting in the library, and she didn't want to delay it any further, but they both needed to tend to their sisters first. As she brushed Lydia's hair and plaited it to the side, Lydia told her what had happened at the Ocean's Hallow Inn. Elizabeth was admittedly quite shocked. Then Lydia related the story Mr. Darcy had told her of Wickham's dissolute history with a "close family friend" and declared, "George Wickham is truly a worm of a man, and I am ever so glad I hit him!" It seemed Lydia knew nothing about Georgiana's involvement with Wickham. Will had been wise not to entrust the full story to her. Then Elizabeth listened as Lydia described how Will had saved the day, and just in time. She even showed Elizabeth her wrists, which were beginning to bruise.

Elizabeth warned her against speaking openly of what almost happened. For the first time, Lydia showed some maturity and agreed readily. The night must have changed her some, but her next statement confirmed that she hadn't changed completely:

"But I have to tell you, Lizzy, talking to the magistrate was so droll! La, he just kept asking the same thing in different ways! Mr. Darcy kept answering the questions for me anyway—to protect my reputation, so he says. Colonel Whats-His-Name is still there with the magistrate now. And so everyone thinks that my companion stepped out to ask for some fresh water when Wickham attacked me. It was very kind of Darcy and the colonel not to say what *really* happened. But I would never have gone through with it, Lizzy—not unless we were married. You know that, do you not?"

Elizabeth carefully considered her thoughts and replied, "I never lost hope for Mr. Darcy to find you in time."

Lydia shrugged her shoulders. "He did, I suppose. But I still cannot believe you are going to marry him! He seems so cross all the time! He *is* wealthy. But are you sure you want spend the rest of your life with someone so dull?"

Elizabeth guided her to her bed and tucked her in as she had done many times when Lydia was young. "Yes, I will be most happy. He is not as he seems to people at first. He is the perfect gentleman. Now, get some rest, Lydia." She backed out of the door, closed it behind her, and hurried down to the library.

The door was cracked open just wide enough for her to sneak in. Will stood by the window with his hands clasped behind his back, looking out at the moon. He had already changed from the dirty, singed clothes. Now, he only wore a white shirt, trousers, shoes, and a gold-and-burgundy-striped silk vest. His knee high boots accentuated the muscular legs above them. Her heart started to race, and she felt suddenly warm. She could tell he had stoked the coals, but she knew her reactions well enough to know that the fire in the room was not the source of her heat. She took a bold step further into the room and with each step closer to him, her heart picked up speed. Never had they had such an opportunity to be alone like this. All their moments in the past had been stolen moments—a minute here or there outside, or tarrying for a moment in a room where someone could come across them at any moment.

She was overcome with the love and admiration she had for Will. He had stayed by her, through her illness and had even risked coming back into her life after she rejected him a second time. He had stepped in without being asked and had saved her family from ruin. He had been so kind to Lydia, regardless of the fact that she may not have deserved it. This was no ordinary man. This was her man. She felt eager to express her love and took the last few steps and closed the gap.

As she reached him, she could tell he had detected her behind him. His shoulders relaxed, and he unclasped his hands from behind his back, and yet he did not turn around. She slid her arms around his waist from behind and allowed her hands to fully take in the feel of the fabric and his muscles. He was tight and sculpted, and he let out an audible sigh as her hands examined his abdomen and chest blindly. With her cheek pressed to his back, she could feel that his breathing had increased in pace and depth, but so had hers. She continued to hold him, even stepping closer to feel more of him.

"Elizabeth." His voice was barely heard and came out more like a caress.

"Elizabeth." He repeated in a sultry baritone that she had only heard a few times. She still did not respond, but kept her hands moving along his chest, delighting in this newfound thrill.

"Elizabeth," he whispered again.

She felt him cover her hands with his and he brought one up to his mouth and kissed it in that reverent way that she never thought possible. So many gentlemen had kissed her hand, but Will did it reverently, with all the feeling his eyes betrayed. He pulled her around to face him and she let her free hand slide along the muscles of his back. As she looked up at him, his eyes devoured her, and shortly after he looked at her, he kissed her fervently.

His kisses were hungry and passionate, and his lips caressed her in the perfect mixture of light graze and firm, undaunted energy. His lips pressed sensually to hers, and he deepened the kiss for the first time. She could hear her heart racing as their mouths intertwined like they had never done before. His hands wrapped around her and held her so close to him that she could not tell where she ended and he began. His lips parted from hers, but only momentarily, as they began a path along her jaw down to her ear where she couldn't help but moan.

The room had gotten entirely too warm. How one could feel so warm yet have goose bumps along their spine was still unclear, but that was not the only thing that was unclear. She had no rational thought at the moment. Moaning once again as his lips started down her neck, she felt him pull away slightly, only to pause and place his forehead on hers, their heavy breaths mixing and dissipating into the library as one. With time, their breathing slowed.

"Elizabeth," He said a fourth time, his breath catching as he said it. "If you continue to let me kiss you like that, you will bring me to my knees. I am powerless right now with you here."

She smirked and looked up at him. "I am suddenly very grateful for my knees."

He looked at her confused and asked, "Pardon me?"

"I mean to say that my knees have never felt so weak before, yet they surprise me and are holding my weight admirably. You should be very proud of them."

He chuckled and said, "Indeed, I am very proud of your knees. I am proud of every bit of you." He reached up and touched her smiling lips. He took her hand and led her to the chaise. They sat down and he placed his arm around her shoulders, gently guiding her head to his chest.

She took in the moonlight shining through the window and just breathed. "Will, I was so very scared tonight. When I heard that you had summoned Colonel Fitzwilliam, it suddenly occurred to me that you could be in danger. I felt so helpless. I felt alone. It reminded me of one part of the dream when I was ill."

Darcy frowned. "But you always describe feeling only peace and love in your dream," he replied.

"Most of the time I did. But there was a moment . . . I have not told you this part, because it is very difficult to discuss."

"You can tell me anything, dearest Elizabeth."

"I had gone on to the Son, and yet I heard you calling me from behind. You had told me that I had a mission left on Earth and that my family still needed me. Although God knew I could still choose whether or not to stay with Him or return to you, He also knew me well enough to know what I would choose. Even though I didn't understand the depth of the love you had for me, and even though I didn't fully realize the love I had developed for you, God knew I would choose you."

Will held her closer and kissed the top of her head. "And I will forever be glad you did. But you said, *most of the time* you felt peace and love in the garden. When did you not?"

Elizabeth took a deep breath and tucked her feet under her and leaned into him further. "After I made my choice, you were gone. The moment I knew I wanted to be with you, you left. I was alone in a place that no longer was heaven to me without you. That is when I knew I had to find you and tell you how important you were to me. You were vital to my happiness. *You* were my heaven, and God knew it before I knew it. That is why I was so determined to walk back to you, even if I had to do it alone."

Will took his hand and tilted her chin up to him. She had to reach a bit but her lips met his, and, for a moment, she felt in her heart everything that he was trying to tell her, before he even said it, just like in her dream. "I will never leave you. You are my love. My life. You are the love of my life. I cannot go through life without you anymore, for you have altered me so permanently that I do not think I can return to that selfish existence. You will never, ever, have to walk in the garden looking for me. You will never be alone again—not if I can help it."

"I know, Will. It was only because I doubted my ability to find you and tell you how important you were to me that I had any fear at all. Somehow I knew that once I found you, you would never leave me again."

"What we have is real, Elizabeth. It is not some dream you have imagined. It is not some faraway place that you thought was heaven. Pemberley is real. I am real. My love for you is real. All of it, from the yellow plum tree to the rose-colored path. It exists. I cannot wait to share it with you. I do not know how you were able to see Pemberley's garden. I do not know how you survived when Mr. Collins did not. I do not know how you had the courage to seek me out, using my cousin to relay the message that you were in London, but you did. We are meant to be together. Our love is the kind people write about. Although I do not know how someone could truly write it, because it is too beautiful to put to words."

"Sometimes there are no words."

He looked down at her and kissed her lips again tenderly. "But there are ways to communicate besides words." He smiled so widely his dimples showed.

"And what are you suggesting, sir?"

"Let us just say your 'family' still needs you."

Elizabeth smiled back and kissed him just as fervently as before. He leaned forward to make her more comfortable, and their lips communicated quite effectively. After a moment, he pulled her onto his lap with strong arms. Now she was as tall as he was, and they spent a few minutes kissing and exploring each other's hair with their hands. He discovered how to unpin her hair, and she found the perfect curls to twirl in her fingers. When her breathing seemed impossible to control, she finally pulled back and uttered, "I should retire."

"You should."

"You should retire too."

"I should, but I will not."

"Why not?"

"I just found my kind of heaven, and it has nothing to do with a garden."

"You wicked man!"

"But I am *your* wicked man."

"Indeed, you are."

"Can you just stay a little longer? I promise to do nothing more than hold your hand."

"What kind of promise is that? Is that supposed to convince me to stay?"

He chuckled softly. "It is supposed to keep your reputation intact, my dear."

"Ah, that. Yes, I suppose that would be a wise choice. But I will stay on one condition. I would like a goodnight kiss."

"You drive a hard bargain, madam."

"Yes, such a sacrifice on your part!"

"Indeed." He lifted her off his lap and took her hand in his, and with both hands, he caressed it as if he were a drowning man being offered a life vest. It was vital that he hold her hand. It was unthinkable that she should remove it from his soft touch.

They had a great deal to discuss. Elizabeth did not hesitate to ask if they could offer Charlotte a home at Pemberley through her confinement, and Will thought that would be a wonderful idea. Doing so would also allow him more time to consult with her about the mysterious ledger.

They both agreed that Lydia needed to return home to Longbourn very quickly to silence any rumors that might have surfaced. Will told her that the magistrate would only hold Wickham for a week without knowing what debts he held in Meryton even though Darcy had assured him they were substantial. So Will offered to return Elizabeth, Lydia, and Avelina to Longbourn tomorrow instead of taking Elizabeth and Avelina on to Rosings as planned.

But Will would need to return to London, and that would mean more time apart. Besides continuing his research about the mysterious C. W. Pastel, he desired to work with his solicitor further on the settlement. Elizabeth protested the amounts that he insisted upon, but he told her his mind was already made up. There was nothing he wanted more than to give all he had to Elizabeth. And if he were to someday die and leave her a widow, he would do everything he could now to secure her future and not leave her to Charlotte's fate. But Elizabeth would not hear of such talk. There was Pemberley and Georgiana to consider as well. And the sums he had in mind were ridiculous.

They seemed to be on the verge of an argument when Will kissed her hand in that reverent way, looking at her longingly, and her heart was lost to him again. She apologized, and they compromised, and then they both eagerly turned to happier subjects. Elizabeth said that she would like to be married in Pemberley's garden. He was delighted by the idea but wanted to make sure that her parents would agree to it. She simply laughed.

"Of course my parents would agree to a wedding at Pemberley!" she replied. "And I think I would like Jane to stand up with me."

Will smiled mischievously and said, "I do not think she will be able to do so."

"Why not?"

"I have news that will not surprise you, but will prevent her from being at your side like you are imagining."

"What is it?"

"Bingley asked your sister to marry him as soon as we left for Longbourn. They are engaged."

Elizabeth squealed in delight, but Will clasped his hand over her mouth and said, "Shhh! Do you want all my servants to know I have clandestine visits with unmarried ladies in my library?"

She shook her head, and he removed his hand. "Why, then, can I not have Jane there?"

"You must be quite tired, my dear. I think even Avelina could figure that answer out."

Elizabeth furrowed her brows and tried to ponder what he could mean. "Will, we are to be married in three weeks. Surely they will not be on their honeymoon by that time."

"No, they will not be on their honeymoon."

"And surely my father will give him permission."

He leaned over and kissed the creases out of her brows and said, "Do not overthink it. Consider your mother's excitement over having *two* daughters marrying at roughly the same time . . ."

It dawned on her. "A double wedding!" she cried. He laughed and nodded. "I should think that Jane would like that very much! I admit

I agree that I must be terribly tired to not have figured that one out sooner."

He pulled her close to him and held her head to his chest. "Then rest for a moment."

"Mmm . . ." she murmured sleepily. She listened to his deep breathing and felt her body relaxing. "Do not fall asleep, Will. I would not want to be found in your arms like this by Avelina or Georgiana."

"I do not think I can sleep right now anyway. Go ahead, my love, my life. Sleep. I will be sure to give you your goodnight kiss."

"Such a sacrifice," she said while yawning. She vaguely remembered him draping a blanket over her shoulders. The last thing she heard was the clock chiming three o'clock.

CHAPTER 28

Darcy now had a taste of what it would be like to have Elizabeth in his arms, and as each quarter hour passed, with her sweet lavender scent wafting up at him, he struggled to let her go. Maybe spending some time apart before the wedding was not such a bad idea. His self-control seemed to dissipate in her presence.

As he brushed the curls away from her face, he reconsidered his plan. Perhaps his business in London could wait until after their marriage. But once he was married, he would have her all night. He knew it would be impossible to part from her then. No, his business in London was vital. Five chimes alerted him to the hour, and he decided the debate was over. He would take her to Longbourn, and immediately return to London to finish his business. The sooner he finished it, the sooner he could return.

He gently rubbed her shoulders. "Elizabeth, you had best return to your room. I hear the morning birds chirping."

She moaned slightly and snuggled her face into his chest. "I suppose I must." She got up to leave, and Darcy cleared his throat loudly, making her turn back to him.

"Are you going to make a liar out of me?" he asked trying to hide his smile. "Anything less than the truth is the devil's snare, Elizabeth."

Her brows knit together. "What do you mean?"

"My very reputation as a man of honor is in question if you leave now."

"Will, your honor was in jeopardy as soon as I entered the library."

"Nevertheless, when a gentleman makes a promise, he must sacrifice everything to fulfill that promise. Now, I believe I am to give you a goodnight kiss." He stood, walked to her and unashamedly took in her beauty. Her hair was down, and the curls framed her face in such a beautiful way.

Her tired eyes smiled, and she arched an eyebrow at him. "Well? Are you going to keep your word as a gentleman?"

"On my honor." He wrapped both arms around her waist and pulled her to him and pressed his lips to hers. He drank her in, every bit of her, until he could hold his control no further. He had allowed himself to be tempted in ways he never knew existed, but what he hadn't realized was that he affected her as much as she did him. Realizing this only meant he had to be more in control than ever. He would not sacrifice her virtue because of his selfishness; he was not that man anymore. He kissed her once more on the lips then pulled away.

Her eyes spoke of the effect he had on her, and he felt guilty for kissing her so thoroughly. "Forgive me. I admit I am a little afraid of how far distant our next moment like that will be."

She reached up and cupped her hand to his jaw and said, "I know, Will, I know."

*****

Darcy was sitting across from Georgiana, Miss Lydia, and Miss Gardiner. His hand gently caressing Elizabeth's hand under the blanket, he remembered with pleasure how helpful Georgiana could be.

He had gotten two hours of sleep before he could rest no further. He arose and breakfasted early, where he found Georgiana eager to hear what his plans were. Last night Darcy had told her that Elizabeth's sister had been in danger, but that Darcy had found her in time. He had been vague on the details and most certainly did not mention Wickham's involvement.

As he mentioned that they would be leaving for Hertfordshire today, Georgiana perked up and looked like she was ready to pounce.

"When will we be leaving for Hertfordshire?" she asked.

"I am sorry, Georgiana, when I said *we*, I meant Miss Gardiner, Miss Lydia, Elizabeth, and I. But I will return to London tomorrow. And as soon as I finish my business here, I will take you on my return trip to Hertfordshire if you would like."

"But, William, is there not some way to allow me to go? Could I not stay in Hertfordshire while you finish your business in London? I am sure I could stay at Netherfield with Bingley. I would dearly like to spend some more time with my future sister."

"But Bingley is a single man. You cannot be a guest at Netherfield without either me or his sisters present, and none of us will be there. I am sorry."

Georgiana whined slightly. "But Mr. Bingley is like a brother to me. I do not think of him that way."

"He will be a brother shortly. He is planning to marry Elizabeth's older sister," Darcy grinned.

"That is wonderful! But can we not think of someway to let me come? Did you not say that Colonel Fitzwilliam will be going to Hertfordshire as well?"

"Yes, but not today. He has urgent business in town this week. Do not fret. You will be able to see everyone at the wedding at Pemberley soon enough."

"But, Will, I want to get to know Elizabeth better *before* the wedding. And I am sick to death of my companion. Please. We will all be family soon enough."

"I am sorry, Georgie. You will be staying here. That is final."

Elizabeth walked into the room and asked, "What is final?"

Georgiana rushed to Elizabeth's side. "My brother says I cannot go with you to Hertfordshire because Mr. Bingley's sisters will not be at Netherfield."

Elizabeth smiled, "Then stay at Longbourn. We have two guest rooms, and Avelina will only be using one."

Georgiana clapped her hands and jumped up and down. "What a wonderful idea! I have been invited to Longbourn! I shall order my bags packed immediately. See, William? Good things come when great minds are put together. I can be very helpful, you just watch." She skipped out of the breakfast room.

Elizabeth walked to Darcy and asked, "I hope that is acceptable to you."

He stole a quick kiss and said, "It means there will be one more person to chaperone to us, which I consider completely unacceptable. But it was very kind of you to invite her."

Now, as the carriage rocked back and forth, he had to admit that Georgiana had been quite helpful. She had taken the seat between Miss Lydia and Miss Gardiner and had pretended to look the other way when Elizabeth was handed in. He had several hours to spend next to Elizabeth, and her intoxicating lavender scent was engulfing his senses.

He drifted off into a blissful sleep all too quickly. In what seemed like minutes, he was jolted awake to find they were already pulling into Meryton. Disappointment flooded him as he realized he had wasted their precious time together by sleeping. Elizabeth's head was resting on his shoulder, and as he leaned down to kiss the chocolate curls, he caught Georgiana's smiling eyes on him. She winked and conveniently turned her head and pointed out the window, causing both Miss Lydia and Miss Gardiner's gaze to be diverted as well. Darcy kissed Elizabeth's hair and squeezed her hand under the blanket. "We have arrived in Meryton, Elizabeth."

She awoke and looked out the window. "Oh, my! I did not think I would sleep the whole way."

The carriage stirred to life as everyone started to fold blankets and tuck away books into bags.

While the other passengers were distracted, he whispered to Elizabeth, "I will have a great deal to discuss with your father. I hope you do not mind me doing so right away."

"Not at all. But please finish your business as soon as possible. I must inform my mother she will be going to Pemberley far sooner than she expected. I would appreciate having you by my side to deflect some of her excess happiness."

He agreed, eager to seal up the business with Wickham as quickly as possible, "I will."

Elizabeth smiled back at him and said, "It is close enough to the dinner hour that you might as well plan to stay for dinner."

"Certainly. I would never deny your mother the chance to overfeed her future son," he said with a grin.

The carriage pulled to a stop, and Darcy exited and handed each one out. He heard the rest of the Bennets coming to meet them, and both Mrs. Bennet and Kitty ran to embrace Lydia.

"Oh, my dear child! Are you well?" Mrs. Bennet pestered. She embraced Miss Lydia over and over again and seemed to be at a loss for words, but the fierceness of the embrace was not lost on Darcy. He would have to add *devoted* to the list of Mrs. Bennet's admirable qualities. There was no doubt that she had been deeply worried and that she could not contain her relief.

Miss Lydia said, "La, Mamma! It is not as if I died! I only spent a few nights in an inn! Oops! I promised Elizabeth that I would not talk about what happened! But I am well, thanks to Mr. Darcy."

Darcy looked away in embarrassment when Mrs. Bennet's eyes landed on him. But diverting his eyes only made him notice that Mr. Bennet was standing behind her with his arms clasped behind him. He too had been worried.

"Mr. Bennet." Darcy bowed. "I believe I have yet to sample your French brandy."

Darcy nodded to Mr. Bennet, tipped his hat, and smiled reassuringly. A softness came across Mr. Bennet's face, and that look alone was enough to have made it all worthwhile. He knew that look well. He himself had worn it when the threat of Georgiana eloping had abated and Wickham had departed. Mr. Bennet just silently turned, and Darcy followed him into the study.

Mr. Bennet opened a cupboard with a key and brought out a bottle similar to the ones he recognized from Bingley's stash. *The two of them will get along nicely*, Darcy thought. Mr. Bennet poured slowly and then while handing it to Darcy said, "Since you are back so soon, and I do not have a daughter named Mrs. Wickham, I must presume you have good news. Tell me what happened, but please, spare me the unpleasant details."

Darcy then shared how they were able to locate Wickham in London, glossing over the fact that he had paid Mrs. Younge handsomely for the information. He reassured Mr. Bennet that they had every reason to believe that Lydia had not allowed Wickham such liberties as a man and a wife would share—omitting the part when Miss Lydia had given

Wickham entry into her room, wearing only her night clothes. Then he finished up by praising Miss Lydia's moral courage. And her very good arm.

Mr. Bennet looked pensive and drank his brandy but paid close attention. Darcy continued to tell him that they only had limited time to prove his debts or the magistrate would have to let him go.

Mr. Bennet pulled out a piece of paper. "That will not be a problem," he said. "I met with great success, for every shopkeeper and tradesperson in the village eagerly assisted me in my quest. It is quite shocking to tell you the staggering sum, they are, impressive, to say the least. Well, here is the list. I believe it is all inclusive. I hope you do not still intend to pay them, Mr. Darcy."

"No," Darcy agreed. "I plan to use them to keep him in debtor's prison until the trial. I will rest more easily at night knowing he is not a free man." Mr. Bennet nodded.

"I have a bit more work to do in London and must leave at first light," Darcy continued. "But when I am finished, sometime next week, I should like to escort your family to Pemberley so that you may be our guests for the ten days before the wedding. Elizabeth and I would like to be married in the gardens there."

"I should think I would like that very much. Jane will be here tomorrow, and I imagine Elizabeth wishes her sister to stand up with her."

Darcy knew it was not his place to inform him that Miss Bennet and Bingley were now engaged. Mr. Bennet would no doubt hear it soon enough when Bingley delivered her to Longbourn. "I believe you are correct."

*****

Dinner had been more subdued than the last time Will was fed by the Bennets. Elizabeth and Will were able to spend some time talking privately in the corner of the room afterwards while Georgiana occupied the three youngest Bennets. Avelina had found time to sketch by herself, and Mrs. Bennet was busy making plans for the wedding. Mr. Bennet, surprisingly not secluded in his study, was reading by the fire.

Elizabeth spoke quietly, "So you will write to me? You will tell me all that you find in London?"

"Of course," Will promised. "I will miss your teasing and sweet smile. But might I leave you with a challenge? It is one I feel confident you will excel at."

"And what is that?"

"I would very much like to see you make a certain gentleman blush."

"Oh, no, sir, I could not do that, not in a letter."

"Hmm, then what will your letters contain? Although I love Hertfordshire, I prefer not to receive an exhaustive examination of its weather or plants." He smiled charmingly back at her.

"Well, a study of London would not suit my purposes either, but I admit there is still quite a bit of learning to be done about the two cities."

"Very well, then. I will write every day about London, and you will write me novels about Hertfordshire. We will know more about the towns than ever before."

There was a sense of excitement in this challenge. A game to keep them occupied was indeed something to look forward to.

*****

The next morning, Darcy had stopped by Longbourn to deliver his first letter before heading to London. Elizabeth did not get a chance to see him, but his letter brought great comfort.

My love,

London is full of resources. The city is equipped better than any other city to accommodate ladies and gentlemen from all over, especially ladies from Hertfordshire.

I hear ladies from Hertfordshire tend to be impertinent and yet exquisitely attractive. You must validate this rumor, for I fear I have a dear friend who has lost his heart to one. Although I sympathize with him as he must still wait to enjoy wedded bliss, I feel a certain amount of satisfaction in seeing him happy. And a certain amount of jealousy that he remains in Hertfordshire, so near to the object of his affection.

But perhaps my removal to London is for the best. My very self-control is in question every time I visit Hertfordshire. I always get warm under the cravat and find myself anxious to wet my lips with something satisfying. You would not have any suggestions, do you? Although London boasts many desserts and cakes, I fear my lips will be quite melancholy while I am here.

I have written to my housekeeper, Mrs. Reynolds, to inform her of our engagement and the upcoming wedding. I asked her to start drawing up a small guest list, but you and your mother may have free rein with the other details. Mrs. Reynolds stands ready to assist you. Just have your mother forward her instructions directly to Pemberley, and she will arrange everything perfectly.

London misses you already.

Will

Elizabeth smiled at his wickedness. She pulled out a pen and paper and wrote him immediately.

Will,

I suffer with dry lips myself here in Hertfordshire as well. I had hoped your letter might offer some suggestion for alleviating the situation. Very well, I shall suggest that you take a bit more lemon in your tea; I hear that lemon in tea offers hope in ways that one would never have imagined.

Do not fret about your fever. Hertfordshire has a tendency to make out-of-town visitors, even those from cities like London, question their strength of constitution. But I have little doubt that men from London, although tempted to partake in questionable activities, have the fortitude to endure at least another two weeks. At that time, I hear the governments of the two cities may form a union, or a merger, of some sort. It is a happy thought, one I find myself thinking on a great deal.

Hertfordshire is already feeling the absence of fine gentlemen.

Elizabeth

*****

It was a full four days before she heard back from him. The only thing that kept her busy was that Jane had arrived with Charlotte and Mr. Bingley, and, of course, her mother's wedding plans. Mr. Bennet had given his permission for Mr. Bingley to marry Jane, and, according to her mother, the double wedding at Pemberley would be so fine it would be talked about for years. Her mother had written daily to Mrs. Reynolds, detailing her desires for flowers, decorations, and food—even declaring the time of day the ceremony would be held.

But Elizabeth had had to put her foot down on that detail. Her mother insisted that all weddings happen in the morning, but it was vital that the wedding occur at sunset, just like when she walked with Will to the Son in her dream.

It had been a long four days, but when the letter came, she ran quickly to her room and opened it. In it was a pressed iris petal, the exact shade as the one in her dream.

To the love of my life,

Gentlemen? As in plural? Hertfordshire is missing more than one gentleman? I daresay I learned to be thankful for my knees when I read that. For it is my understanding that ladies from Hertfordshire find only one man irresistibly charming, if not a little selfish and prideful, and—it cannot be denied—wicked.

As to the business I have been attempting, this London gentleman has met with several roadblocks. I have been very busy. The conservatory only keeps two years of old newspapers locally. I had to sign my life away to request anything further back, but the newspapers should be delivered tomorrow. I hope I will find the advertisement in the ones I requested.

My solicitor has also asked around about who C. W. Pastel may be or what kind of company P&S is. After I showed him the letter, he feels confident Pastel is a fellow solicitor or some form of estate planner.

There seems to be no information at the docks regarding the Horizon's Challenge *or the* Winter's Night *or their captains. I have an impression that one sailor might have heard about Captain Blackhurst. I will follow up with him today and see if he can be bribed. Colonel Fitzwilliam has offered to go in his uniform to see if the sailors' loyalties can be swayed. Perhaps they will be more forthcoming to an officer. I am sorry that I have nothing substantial to report.*

How is Mrs. Collins? I have been asked several times by my cousin how she is doing. I find it somewhat odd that he seems so invested in her welfare. It was not just his inquiry that is curious; it is the frequency and the anxious tones of his inquiries. More than once, while helping with the funeral, he seemed to give extra attention to her needs, but I do not doubt his sincerity in the slightest. Please let her know that she has a great deal of support. Just because I am away does not mean I cannot assist her.

Oh, and let her know that Colonel Fitzwilliam was able to balance the parish ledger. There were no concerns. Mr. Collins paid himself the appropriate amount, and there were no undue or suspicious expenses. My success in the household ledgers is making progress. I started with the most recent but had to go back to the ledger he had before he married Mrs. Collins. It seems he was very frugal. It astonishes me that Mrs. Collins was able to run the household with such a small budget. You may pass on my admiration for her fiscal sense.

You may be surprised to learn that I saw Wickham today. I was told he was ill in prison, and the warden asked me to bring an apothecary. Out of pure loyalty to my father, I did so.

I admit I was curious to see for myself whether he was truly sick, but he does seem very ill. He also seemed confused. He called me by my father's name and treated me as if nothing had ever happened between us. When I mentioned it to the apothecary, he said that it could be the residual effect from hitting his head. I admit I took pity on him and have funded his care. As he may not survive the environment of debtor's prison in his current state of poor health, he is being kept at the local jail for now.

The settlement papers are complete. As of noon today, the merger between London and Hertfordshire is legal. Hertfordshire has full decision-making power if London were ever incapacitated or unavailable. You are to receive fifty thousand pounds upon my death and another four thousand every year thereafter.

Speaking of London, are you aware that the city is anticipating a population boom in the near future? I understand it is anxious to see its population grow by three, four, or even five more inhabitants in coming years. I believe this London gentleman is very confident, and as you have declared in the past, he has a healthy strength of constitution. He anticipates dedicating hours, even days and nights on end, to the subject of population growth.

Now, I suspect Hertfordshire is in full bloom with that news. If you could only hear the rolling laughter here in London right now. Too bad there was no challenge to see Hertfordshire bloom scarlet. I am confident it has happened despite the distance between the two municipalities.

London has a lot to offer, but there are big plans being made for an immediate departure once the merger has taken place. However, the plans are quite secretive, and I cannot give you any intelligence on the particulars. I know I have said before that all you need to do is ask and it shall be given, but in this instance, you will just have to trust this wicked man.

Will

Elizabeth touched the back of her hand to her face and felt the warmth. She smiled at how open they had become with each other. In such a short amount of time, they had built something that she knew would never be broken down. This thought gave her an idea. She immediately took up her pen and wrote him back.

Dear irresistible, charming, and wicked man,

London wishes for a population explosion? There will have to be a significant amount of hard work and fortitude to accomplish such a task. But Hertfordshire women are known for their healthy drive and determination. Need I remind you of her ability to communicate effectively without words? I admit that London is enticing, but Derbyshire provides things that cannot be found anywhere else. If you wish to see any city grow, let it be Derbyshire. Men from that area tend to be taciturn yet tenacious in their pursuit of Hertfordshire women.

As to the blooms in Hertfordshire, I confess the reds and pinks are quite apparent after reading your letter. And on that subject, I have included some lavender for you to remember me by. This particular sprig has touched my new nightdress, which article of clothing I know London will be most impressed with. Although I do not expect that the weather and heat in London will require such attire to be worn for long. How are the blooms in London now, my good sir?

Charlotte is doing well. Let Colonel Fitzwilliam know she trusts you both a great deal. I will check in on her again today. I admit I have noticed a familiarity laced with resistance between the two. I extended the invitation for Charlotte to come to Pemberley, and she very nearly cried with joy. She has agreed to come for the wedding, and I hope you do not mind, but I told her to not to plan to return with my parents—to make it her home immediately. It will be good for someone to be with Georgiana while we honeymoon. And Charlotte has taken such a liking to Georgiana that they will be quite happy together.

I admit that I hope to see you before the next news from London comes. Hertfordshire is lonely.

Elizabeth

*****

Darcy hated to write this next letter. He had put it off for as long as he could, but it was time to make a decision.

Late that morning, while returning to the Ocean's Hallow Inn to confirm Wickham's debts there, he had overheard a finely dressed sailor, who seemed out of his element in that part of town, being referred to as

Captain Jersey. Upon examining him, he seemed to be older than the average sailor, and his gloves were pristine white. Darcy followed him for a short while to see where he might be headed. The man walked purposefully but took a great deal of turns. And at one point, Darcy thought they were about to make a complete circle. After seeing Captain Jersey turn the corner behind a building, Darcy lengthened his stride and increased his pace to catch up, but as he turned, Darcy nearly ran into the end of the captain's sword that was thrust at his chest.

Darcy backed away and put up his hands. He hadn't thought to come armed. "There is no need for that, now. Put it down."

"Who might you be, and why are you pursuing me?" the captain asked with a stern face.

Darcy knew that only honesty could get him out of the situation. "I am afraid I heard you being referred to as Captain Jersey. My name is Fitzwilliam Darcy; I am a friend of Mr. William Collins. You would not happen to know him, do you?"

"Collins? No, I do not think I do. Why do you ask? Is he a sailor?"

"Actually, he is dead." Captain Jersey finally lowered his sword. "Thank you. I am trying to help his widow make sense of the assets that he left her. Your name would not be Captain Conrad Jersey, would it?"

The man tilted his head, squinted, and said, "Indeed. You have my curiosity piqued. How am I involved with this man and his assets?"

"A few years ago, I believe you applied for the captaincy of a ship called the *Horizon's Challenge*. I believe Mr. William Collins was the ship's owner. I am trying to locate the ship or the company that advertised the captaincy: P&S. So far you are my best lead. Do you remember anything? It would have been in August 1808."

"Yes, I remember the job interview, but it was not for the *Horizon's Challenge.* It also was in June, not August. I met with them briefly to discuss the position. They were quite vague in what cargo I would be transporting, but I still gave them my credentials. However, by the time I got back into port in late August, the position had been filled. To be honest, I was somewhat relieved. I have always been an honest gentleman—a second son forced to find a career—and something about the arrangement felt . . . well, less than honest."

Darcy felt his heart gallop with this glimmer of hope. He, his cousin, and his solicitor had been searching for P&S for the last six days with no leads. Captain Jersey had just given him more information in two minutes than he had found that entire week. "Would you have time to discuss this a little more?"

Captain Jersey looked at his pocket watch and said, "I am afraid not. I am overseeing my ship's cargo being loaded. But I will have a few minutes tomorrow morning before we set sail."

This news was both relieving and reassuring at the same time. At least he would get some answers, but that meant delaying his departure for Hertfordshire and seeing Elizabeth.

Darcy pulled out his calling card and handed it to him. "Here is my contact information. What time can I expect you?"

"Perhaps around ten o'clock. I am not sure I will have too much to tell you but I will tell you what I know."

"Thank you. You will help me a great deal."

"I do not know about that." Captain Jersey bowed and left, sliding his sword back into its sheath.

Now, an hour later, as he prepared to write to Elizabeth saying his departure would be delayed, he leaned back in his chair and rehearsed what he should tell her. He was expected back in Hertfordshire today, but now he would not be able to leave until after tomorrow's meeting with Captain Jersey. And if the captain gave him another lead to follow, that would delay him even further.

It was killing him to be so far, yet so near, to Elizabeth. If he wanted to, it was early enough in the day that he could take a trip down to Longbourn now, spend the evening with her, and leave at first light to arrive in time to meet Captain Jersey. It was a very tempting plan.

Mindlessly he passed the pen from finger to finger and he debated the ride. He would be on horseback, which meant if he rode quickly, he could make the trip by four o'clock. It would still be daylight at that time, and they could go on a walk. If he did not go, he would spend a lonely night just thinking of her. And she would be alone as well. Suddenly the decision was made for him. He had promised her that she would never be alone if he could help it.

He put his pen down and found Poole, who had been dropped off in London by Bingley on the way to Hertfordshire. Poole looked up at him and said, "Mr. Darcy, you should have told me that there were tea stains on this cravat. Now that it has set in, I do not know how I will get them out."

"Never mind," Darcy replied. "I need you to put one change of clothes in my satchel, but leave my trunk packed. I know I told you we were heading to Hertfordshire today, but I have important business tomorrow morning that delays our original plans. I am, however, going to go on horseback for one night. You should expect me back by nine tomorrow morning. I will probably need an immediate bath at that time. A Captain Jersey will be calling on me at ten o'clock tomorrow, and I will need to be presentable."

Then he looked at the cravat in Poole's hands. It was the one he had spattered his tea on when Elizabeth had asked if he knew her sister was in London. The sight of it made him realize just how far he had come. "Oh, Poole, I would rather you not try to remove those tea stains. You might say they are a reminder of the man I used to be. In fact, I would like you to frame that cravat and hang in my sitting room, above the full-length mirror, the one I stand in front of every day as you place the finishing touches on my attire."

Mr. Darcy then turned and left, still oblivious of the strange look coming from Poole. He was much too excited to notice such things. In a few short hours, he would see his lovely Elizabeth. Perhaps, if he rode hard, he might make it before three.

CHAPTER 29

Elizabeth could not contain her delight. When Mr. Darcy was announced, she immediately ran to him and threw her arms around him. He nestled his face in her hair and held her close.

"Was my absence so painful that you have decided to abandon propriety entirely? What will your sisters say?" Darcy asked.

She pulled away and said, "My dear, you and I are the only ones here. My mother took my sisters and Georgiana into Meryton to get more ribbon and lace for Jane's dress."

"And your father?" He asked hopefully.

"He was needed at a tenant's house. I am entirely alone at the present."

He looked at her wickedly and then without hesitation he took her face in his hands and kissed her on the lips gently but hungrily. "How fortunate I am!"

"I admit that I stayed home in case you were to arrive. But my sisters, mother, and Georgiana will most likely be arriving home shortly. I feel the need to stretch my legs. Would you escort me to Oakham Mount?"

"It would be my pleasure."

Elizabeth picked up her shawl, and he assisted placing it around her shoulders, letting his fingers smooth it out, caressing her shoulders and neckline. His touch was exquisite and had been sorely missed.

They walked arm in arm on the path that Elizabeth had known her whole life. For a few minutes, neither one felt the need to say anything, but Will finally broke the silence and said, "I regret to inform you that I must return to London at first light. I hope to only be gone two more days, at most, but I could not risk having you here by yourself when you were expecting me to arrive. I know *I* would have been disappointed if I received a letter instead of the real thing."

"But why must you return so quickly?"

"I found Captain Conrad Jersey. It was quite by accident, but he has agreed to meet with me tomorrow morning. He had applied for the captain's position, but by the time he returned to port, he had decided to withdraw his application."

"Did he give a reason why?"

"He mentioned that P&S were very vague about the cargo he would be transporting, and he felt that his integrity would not allow him to go into business with them."

Elizabeth pondered this for a moment. It brought her thoughts around to Charlotte, and it reminded her she needed to tell him something. "Will, I spoke with Charlotte the other day after I got your last letter. I took her aside, and very carefully asked her if she felt uncomfortable around Colonel Fitzwilliam. If it had not been for her deep blush when she said, 'No, not in the slightest. He is the perfect gentleman', I think I would have believed her."

Darcy's brows furrowed. "You think he has not been the perfect gentleman? I can speak with him as soon as I get into town."

"Oh, no, that is not my impression of the situation. I felt like Charlotte was holding back in her opinion of him. I think she might have some feelings toward the man and be embarrassed to say anything further."

"You think she admires him?"

"I do, but she is in mourning, and will be for at least another eleven months. And at the end of that, she will have a six-month-old child. The only reason I bring it up is that Colonel Fitzwilliam has been solicitous to her care and situation, but he is a second son, and has stated multiple times that he must marry an heiress."

"And you do not wish for Charlotte to get her hopes up."

"Precisely. That is, unless you think his heart might actually be engaged . . ."

Elizabeth looked at Darcy and saw a very pensive look. "Elizabeth, I do not feel it is my place to ask him directly if he admires her, especially since it will be nearly a year before he can act on any of those feelings," he sighed. "But perhaps we can help them the way they helped us. Let us nudge them in the right direction."

Elizabeth smiled. "What exactly do you have in mind, Cupid?" she teased.

"Well, let us begin by making sure Colonel Fitzwilliam spends *plenty* of time at Pemberley while Mrs. Collins is there with us. Maybe there will be *hope for Fitzwilliam*."

Elizabeth laughed, "Yes, and maybe Charlotte can *hope for Fitzwilliam.*"

*****

Colonel Fitzwilliam had put this off as long as possible. He knocked on Bingley's townhouse door. The last time he had been here was when he told Bingley about Mr. Collins's death in hopes that he would want to escort the ladies to Kent.

Remembering it like it was yesterday stirred torrents of emotions. So much had happened in such a short amount of time. He had felt so many things. He shook off the distracting feelings that had begun to infiltrate his mind and dreams so often of late. He had two jobs to do, and he was good at performing tasks. He took a breath and went to business.

The door opened and the butler answered. "Good day, Wilder," Colonel Fitzwilliam said. "I wondered if Miss Bingley was available. I have a letter from her brother."

"She is, sir. Come in. May I take your hat?"

Colonel Fitzwilliam took off his hat and handed it over; a much easier task than the one he was about to do. He followed the butler into the parlor and immediately Miss Bingley stood and, with a faux smile that spoke of her dull, dark soul, she curtsied. Miss Bingley looked around him at the open door as if she were expecting someone else to follow after him.

He cursed his cousin and Bingley once again for delegating this onerous task to him. Apparently the news would be taken better coming from a bachelor. And they had argued that he was more skilled at bending the truth to appease the enemy. That much was true; Bingley and Darcy were both dreadful liars. He had countered that he did not know her well enough. But Bingley merely instructed to think of her as the most selfish, shallow, conceited, status-minded fortune hunter he had ever met, and then he would know everything he needed to handle the situation.

As she looked behind him expectantly, he bowed and waited for her greeting.

"Colonel Fitzwilliam, how good of you to come. Will Mr. Darcy be joining us?"

"No, Miss Bingley, it will only be me. As you well know, your brother and Mr. Darcy and I recently traveled to Rosings. Darcy had a splendid time, and he has wonderful news—life-changing, in fact. I have it here in a letter for you. He would have sent this by post, but since I was on my way back to London, I offered to deliver it personally."

Miss Bingley looked puzzled but she said, "Come in. Mr. Darcy does not wish to deliver this life-changing news himself?"

"Unfortunately not, as he is very occupied of late. He sends his greetings."

The poor lady noticeably flinched. "I see. Well, would you like to stay for tea? You can tell me about this news."

"No, thank you, madam. I just came to deliver this letter. I cannot stay, and I am afraid I must prepare to leave the city as well. I am sure we will meet up at Pemberley soon."

Her eyes brightened and a smile graced her lips.

Truth. That is what she needs right now. No more bending the truth, no half-truths. "That is, when . . ." Fitzwilliam found himself at a loss to finish the sentence.

But it was no matter. Miss Bingley stood up and took his arm and walked him to the front door, prattling on about inconsequential things. As vain as she was, she would fall hard with the news. He handed her the letter and took his hat from Wilder, who then left them at the door to themselves.

He had delivered the letter, now he needed to deliver the rest of the message—the warning. "Miss Bingley?"

"Yes, Colonel Fitzwilliam?"

"I pray you will not take the letter too hard. I hope you can wish Bingley and Darcy joy. Your response will be watched from those in the finest circles. I would hate to have your standing in society be diminished due to an absence of support for their upcoming nuptials."

All color drained from her face.

He bowed once more and cursed Darcy for making him do this. A lady should never look like that. Now he needed a stiff drink, perhaps more than one. He had seen too many ladies of late with that look of despair and deep sadness, and all he wanted to do was drown out the images for at least a year.

*****

Darcy was glad to have arrived back in London without any poor weather impeding his journey. He immediately called for a bath and a shave. Poole was performing his task efficiently, and it allowed Darcy's mind to drift to the previous evening. It had gone very smoothly, except for the one near-argument.

Mrs. Bennet had confronted him as soon as they had returned from Oakham Mount and said, "Mr. Darcy, I am so glad you are here! Surely you can make her see reason! Elizabeth insists she must have a sunset wedding at Pemberley, but weddings need to be in the morning or there will be no wedding breakfast! *Talk* to her!"

Mr. Darcy had looked at Elizabeth in surprise.

"I thought it would be nice to see Pemberley's gardens as the sun sets," she whispered. She seemed to be trying to communicate something very important, but Darcy couldn't quite understand it.

For once, Mrs. Bennet was right. Weddings were always in the morning. He wanted to give her everything she wanted, but it was a very odd request. Perhaps a little nonverbal negotiation could settle the issue.

Darcy picked up her hand and kissed it, looking up at her eyes. He saw her melt from the kiss and knew he had to move quickly to a compromise. "If I walk with you to the sun every day at sunset before the wedding, will you consent to marry in the morning?"

Mrs. Bennet clapped her hands together, "Yes, Lizzy! See the sunset any other day, but be married in the morning!"

Elizabeth looked up at him sweetly and said, "As long as I get to see what I have dreamed of seeing, I will marry you at any time of day you wish." She then leaned into Darcy and whispered, "I see you are aware what your kisses do to my ability to stand my ground. Well played, sir."

He held back his laughter as best he could. Yes, he knew how he affected her, and he most definitely would remember that negotiating power in the future. He winked at her and squeezed the hand he was still holding.

"Then it is settled, Mrs. Bennet. Elizabeth and I will marry in the morning. But I warn you not to plan on having us too long at the wedding breakfast, for we must make good time with our travels for the honeymoon. We would need to leave no later than one o'clock to get to where we are going before dark."

He chuckled as he saw curiosity cross Elizabeth's features.

*****

Poole startled him out of last night's memory. "Will there be anything else, sir?"

"No, thank you."

He made his way to the study, and as he passed Franklin, he said, "There will be a Captain Jersey arriving shortly. Please show him into my study."

"Yes, sir."

Darcy had no new correspondence to respond to, not even from his Aunt Catherine, which was a welcome relief. He paced for a bit but then saw from his study window that Captain Jersey had arrived. He sat back down at his desk and waited for him to be shown in.

Franklin knocked twice and then entered, allowing the gentleman to follow. "Captain Conrad Jersey, sir."

"Thank you, Franklin. Come in, sir. I am anxious to hear what you have to tell me." Darcy motioned to the great twin chairs by the fireplace and took a seat.

Captain Jersey did likewise. "As I told you before, I do not know much. What questions do you have?"

"First of all, who or what is P&S?"

"I assume it was some sort of solicitor's office. The glass on the front door said 'Pastel and Sons'. I only met with the youngest son—Clyde, I believe. The older son manages the Liverpool office. I have seen that office from the outside before. It is right off of Dale Street. A very nice part of town. But the London office where I met Clyde was very small and unimpressive in comparison. It seems most of the company is managed from Liverpool."

Darcy slid to the edge of his chair. Could it be providence? He planned to take Elizabeth through the Lake District and on to Liverpool for their honeymoon. He had always loved Liverpool, and it was growing so fast these days. He wanted her to see the amazing architecture. She had expressed her admiration for the architecture of Darcy House, both inside and out, and he wanted to take her to tour one of his favorite cities. But could it really be a coincidence that he was going to the very city that could offer answers?

Darcy asked, "What else can you tell me? You said they were vague about what cargo you would be shipping. What was it they said that led you to reconsider the job?"

"I was told that my job would be to take a crew of ten men of their picking, no more, no less, and travel from Scarborough to London. I was to meet with Pastel's contact in Scarborough and sign that I would not open any of the crates for any reason, and then deliver said crates directly to the hands of Clyde Pastel in London. I was to speak to no one about my cargo and not leave the ship for any reason while they were in my possession. They wanted the trip to be made as often and as quickly as possible. It just felt like there was some sort of illegal actions involved. My father gave me a good name, and I intend to keep it that way, even if I must work to earn a living."

They discussed things for a few minutes. Darcy stood and went to his desk and wrote down the address of the offices in London and Liverpool. Darcy noticed Captain Jersey kept checking his pocket watch.

"Mr. Darcy, I am sorry, but my ship is waiting for me, and from the looks of the weather out there, I had best gather my crew and set sail. One does not leave a ship that size docked fully loaded with the wind picking up like it is."

"Yes, of course. I apologize for keeping you so long. Can you think of anything else that might be helpful to me?"

Captain Jersey shrugged his shoulders. "No. I never heard from them again, and that was over two years ago, nearly three. I cannot tell you if the company is still in business, nor can I tell you how Mr. Collins was involved with them."

Darcy said, "Have you ever heard of the *Horizon's Challenge* or the *Winter's Night*? I believe they are the ships that Pastel and Sons used and were possibly owned by Mr. Collins."

"No, sir, I have not heard of them. I have heard of the *Eastern Challenge* and the *Summer's Night*. They are both handsome ships. Do you think they are the same ships as the ones you asked about? They are sister ships, but I have not seen them in port for some time." He stood and bowed. "I really must go, sir. I wish you luck in your endeavors."

"Certainly, I will show you out. Would you like my driver to take you to the dock?"

"No, thank you. I have my horse. You saw for yourself that a carriage as fine as yours probably has no business in that part of town."

Darcy walked him out and bid him farewell. He instructed the footman to saddle his horse immediately. The sooner he paid a visit to Clyde Pastel, the sooner he could return to Hertfordshire and escort all of the Bennets to Pemberley.

Devon came and knocked on the door. "Sir, your horse is ready."

Darcy thanked him and exited the house and traveled as quickly as possible through the busy streets to the address that Captain Jersey had given him. It wasn't the finest part of town, but still respectable. He remembered that the captain had said it was a white stone building and that it was on the second floor. There was only one white building. So he dismounted, tied up his horse, and said to the two young boys playing chess on the steps, "Keep your eyes on my horse, and I will pay you handsomely." They nodded their agreement, and he entered the building.

The lobby was fairly quiet, but there was a man at the front desk that looked up from his book and adjusted his spectacles. "May I help you?"

"I am here for Pastel and Sons. Could you direct me to the second floor?"

For a brief moment, Darcy felt like he was being examined from head to toe. The man said, "I can direct you to the second floor, but that will not get you to Pastel and Sons."

"I was told their office was on the second floor of this building."

The man made a tsk-tsk sound with his tongue. "Either you want the second floor or you want Pastel and Sons. Make up your mind. A man must have a sound commitment to what he wants."

Darcy could sense when a man was asking for money. He pulled out his purse and placed a few coins in his hand. "Is that enough commitment for you?"

He grinned slightly. "Indeed, it is. Pastel and Sons has not been on the second floor for over a year now."

Darcy waited to be told where they had moved to but the man stayed silent. Darcy rolled his eyes and produced two more coins.

"They now are on the third floor. But you will not find him there now."

"Where will I find him?"

The man took a deep breath and waited until Darcy handed him one more coin. "Mr. Pastel, the younger, has traveled to the Liverpool office for a month. Do you need that address?" The man glanced at Darcy's coin purse.

Darcy was disgusted. "No, thank you. I have that address. I believe it is on Dale Street." Darcy noticed that the man looked disappointed that he couldn't finagle more money for the information he held. But seeing this reaction only proved that the address in Liverpool was still correct. This was good news indeed. For that meant he had no other business in London but a stop to see his cousin.

*****

Fitzwilliam slurred his words and tried to block the light coming from the curtains that Darcy had just opened. "Darcy, what are you doing here? I thought 'your love, your life' was waiting in Hertfordshire for you."

He must have drunk a great deal last night to still be hungover at noon. This worried Darcy considerably. As he got closer, he could smell the alcohol. Darcy ignored his question and gathered the empty glass and decanter and set them aside.

His cousin rubbed his eyes and sat up slowly, reaching a hand out to steady himself. “Is everything all right, Darcy?”

“Yes, Fitzwilliam. But I think from the look of things, I should be asking that of you.”

“Oh, do not mind me. I just imbibed a little too much. A man has got to lose himself sometimes, you know. I gave the damn letter to Miss Bingley.”

Darcy went and sat next to him. Truth be told, he hadn’t really examined his cousin for some time. Darcy admitted his thoughts for the last month had been focused exclusively on Elizabeth. And he was long overdue for a conversation. “Fitzwilliam, I need to thank you for offering me hope when my heart was blind to what was sitting in front of me.”

His cousin huffed a little and quipped, “A man in love is always blind. But you have no need to thank me. There was nothing I did that you would not have figured out eventually.”

“Believe what you wish.”

“What?”

“My motto. Believe what you wish. I say I need to thank you, and you believe I would have figured it out eventually, so you may believe what you wish.”

“Darcy, my mind is a little slow right now. Are you well into your cups too? You have a most unfortunate tendency to get obstinate when you drink.”

“No, Richard, I have not drunk anything today. But I might ask if you are a little blind yourself.”

Fitzwilliam rolled his eyes and then closed them, leaning his head back against the back of his chair. “You know, Darcy,” he chuckled, “it is a good thing you made me deliver Miss Bingley’s letter, because you are no good at manipulating the enemy. I know what you are up to.”

Darcy wasn’t sure himself. “And what is that?”

“You are trying to get me to talk about her.”

“Who, Miss Bingley?”

"You know who. And it simply will not work. An amateur like you cannot possibly wield my own tactics against me."

"If it is not Miss Bingley, whoever could you be talking about? Hmm . . . Elizabeth is well. The Miss Bennets are well. Miss Gardiner is well. Oh, by the way, did you hear that Elizabeth and I have invited Mrs. Collins to come live with us at Pemberley?"

Darcy had noticed a slight wince as he mentioned Mrs. Collins's name. He felt bad, but it confirmed everything he suspected.

"I told you, I do not want to talk about her," Fitzwilliam said, opening one eye to peer at his cousin.

Darcy pushed a little further. "Then I will not mention that she is grateful for your help with the parish ledger."

"Quit it, man."

"And I will not mention that she hopes that when you return from your duties with the army, you come visit us all at Pemberley."

Fitzwilliam's head snapped up, but then he groaned, and his hand went to his aching head. Clearly he regretted such a sudden movement. "It will never work, Fitz. How can she even consider me? I have nothing to offer her."

Darcy stood and adjusted his vest and cravat. He patted his cousin on the shoulder and said very clearly, "Believe what you wish."

*****

The Darcys and the Bingleys—including his sisters, who were warned to be on their best behavior—joined by the Gardiners, the Bennets, Charlotte, and Colonel Fitzwilliam, spent the next nine days together at Pemberley.

Although it was sometimes difficult to evade their guests, Will and Elizabeth learned quickly how invaluable their walk to the sun was each and every night. Sometimes they would simply glance at each other from across the crowded room, signaling that it was time to rendezvous in Pemberley's garden. Other times it was a not-so-subtle wink from Darcy, along with an obvious tap on his pocket watch. But most of the time, they didn't say anything at all; they simply found each other at the same time in the same spot along the rose-colored pebbled path.

The night before the wedding found them there as well. Elizabeth relished in the closeness of the man beside her as they walked together. She could feel the strength of his constitution. She could feel his integrity. She could feel his compassion and devotion. She could feel his love. It was all so familiar, yet she knew it would never get old. He was a good man, a great man, and tomorrow he would be *her* man.

She was so grateful that she had gotten ill. It was something that she hadn't explained fully to him, although she had tried several times over the last few sunsets. How could she ever have known such happiness if she had not had her experience of walking to the Son?

She tried to explain it again. "It still amazes me to think of us here together, Will. Just imagine what would have happened if I had not gotten sick. I do not think I would have had the impulse, let alone the courage, to accept your letter nor to write you back. There were too many rules against it. I would have never dismissed propriety like that if I had been in my right mind."

Will rubbed her arm with his ungloved hand. They had both stopped wearing gloves on these walks several days ago. Their subtle tenderness was transparent to those around them. They had exchanged a few kisses in stolen moments, but most of the time they were content to simply walk together.

"If you had never written me that letter," Will replied, "I would have given up all hope of your opinion of me ever changing. It was not any one word or phrase or apology that you said in the letter, it was the whole tone of it. There was a pressure, an intensity, in your writing. In it, I saw a new level of passion in you. You had been passionate the day before, during the refusal, of course, but the letter was different. The passion in your letter . . . well, it gave me hope. It was obvious you were not thinking clearly, but yet, at the same time, the letter made it clearer than I could have hoped."

"Made what clear?"

"Your admiration for me," he explained. She cast him a doubtful look. "No, it is true. Reading that letter was like lighting a candle in a dark room. Mr. Cress, the curate who officiated at Mr. Collins's funeral, talked about how hope is like a candle that we light when we hear a baby cry. Before I read it, the world felt dark and hopeless. But when I read your words, the hope of winning your affection ignited my heart. It gave me faith. It was like I was seeing myself and the world for the first time. It kept me going when I felt the darkest. It helped me see the light."

Elizabeth was spellbound, but she managed to say, "That is exactly what the sun did for me. I was able to see the light."

"I know. There was a time after that when I thought all hope for Mr. Darcy had been extinguished, but Fitzwilliam helped me find it again."

"Just as Charlotte helped me," Elizabeth agreed. "How can we ever thank them enough?"

Darcy shook his head. "I do not know. But I *hope* an opportunity will present itself. And I believe that when we hope for something good, for something greater than ourselves, God blesses us. I know that is true because I hoped for you and summoned all my faith, and tomorrow we will bind ourselves together.

"The hardest thing I ever did was find the hope to seek you out and offer for you again. I thought I had been humbled when you refused me, but that was nothing compared to the moment when I had held your hand, embraced you, smelled your lavender scent, and then had you ripped from my arms." He stopped walking and reached down and caressed her cheek. "But you did not refuse me the second time."

The heat from his gentle fingers made her cheek burn and her heart race with its kindness. "Indeed I did not," Elizabeth murmured.

"Indeed," he echoed in a ragged voice. "Can you ever forgive me for leaving you in the garden, my dear?"

Elizabeth's heart ached at his words. "Only if you can forgive me for saying your pride and selfish disdain for others made you the last man I could ever be prevailed upon to marry." She placed her hand on his jaw and cupped it, allowing her thumb to brush against his cheek. He leaned into her hand and looked deep into her eyes.

"I was so blind to who you really are," she said. "Did my letter not teach you anything? It was I who misjudged you and very nearly lost the chance to have you in my arms forever. That is why God gave me that experience while I was ill. He knew I needed to see who you really are. He knew that I needed hope—not for just any Mr. Darcy, but for *the* Mr. Darcy. I was the one who needed correction."

He pulled her into an embrace and kissed her hair. "My dear, sweet, Elizabeth, you are my love, my life. You are the love of my life. Let us not argue who was more wrong. We have a lifetime to create memories that will replace all those old ones."

"But I do not want to replace them; I simply want to add to them. It is part of our story."

Darcy kissed her once and turned her around to face the sun. "It is time."

Arm in arm, they walked the rose-colored path of Pemberley's gardens for the last time as individuals. The next time they would walk this path, they would be husband and wife, united in body and spirit. The sun's warmth spread hope through both of their hearts.

Sometimes there is no need for words.

And sometimes the story never ends.

THE END

Acknowledgments

This book could not have come about if not for my "pop", Ronald Putnam. He has a strength to him that can only be described as a "strength of constitution", just like Mr. Darcy. I felt that strength many times growing up as he engaged me in hours of discussion about God, my intimate hopes, and my kind of heaven. These special moments offered me vision and perspective. I am so blessed to still have him in my life because—without a doubt—his family still needs him and he has a mission left on Earth.

Next book in the *Hope Series Trilogy*:

Hope for Fitzwilliam

Due to be published August 2016

Colonel Fitzwilliam has always been a ladies' man, confident and suave. But when his heart falls for the recently widowed Charlotte Collins, he discovers all of his experience does him little good. And as he prepares to depart for war in the Americas, he fears he is leaving Charlotte behind at Pemberley with a more dangerous foe—one he does not know how to fight.

Charlotte Collins, ill prepared to understand the workings of a heart that has been touched, is determined to find a way to provide a new life for her and her unborn child. But as she quietly observes the daily, tender expressions of love between Mr. and Mrs. Darcy, she is forced to reexamine her own beliefs about love and marriage.

With battles looming inside them both, Colonel Fitzwilliam prepares to fight the greatest battle he has ever faced. As the conflict unfolds, even a decorated colonel finds himself helpless against the foe. He can only hope for something greater than himself to intervene—for more than one person has hope for Fitzwilliam to return home safely and secure Charlotte's fragile, independent heart.

About the Author

Jeanna Ellsworth Lake entered a new era in her life in December 2015. Through all her single years, she kept searching for a Mr. Darcy, but didn't realize that what she *needed* was a Colonel Fitzwilliam! And she found him: a second son with a passionate heart, who never fails to make her laugh. She is so proud of her three daughters, who have supported her through her writing, and have always been her inspiration.

She also proudly states she is the eighth of thirteen children. When she isn't writing, blogging, gardening, cooking, or raising chickens, she is thoroughly ignoring her house for a few hours at a time in order to read yet another romance novel, and does not feel the least bit guilty in doing so. She absolutely loves her chance to influence lives as a Registered Nurse in a Neurological ICU. She finds great joy in her many roles she juggles, but writing especially has been her therapy. She claims she has never been happier.

Jeanna fell in love again with Jane Austen when she was introduced to the incredible world of Jane Austen-inspired fiction. She can never adequately thank the fellow authors who mentored her and encouraged her to write her first novel.

She is a member of Austen Authors and regularly blogs at www.austenauthors.net. She loves hearing from her readers and cherishes the chance to interact with them. For more information on her books and writing, please visit her website:

www.HeyLadyPublications.com.

Other books by Jeanna Ellsworth

Pride and Prejudice variations

Mr. Darcy's Promise
How can an honorable promise become so vexing?

Pride and Persistence
At some point, a good memory is a bad thing.

To Refine Like Silver
Our trials do not define us; rather they refine us.

The Hope Series Trilogy:

Hope for Mr. Darcy
Hope is all they have left, will it be enough?

Hope for Fitzwilliam (Coming August 2016)
For two destined to be together, hope is their only defense.

Hope for Georgiana (Coming November 2016)
Hope has become vital—*especially* when it comes to love.

Regency Romance

Inspired by Grace
What started as friendship has evolved into something quite tangible.

Buying the Duke's Silence
(Sequel to *Inspired by Grace*—Coming September 2017)
Eventually Evelyn learns that Silence is golden.

Made in the USA
Middletown, DE
28 December 2017